THE CLARION

THE CLARION

SAMUEL HOPKINS ADAMS

WILDSIDE PRESS

THE CLARION

This edition published 2005 by Wildside Press, LLC.
www.wildsidepress.com

CHAPTER I

THE ITINERANT

Between two flames the man stood, overlooking the crowd. A soft breeze, playing about the torches, sent shadows billowing across the massed folk on the ground. Shrewdly set with an eye to theatrical effect, these phares of a night threw out from the darkness the square bulk of the man's figure, and, reflecting garishly upward from the naked hemlock of the platform, accentuated, as in bronze, the bosses of the face, and gleamed deeply in the dark, bold eyes. Half of Marysville buzzed and chattered in the park-space below, together with many representatives of the farming country near by, for the event had been advertised with skilled appeal: cf. the "Canoga County Palladium," April 15, 1897, page 4.

The occupant of the platform, having paused, after a self-introductory trumpeting of professional claims, was slowly and with an eye to oratorical effect moistening lips and throat from a goblet at his elbow. Now, ready to resume, he raised a slow hand in an indescribable gesture of mingled command and benevolence. The clamor subsided to a murmur, over which his voice flowed and spread like oil subduing vexed waters.

"Pain. Pain. Pain. The primal curse, the dominant tragedy of life. Who among you, dear friends, but has felt it? You men, slowly torn upon the rack of rheumatism; you women, with the hidden agony gnawing at your breast" (his roving regard was swift, like a hawk, to mark down the sudden, involuntary quiver of a faded slattern under one of the torches); "all you who have known burning nights and pallid mornings, I offer you r-r-r-release!"

On the final word his face lighted up as from an inner fire of inspiration, and he flung his arms wide in an embracing benediction. The crowd, heavy-eyed, sodden, wondering, bent to him as the torch-fires bent to the breath of summer. With the subtle sense of the man who wrings his livelihood from human emotions, he felt the moment of his mastery approaching. Was it fully come yet? Were his fish securely in the net? Betwixt hovering hands he studied his audience.

His eyes stopped with a sense of being checked by the steady regard of one who stood directly in front of him only a few feet away; a solid-built, crisply outlined man of forty, carrying himself with a practical erectness, upon whose face there was a rather disturbing half-smile. The stranger's hand was clasped in that of a little girl, wide-eyed, elfin, and lovely.

"Release," repeated the man of the torches. "Blessed release from your torments. Peace out of pain."

The voice was of wonderful quality, rich and unctuous, the labials dropping, honeyed, from the lips. It wooed the crowd, lured it, enmeshed it. But the magician had, a little, lost confidence in the power of his spell. His mind dwelt uneasily upon his well-garbed auditor. What was he doing there, with his keen face and worldly, confident carriage, amidst those clodhoppers? Was there peril in his presence? Your predatory creature hunts ever with fear in his heart.

"Guardy," the voice of the elfin child rang silvery in the silence, as she pressed close to her companion. "Guardy, is he preaching?"

"Yes, my dear little child." The orator saw his opportunity and swooped upon it, with a flash of dazzling teeth from under his pliant lips. "This sweet little girl asks if I am preaching. I thank her for the word. Preaching, indeed! Preaching a blessed gospel, for this world of pain and suffering; a gospel of hope and happiness and joy. I offer you, here, now, this moment of blessed opportunity, the priceless boon of health. It is within reach of the humblest and poorest as well as the millionaire. The blessing falls on all like the gentle rain from heaven."

His hands, outstretched, quivering as if to shed the promised balm, slowly descended below the level of the platform railing. Behind the tricolored cheese-cloth which screened him from the waist down something stirred. The hands ascended again into the light. In each was a bottle. The speaker's words came now sharp, decisive, compelling.

"Here it is! Look at it, my friends. The wonder of the scientific world, the never-failing panacea, the despair of the doctors. All diseases yield to it. It revivi-fies the blood, reconstructs the nerves, drives out the poisons which corrupt the human frame. It banishes pain, sickness, weakness, and cheats death of his prey. Oh, grave, where is thy victory? Oh, death, where is thy power? Overcome by my marvelous discovery! Harmless as water! Sweet on the tongue as honey! Potent as a miracle! By the grace of Heaven, which has bestowed this secret upon me, I have saved five thousand men, women, and children from sure doom, in the last three years, through my swift and infallible remedy, Professor Certain's Vital-izing Mixture; as witness my undenied affidavit, sworn to before Almighty God and a notary public and published in every newspaper in the State."

Wonder and hope exhaled in a sigh from the assemblage. People began to stir, to shift from one foot to another, to glance about them nervously. Professor Certain had them. It needed but the first thrust of hand into pocket to set the avalanche of coin rolling toward the platform. From near the speaker a voice piped thinly:—

"Will it ease my cough?"

The orator bent over, and his voice was like a benign hand upon the brow of suffering.

"Ease it? You'll never know you had a cough after one bottle."

"We-ell, gimme—"

"Just a moment, my friend." The Professor was not yet ready. "Put your dollar back. There's enough to go around. Oh, Uncle Cal! Step up here, please."

An old negro, very pompous and upright, made his way to the steps and mounted.

"You all know old Uncle Cal Parks, my friends. You've seen him hobbling and hunching around for years, all twisted up with rheumatics. He came to me yesterday, begging for relief, and we began treatment with the Vitalizing Mixture right off. Look at him now. Show them what you can do, uncle."

Wild-eyed, the old fellow gazed about at the people. "Glory! Hallelujah!" Emotional explosives left over from the previous year's revival burst from his lips. He broke into a stiff, but prankish double-shuffle.

"I'd like to try some o' that on my old mare," remarked a facetious-minded rustic, below, and a titter followed.

"Good for man or beast," retorted the Professor with smiling amiability.

"You've seen what the Vitalizing Mixture has done for this poor old colored man. It will do as much or more for any of you. And the price is Only One Dollar!" The voice double-capitalized the words. "Don't, for the sake of one hundred little cents, put off the day of cure. Don't waste your chance. Don't let a miserable little dollar stand between you and death. Come, now. Who's first?"

The victim of the "cough" was first, closely followed by the mare-owning wit. Then the whole mass seemed to be pressing forward, at once. Like those of a conjurer, the deft hands of the Professor pushed in and out of the light, snatching from below the bottles handed up to him, and taking in the clinking silver and fluttering greenbacks. And still they came, that line of grotesques, hobbling, limping, sprawling their way to the golden promise. Never did Pied Piper flute to creatures more bemused. Only once was there pause, when the dispenser of balm held aloft between thumb and finger a cart-wheel dollar.

"Phony!" he said curtly, and flipped it far into the darkness. "Don't any more of you try it on," he warned, as the thwarted profferer of the counterfeit sidled away, and there was, in his tone, a dominant ferocity.

Presently the line of purchasers thinned out. The Vitalizing Mixture had exhausted its market. But only part of the crowd had contributed to the levy. Mainly it was the men, whom the "spiel" had lured. Now for the women. The voice, the organ of a genuine artist, took on a new cadence, limpid and tender.

"And now, we come to the sufferings of those who bear pain with the fortitude of the angels. Our women-folk! How many here are hiding that dreadful malady, cancer? Hiding it, when help and cure are at their beck and call. Lady," he bent swiftly to the slattern under the torch and his accents were a healing effluence, "with my soothing, balmy oils, you can cure yourself in three weeks, or your money back."

"I do' know haow you knew," faltered the woman. "I ain't told no one yet. Kinder hoped it wa'n't thet, after all."

He brooded over her compassionately. "You've suffered needlessly. Soon it would have been too late. The Vitalizing Mixture will keep up your strength, while the soothing, balmy oils drive out the poison, and heal up the sore. Three and a half for the two. Thank you. And is there some suffering friend who you can lead to the light?"

The woman hesitated. She moved out to the edge of the crowd, and spoke earnestly to a younger woman, whose comely face was scarred with the chiseling of sleeplessness.

"Joe, he wouldn't let me," protested the younger woman. "He'd say 't was a waste."

"But ye'll be cured," cried the other in exaltation. "Think of it. Ye'll sleep again o' nights."

The woman's hand went to her breast, with a piteous gesture. "Oh, my God! D'yeh think it could be true?" she cried.

"Accourse it's true! Didn't yeh hear whut he sayed? Would he dast swear to it if it wasn't true?"

Tremulously the younger woman moved forward, clutching her shawl about her.

"Could yeh sell me half a bottle to try it, sir?" she asked.

The vender shook his head. "Impossible, my dear madam. Contrary to my fixed professional rule. But, I'll tell you what I will do. If, in three days you're not better, you can have your money back."

She began painfully to count out her coins. Reaching impatiently for his price, the Professor found himself looking straight into the eyes of the well-dressed stranger.

"Are you going to take that woman's money?"

The question was low-toned but quite clear. An uneasy twitching beset the corners of the professional brow. For just the fraction of a second, the outstretched hand was stayed. Then:—

"That's what I am. And all the others I can get. Can I sell *you* a bottle?"

Behind the suavity there was the impudence of the man who is a little alarmed, and a little angry because of the alarm.

"Why, yes," said the other coolly. "Some day I might like to know what's in the stuff."

"Hand up your cash then. And here you are—Doctor. It *is* 'Doctor,' ain't it?"

"You've guessed it," returned the stranger.

At once the platform peddler became the opportunist orator again.

"A fellow practitioner, in my audience, ladies and gentlemen; and doing me the honor of purchasing my cure. Sir," the splendid voice rose and soared as he addressed his newest client, "you follow the noblest of callings. My friends, I would rather heal a people's ills than determine their destinies."

Giving them a moment to absorb that noble sentiment, he passed on to his next source of revenue: Dyspepsia. He enlarged and expatiated upon its symptoms until his subjects could fairly feel the grilling at the pit of their collective stomach. One by one they came forward, the yellow-eyed, the pasty-faced feeders on fried breakfasts, snatchers of hasty noon-meals, sleepers on gorged stomachs. About them he wove the glamour of his words, the arch-seducer, until the dollars fidgeted in their pockets.

"Just one dollar the bottle, and pain is banished. Eat? You can eat a cord of hickory for breakfast, knots and all, and digest it in an hour. The Vitalizing Mixture does it."

Assorted ills came next. In earlier spring it would have been pneumonia and coughs. Now it was the ailments that we have always with us: backache, headache, indigestion and always the magnificent promise. So he picked up the final harvest, gleaning his field.

"Now,"—the rotund voice sunk into the confidential, sympathetic register, yet with a tone of saddened rebuke,—"there are topics that the lips shrink from when ladies are present. But I have a word for you young men. Young blood! Ah, young blood, and the fire of life! For that we pay a penalty. Yet we must not overpay the debt. To such as wish my private advice—*private*, I say, and sacredly confidential—" He broke off and leaned out over the railing. "Thousands have lived to bless the name of Professor Certain, and his friendship, at such a crisis; thousands, my friends. To such, I shall be available for consultation from nine to twelve tomorrow, at the Moscow Hotel. Remember the time and place. Men only. Nine to twelve. And all under the inviolable seal of my profession."

Some quality of unexpressed insistence in the stranger—or was it the speaker's own uneasiness of spirit?—brought back the roving, brilliant eyes to the square face below.

"A little blackmail on the side, eh?"

The words were spoken low, but with a peculiar, abrupt crispness. This, then, was direct challenge. Professor Certain tautened. Should he accept it, or was it safer to ignore this pestilent disturber? Craft and anger thrust opposing counsels upon him. But determination of the issue came from outside.

"Lemme through."

From the outskirts of the crowd a rawboned giant forced his way inward. He was gaunt and unkempt as a weed in winter.

"Here's trouble," remarked a man at the front. "Allus comes with a Hardscrabbler."

"What's a Hardscrabbler?" queried the well-dressed man.

"Feller from the Hardscrabble Settlement over on Corsica Lake. Tough lot, they are. Make their own laws, when they want any; run their place to suit themselves. Ain't much they ain't up to. Hoss-stealin', barn-burnin', boot-leggin', an' murder thrown in when—"

"Be you the doctor was to Corsica Village two years ago?" The newcomer's high, droning voice cut short the explanation.

"I was there, my friend. Testimonials and letters from some of your leading citizens attest the work—"

"You give my woman morpheean." There was a hideous edged intonation in the word, like the whine of some plaintive and dangerous animal.

"My friend!" The Professor's hand went forth in repressive deprecation. "We physicians give what seems to us best, in these cases."

"A reg'lar doctor from Burnham seen her," pursued the Hardscrabbler, in the same thin wail, moving nearer, but not again raising his eyes to the other's face. Instead, his gaze seemed fixed upon the man's shining expanse of waistcoat. "He said you doped her with the morpheean you give her."

"So your chickens come home to roost, Professor," said the stranger, in a half-voice.

"Impossible," declared the Professor, addressing the Hardscrabbler. "You misunderstood him."

"They took my woman away. They took her to the 'sylum."

Foreboding peril, the people nearest the uncouth visitor had drawn away. Only the stranger held his ground; more than held it, indeed, for he edged almost imperceptibly nearer. He had noticed a fleck of red on the matted beard, where the lip had been bitten into. Also he saw that the Professor, whose gaze had so timorously shifted from his, was intent, recognizing danger; intent, and unafraid before the threat.

"She used to cry fer it, my woman. Cry fer the morpheean like a baby." He sagged a step forward. "She don't haff to cry no more. She's dead."

Whence had the knife leapt, to gleam so viciously in his hand? Almost as swiftly as it was drawn, the healer had snatched one of the heavy torch-poles from its socket. Almost, not quite. The fury leapt and struck; struck for that shining waistcoat, upon which his regard had concentrated, with an upward lunge, the most surely deadly blow known to the knife-fighter. Two other movements coincided, to the instant. From the curtain of cheesecloth the slight form of a boy shot upward, with brandished arms; and the square-built man reached the Hardscrabbler's jaw with a powerful and accurate swing. There was a scream of pain, a roar from the crowd, and an answering bellow from the quack in midair, for he had launched his formidable bulk over the rail, to plunge, a crushing weight, upon the would-be murderer, who lay stunned on the grass. For a moment the avenger ground him, with knees and fists; then was up and back on the platform. Already the city man had gained the flooring, and was bending above the child. There was a sprinkle of blood on the bright, rough boards.

"Oh, my God! Boy-ee! Has he killed you?"

"No: he isn't killed," said the stranger curtly. "Keep the people back. Lift down that torch."

The Professor wavered on his legs, grasping at the rail for support.

"You *are* a doctor?" he gasped.

"Yes."

"Can you save him? Any money—"

"Set the torch here."

"Oh, Boyee, Boyee!" The great, dark man had dropped to his knees, his face a mask of agony.

"Oh, the devil!" said the physician disgustedly. "You're no help. Clear a way there, some of you, so that I can get him to the hotel." Then, to the other. "Keep quiet. There's no danger. Only a flesh wound, but he's fainted."

Carefully he swung the small form to his shoulder, and forced a way through the crowd, the little girl, who had followed him to the platform, composedly trotting along in his wake, while the Hardscrabbler, moaning from the pain of two broken ribs, was led away by a constable. Some distance behind, the itinerant wallowed like a drunken man, muttering brilliant bargain offers of good conduct to Almighty God, if "Boyee" were saved to him.

Once in the little hotel room, the physician went about his business with swift decisiveness, aided by the mite of a girl, who seemed to know by instinct where to be and what to do in the way of handling towels, wash-basin, and the other simple paraphernalia required. Professor Certain was unceremoniously packed off to the drug store for bandages. When he returned the patient had recovered consciousness.

"Where's Dad?" he asked eagerly. "Did he hurt Dad?"

"No, Boyee." The big man was at the bedside in two long, velvety-footed steps. Struck by the extenuation of the final "y" in the term, the physician for the first time noted a very faint foreign accent, the merest echo of some alien tongue. "Are you in pain, Boyee?"

"Not very much. It doesn't matter. Why did he want to kill you?"

"Never mind that, now," interrupted the physician. "We'll get that scratch bound up, and then, young man, you'll go to sleep."

Pallid as a ghost, the itinerant held the little hand during the process of binding the wound. "Boyee" essayed to smile, at the end, and closed his eyes.

"Now we can leave him," said the physician. "Poppet, curl up in that chair and keep watch on our patient while this gentleman and I have a little talk in the outer room."

With a brisk nod of obedience and comprehension, the elfin girl took her place, while the two men went out.

"What do I owe you?" asked Professor Certain, as soon as the door had closed.

"Nothing."

"Oh, that won't do."

"It will have to do."

"Courtesy of the profession? But—"

The other laughed grimly, cutting him short. "So you call yourself an M.D., do you?"

"Call myself? I am. Regular degree from the Dayton Medical College." He sleeked down his heavy hair with a complacent hand.

The physician snorted. "A diploma-mill. What did you pay for your M.D.?"

"One hundred dollars, and it's as good as your four-year P. and S. course or any other, for my purposes," retorted the other, with hardihood. "What's more, I'm a member of the American Academy of Surgeons, with a special diploma from St. Luke's Hospital of Niles, Michigan, and a certificate of fellowship in the National Medical Scientific Fraternity. Pleased to meet a brother practitioner." The sneer was as palpable as it was cynical.

"You've got all the fake trimmings, haven't you? Do those things pay?"

"Do they! Better than your game, I'll bet. Name your own fee, now, and don't be afraid to make it strong."

"I'm not in regular practice. I'm a naval surgeon on leave. Give your money to those poor devils you swindled tonight. I don't like the smell of it."

"Oh, you can't rile me," returned the quack. "I don't blame you regulars for getting sore when you see us fellows culling out coin from under your very noses, that you can't touch."

"Cull it, and welcome. But don't try to pass it on to me."

"Well, I'd like to do something for you in return for what you did for my son."

"Would you? Pay me in words, then, if you will and dare. What is your Vitalizing Mixture?"

"That's my secret."

"Liquor? Eh?"

"Some."

"Morphine?"

"A little."

"And the rest syrup and coloring matter, I suppose. A fine vitalizer!"

"It gets the money," retorted the other.

"And your soothing, balmy oils for cancer? Arsenious acid, I suppose, to eat it out?"

"What if it is? As well that as anything else—for cancer."

"Humph! I happened to see a patient you'd treated, two years ago, by that mild method. It wasn't cancer at all; only a benign tumor. Your soothing oils burned her breast off, like so much fire. She's dead now."

"Oh, we all make mistakes."

"But we don't all commit murder."

"Rub it in, if you like to. You can't make me mad. Just the same, if it wasn't for what you've done for Boyee—"

"Well, what about 'Boyee'?" broke in his persecutor quite undisturbed. "He seems a perfectly decent sort of human integer."

The bold eyes shifted and softened abruptly. "He's the big thing in my life."

"Bringing him up to the trade, eh?"

"No, damn you!"

"Damn me, if you like. But don't damn him. He seems to be a bit too good for this sort of thing."

"To tell you the truth," said the other gloomily, "I was going to quit at the end of this year, anyway. But I guess this ends it now. Accidents like this hurt business. I guess this closes my tour."

"Is the game playing out?"

"Not exactly! Do you know what I took out of this town last night? One hundred and ten good dollars. And tomorrow's consultation is good for fifty more. That 'spiel' of mine is the best high-pitch in the business."

"High-pitch?"

"High-pitching," explained the quack, "is our term for the talk, the patter. You can sell sugar pills to raise the dead with a good-enough high-pitch. I've done it myself—pretty near. With a voice like mine, it's a shame to drop it. But I'm getting tired. And Boyee ought to have schooling. So, I'll settle down and try a regular proprietary trade with the Mixture and some other stuff I've got. I guess I can make printer's ink do the work. And there's millions in it if you once get a start. More than you can say of regular practice. I tried that, too, before I took up itinerating." He grinned. "A midge couldn't have lived on my receipts. By the way," he added, becoming grave, "what was your game in cutting in on my 'spiel'?"

"Just curiosity."

"You ain't a government agent or a medical society investigator?"

The physician pulled out a card and handed it over. It read, "Mark Elliot, Surgeon, U.S.N."

"Don't lose any sleep over me," he advised, then went to open the outer door, in response to a knock.

A spectacled young man appeared. "They told me Professor Certain was here," he said.

"What is it?" asked the quack.

"About that stabbing. I'm the editor of the weekly 'Palladium.'"

"Glad to see you, Mr. Editor. Always glad to see the Press. Of course you won't print anything about this affair?"

The visitor blinked. "You wouldn't hardly expect me to kill the story."

"Not? Does anybody else but me give you page ads.?"

"Well, of course, we try to favor our advertisers," said the spectacled one nervously.

"That's business! I'll be coming around again next year, if this thing is handled right, and I think my increased business might warrant a double page, then."

"But the paper will have to carry something about it. Too many folks saw it happen."

"Just say that a crazy man tried to interrupt the lecture of Professor Andrew Leon Certain, the distinguished medical savant, and was locked up by the authorities."

"But the knifing. How is the boy?"

"Somebody's been giving you the wrong tip. There wasn't any knife," replied the Professor with a wink. "You may send me two hundred and fifty copies of the paper. And, by the way, do what you can to get that poor lunatic off easy, and I'll square the bills—with commission."

"I'll see the Justice first thing in the morning," said the editor with enthusiasm. "Much obliged, Professor Certain. And the article will be all right. I'll show you a proof. It mightn't be a bad notion for you to drop in at the jail with me, and see Neal, the man that stab—that interrupted the meeting, before he gets talking with any one else."

"So it mightn't. But what about my leaving, now?" Professor Certain asked of the physician.

"Go ahead. I'll keep watch."

Shortly after the itinerant had gone out with the exponent of free and untrammeled journalism, the boy awoke and looked about with fevered anxiety for his father. The little nurse was beside him at once.

"You mustn't wiggle around," she commanded. "Do you want a drink?"

Gratefully he drank the water which she held to his lips.

"Where's my Dad?" he asked.

"He's gone out. He'll come back pretty soon. Lie down."

He sank back, fixing his eyes upon her. "Will you stay with me till he comes?"

She nodded. "Does it hurt you much?" Her cool and tiny fingers touched his forehead, soothingly. "You're very hot. I think you've got a little fever."

"Don't take your hand away." His eyes closed, but presently opened again. "I think you're very pretty," he said shyly.

"Do you? I like to have people think I'm pretty. Uncle Guardy scolds me for it. Not really, you know, but just pretending. He says I'm vain."

"Is that your uncle, the gentleman that fixed my arm?"

"Yes. I call him Uncle Guardy because he's my guardian, too."

"I like him. He looks good. But I like you better. I like you a lot."

"Everybody does," replied the girl with dimpling complacency. "They can't help it. It's because I'm me!"

For a moment he brooded. "Am I going to die?" he asked quite suddenly.

"Die? Of course not."

"Would you be sorry if I did?"

"Yes. If you died you couldn't like me any more. And I want everybody to like me and think me pretty."

"I'm glad I'm not. It would be tough on Dad."

"My Uncle Guardy thinks your father is a bad man," said the fairy, not without a spice of malice.

Up rose the patient from his pillow. "Then I hate him. He's a liar. My Dad is the best man in the world." A brighter hue than fever burnt in his cheeks, and his hand went to his shoulder. "I won't have his bandages on me," he cried.

But she had thrown herself upon his arm, and pushed him back. "Oh, don't! Please don't," she besought. "Uncle Guardy told me to keep you perfectly quiet. And I've made you sit up—"

"What's all this commotion?" demanded Dr. Elliot brusquely, from the door.

"You said my father was a bad man," cried the outraged patient.

"Lie back, youngster." The physician's hand was gentle, but very firm. "I don't recall saying any such thing. Where did you get it?"

"I said you *thought* he was a bad man," declared the midget girl. "I know you do. You wouldn't have spoken back to him down in the square if you hadn't."

Her uncle turned upon her a slow, cool, silent regard. "Esmé, you talk too much," he said finally. "I'm a little ashamed of you, as a nurse. Take your place there by the bedside. And you, young man, shut your ears and eyes and go to sleep."

Hardly had the door closed behind the autocrat of the sick-room, when his patient turned softly.

"You're crying," he accused.

"I'm not!" The denial was the merest gasp. The long lashes quivered with tears.

"Yes, you are. He was mean to you."

"He's *never* mean to me." The words came in a sobbing rush. "But he—he—stopped loving me just for that minute. And when anybody I love stops loving me I want to die!"

The boy's brown hands crept timidly to her arm. "I like you awfully," he said. "And I'll never stop, not even for a minute!"

"Won't you?" Again she was the child coquette. "But we're going away tonight. Perhaps you won't see me any more."

"Oh, yes, I shall. I'll look for you until I find you."

"I'll hide," she teased.

"That won't matter, little girl." He repeated the form softly and drowsily. "Little girl; little girl; I'd do anything in the world for you, little girl, if ever you asked me. Only don't go away while I'm asleep."

Back of them the door had opened quietly and Professor Certain, who, with Dr. Elliot, had been a silent spectator of the little drama, now closed it again, withdrawing, on the further side, with his companion.

"He'll sleep now," said the physician. "That's all he needs. Hello! What's this?"

In a corner of the sofa was a tiny huddle, outlined vaguely as human, under a faded shawl. Drawing aside the folds, the quack disclosed a wild little face, framed in a mass of glowing red hair.

"That Hardscrabbler's young 'un," he said. "She was crying quietly to herself, in the darkness outside the jail, poor little tyke. So I picked her up, and" (with a sort of tender awkwardness) "she was glad to come with me. Seemed to kind of take to me. Kiddies generally do."

"Do they? That's curious."

"I suppose you think so," replied the quack, without rancor.

"What are you going to do with her?"

"I'll see, later. At present I'm going to keep her here with us. She's only seven, and her mother's dead. Are you staying here tonight?"

"Got to. Missed my connection."

"Then at least you'll let me pay your hotel bill, if you won't take my money."

"Why, yes: I suppose so," said the other grudgingly. "I'll look at the boy in the morning. But he'll be all right. Only, don't take up your itinerating again for a few days."

"I'm through, I tell you. Give me a growing city to settle in and I'll go in for the regular proprietary manufacturing game. Know anything about Worthington?"

"Yes."

"Pretty good, live town?"

"First-class, and not too critical, I suppose, to accept your business," said Dr. Elliot dryly. "I'm on my way there now for a visit. Well, I must get my little girl."

The itinerant opened the door, looked, and beckoned. The boy lay on his pillow, the girl was curled in her chair, both fast asleep. Their hands were lightly clasped.

Dr. Elliot lifted his ward and carried her away. The itinerant, returning to the Hardscrabbler girl, took her out to arrange the night's accommodation for her. So, there slept that night under one roof and at the charge of Professor Andrew L. Certain, five human beings who, long years after, were destined to meet and mingle their fates, intricate, intimate strands in the pattern of human weal and woe.

CHAPTER II

OUR LEADING CITIZEN

The year of grace, 1913, commended itself to Dr. L. André Surtaine as an excellent time in which to be alive, rich, and sixty years old. Thoroughly, keenly, ebulliently alive he was. Thoroughly rich, also; and if the truth be told, rather ebulliently conscious of his wealth. You could see at a glance that he had paid no usurious interest to Fate on his success; that his vigor and zest in life remained to him undiminished. Vitality and a high satisfaction with his environment and with himself as well placed in it, radiated from his bulky and handsome person; but it was the vitality that impressed you first: impressed and warmed you; perhaps warned you, too, on shrewder observation. A gleaming personality, this. But behind the radiance one surmised fire. Occasion given, Dr. Surtaine might well be formidable.

The world had been his oyster to open. He had cleaved it wide. Ill-natured persons hinted, in reference to his business, that he had used poison rather than the knife wherewith to loosen the stubborn hinges of the bivalve. Money gives back small echo to the cries of calumny, however. And Dr. Surtaine's Certina, that infallible and guaranteed blood-cure, eradicator of all known human ills, "famous across the map of the world," to use one of its advertising phrases, under the catchword of "Professor Certain's Certina, the Sure-Cure" (for he preserved the old name as a trade-mark), had made a vast deal of money for its proprietor. Worthington estimated his fortune at fifteen millions, growing at the rate of a million yearly, and was not preposterously far afield. In a city of two hundred thousand inhabitants, claimed (one hundred and seventy-five thousand allowed by a niggling and suspicious census), this is all that the most needy of millionaires needs. It was all that Dr. Surtaine needed. He enjoyed his high satisfaction as a hard-earned increment.

Something more than satisfaction beamed from his face this blustery March noon as he awaited the Worthington train at a small station an hour up the line. He fidgeted like an eager boy when the whistle sounded, and before the cars had fairly come to a stop he was up the steps of the sleeper and inside the door. There rose to meet him a tall, carefully dressed and pressed youth, whose exclamation was evenly apportioned between welcome and surprise.

"Dad!"

"Boy-ee!"

To the amusement of the other passengers, the two seized each other in a bear-hug.

"Oof!" panted the big man, releasing his son. "That's the best thing that's happened to me this year. George" (to the porter), "get me a seat. Get us two seats together. Aren't any? Perhaps this gentleman," turning to the chair back of him, "wouldn't mind moving across the aisle until we get to Worthington."

"Certainly not. Glad to oblige," said the stranger, smiling. People usually were "glad to oblige" Dr. Surtaine whether they knew him or not. The man inspired good will in others.

"It's nearly a year since I've set eyes on my son," he added in a voice which took the whole car into his friendly confidence; "and it seems like ten. How are you feeling, Hal? You look chirp as a cricket."

"Couldn't possibly feel better, sir. Where did you get on?"

"Here at State Crossing. Thought I'd come up and meet you. The office got on my nerves this morning. Work didn't hold me worth a cent. I kept figuring you coming nearer and nearer until I couldn't stand it, so I banged down my desk, told my secretary that I was going to California on the night boat and mightn't be back till evening, hung the scrap-basket on the stenographer's ear when she tried to hold me up to sign some letters, jumped out of the fifth-story window, and here I am. I hope you're as tickled to see me as I am to see you."

The young man's hand went out, fell with a swift movement, to touch his father's, and was as swiftly withdrawn again.

"Worthington's just waiting for you," the Doctor rattled on. "You're put up at all the clubs. People you've never heard of are laying out dinners and dances for you. You're a distinguished stranger; that's what you are. Welcome to our city and all that sort of thing. I'd like to have a brass band at the station to meet you, only I thought it might jar your quiet European tastes. Eh? At that, I had to put the boys under bonds to keep 'em from decorating the factory for you."

"You don't seem to have lost any of your spirit, Dad," said the junior, smiling.

"Noticed that already, have you? Well, I'm holding my own, Boyee. Up to date, old age hasn't scratched me with his claws to any noticeable extent—is that the way it goes?—see 'Familiar Quotations.' I'm getting to be a regular book-worm, Hal. Shakespeare, R.L.S., Kipling, Arnold Bennett, Hall Caine—all the high-brows. And I *get* 'em, too. Soak 'em right in. I love it! Tell me, who's this Balzac? An agent was in yesterday trying to make me believe that he invented culture. What about him? I'm pretty hot on the culture trail. Look out, or I'll over-haul you."

"You won't have to go very far or fast. I've got only smatterings." But the boy spoke with a subdued complacency not wholly lost upon the shrewd father.

"Not so much that you'll think Worthington dull and provincial?"

"Oh, I dare say I shall find it a very decent little place."

But here Hal touched another pride and loyalty, quite as genuine as that which Dr. Surtaine felt for his son.

"Little place!" he cried. "Two hundred thousand of the livest people on God's earth. A gen-u-wine American city if there ever was one."

"Evidently it suits you, sir."

"Couldn't suit better if I'd had it made to order," chuckled the Doctor. "And I did pretty near make it over to order. It was a dead-and-alive town when we opened up here. Didn't care much about my business, either. Now we're the biggest thing in town. Why Certina is the cross-mark that shows where Worthington is on the map. The business is sim-plee BOOMING." The word exploded in rapture. "Nothing like it ever known in the proprietary trade. Wait till you see the shop."

"That will be soon, won't it, sir? I think I've loafed quite long enough."

"You're only twenty-five," his father defended him. "It isn't as if you'd been idling. Your four years abroad have been just so much capital. Educational capital, I mean. I've got plenty of the other kind, for both of us. You don't need to go into the business unless you want to."

"Being an American, I suppose I've got to go to work at something."

"Not necessarily."

"You don't want me to live on you all my life, though, I suppose."

"Well, I don't want you to want me to want you to," returned the other, laughing. "But there's no hurry."

"To tell the truth, I'm rather bored with doing nothing. And if I can be of any use to you in the business—"

"You're ready to resume the partnership," his father concluded the sentence for him. "That was the foundation of it all; the old days when I did the 'spieling' and you took in the dollars. How quick your little hands were! Can you remember it? The smelly smoke of the torches, and the shadows chasing each other across the crowds below. And to think what has grown out of it. God, Boyee! It's a miracle," he exulted.

"It isn't very clear in my memory. I used to get pretty sleepy, I remember," said the son, smiling.

"Poor Boyee! Sometimes I hated the life, for you. But there was nobody to leave you with; and you were all I had. Anyway, it's turned out well, hasn't it?"

"That remains to be seen for me, doesn't it? I'm rather at the start of things."

"Most youngsters would be content with an unlimited allowance, and the world for a playground."

"One gets tired of playing. *And* of globe-trotting."

"Good! Do you think you can make Worthington feel like home?"

"How can I tell, sir? I haven't spent two weeks altogether in the place since I entered college eight years ago."

"Did it ever strike you that I'd carefully planned to keep you away from here, and that our periods of companionship have all been abroad or at summer places?"

"Yes."

"You've never spoken of it."

"No."

"Good boy! Now I'll tell you why. I wanted to be absolutely established before I brought you back here. Not in business, alone. That came long ago. There have been obstacles, in other ways. They're all overcome. Today we come pretty near to being king-pins in this town, you and I, Hal. Do you feel like a prince entering into his realm?"

"Rather more like a freshman entering college," said the other, laughing. "It isn't the town, it's the business that I have misgivings about."

"Misgivings? How's that?" asked the father quickly.

"What I can do in it."

"Oh, that. My doubts are whether it's the best thing for you."

"Don't you want me to go into it, Dad?"

"Of course I want you with me, Boyee. But—well, frank and flat, I don't know whether it's genteel enough for you."

"Genteel?" The younger Surtaine repeated the distasteful adjective with surprise.

"Some folks make fun of it, you know. It's the advertising that makes it a fair mark. 'Certina,' they say. 'That's where he made his money. Patent-medicine millions.' I don't mind it. But for you it's different."

"If the money is good enough for me to spend, it's good enough for me to earn," said Hal Surtaine a little grandiloquently.

"Humph! Well, the business is a big success, and I want you to be a big success. But that doesn't mean that I want to combine the two. Isn't there anything else you've ever thought of turning to?"

"I've got something of a leaning toward your profession, Dad."

"My prof—oh, you mean medicine."

"Yes."

"Nothing in it. Doctors are a lot of prejudiced pedants and hypocrites. Not one in a thousand is more than an inch wide. What started you on that?"

"I hardly know. It was just a notion. I think the scientific and sociological side is what appeals to me. But my interest is only theoretical."

"That's very well for a hobby. Not as a profession. Here we are, half an hour late, as usual."

The sudden and violent bite of the brakes, a characteristic operation of that mummy among railroads, the Mid-State and Great Muddy River, commonly known as the "Mid-and-Mud," flung forward in an involuntary plunge the incautious who had arisen to look after their things. Hal Surtaine found himself supporting the weight of a fortuitous citizen who had just made his way up the aisle.

"Thank you," said the stranger in a dry voice. "You're the prodigal son of whom we've heard such glowing forecast, I presume."

"Well met, Mr. Pierce," called Dr. Surtaine's jovial voice. "Yes, that's my son, Harrington, you're hanging to. Hal, this is Mr. Elias M. Pierce, one of the men who run Worthington."

Releasing his burden Hal acknowledged the introduction. Elias M. Pierce, receding a yard or so into perspective, revealed himself as a spare, middle-aged man who looked as if he had been hewn out of a block, square, and glued into a permanent black suit. Under his palely sardonic eye Hal felt that he was being appraised, and in none too amiable a spirit.

"A favorite pleasantry of your father's, Mr. Surtaine," said Pierce. "What became of Douglas? Oh, here he is."

A clean-shaven, rather floridly dressed man came forward, was introduced to Hal, and inquired courteously whether he was going to settle down in Worthington.

"Probably depends on how well he likes it," cut in the dry Mr. Pierce. "You might help him decide. I'm sure William would be glad to have you lunch with him one day this week at the Huron Club, Mr. Surtaine."

Somewhat surprised and a little annoyed at this curiously vicarious suggestion of hospitality, the newcomer hesitated, although Douglas promptly supported the offer. Before he had decided what to reply, his father eagerly broke in.

"Yes, yes. You must go, Hal," he said, apparently oblivious of the fact that he had not been included in the invitation.

"I'll try to be there, myself," continued Pierce, in a flat tone of condescension. "Douglas represents me, however, not only legally but in other matters that I'm too busy to attend to."

"Mr. Pierce is president of the Huron Club," explained Dr. Surtaine. "It's our leading social organization. You'll meet our best business men there." And Hal had no alternative but to accept.

Here William Douglas turned to speak to Dr. Surtaine. "The Reverend Norman Hale has been looking for you. It is some minor hitch about that Mission matter, I believe. Just a little diplomacy wanted. He said he'd call to see you day after tomorrow."

"Meaning more money, I suppose," said Dr. Surtaine. Then, more loudly: "Well, the business can stand it. All right. Send him along."

With Hal close on his heels he stepped from the car. But Douglas, having the cue from his patron, took the younger man by the arm and drew him aside.

"Come over and meet some of our fair citizens," he said. "Nothing like starting right."

The Pierce motor car, very large, very quietly complete and elegant, was waiting near at hand, and in it a prematurely elderly, subdued nondescript of a woman, and a pretty, sensitive, sensuous type of brunette, almost too well dressed. To Mrs. Pierce and Miss Kathleen Pierce, Hal was duly presented, and by them graciously received. As he stood there, bareheaded, gracefully at ease, smiling up into the interested faces of the two ladies, Dr. Surtaine, passing to his own car to await him, looked back and was warmed with pride and gratitude for this further honorarium to his capital stock of happiness, for he saw already in his son the assurance of social success, and, on the hour's reckoning, summed him up. And since we are to see much of Harrington Surtaine, in evil chance and good, and see him at times through the eyes of that shrewd observer and capitalizer of men, his father, the summing-up is worth our present heed, for all that it is to be considerably modified in the mind of its proponent, as events develop. This, then, is Dr. Surtaine's estimate of his beloved "Boyee," after a year of separation.

"A little bit of a prig. A little bit of a cub. Just a *little* mite of a snob, too, maybe. But the right, solid, clean stuff underneath. And my son, thank God! *My* son all through."

CHAPTER III

ESMÉ

Hal saw her first, vivid against the lifeless gray of the cement wall, as he turned away from the Pierce car. A little apart from the human current she stood, still and expectant. As if to point her out as the chosen of gods and men, the questing sun, bursting in triumph through a cloud-rift, sent a long shaft of gold to encompass and irradiate her. To the end, whether with aching heart or glad, Hal was to see her thus, in flashing, recurrent visions; a slight, poised figure, all gracious curves and tender consonances, with a cluster of the trailing arbutus, that first-love of the springtide, clinging at her breast. The breeze bore to him the faint, wild, appealing fragrance which is the very breath and soul of the blossom's fairy-pink.

Half-turning, she had leaned a little, as a flower leans, to the warmth of the sunlight, uplifting her face for its kiss. She was not beautiful in any sense of regularity of outline or perfection of feature, so much as lovely, with the lustrous loveliness which defiantly overrides the lapse of line and proportion, and imperiously demands the homage of every man born of woman. Chill analysis might have judged the mouth, with its delicate, humorous quirk at the corners, too large; the chin too broad, for all its adorable baby dimple; the line of the nose too abrupt, the wider contours lacking something of classic exactitude. But the chillest analysis must have warmed to enthusiasm at the eyes; wide-set, level, and of a tawny hazel, with strange, wine-brown lights in their depths, to match the brownish-golden sheen of the hair, where the sun glinted from it. As it were a higher power of her physical splendor, there emanated from the girl an intensity and radiance of joy in being alive and lovely.

Involuntarily Hal Surtaine paused as he approached her. Her glance fell upon him, not with the impersonal regard bestowed upon a casual passer-by, but with an intent and brightening interest,—the thrill of the chase, had he but known it,—and passed beyond him again. But in that brief moment, the conviction was borne in upon him that sometime, somewhere, he had looked into those eyes before. Puzzled and eager he still stared, until, with a slight flush, she moved forward and passed him. At the head of the stairs he saw her greet a strongly built, grizzled man; and then became aware of his father beckoning to him from the automobile.

"Bewitched, Hal?" said Dr. Surtaine as his son came to him.

"Was I staring very outrageously, sir?"

"Why, you certainly looked interested," returned the older man, laughing. "But I don't think you need apologize to the young lady. She's used to attention. Rather lives on it, I guess."

The tone jarred on Hal. "I had a queer, momentary feeling that I'd seen her before," he said.

"Don't you recall where?"

"No," said Hal, startled. "*Do* I know her?"

"Apparently not," taunted the other good-humoredly. "You should know.

Hers is generally considered a face not difficult to remember."

"Impossible to forget!"

"In that case it must be that you haven't seen her before. But you will again. And, then look out, Boy-ee. Danger ahead!"

"How's that, sir?"

"You'll see for yourself when you meet her. Half of the boys in town are crazy over her. She eats 'em alive. Can't you tell the man-killer type when you see it?"

"Oh, that's all in the game, isn't it?" returned Hal lightly. "So long as she plays fair. And she looks like a girl of breeding and standards."

"All of that. Esmé Elliot is a lady, so far as that goes. But—well, I'm not going to prejudice you. Here she comes now."

"Who is it with her?"

"Her uncle, Dr. Elliot. He doesn't altogether approve of us—me, I mean."

Uncle and niece were coming directly toward them now, and Hal watched her approach with a thrill of delight in her motion. It was a study in harmonies. She moved like a cloud before the wind; like a ship upon the high seas; like the swirl of swift waters above hidden depths. As the pair passed to their car, which stood next to Dr. Surtaine's, the girl glanced up and nodded, with a brilliant smile, to the doctor, who returned to the salutation an extra-gallant bow.

"You seem to be friends," commented Hal, somewhat amused.

"That was more for you than for me. But the fair Esmé can always spare one of those smiles for anything that wears trousers."

Hal moved uneasily. He felt a sense of discord. As he cast about for a topic to shift to, the Elliot car rolled ahead slowly, and once more he caught the woodsy perfume of the pink bloom. Strangely and satisfyingly to his quickened perceptions, it seemed to express the quality of the wearer. Despite her bearing of worldly self-assurance, despite the atmosphere of modishness about her, there was in her charm something wild and vivid, vernal and remote, like the arbutus which, alone among flowers, keeps its life-secret virgin and inviolate, resisting all endeavors to make it bloom except in its own way and in its own chosen places.

CHAPTER IV

THE SHOP

Certina had found its first modest home in Worthington on a side street. As the business grew, the staid tenement which housed it expanded and drew to itself neighboring buildings, until it eventually gave way to the largest, finest, and most up-to-date office edifice in the city. None too large, fine, or modern was this last word in architecture for the triumphant nostrum and the minor medical enterprises allied to it. For though Certina alone bore the name and spread the fame and features of its inventor abroad in the land, many lesser experiments had bloomed into success under the fertilizing genius of the master-quack.

Inanimate machinery, when it runs sweetly, gives forth a definite tone, the bee-song of work happily consummated. So this great human mechanism seemed, to Harrington Surtaine as he entered the realm of its activities, moving to music personal to itself. Through its wide halls he wandered, past humming workrooms, up spacious stairways, resonant to the tread of brisk feet, until he reached the fifth floor where cluster the main offices. Here through a succession of open doors he caught a glimpse of the engineer who controlled all these lively processes, leaning easily back from his desk, fresh, suavely groomed, smiling, an embodiment of perfect satisfaction. Before Dr. Surtaine lay many sheaves of paper, in rigid order. A stenographer sat in a far corner, making notes. From beyond a side door came the precise, faint clicking of a typewriter. The room possessed an atmosphere of calm and poise; but not of restfulness. At once and emphatically it impressed the visitor with a sense that it was a place where things were done, and done efficiently.

Upon his son's greeting, Dr. Surtaine whirled in his chair.

"Come down to see the old slave at work, eh?" he said.

"Yes, sir." Hal's hand fell on the other's shoulder, and the Doctor's fingers went up to it for a quick pressure. "I thought I'd like to see the wheels go 'round."

"You've come to the right spot. This is the good old cash-factory, and yours truly is the man behind the engine. The State, I'm It, as Napoleon said to Louis the Quince. Where McBeth sits is the head of the table."

"In other words, a one-man business."

"That's the secret. There's nothing in this shop that I can't do, and don't do, every now and then, just to keep my hand in. I can put more pull into an ad today than the next best man in the business. Modesty isn't my besetting sin, you see, Hal."

"Why should it be? Every brick in this building would give the lie to it."

"Say every frame on these four walls," suggested Dr. Surtaine with an expansive gesture.

Following this indication, Hal examined the decorations. On every side were ordinary newspaper advertisements, handsomely mounted, most of them bearing dates on brass plates. Here and there appeared a circular, or a typed letter, similarly designated.

Above Dr. Surtaine's desk was a triple setting, a small advertisement, a larger one, and a huge full-newspaper-page size, each embodying the same figure, that of a man half-bent over, with his hand to his back and a lamentable expression on his face.

Certain strongly typed words fairly thrust themselves out of the surrounding print: **"Pain—Back—Take Care—Means Something—Your Kidneys."** And then in dominant presentment—

CERTINA CURES.

"What do you think of Old Lame-Boy?" asked Dr. Surtaine.

"From an æsthetic point of view?"

"Never mind the æsthetics of it. 'Handsome is as handsome does.'"

"What has that faded beauty done, then?"

"Carried many a thousand of our money to bank for us, Boyee. That's the ad that made the business."

"Did you design it?"

"Every word and every line, except that I got a cheap artist to touch up the drawing a little. Then I plunged. When that copy went out, we had just fifty thousand dollars in the world, you and I. Before it had been running three months, I'd spent one hundred thousand dollars more than we owned, in the newspapers, and had to borrow money right and left to keep the manufacturing and bottling plant up to the orders. It was a year before we could see clear sailing, and by that time we were pretty near quarter of a million to the good. Talk about ads. that pull! It pulled like a mule-team and a traction engine and a fifty-cent painless dentist all in one. I'm still using that copy, in the kidney season."

"Do kidneys have seasons?"

"Kidney troubles do."

"I'd have thought such diseases wouldn't depend on the time of year."

"Maybe they don't, actually," admitted the other. "Maybe they're just crowded out of the public mind by the pressure of other sickness in season, like rheumatism in the early winter, and pneumonia in the late. But there's no doubt that the kidney season comes in with the changes of the spring. That's one of my discoveries, too. I tell you, Boyee, I've built my success on things like that. It's psychology: that's what it is. That's what you've got to learn, if you're going into the concern."

"I'm ready, Dad. It sounds interesting. More so than I'd have thought."

"Interesting! It's the very heart and core of the trade." Dr. Surtaine leaned forward, to tap with an earnest finger on his son's knee, a picture of expository enthusiasm. "Here's the theory. You see, along about March or April people begin to get slack-nerved and out-of-sortsy. They don't know what ails 'em, but they think there's something. Well, one look at that ad sets 'em wondering if it isn't their kidneys. After wonder comes worry. He's the best little worrier in the trade, Old Lame-Boy is. He just pesters folks into taking proper care of themselves. They get Certina, and we get their dollars. And they get their money's worth, too," he added as an afterthought for Hal's benefit, "for it's a mighty good thing to have your kidneys tonicked up at this time of year."

"But, Dad," queried Hal, with an effort of puzzled reminiscence, "in the old days Certina wasn't a kidney remedy, was it?"

"Not specially. It's always been *good* for the kidneys. Good for everything, for that matter. Besides, the formula's been changed."

"Changed? But the formula's the vital thing, isn't it?"

"Yes, yes. Of course. Certainly it's the vital thing: certainly. But, you see,—well,—new discoveries in medicine and that sort of thing."

"You've put new drugs in?"

"Yes: I've done that. Buchu, for instance. That's supposed to be good for the kidneys. Dropped some things out, too. Morphine got sort of a bad name. The muckrakers did that with their magazine articles."

"Of course I don't pretend to know about such things, Dad. But morphine seems a pretty dangerous thing for people to take indiscriminately."

"Well, it's out. There ain't a grain of it in Certina today."

"I'm glad of it."

"Oh, I don't know. It's useful in its place. For instance, you can't run a soothing-syrup without it. But when the Pure Food Law compelled us to print the amount of morphine on the label, I just made up my mind that I'd have no government interference in the Certina business, so I dropped the drug."

"Did the law hurt our trade much?"

"Not so far as Certina goes. I'm not even sure it didn't help. You see, now we can print 'Guaranteed under the U.S. Food and Drugs Act' on every bottle. In fact we're required to."

"What does the guaranty mean?"

"That whatever statement may be on the label is accurate. That's all. But the public takes it to mean that the Government officially guarantees Certina to do everything we claim for it," chuckled Dr. Surtaine. "It's a great card. We've done more business under the new formula than we ever did under the old."

"What is the formula now?"

"Prying into the secrets of the trade?" chuckled the elder man.

"But if I'm coming into the shop, to learn—"

"Right you are, Boyee," interrupted his father buoyantly. "There's the formula for making profits." He swept his hand about in a spacious circle, grandly indicating the advertisement-bedecked walls. "There's where the brains count. Come along," he added, jumping up; "let's take a turn around the joint."

Every day, Dr. Surtaine explained to his son, he made it a practice to go through the entire plant.

"It's the only way to keep a business up to mark. Besides, I like to know my people."

Evidently he did know his people and his people knew and strongly liked him. So much Hal gathered from the offhand and cheerily friendly greetings which were exchanged between the head of the vast concern and such employees, important or humble, as they chanced to meet in their wanderings. First they went to the printing-plant, the Certina Company doing all its own printing; then to what Dr. Surtaine called "the literary bureau."

"Three men get out all our circulars and advertising copy," he explained in an aside. "One of 'em gets five thousand a year; but even so I have to go over all his stuff. If I could teach him to write ads. like I do it myself, I'd pay him ten thousand—yes, twenty thousand. I'd have to, to keep him. The circulars they do better; but I edit those, too. What about that name for the new laxative pills, Con? Hal, I want you to meet Mr. Conover, our chief ad-man."

Conover, a dapper young man with heavy eye-glasses, greeted Hal with some interest, and then turned to the business in hand.

"What'd you think of 'Anti-Pellets'?" he asked. "Anti, opposed to, you know. In the sub-line, tell what they're opposed to: indigestion, appendicitis, and so on."

"Don't like it," returned Dr. Surtaine abruptly. "Anti-Ralgia's played that to death. Lemme think, for a moment."

Down he plumped into Conover's chair, seized a pencil and made tentative jabs at a sheet of paper. "Pellets, pellets," he muttered. Then, in a kind of subdued roar, "I've got it! I've got it, Con! 'Pro-Pellets.' Tell people what they're for, not what they're against. Besides, the name has got the idea of pro-pulsion. See? Pro-Pellets, pro-pel!" His big fist shot forward like a piston-rod. "Just the idea for a laxative. Eh?"

"Fine!" agreed Conover, a little ruefully, but with genuine appreciation of the fitness of the name. "I wish I'd thought of it."

"You did—pretty near. Anyway, you made me think of it. Anti-Pellets, Pro-Pellets: it's just one step. Like as not you'd have seen it yourself if I hadn't butted in. Now, go to it, and figure out your series on that."

With kindly hands he pushed Conover back into his chair, gave him a hearty pat on the shoulder, and passed on. Hal began to have an inkling of the reasons for his father's popularity.

"Have we got other medicines besides Certina?" he asked.

"Bless you, yes! This little laxative pills business I took over from a concern that didn't have the capital to advertise it. Across the hall there is the Sure Soother department. That's a teething syrup: does wonders for restless babies. On the floor below is the Cranicure Mixture for headaches, Rub-it-in Balm for rheumatism and bruises, and a couple of small side issues that we're not trying to push much. We're handling Stomachine and Relief Pills from here, but the pills are made in Cincinnati, and we market 'em under another trade name."

"Stomachine is for stomach troubles, I assume," said Hal. "What are the Relief Pills?"

"Oh, a female remedy," replied his father carelessly. "Quite a booming little trade, too. Take a look at the Certina collection of testimonials."

In a room like a bank vault were great masses of testimonial letters, all listed and double-catalogued by name and by disease.

"Genuine. Provably genuine, every one. There's romance in some of 'em. And gratitude; good Lord! Sometimes when I look 'em over, I wonder I don't run for President of the United States on a Certina platform."

From the testimonial room they went to the art department where Dr. Surtaine had some suggestions to make as to bill-board designs.

"You'll never get another puller like Old Lame-Boy," Hal heard the head designer say with a chuckle, and his father reply: "If I could I'd start another pro-prietary as big as Certina."

"Where does that lead to?" inquired Hal, as they approached a side passage sloping slightly down, and barred by a steel door.

"The old building. The manufacturing department is over there."

"Compounding the medicine, you mean?"

"Yes. Bottling and shipping, too."

"Aren't we going through?"

"Why, yes: if you like. You won't find much to interest you, though."

Nor, to Hal's surprise, did Dr. Surtaine himself seem much concerned with this phase of the business. Apparently his hand was not so close in control here as in the other building. The men seemed to know him less well.

"All this pretty well runs itself," he explained negligently.

"Don't you have to keep a check on the mixing, to make sure it's right?"

"Oh, they follow the formula. No chance for error."

They walked amidst chinking trucks, some filled with empty, some with filled and labeled bottles, until they reached the carton room where scores of girls were busily inserting the bottles, together with folded circulars and advertising cards, into pasteboard boxes. At the far end of this room a pungent, high-spiced scent, as of a pickle-kitchen with a fortified odor underlying it, greeted the unaccustomed nose of the neophyte.

"Good!" he sniffed. "How clean and appetizing it smells!"

Enthusiasm warmed the big man's voice once more.

"Just what it is, too!" he exclaimed. "Now you've hit on the second big point in Certina's success. It's easy to take. What's the worst thing about doctors' doses? They're nasty. The very thought of 'em would gag a cat. Tell people that here's a remedy better than the old medicine and pleasant to the taste, and they'll take to it like ducks to water. Certina is the first proprietary that ever tasted good. Next to Old Lame-Boy, it's my biggest idea."

"Are we going into the mixing-room?" asked his son.

"If you like. But you'll see less than you smell."

So it proved. A heavy, wet, rich vapor shrouded the space about a huge cauldron, from which came a sound of steady plashing. Presently an attendant gnome, stripped to the waist, appeared, nodded to Dr. Surtaine, called to some one back in the mist, and shortly brought Hal a small glass brimming with a pale-brown liquid.

"Just fresh," he said. "Try it."

"My kidneys are all right," protested Hal. "I don't need any medicine."

"Take it for a bracer. It won't hurt you," urged the gnome.

Hal looked at his father, and, at his nod, put his lips to the glass.

"Why, it tastes like spiced whiskey!" he cried.

"Not so far out of the way. Columbian spirits, caramel, cinnamon and cardamom, and a touch of the buchu. Good for the blues. Finish it."

Hal did so and was aware of an almost instantaneous glow.

"Strong stuff, sir," he said to his father as they emerged into a clearer atmosphere.

"They like it strong," replied the other curtly. "I give 'em what they like."

The attendant gnome followed. "Mr. Dixon was looking for you, Dr. Surtaine. Here he comes, now."

"Dixon's our chief chemist," explained Dr. Surtaine as a shabby, anxious-looking man ambled forward.

"We're having trouble with that last lot of cascara, sir," said he lugubriously.

"In the Number Four?"

"Yes, sir. It don't seem to have any strength."

"Substitute senna." So offhand was the tone that it sounded like a suggestion rather than an order.

As the latter, however, the chemist contentedly took it.

"It'll cost less," he observed; "and I guess it'll do the work just as well."

To Hal it seemed a somewhat cavalier method of altering a medical formula. But his mind, accustomed to easy acceptance of the business which so luxuriously supplied his wants, passed the matter over lightly.

"First-rate man, Dixon," remarked Dr. Surtaine as they passed along. "College-bred, and all that. Boozes, though. I only pay him twenty-five a week, and he's mighty glad to get it."

On the way back to the offices, they traversed the checking and accounting rooms, the agency department, the great rows of desks whereat the shipping and mailing were looked after, and at length stopped before the door of a small office occupied by a dozen women. One of these, a full-bosomed, slender, warm-skinned girl with a wealth of deep-hued, rippling red hair crowning her small, well-poised head, rose and came to speak to Dr. Surtaine.

"Did you get the message I sent you about Letter Number Seven?" she asked.

"Hello, Milly," greeted the presiding genius, pleasantly. "Just what was that about Number Seven?"

"It isn't getting results."

"No? Let's see it." Dr. Surtaine was as interested in this as he had been casual about the drug alteration.

"I don't think it's personal enough," pursued the girl, handing him a sheet of imitation typewriter print.

"Oh, you don't," said her employer, amused. "Maybe you could better it."

"I have," said the girl calmly. "You always tell us to make suggestions. Mine are on the back of the paper."

"Good for you! Hal, here's the prettiest girl in the shop, and about the smartest. Milly, this is my boy."

The girl looked up at Hal with a smile and brightened color. He was suddenly interested and appreciative to see to what a vivid prettiness her face was lighted by the raised glance of her swift, gray-green eyes.

"Are you coming into the business, Mr. Surtaine?" she asked composedly, and with almost as proprietary an air as if she had said "our business."

"I don't know. Is it the sort of business you would advise a rather lazy person to embark in, Miss—"

"Neal," she supplied; adding, with an illustrative glance around, upon her busy roomful, all sorting and marking correspondence, "You see, I only give advice by letter."

She turned away to answer one of the subordinates, and, at the same time, Dr. Surtaine was called aside by a man with a shipping-bill. Looking down the line of workers, Hal saw that each one was simply opening, reading, and marking with a single stroke, the letters from a distributing groove. To her questioner Milly Neal was saying, briskly:

"That's Three and Seven. Can't you see, she says she has spots before her eyes. That's stomach. And the lameness in the side is kidneys. Mark it 'Three pass to Seven.' There's a combination form for that."

"What branch of the work is this?" asked Hal, as she lifted her eyes to his again.

"Symptom correspondence. This is the sorting-room."

"Please explain. I'm a perfect greenhorn, you know."

"You've seen the ads. of course. Nobody could help seeing them. They all say, 'Write to Professor Certain'—the trade name, you know. It's the regular stock line, but it does bring in the queries. Here's the afternoon mail, now."

Hundreds upon hundreds of letters came tumbling from a bag upon the receiving-table. All were addressed to "Prof." or "Dr." Certain.

"How can my father hope to answer all those?" cried Hal.

The girl surveyed him with a quaint and delicious derision. "He? You don't suppose he ever sees them! What are *we* here for?"

"You do the answering?"

"Practically all of it, by form-letters turned out in the printing department. For instance, Letter One is coughs and colds; Two, headaches; Three, stomach; and so on. As soon as a symp-letter is read the girl marks it with the form-letter number, underscores the address, and it goes across to the letter room where the right answer is mailed, advising the prospect to take Certina. Orders with cash go direct to the shipping department. If the symp-writer wants personal advice that the form-letters don't give, I send the inquiry upstairs to Dr. De Vito. He's a regular graduate physician who puts in half his time as our Medical Adviser. We can clear up three thousand letters a day, here."

"I can readily see that my father couldn't attend to them personally," said Hal, smiling.

"And it's just as good this way. Certina is what the prospects want and need. It makes no difference who prescribes it. This is the Chief's own device for handling the correspondence."

"The Chief?"

"Your father. We all call him that, all the old hands."

Hal's glance skimmed over the fresh young face, and the brilliant eyes. "You wouldn't call yourself a very old hand, Miss Neal."

"Seven years I've worked for the Chief, and I never want to work in a better place. He's been more than good to me."

"Because you've deserved it, young woman," came the Doctor's voice from behind Hal. "That's the one and only reason. I'm a flint-livered old divvle to folks that don't earn every cent of their wages."

"Don't you believe him, Mr. Surtaine," controverted the girl, earnestly. "When one of my girls came down last year with tuber—"

"Whoof! Whoof! Whoof!" interrupted the big man, waving his hands in the air. "Stop it! This is no experience meeting. Milly, you're right about this letter. It's the confidential note that's lacking. It'll work up all right along the line of your suggestion. I'll have to send Hal to you for lessons in the business."

"Miss Neal would have to be very patient with my stupidity."

"I don't think it would be hard to be patient with you," she said softly; and though her look was steady he saw the full color rise in her cheeks, and, startled, felt an answering throb in his pulses.

"But you mustn't flirt with her, Hal," warned the old quack, with a joviality that jarred.

Uncomfortably conscious of himself and of the girl's altered expression, Hal spoke a hasty word or two of farewell, and followed his father out into the hallway. But the blithe and vivid femininity of the young expert plucked at his mind. At the bend of the hall, he turned with half a hope and saw her standing at the door. Her look was upon him, and it seemed to him to be both troubled and wistful.

CHAPTER V

THE SCION

To Harrington Surtaine, life had been a game with easy rules. Certain things one must not do. Decent people didn't do them. That's all there was to that. In matters of morals and conduct, he was guided by a natural temperance and an innate sense of responsibility to himself. Difficult questions had not come up in his life. Consequently he had not found the exercise of judgment troublesome. His tendency, as regarded his own affairs, was to a definite promptness of decision, and there was an end of the matter. Others he seldom felt called upon to judge, but if the instance were ineluctable, he was prone to an amiable generosity. Ease of living does not breed in the mind a strongly defined philosophy. All that young Mr. Surtaine required of his fellow beings was that they should behave themselves with a due and respectable regard to the rights of all in general and of himself in particular—and he would do the same by them. Rather a pallid attenuation of the Golden Rule; but he had thus far found it sufficient to his existence.

Into this peaceful world-scheme intruded, now, a disorganizing factor. He had brought it home with him from his visit to the "shop." An undefined but pervasive distaste for the vast, bustling, profitable Certina business formed the nucleus of it. As he thought it over that night, amidst the heavily ornate elegance of the great bedroom, which, with its dressing-room and bath, his father had set aside for his use in the Surtaine mansion, he felt in the whole scheme of the thing a vague offense. The air which he had breathed in those spacious halls of trade had left a faintly malodorous reminiscence in his nostrils.

One feature of his visit returned insistently to his mind: the contrast between the semi-contemptuous carelessness exhibited by his father toward the processes of compounding the cure and the minute and insistent attention given to the methods of expounding it. Was the advertising really of so much more import than the medicine itself? If so, wasn't the whole affair a matter of selling shadow rather than substance?

But it is not in human nature to view with too stern a scrutiny a business which furnishes one's easeful self with all the requisites of luxury, and that by processes of almost magic simplicity. Hal reflected that all big businesses doubtless had their discomforting phases. He had once heard a lecturing philosopher express a doubt as to whether it were possible to defend, ethically, that prevalent modern phenomenon, the millionaire, in any of his manifestations. By the counsel of perfection this might well be true. But who was he to judge his father by such rigorous standards? Of the medical aspect of the question he could form no clear judgment. To him the patent medicine trade was simply a part of the world's business, like railroading, banking, or any other form of merchandising. His own precocious commercial experience, when, as a boy, he had played his little part in the barter and trade, had blinded him on that side. Nevertheless, his mind was not impregnably fortified. Old Lame-Boy, bearer of dollars to the bank, loomed up, a disturbing figure.

Then, from a recess in his memory, there popped out the word "genteel."

His father had characterized the Certina business as being, possibly, not sufficiently "genteel" for him. He caught at the saving suggestion. Doubtless that was the trouble. It was the blatancy of the business, not any evil quality inherent in it, which had offended him. Kindest and gentlest of men and best of fathers as Dr. Surtaine was, he was not a paragon of good taste; and his business naturally reflected his personality. Even this was further than Hal had ever gone before in critical judgment. But he seized upon the theory as a defense against further thought, and, having satisfied his self-questionings with this sop, he let his mind revert to his trip through the factory. It paused on the correspondence room and its attractive forewoman.

"She seemed a practical little thing," he reflected. "I'll talk to her again and get her point of view." And then he wondered, rather amusedly, how much of this self-suggestion arose from a desire for information, and how much was inspired by a memory of her haunting, hungry eyes.

On the following morning he kept away from the factory, lunched at the Huron Club with William Douglas, Elias M. Pierce, who had found time to be present, and several prominent citizens whom he thought quite dully similar to each other; and afterward walked to the Certina Building to keep an appointment with its official head.

"Been feeding with our representative citizens, eh?" his father greeted him. "Good! Meantime the Old Man grubbed along on a bowl of milk and a piece of apple pie, at a hurry-up lunch-joint. Good working diet, for young or old. Besides, it saves time."

"Are you as busy as all that, Dad?"

"Pretty busy this morning, because I've had to save an hour for you out of this afternoon. We'll take it right now if you're ready."

"Quite ready, sir."

"Hal, where's Europe?"

"Europe? In the usual place on the map, I suppose."

"You didn't bring it back with you, then?"

"Not a great deal of it. They mightn't have let it through the customs."

Dr. Surtaine snapped a rubber band from a packet of papers lying on his desk. "Considering that you seem to have bought it outright," he said, twinkling, "I thought you might tell me what you intend doing with it. There are the bills."

"Have I gone too heavy, sir?" asked Hal. "You've never limited me, and I supposed that the business—"

"The business," interrupted his father arrogantly, "could pay those bills three times over in any month. That isn't the point. The point is that you've spent something more than forty-eight thousand dollars this last year."

Hal whistled ruefully. "Call it an even fifty," he said. "I've made a little, myself."

"No! Have you? How's that?"

"While I was in London I did a bit of writing; sketches of queer places and people and that sort of thing, and had pretty good luck selling 'em. One fellow I know there even offered me a job paragraphing. That's like our editorial writing, you know."

"Fine! That makes me feel easier. I was afraid you might be going soft, with so much money to spend."

"How I ever spent that much—"

"Never mind that. It's gone. However, we'll try another basis. I'd thought of an allowance, but I don't quite like the notion. Hal, I'm going to give you your own money."

"My own money? I didn't know that I had any."

"Well, you have."

"Where did I get it?"

"From our partnership. From the old days on the road."

"Rather an intangible fortune, isn't it?"

"That old itinerant business was the nucleus of the Certina of today. You had a profit-sharing right in that. You've still got it—in this. Hal, I'm turning over to you today half a million dollars."

"That's a lot of money, Dad," said the younger man soberly.

"The interest doesn't come to fifty thousand dollars a year, though."

"More than half; and that's more than plenty."

"Well, I don't know. We'll try it. At any rate, it's your own. Plenty more where it comes from, if you need extra."

"I shan't. It's more than generous of you—"

"Not a bit of it. No more than just, Boyee. So let the thanks go."

"All right, sir. But—you know how I feel about it."

"I guess I know just about how you and I feel toward each other on anything that comes up between us, Boyee." There was a grave gentleness in Dr. Surtaine's tone. "Well, there are the papers," he added, more briskly. "I haven't put all your eggs in one basket, you see."

Going over the certificates Hal found himself possessed of fifty thousand dollars in the stock of the Mid-State and Great Muddy Railroad: an equal sum in the Security Power Products Company; twenty-five thousand each in the stock of the Worthington Trust Company and the Remsen Savings Bank; one hundred thousand in the Certina Company, and fifty thousand in three of its subsidiary enterprises. Besides this, he found five check-books in the large envelope which contained his riches.

"What are these, Dad?" he asked.

"Cash on deposit in local and New York banks. You might want to do some investing of your own. Or possibly you might see some business proposition you wanted to buy into."

"I see some Security Power Products Company certificates. What is that?"

"The local light, heat, and power corporation. It pays ten per cent. Certina never pays less than twenty. The rest is all good for six, at least and the Mid-and-Mud averages eight. You've got upwards of thirty-seven thousand income there, not counting your deposits. While you're looking about, deciding what you're going to do, it'll be your own money and nobody else's that you're spending."

"Do you think many fathers would do this sort of thing, Dad?" said Hal warmly.

"Any sensible one would. I don't want to own you, Boyee. I want you to own yourself. And to make yourself," he added slowly.

"If I can make myself like you, Dad—"

"Oh, I'm a good-enough piece of work, for my day and time," laughed the father. "But I want a fine finish on you. While you're looking around for your life-work, how about doing a little unpaid job for me?"

"Anything," cried Hal. "Just try me."

"Do you know what an Old Home Week is?"

"Only what I read in today's paper announcing the preliminary committee."

"That gave you enough idea. We make a big thing of Old Home Week in Worthington. This year it will be particularly big because it's the hundredth anniversary of the city. The President of the United States will be here. I'm to be chairman of the general committee, and I want you for my secretary."

"Nothing I'd like better, sir."

"Good! All the moneyed men in town will be on the committee. The work will put you in touch with the people who count. Well, that settles our business. Good luck to you in your independence, Boyee." He touched a bell. "Any one waiting to see me, Jim?" he asked the attendant.

"Yes, sir. The Reverend Norman Hale."

"Send him in."

"Shall I go, Dad?" asked Hal.

"Oh, you might take a little ramble around the shop. Go anywhere. Ask any questions of anybody. They all know you."

At the door, Hal passed a tall, sinewy young man with heavy brows and rebellious hair. A slight, humorous uptilt to his mouth relieved the face of impassivity and saved it from a too formal clericalism. The visitor was too deeply concerned with some consideration of his inner self to more than glance at Hal, who heard Dr. Surtaine's hearty greeting through the closing door.

"Glad to see you, Mr. Hale. Take a chair."

The visitor bowed gravely and sat down.

"You've come to see me about—?"

"Your subscription to the East End Church Club Fund."

"I am heartily in sympathy with the splendid work your church is doing in the—er—less salubrious parts of our city," said Dr. Surtaine.

"Doubtless," returned the young clergyman dryly.

"Seems to be saving his wind," thought Dr. Surtaine, a little uneasily. "I suppose it's a question," he continued, aloud, "of the disposition of the sum—"

"No: it is not."

If this bald statement required elucidation or expansion, its proponent didn't seem to realize the fact. He contemplated with minute scrutiny a fly which at that moment was alighting (in about the proportion of the great American eagle) upon the pained countenance of Old Lame-Boy.

"Well?" queried the other, adding to himself, "What the devil ails the man!"

The scrutinized fly rose, after the manner of its kind, and (now reduced to normal scale) touched lightly in its exploratory tour upon Dr. Surtaine's domed forehead. Following it thus far, the visitor's gaze rested. Dr. Surtaine brushed off the insect. He could not brush off the regard. Under it and his caller's continued silence he grew fidgety.

"While I'm very glad," he suggested, "to give you what time you need—"

"I've come here because I wanted to have this thing out with you face to face."

"Well, have it out," returned the other, smiling but wary.

The young clergyman drew from his pocket a folded newspaper page to which was pinned an oblong of paper. This he detached and extended to the other.

"What's that?" asked the doctor, making no motion to receive it, for he instantly recognized it.

"Your check."

"You're returning it?"

"Without thanks."

"You mean to turn down two thousand dollars!" demanded the other in slow incredulity.

"Exactly."

"Why?"

"Is that question asked in good faith?"

"It is."

"Then you haven't seen the letter written by the superintendent of our Sunday School to the Certina Company."

"What kind of a letter?"

"A testimonial letter—for which your two thousand dollars is payment, I suppose."

"Two thousand for a church testimonial!" Dr. Surtaine chuckled at his caller's innocence. "Why, I wouldn't pay that for a United States Senator. Besides," he added virtuously, "Certina doesn't buy its testimonials."

"Then it's an unfortunate coincidence that your check should have come right on top of Mr. Smithson's very ill-advised letter."

By a regular follow-up mechanism devised by himself, every donation by Dr. Surtaine was made the basis of a shrewd attempt to extract from the beneficiary an indorsement of Certina's virtues, or, if not that, of the personal character and professional probity of its proprietor. This is what had happened in the instance of the check to Mr. Hale's church, Smithson being the medium through whom the attempt was made.

The quack saw no occasion to explain this to his inquisitor. So he merely said: "I never saw any such letter," which was, in a literal sense, true.

"Nor will you know anything about it, I suppose, until the name of the church is spread broadcast through your newspaper advertising."

Now, it is a rule of the patent medicine trade never to advertise an unwilling testimonial because that kind always has a kick-back. Hence:—

"Oh, if you feel that way about it," said Dr. Surtaine disdainfully, "I'll keep it out of print."

"And return it to me," continued the other, in a tone of calm sequentiality, which might represent either appeal, suggestion, or demand.

"Don't see the point," said the quack shortly.

"Since you do not intend to use it in your business, it can't be of any value to you," countered the other.

"What's its value to you?"

"In plain words, the honor of my church is involved. The check is a bribe. The letter is the graft."

"Nothing of the sort. You come here, a minister of the gospel," Dr. Surtaine reproached him sorrowfully, "and use hard words about a transaction that is perfectly straight business and happens every day."

"Not in my church."

"It isn't your letter, anyhow. You didn't write it."

"It is written on the official paper of the church. Smithson told me so. He didn't understand what use would be made of it when he wrote it. Take your check back, Dr. Surtaine, and give me the letter."

"Persistency, thy name is a jewel," said Dr. Surtaine with an air of scholarliness. "You win. The letter will be returned tomorrow. You'll take my word, I suppose?"

"Certainly; and thank you."

"And now, suppose I offered to leave the check in your hands?" asked the Doctor curiously.

"I couldn't take it," came the decisive reply.

"Do you mind telling me why?"

The visitor spread out upon the table the newspaper page which he had taken from his pocket. "This morning's 'Clarion,'" he said.

"So that's the trouble! You've been reading that blackmailing sheet. Why, what's the 'Clarion,' anyway? A scandal-mongering, yellow blatherskite, on its last legs financially. It's for sale to any bidder who'd be fool enough to put up money. The 'Clarion' went after me because it couldn't get our business. It ain't any straighter than a corkscrew's shadow."

"Do I understand you to say that this attack is due to your refusal to advertise in the 'Clarion'?"

"That's it, to a T. And now, you see, Mr. Hale," continued Dr. Surtaine in a tone of long-suffering and dignified injury, "how believing all you see in print lures you into chasing after strange dogs."

The visitor's mouth quivered a little at this remarkable paraphrase of the Scripture passage; but he said gravely enough:

"Then we get back to the original charges, which the 'Clarion' quotes from the 'Church Standard.'"

"And there you are! Up to three years ago the 'Standard' took all the advertising we'd give them, and glad to get it. Then it went daffy over the muckraking magazine exposures, and threw out all the proprietary copy. Now nothing will do but it must roast its old patrons to show off its new virtue."

"Do you deny what the editor of the 'Standard' said about Certina?"

Dr. Surtaine employed the stock answer of medical quackery when challenged on incontrovertible facts. "Why, my friend," he said with elaborate carelessness, "if I tried to deny everything that irresponsible parties say about me, I wouldn't have any time left for business. Well, well; plenty of other people will be glad of that two thousand. Turn in the check at the cashier's window, please. Good-day to you."

The Reverend Norman Hale retired, leaving the "Clarion's" denunciation lying outspread on the table.

Meantime, wandering in the hallway, Hal had encountered Milly Neal.

"Are you very busy, Miss Neal?" he asked.

"Not more than usual," she answered, regarding him with bright and kindly eyes. "Did you want me?"

"Yes. I want to know some things about this business."

"Outside of my own department, I don't know much."

"Well; inside your own department, then. May I ask some questions?"

With a businesslike air she consulted a tiny watch, then glanced toward a settee at the end of the hall. "I'll give you ten minutes," she announced. "Suppose we sit down over there."

"Do the writers of those letters—symp-letters, I believe, you call them—" he began; "do they seem to get benefit out of the advice returned?"

"What advice? To take Certina? Why, yes. Most of 'em come back for more."

"You think it good medicine for all that long list of troubles?"

The girl's eyes opened wide. "Of course it's a good medicine!" she cried. "Do you think the Chief would make any other kind?"

"No; certainly not," he hastened to disclaim. "But it seems like a wide range of diseases to be cured by one and the same prescription."

"Oh, we've got other proprietaries, too," she assured him with her pretty air of partnership. "There's the Stomachine, and the headache powders and the Relief Pills and the liniment; Dr. Surtaine runs 'em all, and every one's a winner. Not that I keep much track of 'em. We only handle the Certina correspondence in our room. I know what that can do. Why, I take Certina myself when there's anything the matter with me."

"Do you?" said Hal, much interested. "Well, you're certainly a living testimonial to its efficacy."

"All the people in the shop take it. It's a good tonic, even when you're all right."

The listener felt his vague uneasiness soothed. If those who were actually in the business had faith in the patent medicine's worth, it must be all that was claimed for it.

"I firmly believe," continued the little loyalist, "that the Chief has done more good and saved more lives than all the doctors in the country. I'd trust him further than any regular doctor I know, even if he doesn't belong to their medical societies and all that. They're jealous of him; that's what's the matter with them."

"Good for you!" laughed Hal, feeling his doubts melt at the fire of her enthusiasm. "You're a good rooter for the business."

"So's the whole shop. I guess your father is the most popular employer in Worthington. Have you decided to come into the business, Mr. Surtaine?"

"Do you think I'd make a valuable employee, Miss Milly?" he bantered.

But to Milly Neal the subject of the Certina factory admitted of no jocularity. She took him under advisement with a grave and quaint dubiety.

"Have you ever worked?"

"Oh, yes; I'm not wholly a loafer."

"For a living, I mean."

"Unfortunately I've never had to."

"How old are you?"

"Twenty-five."

"I don't believe I'd want you in my department, if it was up to me," she pronounced.

"Do you think I wouldn't be amenable to your stern discipline?"

Still she refused to meet him on his ground of badinage. "It isn't that. But I don't think you'd be interested enough to start in at the bottom and work up."

"Perhaps you're right, Miss Neal," said Hal, a little startled by the acuteness of her judgment, and a little piqued as well. "Though you condemn me to a life of uselessness on scant evidence."

She went scarlet. "Oh, please! You know I didn't mean that. But you seem too—too easy-going, too—"

"Too ornamental to be useful?"

Suddenly she stamped her foot at him, flaming into a swift exasperation. "You're laughing at me!" she accused. "I'm going back to my work. I won't stay and be made fun of." Then, in another and rather a dismayed tone, "Oh, I'm forgetting about your being the Chief's son."

Hal jumped to his feet. "Please promise to forget it when next we meet," he besought her with winning courtesy. "You've been a kind little friend and adviser. And I thank you for what you have said."

"Not at all," she returned lamely, and walked away, her face still crimson.

Returning to the executive suite, the young scion found his father immersed in technicalities of copy with the second advertising writer.

"Sit down, Boyee," said he. "I'll be through in a few minutes." And he resumed his discussion of "black-face," "36-point," "indents," "boxes," and so on.

Left to his own devices Hal turned idly to the long table. From the newspaper which the Reverend Norman Hale had left, there glared up at him in savage black type this heading:—

CERTINA A FAKE
Religious Editor Shows Up Business and Professional Methods of Dr. L. André Surtaine

The article was made up of excerpts from a religious weekly's exposé, interspersed with semi-editorial comment. As he skimmed it, Hal's wrath and loyalty waxed in direct ratio. Malice was obvious in every line, to the incensed reader. But the cause and purpose were not so clear. As he looked up, brooding upon it, he caught his father's eye.

"Been reading that slush, Hal?"

"Yes, sir. Of course it's all a pack of lies. But what's the reason for it?"

"Blackmail, son."

"Do they expect to get money out of you this way?"

"No. That isn't it. I've always refused to have any business dealings with 'em, and this is their way of revenge."

"But I didn't know you advertised Certina in the local papers."

"We don't. Proprietaries don't usually advertise in their own towns. We're so well known at home that we don't have to. But some of the side lines, like the Relief Pills, that go out under another trade name, use space in the Worthington papers. The 'Clarion' isn't getting that copy, so they're sore."

"Can't you sue them for libel, Dad?"

"Hardly worth while. Decent people don't read the 'Clarion' anyway, so it can't hurt much. It's best just to ignore such things."

"Something ought to be done about it," declared Hal angrily.

Stuffing the paper into his pocket he took his wrath out into the open air. Hard and fast he walked, but the farther he went the hotter burned his ire.

There was in Harrington Surtaine a streak of the romantic. His inner world was partly made up of such chimerical notions as are bred in a lively mind, not in very close touch with the world of actualities, by a long course of novel-reading and theater-going. Deep within him stirred a conviction that there was a proper and suitable, nay, an almost obligatory, method made and provided for just such crises as this: something that a keen-spirited and high-bred youth ought to do about it. Suddenly it came to him. Young Surtaine returned home with his resolve taken. In the morning he would fare forth, a modern knight redressing human wrongs, and lick the editor of the "Clarion."

Overnight young Mr. Surtaine revised his project. Horsewhipping would be no more than the offending editor deserved. However, he should have his chance. Let him repent and retract publicly, and the castigation should be remitted. Forthwith the avenger sat him down to a task of composition. The apology which, after sundry corrections and emendations, he finally produced in fair copy, was not alone complete and explicit: it was fairly abject. In such terms might a confessed and hopeless criminal cast himself desperately upon the mercy of the court. Previsioning this masterly *apologium* upon the first page of the morrow's "Clarion,"—or perhaps at the top of the editorial columns,—its artificer thrilled with the combined pride of authorship and poetic justice.

On the walls of the commodious room which had been set aside in the Surtaine mansion for the young master's study hung a plaited dog-whip. The agent of just reprisals curled this neatly inside his overcoat pocket and set forth upon his errand. It was then ten o'clock in the morning.

Now, in hunting the larger fauna of the North American continent with a dog-whip, it is advantageous to have some knowledge of the game's habits. Mr. Harrington Surtaine's first error lay in expecting to find the editorial staff of a morning newspaper on duty in the early forenoon. So much a sweeper, emerging from a pile of dust, communicated to him across a railing, further volunteering that three o'clock would be a well-chosen hour for return, as the boss would be less pressed upon by engagements then, perhaps, than at other hours.

In the nature of things, the long delay might well have cooled the knightliest ardor. But as he departed from the office, Mr. Surtaine took with him a copy of that day's "Clarion" for perusal, and in its pages discovered a "follow-up" of the previous day's outrage. Back home he went, and added to his literary effort a few more paragraphs wherein the editorial "we" more profoundly cringed, cowered, and crawled in penitential abasement. Despite the relish of the words, Hal rather hoped that the editor would refuse to publish his masterpiece. He itched to use that whip.

CHAPTER VI
LAUNCHED

For purposes of vital statistics, the head office boy of the Worthington "Daily Clarion" was denominated Reginald Currier. As this chaste cognomen was artistically incompatible with his squint eye, his militant swagger, and a general bearing of unrepressed hostility toward all created beings, he was professionally known as "Bim." Journalism, for him, was comprised in a single tenet; that no visitor of whatsoever kind had or possibly could have any business of even remotely legitimate nature within the precincts of the "Clarion" office. Tradition of the place held that a dent in the wall back of his desk marked the termination of an argument in which Reginald, all unwitting, had essayed to maintain his thesis against the lightweight champion of the State who had come to call on the sporting editor.

There had been a lull in the activities of this minor Cerberus when the light and swinging footfall of one coming up the dim stairway several steps at a time aroused his ready suspicions. He bristled forth to the rail to meet a tall and rather elegant young man whom he greeted with a growl to this effect:

"Hoojer wanter see?"

"Is the editor in?"

"Whajjer want uvvum?"

The tall visitor stepped forward, holding out a card. "Take this to him, please, and say that I'd like to see him at once."

Unwisely, Reginald disregarded the card, which fluttered to the floor. More unwisely, he ignored a certain tensity of expression upon the face of his interlocutor. Most unwisely he repeated, in his very savagest growl:

"Whajjer want uvvum, I said. Didn' chu hear me?"

Graceful and effortless as the mounting lark, Reginald Currier rose and soared. When he again touched earth, it was only to go spinning into a far corner where he first embraced, then strove with and was finally tripped and thrown by a large and lurking waste-basket. Somewhat perturbed, he extricated himself in time to see the decisive visitor disappear through an inner door. Retrieving the crumpled and rejected card from its resting-place, he examined it with interest. The legend upon it was "Mr. Harrington Surtaine."

"Huh!" grunted Reginald Currier; "I never seen *that* in no sporting column."

Once within the sacred precincts, young Mr. Surtaine turned into an inner room, bumped against a man trailing a kite-tail of proof, who had issued from a door to the right, asked a question, got a response, and entered the editor's den. Two littered desks made up the principal furniture of the place. Impartially distributed between the further desk and a chair, the form of one lost in slumber sprawled. At the nearer one sat a dyspeptic man of middle age waving a heavy pencil above a galley proof.

"Are you the editor?" asked Hal.

"One editor. I'm Mr. Sterne. How the devil did you get in here?"

"Are you responsible for this?" Hal held up the morning's clipping, headed "Surtaine Fakeries Explained."

"Who are you?" asked Sterne, nervously hitching in his chair.

"I am Harrington Surtaine."

The journalist whistled, a soft, long-drawn note. "Dr. Surtaine's son?" he inquired.

"Yes."

"That's awkward." "Not half as awkward as it's going to be unless you apologize privately and publicly."

Mr. Sterne looked at him estimatingly, at the same time wadding up a newspaper clipping from the desk in front of him. This he cast at the slumberer with felicitous accuracy.

"Hoong!" observed that gentleman, starting up and caressing his cheek.

"Wake up, Mac. Here's a man from the Trouble Belt, with samples to show."

The individual thus addressed slowly rose out of his chair, exhibiting a squat, gnarly figure surmounted by a very large head.

Hal's hand came up out of his pocket, with the dog-whip writhing unpleasantly after it. Simultaneously, the ex-sleeper projected himself, without any particular violence but with astonishing quickness, between the caller and his prey. Without at all knowing whence it was derived, Hal became aware of a large, black, knobby stick, which it were inadequate to call a cane, in his new opponent's grasp.

Of physical courage there was no lack in the scion of the Surtaine line. Neither, however, was he wholly destitute of reasoning powers and caution. The figure before him was of an unquestionable athleticism; the weapon of obvious weight and fiber. The situation was embarrassing.

"Please don't lick the editor," said the interrupter of poetic justice good-humoredly. "Appropriately framed and hung upon the wall, fifteen cents apiece. Yah-ah-ah-oo!" he yawned prodigiously. "Calm down," he added.

Hal stared at the squat and agile figure. "You're the office bully and bouncer, I suppose," he said.

"McGuire Ellis, *at* your service. Bounce only when compelled. Otherwise peaceful. *And* sleepy."

"My business is with this man," said Hal, indicating Sterne. "Put up your toy, then, and state it in words of one syllable."

For a moment the visitor pondered, drawing the whip through his hands, uncertainly. "I'm not fool enough to go up against that war-club," he remarked.

Mr. McGuire Ellis nodded approval. "First sensible thing I've heard you say," he remarked.

"But neither"—here Hal's jaw projected a little—"am I going to let this thing drop."

"Law?" inquired Sterne. "If you think there's any libel in what the 'Clarion' has said, ask your lawyer. What do you want, anyway?"

Thus recalled to the more pacific phase of his errand, Hal produced his document. "If you've got an iota of decency or fairness about you, you'll print that," he said.

Sterne glanced through it swiftly. "Nothing doing," he stated succinctly. "Did Dr. Surtaine send you here with that thing?"

"My father doesn't know that I'm here."

"Oho! So that's it. Knight-errantry, eh? Now, let me put this thing to you straight, Mr. Harrington Surtaine. If your father wants to make a fair and decent statement, without abuse or calling names, over his own signature, the 'Clarion' will run it, at fifty cents a word."

"You dirty blackmailer!" said Hal slowly.

"Hard names go with this business, my young friend," said the other coolly.

"At present you've got me checked. But you don't always keep your paid bully with you, I suppose. One of these days you and I will meet—"

"And you'll land in jail."

"He talks awfully young, doesn't he?" said Mr. Ellis, shaking a solemn head.

"As for blackmail," continued Sterne, a bit eagerly, "there's nothing in that. We've never asked Dr. Surtaine for a dollar. He hasn't got a thing on us." "You never asked him for advertising either, I suppose," said Hal bitterly.

"Only in the way of business. Just as we go out after any other advertising."

"If he had given you his ads.—"

"Oh, I don't say that we'd have gone after him if he'd been one of our regular advertisers. Every other paper in town gets his copy; why shouldn't we? We have to look out for ourselves. We look out for our patrons, too. Naturally, we aren't going to knock one of our advertisers. Others have got to take their chances."

"And that's modern journalism!"

"It's the newspaper business," cried Sterne. "No different from any other business."

"No wonder decent people consider newspaper men the scum of the earth," said Hal, with rather ineffectual generalization.

"Don't be young!" besought McGuire Ellis wearily. "Pretend you're a grown-up man, anyway. You look as if you might have some sense about you somewhere, if you'd only give it a chance to filter through."

Some not unpleasant quirk of speech and manner in the man worked upon Hal's humor.

"Why, I believe you're right about the youngness," he admitted, with a smile. "Perhaps there are other ways of getting at this thing. Just for a test,—for the last time will you or will you not, Mr. Sterne, publish this apology?"

"We will not. There's just one person can give me orders."

"Who is that?"

"The owner."

"I think you'll be sorry."

McGuire Ellis turned upon him a look that was a silent reproach to immaturity.

"Anything more?" queried Sterne. "Nothing," said Hal, with an effort at courtesy. "Good-day to you both."

"Well, what about it?" asked McGuire Ellis of his chief, as the visitor's footsteps died away.

"Nothing about it. When'll the next Surtaine roast be ready?"

"Ought to be finished tomorrow."

"Schedule it for Thursday. We'll make the old boy squeal yet. Do you believe the boy when he says that his father didn't send him?"

"Sounded straight. Pretty straight boy he looked like to me, anyway."

"Pretty fresh kid, *I* think. And a good deal of a pin-head. Distributing agency for the old man's money, I guess. He won't get anywhere."

"Well, I'm not so sure," said Ellis contemplatively. "Of course he acts gosh-awful young. But did you notice him when he went?"

"Not particularly."

"He was smiling."

"Well?"

"Always look out for a guy that smiles when he's licked. He's got a come-back to him."

Eleven o'clock that night saw McGuire Ellis lift his head from the five-minute nap which he allowed himself on evenings of light pressure after the Washington copy was run off, and blink rapidly. At the same moment Mr. David Sterne gave utterance to an exclamation, partly of annoyance, partly of surprise. Mr. Harrington Surtaine, wearing an expression both businesslike and urbane stood in the doorway.

"Good-evening, gentlemen," he remarked.

Mr. Sterne snorted. Mr. Ellis's lips seemed about to form the reproachful monosyllable "young." Without further greeting the visitor took off his hat and overcoat and hung them on a peg. "You make yourself at home," growled Sterne.

"I do," agreed Hal, and, discarding his coat, hung that on another peg. "I've got a right to."

Tilting a slumber-burdened head, McGuire Ellis released his adjuration against youthfulness.

"What's the answer?" demanded Sterne.

"I've just bought out the 'Clarion,'" said Hal.

CHAPTER VII

THE OWNER

Some degree of triumph would perhaps have been excusable in the new owner. Most signally had he turned the tables on his enemies. Yet it was with no undue swagger that he seated himself upon a chair of problematical stability, and began to study the pages of the morning's issue. Sterne regarded him dubiously.

"This isn't a bluff, I suppose?" he asked.

"Ask your lawyers."

"Mac, get Rockwell's house on the 'phone, will you, and find out if we've been sold."

Presently the drawl of Mr. Ellis was heard, pleading with a fair and anonymous Central, whom he addressed with that charming impersonality employed toward babies, pet dogs, and telephone girls, as "Tootsie," to abjure juvenility, and give him 322 Vincent, in a hurry.

"You'll excuse me, Mr. Surtaine," said Sterne, in a new and ingratiating tone, for which Hal liked him none the better, "but verifying news has come to be an instinct with me."

"It's straight," said Ellis, turning his heavy face to his principal, after a moment's talk over the wire. "Bought *and* sold, lock, stock, and barrel."

"Have you had any newspaper experience, Mr. Surtaine?" inquired Sterne.

"Not on the practical side."

"As owner I suppose you'll want to make changes."

"Undoubtedly."

"They all do," sighed Sterne. "But my contract has several months—" "Yes: I've been over the contracts with a lawyer. Yours and Mr. Ellis's. He says they won't hold."

"All newspaper contracts are on the cheese," observed McGuire Ellis philosophically. "Swiss cheese, at that. Full of holes."

"I don't admit it," protested Sterne. "Even so, to turn a man out—"

A snort of disgust from Ellis interrupted the plea. The glare with which that employee favored his boss fairly convicted the seamed and graying editor of willful and captious immaturity.

"Contract or no contract, you'll both be fairly treated," said the new owner shortly.

"Who, me?" inquired Ellis. "You can go rapidly to hell and take my contract with you. I know when I'm fired."

"Who fired you?"

"I did. To save you the satisfaction."

"Very good of you, I'm sure," drawled Hal in a tone of lofty superiority, turning away. Out of the corner of his eye, however, he could see McGuire Ellis making pantomime as of one spanking a baby with fervor. Amusement helped him to the recovery of his temper.

"Working under an amateur journalist will just suit Sterne," observed Ellis, in a tone quite as offensive as Hal's.

"Cut it out, Mac," suggested his principal. "There's no occasion for hard words."

"Amateur isn't the hardest word in the dictionary," said Hal quietly. "Perhaps I'll become a professional in time."

"Buying a newspaper doesn't make a newspaper man."

"Well, I'm not too old to learn. But see here, Mr. Ellis, doesn't your contract hold you?"

"The contract that you said was no good? Do you expect it to work all one way?"

"Well, professional honor, then, I should suppose—"

"Professional honor!" cut in Ellis, with scathing contempt. "You step in here and buy a paper out of a freak of revenge—"

"Hold on, there! How can you know my motive?"

"What else could it be?"

Hal was silent, finding no answer.

"You see! To feed your mean little spite, you've taken over control of the biggest responsibility, for any one with any decent sense of responsibility, that a man could take on his shoulders. And what will you make of it? A toy! A rich kid's plaything."

"Well, what would you make of it, yourself?" asked Hal.

"A teacher and a preacher. A force to tear down and to build up. To rip this old town wide open, and remould it nearer to the heart's desire! That's what a newspaper might be, and ought to be, and could be, by God in Heaven, if the right man ever had a free hand at it."

"Don't get profane, my boy," tittered Sterne.

"You think that's swearing?" retorted Ellis. "Yes; *you* would. But I was nearer praying then than I've ever been since I came to this office. We'll never live to see that prayer answered, you and I."

"Perhaps," began Hal.

"Oh, perhaps!" Ellis snatched the word from his lips. "Perhaps you're the boy to do it, eh? Why, it's your kind that's made journalism the sewer of the professions, full of the scum and drainings of every other trade's failures. What chance have we got to develop ideals when you outsiders control the whole business?"

"Hullo!" observed Sterne with a grin. "Where do you come in on the idealist business, Mac? This is new talk from you."

"New? Why wouldn't it be new? Would I waste it on you, Dave Sterne?"

"You certainly never have since I've known you."

"Call it easing up my mind if you like. I can afford that luxury, now that you 're not my boss any longer. Not but what it's all Greek to you."

"Had a drink today, Mac?"

"No, damn you. But I'm going out of here and take a hundred. First, though, I'm going to tell young Bib-and-Tucker over there a thing or two about his new toy. Oh, yes: you can listen, too, Sterne, but it won't get to your shelled-in soul."

"You in'trust muh, strangely," said Sterne, and looked over to Hal for countenance of his uneasy amusement.

But the new owner did not appear amused. He had faced around in his chair and now sat regarding the glooming and exalted Ellis with an intent surprise.

"A plaything! That's what you think you've bought, young Mr. Harrington Surtaine. One of two things you'll do with it: either you'll try to run it yourself, and you'll dip deeper and deeper into Poppa's medicine-bag till he gets sick of it and closes you up; or you'll hire some practical man to manage it, and insist on dividends that'll keep it just where it is now. And that's pretty low, even for a Worthington paper."

"It won't live on blackmail, at any rate," said Hal, his mind reverting to its original grievance.

"Maybe it will. You won't know it if it does. Anyhow, it'll live on suppression and distortion and manipulation of news, because it'll have to, if it's going to live at all."

"You mean that is the basis of the newspaper business as it is today?"

"Generally speaking. It certainly is in Worthington."

"You're frank, at any rate. Where's all your glowing idealism now?"

"Vanished into mist. All idealism goes that way, doesn't it?"

"Not if you back it up with work. You see, Mr. Ellis, I'm something of an idealist myself."

"The Certina brand of idealism. Guaranteed under the Pure Thought and Deed Act."

"Our money may have been made a little—well, blatantly," said Hal, flushing. "But at least it's made honestly." He was too intent on his subject to note either Sterne's half-wink or Ellis's stare of blank amazement. "And I'm going to run this newspaper on the same high principles. I don't quite reconcile your standards with the practices of this paper, Mr. Ellis—"

"Mac has nothing to do with the policy of the paper, Mr. Surtaine," put in Sterne. "He's only an employee."

"Then why don't you get work on some paper that practices your principles?"

"Hard to find. Not having been born with a silver spoon, full of Certina, in my mouth, I have to earn my own living. It isn't profitable to make a religion of one's profession, Mr. Surtaine. Not that I think you need the warning. But I've tried it, and I know."

"Do you know, it's rather a pity you don't like me," said Hal, with ruminative frankness. "I think I could use some of that religion of yours."

"Not on the market," returned Ellis shortly.

"You see," pursued the other, "it's really my own money I've put into this paper: half of all I've got."

"How much did you pay for it?" inquired Ellis: "since we're telling each other our real names."

"Two hundred and thirty thousand dollars."

"Whee-ee-ee-ew!" Both his auditors joined in the whistle.

"They asked two-fifty."

"Half of that would have bought," said Sterne.

Hal digested that information in silence for a minute. "I suppose I was easy. Hurry never yet made a good bargain. But, now that I've got this paper I'm going to run it myself."

"On the rocks," prophesied McGuire Ellis. "Utter and complete shipwreck.

I'm glad I'm off."

"Is it your habit, Mr. Ellis, to run at the first suggestion of disaster?"

Ellis looked his questioner up and down. "Say the rest of it," he barked.

"Why, it seems to me you're still an officer of this ship. Doesn't it enter into your ethics somewhere that you ought to stick by her until the new captain can fill your place, and not quit in the face of the shipwreck you foresee?"

"Humph," grunted McGuire Ellis, "I guess you're not quite as young as I thought you were. How long would you want me to stay?"

"About a year."

"What!"

"On an unbreakable contract. To be editorial manager. You see, I'm prepared to buy ideals."

"What about my opinion of amateur journalism?"

"You'll just have to do the best you can about that."

"Give me till tomorrow to think it over."

"All right."

Ellis put down the hat and cane which he had picked up preparatory to his departure.

"Not going out after those hundred drinks, eh, Mac?" laughed Sterne.

"Indefinitely postponed," replied the other.

"The first thing to do," said Hal decisively, "is to make amends. Mr. Sterne, the 'Clarion' is to print a full retraction of the attacks upon my father, at once."

"Yes, sir," assented Sterne, slavishly responsive to the new authority.

Not so McGuire Ellis. "If you do that you'll make a fool of your own paper," he said bluntly.

"Make a fool of the paper by righting a rank injustice?"

"Just the point. It isn't a rank injustice."

"See here, Mr. Sterne: isn't it a fact that this attack was made because my father doesn't advertise with you?"

The editor twisted uneasily in his chair. "A newspaper's got to look out for its own interests," he asserted defensively.

"Please answer my question."

"Well—yes; I suppose it is so."

"Then you're simply operating a blackmailing scheme to get the Certina advertising for the 'Clarion.'"

"The Certina advertising?" repeated Sterne in obvious surprise.

"Certina doesn't advertise locally. Most patent medicines don't. It's a sort of fashion of the trade not to," explained Ellis.

"What on earth is all this about, then?"

The two newspaper men exchanged a glance. Obviously the new boss understood little of his progenitor's extensive business interests. "Might as well know sooner as later," decided Ellis, aloud. "It's the Neverfail Company of Cincinnati that we got turned down on."

"What is the Neverfail Company?"

"One of Dr. Surtaine's alia—one of the names he does business under. Every other paper in town gets their copy. We don't. Hence the roast."

"What sort of business is it?"

"Relief Pills. Here's the ad in this morning's 'Banner.'"

The name struck chill on Hal's memory. He stared at the sinister oblong of type, vaguely sensing in its covert promises the taint, yet failing to apprehend the full villainy of the lure.

"Whatever the advertising is," said he, "the principle is the same."

"Precisely," chirped Ellis.

"And you call that decent journalism?"

"No: my extremely youthful friend, I do not. What's more, I never did."

"If you want a retraction published," said Sterne, spreading wide his hands as one offering fealty, "wouldn't it be just as well to preface it with an announcement of the taking-over of the paper by yourself?"

"That itself would be tantamount to an announced reversal of policy," mused Hal.

Again Sterne and Ellis glanced at each other, but with a different expression this time. The look meant that they had recognized in the intruder a flash of that mysterious sense vaguely known as "the newspaper instinct," with which a few are born, but which most men acquire by giving mortgages on the blest illusions of youth.

"Cor-*rect*," said Ellis.

"Let the retraction rest for the present. I'll decide it later."

The door was pushed open, and a dark man of perhaps thirty, with a begrimed and handsome face, entered. In one hand he held a proof.

"About this paragraph," he said to Sterne in a slightly foreign accent. "Is it to run tomorrow?"

"What paragraph is that?"

"The one-stick editorial guying Dr. Surtaine."

"Kill it," said Sterne hastily. "This is Mr. Harrington Surtaine. Mr. Surtaine, this is Max Veltman, foreman of our composing-room."

Slowly the printer turned his fine, serious face from one to the other. "Ah," he said presently. "So it is arranged. We do not print this paragraph. Good!"

Impossible to take offense at the tone. Yet the smile which accompanied it was so plainly a sneer that Hal's color rose.

"Mr. Surtaine is the new owner of the 'Clarion,'" explained Ellis.

"In that case, of course," said Veltman quietly. "Good-night, gentlemen."

"Good-looking chap," remarked Hal. "But what a curious expression."

"Veltman's a thinker and a crank," said Ellis. "If he had a little more balance he'd make his mark. But he's a sort of melancholiac. Ill-health, nerves, and a fixed belief in the general wrongness of creation."

"Well. I'll get to know more about the shop tomorrow," said Hal. "I'm for home and sleep just now. See you at—what time, by the way?"

"Noon," said Sterne. "If that suits you."

"Perfectly. Good-night."

Arrived at home, Hal went straight to the big ground-floor library where, as the light suggested, his father sat reading.

"Dad, do you want a retraction printed?"

"Of the 'Clarion' article?"

"Yes."

"From 'Want' to 'Get' the road runs rocky," said the senior Surtaine whimsically.

"I've just come from removing a few of the rocks at the 'Clarion' office."

"Go down to lick the editor?" Dr. Surtaine's eyes twinkled.

"There may have been some such notion in the back of my head."

"Expensive exercise. Did you do it?"

"No. He had a club."

"If I were running a slander-machine like the 'Clarion' I'd want six-inch armor-plate and a quick-fire battery. Well, what did you do?"

"Bought the paper."

"You needn't have gone down town to do that. It comes to the office."

"You don't understand. I've bought the 'Clarion,' presses, plant, circulation, franchise, good-will, ill-will, high, low, jack, and the game."

"You! What for?"

"Why," said Hal thoughtfully; "mainly because I lost my temper, I believe."

"Sounds like a pretty heavy loss, Boy-ee."

"Two hundred and thirty thousand dollars. Oh, the prodigal son hasn't got anything on me, Dad, when it comes to scattering patrimonies," he concluded a little ruefully.

"What are you going to do with it, now you've got it?"

"Run it. I've bought a career."

"Now you're talking." The big man jumped up and set both hands on Hal's shoulders. "That's the kind of thing I like to hear, and in the kind of way it ought to be said. You go to it, Hal. I'll back you, as far as you like."

"No, sir. I thank you just the same: this is my game."

"Want to play it alone, do you?"

"How else can I make a career of it?"

"Right you are, Boyee. But it takes something behind money to build up a newspaper. And the 'Clarion' 'll take some building up."

"Well, I've got aspiration enough, if it comes to that," smiled Hal.

"Aspiration's a good starter: but it's perspiration that makes a business go. Are you ready to take off your coat and work?"

"I certainly am. There's a lot for me to learn."

"There is. Everything. Want some advice from the Old Man?"

"I most surely do, Dad."

"Listen here, then. A newspaper is a business proposition. Never forget that. All these hifalutin' notions about its being a palladium and the voice of the people and the guardian of public interests are good enough to talk about on the editorial page. Gives a paper a following, that kind of guff does. But the duty of a newspaper is the duty of any other business, to make money. There's the principle, the policy, the politics, ethics, and religion of the newspaper in a nutshell. Now, how are you going to make money with the 'Clarion'?"

"By making it a better paper than the others."

"Hm! Better. Yes: that's all right, so long as you mean the right thing by 'better.' Better for the people that want to use it and can pay for using it."

"The readers, you mean?"

"The advertisers. It's the advertisers that pay for the paper, not the readers. You've got to have circulation, of course, to get the advertising. But remember this, always: circulation is only a means to an end. It never yet paid the cost of getting out a daily, and it never will."

"I know enough of the business to understand that."

"Good! Look at the 'Clarion,' as it is. It's got a good circulation. And that lets it out. It can't get the advertising. So it's losing money, hand over fist."

"Why can't it?"

"It's yellow. It doesn't treat the business interests right."

"Sterne says they always look after their own advertisers."

"Oh, that! Naturally they have to. Any newspaper will do that. But they print a lot of stuff about strikes and they're always playing up to the laboring man and running articles about abuses and pretending to be the friend of the poor and all that slush, and the better class of business won't stand for it. Once a paper gets yellow, it has to keep on. Otherwise it loses what circulation it's got. No advertiser wants to use it then. The department stores do go into the 'Clarion' because it gets to a public they can't reach any other way. But they give it just as little space as they can. It isn't popular."

"Well, I don't intend to make the paper yellow."

"Of course you don't. Keep your mind on it as a business proposition and you won't go wrong. Remember, it's the advertiser that pays. Think of that when you write an editorial. Frame it and hang it where every sub-editor and reporter can't help but see it. Ask of every bit of news, 'Is this going to get me an advertiser? Is that going to lose me an advertiser?' Be on the lookout to do your advertisers favors. They appreciate little things like special notices and seeing their names in print, in personals, and that kind of thing. And keep the paper optimistic. Don't knock. Boost. Business men warm up to that. Why, Boy-ee, if you'll just stick to the policy I've outlined, you'll not only make a big success, but you'll have a model paper that'll make a new era in local journalism; a paper that every business man in town will swear by and that'll be the pride of Worthington before you're through."

Fired by the enthusiasm of his fair vision of a higher journalism, Dr. Surtaine had been walking up and down, enlivening, with swinging arms, the chief points of his Pæan of Policy. Now he dropped into his chair and with a change of voice said:

"Never mind about that retraction, Hal."

"No?"

"No. Forget it. When do you start in work?"

"Tomorrow."

"You must save tomorrow evening."

"For what?"

"You're invited to the Festus Willards'. Mrs. Willard was particularly anxious you should come."

"But I don't know them, Dad."

"Doesn't matter. It's about the most exclusive house in town. A cut above me, I can tell you. I've never so much as set foot in it."

"Then I won't go," declared his son, flushing.

"Yes: you must," insisted his father anxiously. "Don't mind about me. I'm not ambitious socially. I told you some folks don't like the business. It's too noisy. But you won't throw out any echoes. You'll go, Boyee?"

"Since you want me to, of course, sir. But I shan't find much time for play if I'm to learn my new trade."

"Oh, you can hire good teachers," laughed his father. "Well, I'm sleepy. Good-night, Mr. Editor."

"Good-night, Dad. I could use some sleep myself." But thought shared the pillow with Hal Surtaine's head. Try as he would to banish the contestants, Dr. Surtaine's Pæan of Policy and McGuire Ellis's impassioned declaration of faith did battle for the upper hand in his formulating professional standards. The Doctor's theory was the clean-cut, comprehensible, and plausible one. But something within Hal responded to the hot idealism of the fighting journalist. He wanted Ellis for a fellow workman. And his last waking notion was that he wanted and needed Ellis mainly because Ellis had told him to go to hell.

CHAPTER VIII

A PARTNERSHIP

All the adjectives in the social register were exhausted by the daily papers in describing Mrs. Festus Willard's dance. Without following them into that verbal borderland wherein "recherché" vies with "exclusive," and "chic" disputes precedence with "distingué," it is sufficient for the purposes of this narrative to chronicle the fact that the pick of Worthington society was there, and not much else. Also, if I may borrow from the Society Editor's convenient phrase-book, "Among those present" was Mr. Harrington Surtaine.

For reasons connected with his new venture, Hal had come late. He was standing near the doorway wondering by what path to attain to an unidentified hostess, when Miss Esmé Elliot, at the moment engaged with that very hostess on some matter of feminine strategy with which we have no concern, spied him.

"Who is the young Greek godling, hopelessly lost in the impenetrable depths of your drawing-room?" she propounded suddenly.

"Who? What? Where?" queried Mrs. Willard, thus abruptly recalled to her duties.

"Yonder by the doorway, looking as if he didn't know a soul."

"It's some stranger," said the hostess, trying to peer around an intervening palm. "I must go and speak to him."

"Wait. Festus has got him."

For the host, a powerful, high-colored man in his early forties, with a slight limp, had noticed the newcomer and was now introducing himself. Miss Elliot watched the process with interest.

"Jinny," she announced presently, "I want that to play with."

The stranger turned a little, so that his full face was shown. "It's Hal Surtaine!" exclaimed Mrs. Willard.

"I don't care who it is. It looks nice. Please, mayn't I have it to play with?"

"Will you promise not to break it? It used to be a particular pet of mine."

"When?"

"Oh, years ago. When you were in your cradle."

"Where?"

"On the St. Lawrence. Several summers. He was my boy-knight, and chaperon, and protector. Such a dear, chivalrous boy!"

"Was he in love with you?" demanded Miss Elliot with lively interest.

"Of course he wasn't. He was a boy of fifteen, and I a mature young woman of twenty-one."

"He *was* in love with you," accused the girl, noting a brightness in her friend's color.

"There was a sort of knightly devotion," admitted the other demurely. "There always is, isn't there, in a boy of that age, for a woman years older?"

"And you didn't know him at first?"

"It's ten years since I've set eyes on him. He doesn't even know that I am the Mrs. Festus Willard who is giving this party."

"Festus is looking around for you. They'll be over here in a minute. No! Don't get up yet. I want you to do something for me."

"What is it, Norrie?"

"I'm not going to feel well, about supper-time."

"Why not?"

"Would *you* feel well if you'd been in to dinner three times in the last week with Will Douglas, and then had to go in to supper with him, too?"

"But I thought you and Will—"

"I'm tired of having people think," said Miss Elliot plaintively. "Too much Douglas! Yes; I shall be quite indisposed, about one dance before supper."

"I'll send you home."

"No, you won't, Jinny, dear. Because I shall suddenly recover, about two minutes before the oysters arrive."

"Norrie!"

"Truly I shall. Quite miraculously. And you're to see that the young Greek godling doesn't get any other partner for supper—"

"Esmé!!"

"—because I'm sure he'd rather have me," she concluded superbly.

"Eleanor Stanley Maxwell Elliot!"

"Oh, you may call me *all* my names. I'm accustomed to abuse from you. But you'll arrange it, *dear* Jinny, won't you!"

"Did you ever fail of anything when you put on that wheedling face and tone?"

"Never," said Miss Elliot with composure, but giving her friend a little hug. "Here they come. I fly. Bring him to me later."

Piloted by Festus Willard, Hal crossed the floor, and beheld, moving to meet him with outstretched hands, a little woman with an elfin face and the smile of a happy child.

"Have you forgotten me, Hal?"

"Lady Jeannette!" he cried, the old boyhood name springing to his lips. "What are you doing here?"

"Didn't Festus tell you?" She looked fondly up at her big husband. "I didn't know that the surprise would last up to the final moment."

"It's the very best surprise that has happened to me in Worthington," declared Hal emphatically.

"We're quite prepared to adopt you, Surtaine," said Willard pleasantly. "Jinny has never ceased to wonder why she heard nothing from you in reply to her note telling of our engagement."

"Never got it," said Hal promptly. "And I've wondered why she dropped me so unaccountably. It's rather luck for me, you know," he added, smiling, "to find friends ready-made in a strange town."

"Oh, you'll make friends enough," declared Mrs. Willard. "The present matter is to make acquaintances. Come and dance this dance out with me and then I'll take you about and introduce you. Are you as good a dancer as you used to be?"

Hal was, and something more. And in his hostess he had one of the best partners in Worthington. Cleverly she had judged that the "Boston" with her, if he were proficient, would be the strongest recommendation to the buds of the place. And, indeed, before they had gone twice about the floor, many curious and interested eyes were turned upon them. Not the least interested were those of Miss Elliot, who privately decided, over a full and overflowing programme, that she would advance her recovery to one dance before the supper announcement.

"You're going to be a social success, Hal," whispered his partner. "I feel it. And *where* did you learn that delightful swing after the dip?"

"Picked it up on shipboard. But I shan't have much time for gayeties. You see, I've become a workingman."

"Tell me about it tomorrow. You're to dine with us; quite *en famille*. You *must* like Festus, Hal."

"I should think that would be easy."

"It is. He is just the finest, cleanest, straightest human being in the world," she said soberly. "Now, come away and meet a million people."

So late was it that most of the girls had no vacancies on their programmes. But Jeannette Willard was both a diplomat and a bit of a despot, socially, and several of the young eligibles relinquished, with surprisingly good grace, so Hal felt, their partners, in favor of the newcomer. He did not then know the tradition of Worthington's best set, that hospitality to a stranger well vouched for should be the common concern of all. Very pleasant and warming he found this atmosphere, after his years abroad, with its happy, well-bred frankness, its open comradeship, and obvious, "first-name" intimacies. But though every one he met seemed ready to extend to him, as a friend of the Willards, a ready welcome, he could not but feel himself an outsider, and at the conclusion of a dance he drew back into a side passage, to watch for a time.

Borne on a draught of air from some invisibly opening door behind him there came to his nostrils the fairy-spice of the arbutus-scent. He turned quickly, and saw her almost at his shoulder, the girl of the lustrous face. Behind her was Festus Willard.

"Ah, there you are, Surtaine," he said. "I've been looking for you to present you to Miss Elliot. Esmé, this is Mr. Harrington Surtaine."

She neither bowed nor moved in acknowledgment of Hal's greeting, but looked at him with still, questioning eyes. The springtide hue of the wild flower at her breast was matched in her cheek. Her head was held high, bringing out the pure and lovely line of chin and throat. To Hal it seemed that he had never seen anything so beautiful and desirable.

"Is it a bet?" Festus Willard's quiet voice was full of amusement. "Have you laid a wager as to which will keep silent longest?"

At this, Hal recovered himself, though stumblingly.

"'Fain would I speak,'" he paraphrased, "'but that I fear to—to—to—'"

"Stutter," suggested Willard, with solicitous helpfulness. The girl broke into a little trill of mirth, too liquid for laughter; being rather the sound of a brooklet chuckling musically over its private delectations.

"If I could have a dance with you," suggested Hal, "I'm sure it would help my aphasia."

"I'm afraid," she began dubiously, "that—No; here's one just before supper. If you haven't that—"

"No: I haven't," said Hal hastily. "It's awfully good of you—and lucky for me."

"I'll be with Mrs. Willard," said the girl, nodding him a cheerful farewell.

Just what or who his partners for the next few dances were, Hal could not by any effort recall the next day. He was conscious, on the floor, only of an occasional glimpse of her, a fugitive savor of the wildwood fragrance, and then she had disappeared.

Later, as he returned from a talk with Festus Willard outside, he became aware of the challenge of deep-hued, velvety eyes, regarding him with a somewhat petulant expression, and recognized his acquaintance of the motor car and the railroad terminal.

"You'd forgotten me," accused Miss Kathleen Pierce, pouting, as he came to greet her.

Hal's disclaimer had sufficient diplomatic warmth to banish her displeasure. She introduced to him as Dr. Merritt a striking-looking, gray-haired young man, who had come up at the same time with an anticipatory expression. This promptly vanished when she said offhandedly to him:

"You've had three dances with me already, Hugh. I'm going to give this one to Mr. Surtaine if he wants it."

"Of course I want it," said Hal.

"Not that you deserve it," she went on. "You should have come around earlier. I'm not in the habit of giving dances this late in the evening."

"How could I break through the solid phalanx of supplicating admirers?"

"At least, you might have tried. I want to try that new step I saw you doing with Mrs. Willard. And I always get what I want."

"Unfortunate young lady!"

"Why unfortunate?"

"To have nothing seem unattainable. Life must pall on you terribly."

"Indeed, it doesn't. I like being a spoiled child, don't you? Don't you think it's fun having everything you want to buy, and having a leading citizen for a father?"

"Is your father a leading citizen?" asked Hal, amused.

"Of course. So's yours. Neither of them quite knows which is the most leading. Dr. Surtaine is the most popular, but I suppose Pop is the most influential. Between the two of them they pretty much run this little old burg. Of course," she added with careless insolence, "Pop has got it all over Dr. Surtaine socially."

"I humbly feel that I am addressing local royalty," said Hal, smiling sardonically.

"Who? Me? Oh, I'm only the irresponsible child of wealth and power. Dr. Merritt called me that once—before I got him tamed." Turning to look at the gray young man who stood not far off, and noting the quiet force and competence of the face, Hal hazarded a guess to himself that the very frank young barbarian with whom he was talking was none too modest in her estimate of her own capacities. "Mrs. Willard is our local queen," she continued. "And Esmé Elliot is the princess. Have you met Esmé yet?"

"Yes."

"Then, of course, nobody else has a chance—so long as you're the newest toy. Still, you might find a spare hour between-times to come and call on us. Come on; let's dance."

"Pert" was the mildest term to which Hal reduced his characterization of Miss Pierce, by the time the one-step ended. Nevertheless, he admitted to himself that he had been amused. His one chief concern now, however, was the engagement with Miss Elliot.

When finally his number came around, he found her calmly explaining to a well-favored young fellow with a pained expression that he must have made a mistake about the number, while Mrs. Willard regarded her with mingled amusement and disfavor.

"Don't expect me to dance," she said as Hal approached. "I've twisted my foot."

"I'm sorry," said he blankly.

"Let's find a quiet place where we can sit. And then you may get me some supper."

His face lighted up. Esmé Elliot remarked to herself that she had seldom seen a more pleasing specimen of the youth of the species.

"This is rather like a fairy-gift," he began eagerly, as they made their way to a nook under the stairway, specially adapted to two people of hermit tastes. "I shouldn't have dared to expect such good fortune."

"You'll find me quite a fairy-godmother if you're good. Besides," she added with calm audacity, "I wanted you to myself."

"Why?" he asked, amused and intrigued.

"Curiosity. My besetting sin. You're a phenomenon."

"An ambiguous term. It may mean merely a freak."

"A new young man in Worthington," she informed him, "is a phenomenon, a social phenomenon. Of course he may be a freak, also," she added judicially.

"Newness is a charm that soon wears off."

"Then you're going to settle down here?"

"Yes. I've joined the laboring classes."

"What kind of labor?"

"Journalism. I've just started in, today."

"Really! Which paper?"

"The 'Clarion.'"

Her expressive face changed. "Oh," she said, a little blankly.

"You don't like the 'Clarion'?"

"I almost never see it. So I don't know. And you're going to begin at the bottom? That's quite brave of you."

"No; I'm going to begin at the top. That's braver. Anyway, it's more reckless. I've bought the paper."

"Have you! I hadn't heard of it."

"Nobody's heard of it yet. No outsider. You're the first."

"How delightful!" She leaned closer and looked into his face with shining eyes. "Tell me more. What are you going to do with it?"

"Learn something about it, first."

"It's rather yellow, isn't it?"

"Putting it mildly, yes. That's one of the things I want to change."

"Oh, I wish I owned a newspaper!"

"Do you? Why?"

"For the power of it. To say what you please and make thousands listen."

The pink in her cheeks deepened. "There's nothing in the world like the thrill of that sense of power. It's the one reason why I'd be almost willing to be a man."

"Perhaps you wouldn't need to be. Couldn't you exert the power without actually owning the newspaper?"

"How?"

"By exercising your potent influence upon the obliging proprietor," he suggested smiling.

There came a dancing light in her eyes. "Do you think I'd make a good Goddess-Outside-the-Machine, to the 'Daily Clarion'?"

"Charming! For a two-cent stamp—no, for a spray of your arbutus, I'll sell you an editorial sphere of influence."

"Generous!" she cried. "What would my duties be?"

"To advise the editor and proprietor on all possible points," he laughed.

"And my privileges?"

"The right of a queen over a slave."

"We move fast," she said. Her fingers went to the cluster of delicate-hued bells in her bodice. But it was a false gesture. Esmé Elliot was far too practiced in her chosen game to compromise herself to comment by allowing a man whom she had just met to display her favor in his coat.

"Am I to have my price?" His voice was eager now. She looked very lovely and childlike, with her head drooping, consideringly, above the flowers.

"Give me a little time," she said. "To undertake a partnership on five minutes' notice—that isn't business, is it?"

"Nor is this—wholly," he said, quite low.

Esmé straightened up. "I'm starved," she said lightly. "Are you not going to get me any supper?"

After his return she held the talk to more impersonal topics, advising him, with an adorable assumption of protectiveness, whom he was to meet and dance with, and what men were best worth his while. At parting, she gave him her hand.

"I will let you know," she said, "about the—the sphere of influence."

Hal danced several more numbers, with more politeness than enjoyment, then sought out his hostess to say good-night.

"I'll see you tomorrow, then," she said: "and you shall tell me all your news."

"You're awfully good to me, Lady Jeannette," said he gratefully. "Without you I'd be a lost soul in this town."

"Most people are good to you, I fancy, Hal," said she, looking him over with approval. "As for being a lost soul, you don't look it. In fact you look like a very well-found soul, indeed."

"It *is* rather a cheerful world to live in," said Hal with apparent irrelevance.

"I hope they haven't spoiled you," she said anxiously. "Are you vain, Hal? No: you don't look it."

"What on earth should I be vain about? I've never done anything in the world."

"No? Yet you've improved. You've solidified. What have you been doing to yourself? Not falling in love?"

"Not that, certainly," he replied, smiling. "Nothing much but traveling."

"How did you like Esmé Elliot?" she asked abruptly.

"Quite attractive," said Hal in a flat tone.

"Quite attractive, indeed!" repeated his friend indignantly. "In all your travelings, I don't believe you've ever seen any one else half as lovely and lovable."

"Local pride carries you far, Lady Jeannette," laughed Hal.

"And I *had* intended to have her here to dine tomorrow; but as you're so indifferent—"

"Oh, don't leave her out on my account," said Hal magnanimously.

"I believe you're more than half in love with her already."

"Well, you ought to be a good judge unless you've wholly forgotten the old days," retorted Hal audaciously.

Jeannette Willard laughed up at him. "Don't try to flirt with a middle-aged lady who is most old-fashionedly in love with her husband," she advised. "Keep your bravo speeches for Esmé! She's used to them."

"Rather goes in for that sort of thing, doesn't she?"

"You mean flirtation? Someone's been talking to you about her," said Mrs. Willard quickly. "What did they say?"

"Nothing in particular. I just gathered the impression."

"Don't jump to any conclusions about Esmé," advised his friend. "Most men think her a desperate flirt. She does like attention and admiration. What woman doesn't? And Esmé is very much a woman."

"Evidently!"

"If she seems heartless, it's because she doesn't understand. She enjoys her own power without comprehending it. Esmé has never been really interested in any man. If she had ever been hurt, herself, she would be more careful about hurting others. Yet the very men who have been hardest hit remain her loyal friends."

"A tribute to her strategy."

"A finer quality than that. It is her own loyalty, I think, that makes others loyal to her. But the men here aren't up to her standard. She is complex, and she is ambitious, without knowing it. Fine and clean as our Worthington boys are, there isn't one of them who could appeal to the imagination and idealism of a girl like Esmé Elliot. For Esmé, under all that lightness, is an idealist; the idealist who hasn't found her ideal."

"And therefore hasn't found herself."

She flashed a glance of inquiry and appraisal at him. "That's rather subtle of you," she said. "I hope you don't know *too* much about women, Hal."

"Not I! Just a shot in the dark."

"I said there wasn't a man here up to her standard. That isn't quite true. There is one,—you met him tonight,—but he has troubles of his own, elsewhere," she added, smiling. "I had hoped—but there has always been a friendship too strong for the other kind of sentiment between him and Esmé."

"For a guess, that might be Dr. Merritt," said Hal.

"How did you know?" she cried.

"I didn't. Only, he seems, at a glance, different and of a broader gauge than the others."

"You're a judge of men, at least. As for Esmé, I suppose she'll marry some man much older than herself. Heaven grant he's the right one! For when she gives, she will give royally, and if the man does not meet her on her own plane—well, there will be tragedy enough for two!"

"Deep waters," said Hal. The talk had changed to a graver tone.

"Deep and dangerous. Shipwreck for the wrong adventurer. But El Dorado for the right. Such a golden El Dorado, Hal! The man I want for Esmé Elliot must have in him something of woman for understanding, and something of genius for guidance, and, I'm afraid, something of the angel for patience, and he must be, with all this, wholly a man."

"A pretty large order, Lady Jeannette. Well, I've had my warning. Good-night."

"Perhaps it wasn't so much warning as counsel," she returned, a little wistfully. "How poor Esmé's ears must be burning. There she goes now. What a picture! Come early tomorrow."

Hal's last impression of the ballroom, as he turned away, was summed up in one glance from Esmé Elliot's lustrous eyes, as they met his across her partner's shoulder, smiling him a farewell and a remembrance of their friendly pact.

"Honey-Jinny," said Mrs. Willard's husband, after the last guest had gone; "I don't understand about young Surtaine. Where did he get it?"

"Get what, dear? One might suppose he was a corrupt politician."

"One might suppose he might be anything crooked or wrong, knowing his old, black quack of a father. But he seems to be clean stuff all through. He looks it. He acts it. He carries himself like it. And he talks it. I had a little confab with him out in the smoking-room, and I tell you, Jinny-wife, I believe he's a real youngster."

"Well, he had a mother, you know."

"Did he? What about her?"

"She was an old friend of my mother's. Dr. Surtaine eloped with her out of her father's country place in Midvale. He was an itinerant peddler of some cure-all then. She was a gently born and bred girl, but a mere child, unworldly and very romantic, and she was carried away by the man's personal beauty and magnetism."

"I can't imagine it in a girl of any sort of family."

"Mother has told me that he had a personal force that was almost hypnotic. There must have been something else to him, too, for they say that Hal's mother died, as desperately in love as she had been when she ran away with him, and that he was almost crushed by her loss and never wholly got over it. He transferred his devotion to the child, who was only three years old when the mother died. When Hal was a mere child my mother saw him once taking in dollars at a country fair booth,—just think of it, dearest,—and she said he was the picture of his girl-mother then. Later, when Professor Certain, as he called himself then, got rich, he gave Hal the best of education. But he never let him have anything to do with the Ellersleys—that was Mrs. Surtaine's name. All the family are dead now."

"Well, there must be some good in the old boy," admitted Willard. "But I don't happen to like him. I do like the boy. Blood does tell, Jinny. But if he's really as much of an Ellersley as he looks, there's a bitter enlightenment before him when he comes to see Dr. Surtaine as he really is."

Meantime Hal, home at a reasonable hour, in the interest of his new profession, had taken with him the pleasantest impressions of the Willards' hospitality. He slept soundly and awoke in buoyant spirits for the dawning enterprise. On the breakfast table he found, in front of his plate, a bunchy envelope addressed in a small, strong, unfamiliar hand. Within was no written word; only a spray of the trailing arbutus, still unwithered of its fairy-pink, still eloquent, in its wayward, woodland fragrance, of her who had worn it the night before.

CHAPTER IX

GLIMMERINGS

Ignorance within one's self is a mist which, upon closer approach, proves a mountain. To the new editor of the "Clarion" the things he did not know about this enterprise of which he had suddenly become the master loomed to the skies. Together with the rest of the outer world, he had comfortably and vaguely regarded a newspaper as a sort of automatic mill which, by virtue of having a certain amount of grain in the shape of information dumped into it, worked upon this with an esoteric type-mechanism, and, in due and exact time, delivered a definite grist of news. Of the refined and articulated processes of acquisition, selection, and elimination which went to the turning-out of the final product, he was wholly unwitting. He could as well have manipulated a linotype machine as have given out a quiet Sunday's assignment list: as readily have built a multiple press as made up an edition.

So much he admitted to McGuire Ellis late in the afternoon of the day after the Willard party. Fascinated, he had watched that expert journalist go through page after page of copy, with what seemed superhuman rapidity and address, distribute the finished product variously upon hooks, boxes, and copy-boys, and, the immediate task being finished, lapse upon his desk and fall asleep. Meantime, the owner himself faced the unpleasant prospect of being smothered under the downfall of proofs, queries, and scribbled sheets which descended upon his desk from all sides. For a time he struggled manfully: for a time thereafter he wallowed desperately. Then he sent out a far cry for help. The cry smote upon the ear of McGuire Ellis, "Hoong!" ejaculated that somnolent toiler, coming up out of deep waters. "Did you speak?"

"I want to know what I'm to do with all of these things," replied his boss, indicating the augmenting drifts.

"Throw 'em on the floor, is *my* advice," said the employee drowsily. "The more stuff you throw away, the better paper you get out. That's a proverb of the business."

"In other words, you think the paper would get along better without me than with me?"

"But you're enjoying yourself, aren't you?" queried his employee. Heaving himself out of his chair, he ambled over to Hal's desk and evolved out of the chaos some semblance of order. "Don't find it as easy as your enthusiasm painted it," he suggested.

"Oh, I've still got the enthusiasm. If only I knew where to begin."

Ellis rubbed his ear thoughtfully and remarked: "Once I knew a man from Phoenix, Arizona, who was so excited the first time he saw the ocean that he borrowed a uniform from an absent friend, shinned aboard a five-thousand-ton brigantine, and ordered all hands to put out to sea immediately in the teeth of a whooping gale. But he," added the narrator in the judicial tone of one who cites mitigating circumstances, "was drunk at the time."

"Thanks for the parallel. I don't like it. But never mind that. The question is, What am I going to do?"

"That's the question all right. Are you putting it to me?"

"I am."

"Well, I was just going to put it to you."

"No use. I don't know."

The two men looked each other in the eye, long and steadily. Ellis's harsh face relaxed to a sort of grin.

"You want me to tell you?"

"Yes."

"What do you think you're hiring, a Professor of Journalism in the infant class?" The tone of the question offset any apparent ill-nature in the wording.

"It might be made worth your while."

"All right; I'm hired."

"That's good," said Hal heartily. "I think you'll find I'm not hard to get along with."

"I think *you'll* find *I* am," replied the other with some grimness. "But I know the game. Well, let's get down to cases. What do you want to do with the 'Clarion'?"

"Make it the cleanest, decentest newspaper in the city."

"Then you don't think it's that, now."

"No. I know it isn't."

"Did you get that from Dr. Surtaine?"

"Partly."

"What's the other part?"

"First-hand impressions. I've been going through the files."

"When?"

"Since nine o'clock this morning."

"With what idea?"

"Why, having bought a piece of property, I naturally want to know about it."

"Been through the plant yet? That's your property, too."

"No. I thought I'd find out more from the files. I've bought a newspaper, not a building."

The characteristic grunt with which Ellis favored his employer in reply to this seemed to have a note of approval in it.

"Well; now that you own the 'Clarion,'" he said after a pause, "what do you think of it?"

"It's yellow, and it's sensational, and—it's vulgar."

There was nothing complimentary in the other's snort this time.

"Of course it's vulgar. You can't sell a sweet-scented, prim old-maidy newspaper to enough people to pay for the z's in one font of type. People are vulgar. Don't forget that. And you've got to make a newspaper to suit them. Lesson Number One."

"It needn't be a muckraking paper, need it, forever smelling out something rotten, and exploiting it in big headlines?"

"Oh, that's all bluff," replied the journalist easily. "We never turn loose on anything but the surface of things. Why, if any one started in really to muckrake this old respectable burg, the smell would drive most of our best citizens to the woods."

"Frankly, Mr. Ellis, I don't like cheap cynicism."

"Prefer to be fed up on pleasant lies?" queried his employee, unmoved.

"Not that either. I can take an unpleasant truth as well as the next man. But it's got to be the truth."

"Do you know the nickname of this paper?"

"Yes. My father told me of it."

"It was his set that pinned it on us. 'The Daily Carrion,' they call us, and they said that our triumphal roosters ought to be vultures. Do you know why?"

"In plain English because of the paper's lies and blackguardism."

"In plainer English, because of its truth. Wait a minute, now. I'm not saying that the 'Clarion' doesn't lie. All papers do, I guess. They have to. But it's when we've cut loose on straight facts that we've got in wrong."

"Give me an instance."

"Well, the sewing-girls' strike."

"Engineered by a crooked labor leader and a notoriety-seeking woman."

"I see the bunch have got to you already, and have filled you up with their dope. Never mind that, now. We're supposed to be a sort of tribune of the common people. Rights of the ordinary citizen, and that sort of thing. So we took up the strike and printed the news pretty straight. No other paper touched it."

"Why not?"

"Didn't dare. We had to drop it, ourselves. Not until we'd lost ten thousand dollars in advertising, though, and gained an extra blot on our reputation as being socialistic and an enemy to capital and all that kind of rot."

"Wasn't it simply a case of currying favor with the working-classes?"

"According as you look at it." Apparently weary of looking at it at all, McGuire Ellis tipped back in his chair and contemplated the ceiling. When he spoke his voice floated up as softly as a ring of smoke. "How honest are you going to be, Mr. Surtaine?"

"What!"

"I asked you how honest you are going to be."

"It's a question I don't think you need to ask me."

"I do. How else will I find out?"

"I intend the 'Clarion' to be strictly and absolutely honest. That's all there is to that."

"Don't be so young," said McGuire Ellis wearily. "'Strictly and absol'—see here, did you ever read 'The Wrecker'?"

"More than once."

"Remember the chap who says, 'You seem to think honesty as simple as blindman's-buff. I don't. It's some difference of definition, I suppose'? Now, there's meat in that."

"Difference of definition be hanged. Honesty is honesty."

"And policy is policy. And bankruptcy is bankruptcy."

"I don't see the connection."

"It's there. Honesty for a newspaper isn't just a matter of good intentions. It's a matter of eternal watchfulness and care and expert figuring-out of things."

"You mean that we're likely to make mistakes about facts—"

"We're certain to. But that isn't what I mean at all. I mean that it's harder for a newspaper to be honest than it is for the pastor of a rich church."

"You can't make me believe that."

"Facts can. But I'm not doing my job. You want to learn the details of the business, and I'm wasting time trying to throw light into the deep places where it keeps what it has of conscience. That'll come later. Now where shall I begin?"

"With the structure of the business."

"All right. A newspaper is divided into three parts. News is the merchandise which it has to sell. Advertising is the by-product that pays the bills. The editorial page is a survival. At its best it analyzes and points out the significance of important news. At its worst, it is a mouthpiece for the prejudices or the projects of whoever runs it. Few people are influenced by it. Many are amused by it. It isn't very important nowadays."

"I intend to make it so on the 'Clarion.'"

Ellis turned upon him a regard which carried with it a verdict of the most abandoned juvenility, but made no comment. "News sways people more than editorials," he continued. "That's why there's so much tinkering with it. I'd like to give you a definition of news, but there isn't any. News is conventional. It's anything that interests the community. It isn't the same in any two places. In Arizona a shower is news. In New Orleans the boll-weevil is news. In Worthington anything about your father is news: in Denver they don't care a hoot about your father; so, unless he elopes or dies, or buys a fake Titian, or breaks the flying-machine record, or lectures on medical quackery, he isn't news away from home. If Mrs. Festus Willard is bitten by a mad dog, every dog-chase for the week following is news. When a martyred suffragette chews a chunk out of the King of England, the local meetings of the Votes-for-Women Sorority become a live topic. If ever you get to the point where you can say with certainty, 'This is news; that isn't,' you'll have no further need for me. You'll be graduated."

"Where does a paper get its news?"

"Through mechanical channels, mostly. If you read all the papers in town,—and you'll have to do it,—you'll see that they've got just about the same stuff. Why shouldn't they have? The big, clumsy news-mill grinds pretty impartially for all of them. There's one news source at Police Headquarters, another at the City Hall, another in the financial department, another at the political headquarters, another in the railroad offices, another at the theaters, another in society, and so on. At each of these a reporter is stationed. He knows his own kind of news as it comes to him, ready-made, and, usually, not much else. Then there's the general, unclassified news of the city that drifts in partly by luck, partly by favor, partly through the personal connections of the staff. One paper is differentiated from another principally by getting or missing this sort of stuff. For instance, the 'Banner' yesterday had a 'beat' about you. It said that you had come back and were going to settle down and go into your father's business."

"That's not true."

"Glad to hear it. Your hands will be full with this job. But it was news. Everybody is interested in the son of our leading citizen. The 'Banner' is strong on that sort of local stuff. I think I'll jack up our boys in the city room by hinting that there may be a shake-up coming under the new owner. Knowing they're on probation will make 'em ambitious."

"And the news of the outside world?"

"Much the same principle as the local matter and just as machine-like. The 'Clarion' is a unit in a big system, the National News Exchange Bureau. Not only has the bureau its correspondents in every city and town of any size, but it covers the national sources of news with special reporters. Also the international. Theoretically it gives only the plainest facts, uncolored by any bias. As a matter of fact, it's pretty crooked. It suppresses news, and even distorts it. It's got a secret financial propaganda dictated by Wall Street, and its policies are always open to suspicion."

"Why doesn't it get honest reporters?"

"Oh, its reporters are honest enough. The funny business is done higher up, in the executive offices."

"Isn't there some other association we can get into?"

"Not very well, just now. The Exchange franchise is worth a lot of money. Besides," he concluded, yawning, "I don't know that they're any worse than we are."

Hal got to his feet and walked the length of the office and back, five times. At the end of this exercise he stood, looking down at his assistant.

"Ellis, are you trying to plant an impression in my mind?"

"No."

"You're doing it."

"Of what sort?"

"I hardly know. Something subtle, and lurking and underhanded in the business. I feel as if you had your hands on a curtain that you might pull aside if you would, but that you don't want to shock my—my youthfulness."

"Plain facts are what you want, aren't they?"

"Exactly."

"Well, I'm giving them to you as plain as you can understand them. I don't want to tell you more than you're ready to believe."

"Try it, as an experiment."

"Who do you suppose runs the newspapers of this town?"

"Why, Mr. Vane runs the 'Banner.' Mr. Ford owns the 'Press.' The 'Telegram'—let me see—"

"No; no; no," cried Ellis, waving his hands in front of his face. "I don't mean the different papers. I mean all of 'em. The 'Clarion,' with the others."

"Nobody runs them all, surely."

"Three men run them all; Pierce, Gibbs, and Hollenbeck."

"E.M. Pierce?"

"Elias Middleton Pierce."

"I had luncheon with him yesterday, and with Mr. Gibbs—"

"Ah! That's where you got your notions about the strike."

"—and neither of them spoke of any newspaper interests."

"Catch them at it! They're the Publication Committee of the Retail Dry Goods Union."

"What is that?"

"The combination of local department stores. And, as such, they can dictate to every Worthington newspaper what it shall or shall not print."

"Nonsense!"

"Including the 'Clarion.'"

"There you're wrong, anyway."

"The department stores are the biggest users of advertising space in the city. No paper in town could get along without them. If they want a piece of news kept out of print, they tell the editor so, and you bet it's kept out. Otherwise that paper loses the advertising."

"Has it ever been done here?"

"Has it? Get Veltman down to tell you about the Store Employees' Federation."

"Veltman? What does he know of it? He's in the printing-department, isn't he?"

"Composing-room; yes. Outside he's a labor agitator and organizer. A bit of a fanatic, too. But an A1 man all right. Get the composing-room," he directed through the telephone, "and ask Mr. Veltman to come to Mr. Surtaine's office."

As the printer entered, Hal was struck again with his physical beauty.

"Did you want to see me?" he asked, looking at the "new boss" with somber eyes.

"Tell Mr. Surtaine about the newspapers and the Store Federation, Max," said Ellis.

The German shook his head. "Nothing new in that," he said, with the very slightest of accents. "We can't organize them unless the newspapers give us a little publicity."

"Explain it to me, please. I know nothing about it," said Hal.

"For years we've been trying to organize a union of department store employees."

"Aren't they well treated?"

"Not quite as well as hogs," returned the other in an impassive voice. "The girls wanted shorter hours and extra pay for overtime at holiday time and Old Home Week. Every time we've tried it the stores fire the organizers among their employees."

"Hardly fair, that."

"This year we tried to get up a public meeting. Reverend Norman Hale helped us, and Dr. Merritt, the health officer, and a number of women. It was a good news feature, and that was what we wanted, to get the movement started. But do you think any paper in town touched it? Not one."

"But why?"

"E.M. Pierce's orders. He and his crowd."

"Even the 'Clarion,' which is supposed to have labor sympathies?"

"The 'Clarion'!" There was a profundity of contempt in Veltman's voice; and a deeper bitterness when he snapped his teeth upon a word which sounded to Hal suspiciously like the Biblical characterization of an undesirable citizeness of Babylon.

"In any case, they won't give the 'Clarion' any more orders."

"Oh, yes, they will," said Veltman stolidly.

"Then they'll learn something distinctly to their disadvantage."

The splendid, animal-like eyes of the compositor gleamed suddenly. "Do you mean you're going to run the paper honestly?"

Hal almost recoiled before the impassioned and incredulous surprise in the question.

"What is 'honestly'?"

"Give the people who buy your paper the straight news they pay for?"

"Certainly, the paper will be run that way."

"As easy as rolling off a log," put in McGuire Ellis, with suspicious smoothness.

Veltman looked from one to the other. "Yes," he said: and again "Yes-s-s." But the life had gone from his voice. "Anything more?"

"Nothing, thank you," answered Hal.

"Brains, fire, ambition, energy, skill, everything but balance," said Ellis, as the door closed. "He's the stuff that martyrs are made of—or lunatics. Same thing, I guess."

"Isn't he a trouble-maker among the men?"

"No. He's a good workman. Something more, too. Sometimes he writes paragraphs for the editorial page; and when they're not too radical, I use 'em. He's brought us in one good feature, that 'Kitty the Cutie' stuff."

"I'd thought of dropping that. It's so cheap and chewing-gummy."

"Catches on, though. We really ought to run it every day. But the girl hasn't got time to do it."

"Who is she?"

"Some kid in your father's factory, I understand. Protégée of Veltman's, He brought her stuff in and we took it right off the bat."

"Well, I'll tell you one thing that is going."

"What?"

"The 'Clarion's' motto. 'We Lead: Let Those Who Can Follow.'" Hal pointed to the "black-face" legend at the top of the first editorial column.

"Got anything in its place?"

"I thought of 'With Malice Toward None: With Charity for All.'"

"Worked to death. But I've never seen it on a newspaper. Shall I tell Veltman to set it up in several styles so you may take your pick?"

"Yes. Let's start it in tomorrow."

That night Harrington Surtaine went to bed pondering on the strange attitude of the newspaper mind toward so matter-of-fact a quality as honesty; and he dreamed of a roomful of advertisers listening in sodden silence to his own grandiloquent announcement, "Gentlemen: honesty is the best policy," while, in a corner, McGuire Ellis and Max Veltman clasped each other in an apoplectic agony of laughter.

On the following day the blatant cocks of the shrill "Clarion" stood guard at either end of the paper's new golden text.

CHAPTER X
IN THE WAY OF TRADE

Dr. Surtaine sat in Little George's best chair, beaming upon the world. By habit, the big man was out of his seat with his dime and nickel in the boot-black's ready hand, almost coincidently with the final clip-clap of the rhythmic process. But this morning he lingered, contemplating with an unobtrusive scrutiny the occupant of the adjoining chair, a small, angular, hard man, whose brick-red face was cut off in the segment of an abrupt circle, formed by a low-jammed green hat. This individual had just briskly bidden his bootblack "hurry it up" in a tone which meant precisely what it said. The youth was doing so.

"George," said Dr. Surtaine, to the proprietor of the stand.

"Yas, suh."

"Were you ever in St. Jo, Missouri?"

"Yas, suh, Doctah Suhtaine; oncet."

"For long?"

"No, suh."

"Didn't live there, did you?"

"No, suh."

"George," said his interlocutor impressively, "you're lucky."

"Yas, suh," agreed the negro with a noncommittal grin.

"While you can buy accommodations in a graveyard or break into a penitentiary, don't you ever live in St. Jo Missouri, George."

The man in the adjacent seat half turned toward Dr. Surtaine and looked him up and down, with a freezing regard.

"It's the sink-hole and sewer-pipe of creation, George. They once elected a chicken-thief mayor, and he resigned because the town was too mean to live in. Ever know any folks there, George?"

"Don't have no mem'ry for 'em, Doctah."

"You're lucky again. They're the orneriest, lowest-down, minchin', pinchin', pizen trash that ever tainted the sweet air of Heaven by breathing it, George."

"You don' sesso, Doctah Suhtaine, suh."

"I do sess precisely so, George. Does the name McQuiggan mean anything to you?"

"Don' mean nothin' at-tall to me, Doctah."

"You got away from St. Jo in time, then. Otherwise you might have met the McQuiggan family, and never been the same afterward."

"Ef you don' stop youah feet a-fidgittin', Boss," interpolated the neighboring bootblack, addressing the green-hatted man in aggrieved tones, "I cain't do no good wif this job."

"McQuiggan was the name," continued the volunteer biographer. "The best you could say of the McQuiggans, George, was that one wasn't much cusseder than the others, because he couldn't be. Human nature has its limitations, George."

"It suttinly have, suh."

"But if you had to allow a shade to any of 'em, it would probably have gone to the oldest brother, L.P. McQuiggan. Barring a scorpion I once sat down on while in swimming, he was the worst outrage upon the scheme of creation ever perpetrated by a short-sighted Providence."

"Get out of that chair!"

The little man had shot from his own and was dancing upon the pavement.

"What for?" Dr. Surtaine's tone was that of inquiring innocence.

"To have your fat head knocked off."

With impressive agility for one of his size and years, the challenged one descended. He advanced, "squared," and suddenly held out a muscular and plump hand.

"Hullo, Elpy."

"Huh?"

The other glared at him, baleful and baffled.

"Hullo, I said. Don't you know me?"

"No, I don't. Neither will your own family after I get through with you."

"Come off, Elpy; come off. I licked you once in the old days, and I guess I could do it now, but I don't want to. Come and have a drink with old Andy."

"Andy? Andy the Spieler? Andy Certain?"

"Dr. L. André Surtaine, at your service. *Now*, will you shake?"

Still surly, Mr. McQuiggan hung back. "What about that roast?" he demanded.

"Wasn't sure of you. Twenty years is a long time. But I knew if it was you you'd want to fight, and I knew if you didn't want to fight it wasn't you. I'll buy you one in honor of the best little city west of the Mississip, and the best bunch of sports that ever came out of it, the McQuiggans of St. Jo, Missouri. Does that go?"

"It goes," replied the representative of the family concisely.

Across the café table Dr. Surtaine contemplated his old acquaintance with friendly interest.

"The same old scrappy Elpy," he observed. "What's happened to you, since you used to itinerate with the Iroquois Extract of Life?"

"Plenty."

"You're looking pretty prosperous."

"Have to, in my line."

"What is it?"

Mr. McQuiggan produced a card, with the legend:—

McQuiggan & Straight

STREAKY MOUNTAIN COPPER COMPANY
Orsten, Palas County, Nev.

L.P. MCQUIGGAN   ARTHUR STRAIGHT
President   Vice-Pres. & Treas.

"Any good?" queried the Doctor.

"Best undeveloped property in the State."

"Why don't you develop it?"

"Capital."

"Get the capital."

"Will you help me?"

"Sure."

"How?"

"Advertise."

"Advertising costs money."

"And brings two dollars for every one you spend."

"Maybe," retorted the other, with a skeptical air. "But my game is still talk."

"Talk gets dimes; print gets dollars," said his friend sententiously.

"You have to show me."

"Show you!" cried the Doctor. "I'll write your copy myself."

"*You* will? What do you know about mining?"

"Not a thing. But there isn't much I don't know about advertising. I've built up a little twelve millions, plus, on it. And I can sell your stock like hot cakes through the 'Clarion.'"

"What's the 'Clarion'?"

"My son's newspaper."

"Thereby keeping the graft in the family, eh?"

"Don't be a fool, Elpy. I'm showing you profits. Besides doing you a good turn, I'd like to bring in some new business to the boy. Now you take half-pages every other day for a week and a full page Sunday—"

"Pages!" almost squalled the little man. "D'you think I'm made of money?"

"Elpy," said Dr. Surtaine, abruptly, "do you remember my platform patter?"

"Like the multiplication table."

"Was it good?"

"Best ever!"

"Well, I'm a slicker proposition with a pen than I ever was with a spiel. And you're securing my services for nothing. Come around to the office, man, and let me show you."

Still suspicious, Mr. McQuiggan permitted himself to be led away, expatiating as he went, upon the unrivaled location and glorious future of his mining property. From time to time, Dr. Surtaine jotted down an unostentatious note.

The first view of the Certina building dashed Mr. McQuiggan's suspicions; his inspection of his old friend's superb office slew them painlessly.

"Is this all yours, Andy? On the level? Did you do it all on your own?"

"Every bit of it! With my little pen-and-ink. Take a look around the walls and you'll see how."

He seated himself at his desk and proceeded to jot down, with apparent carelessness, but in broad, sweeping lines, a type lay-out, while his guest passed from advertisement to advertisement, in increasing admiration. Before Old Lame-Boy he paused, absolutely fascinated.

"I thought that'd get you," exulted the host, who, between strokes of the creative pen had been watching him.

"I've seen it in the newspaper, but never connected it with you. Being out of the medical line I lost interest. Say, it's a wonder! Did it fetch 'em?"

"Fetch 'em? It knocked 'em flat. That picture's the foundation of this business. Talk about suggestion in advertising! He's a regular hypnotist, Old Lame-Boy is. Plants the suggestion right in the small of your back, where we want it. Why, Elpy, I've seen a man walk up to that picture on a bill-board as straight as you or me, take one good, long look, and go away hanging onto his kidneys, and squirming like a lizard. Fact! What do you think of that? Genius, I call it: just flat genius, to produce an effect like that with a few lines and a daub or two of color."

"Some pull!" agreed Mr. McQuiggan, with professional approval. "And then—'Try Certina,' eh?"

"For a starter and, for a finisher 'Certina *Cures*.' Shoves the bottle right into their hands. The first bottle braces 'em. They take another. By the time they've had half a dozen, they love it."

"Booze?"

"Sure! Flavored and spiced up, nice and tasty. Great for the temperance trade. *And* the best little repeater on the market. Now take a look, Elpy."

He tapped the end of his pen upon the rough sketch of the mining advertisement, which he had drafted. Mr. McQuiggan bent over it in study, and fell a swift victim to the magic of the art.

"Why, that would make a wad of bills squirm out of the toe of a stockin'! It's new game to me. I've always worked the personal touch. But I'll sure give it a try-out, Andy."

"I guess it's bad!" exulted the other. "I guess I've lost the trick of tolling the good old dollars in! Take this home and try it on your cash register! Now, come around and meet the boy."

Thus it was that Editor-in-Chief Harrington Surtaine, in the third week of his incumbency received a professional call from his father, and a companion from whose pockets bulged several sheets of paper.

"Shake hands with Mr. McQuiggan, Hal," said the Doctor. "Make a bow when you meet him, too. He's your first new business for the reformed 'Clarion.'"

"In what way?" asked Hal, meeting a grip like iron from the stranger. "News?"

"News! I guess not. Business, I said. Real money. Advertising."

"It's like this, Mr. Surtaine," said L.P. McQuiggan, turning his spare, hard visage toward Hal. "I've got some copper stock to sell—an A1 under-developed proposition; and your father, who's an old pal, tells me the 'Clarion' can do the business for me. Now, if I can get a good rate from you, it's a go."

"Mr. Shearson, the advertising manager, is your man. I don't know anything about advertising rates."

"Then you'd best get busy and learn," cried Dr. Surtaine.

"I'm learning other things."

"For instance?"

"What news is and isn't."

"Look here, Boyee." Dr. Surtaine's voice was surcharged with a disappointed earnestness. "Put yourself right on this. News is news; any paper can get it. But advertising is *Money*. Let your editors run the news part, till you can work into it. *You get next to the door where the cash comes in.*"

In the fervor of his advice he thumped Hal's desk. The thump woke

McGuire Ellis, who had been devoting a spare five minutes to his favorite pastime. For his behoof, the exponent of policy repeated his peroration. "Isn't that right, Ellis?" he cried. "You're a practical newspaper man."

"It's true to type, anyway," grunted Ellis.

"Sure it is!" cried the other, too bent on his own notions to interpret this comment correctly. "And now, what about a little reading notice for McQuiggan's proposition?"

"Yes: an interview with me on the copper situation and prospects might help," put in McQuiggan.

Hal hesitated, looking to Ellis for counsel.

"You've got to do something for an advertiser on a big order like this, Boyee," urged his father.

"Let's see the copy," put in Ellis. The trained journalistic eye ran over the sheets. "Lot of gaudy slush about copper mines in general," he observed, "and not much information on Streaky Mountain."

"It's an undeveloped property," said McQuiggan.

"Strong on geography," continued Ellis. "'In the immediate vicinity,'" he read from one sheet, "'lie the Copper Monarch Mine paying 40 per cent dividends, the Deep Gulch Mine, paying 35 per cent, the Three Sisters, Last Chance, Alkali Spring Mines, all returning upwards of 25 per cent per annum: and immediately adjacent is the famous Strike-for-the-West property which enriches its fortunate stockholders to the tune of 75 per cent a year!' Are you on the same range as the Strike-for-the-West, Mr. McQuiggan?"

"It's an adjacent property," growled the mining man. "What d'you know about copper?"

"Oh, I've seen a little mining, myself. And a bit of mining advertising. That's quite an ad of yours, McQuiggan."

"I wrote that ad," said Dr. Surtaine blandly: "and I challenge anybody to find a single misstatement in it."

"You're safe. There isn't any. And scarcely a single statement. But if you wrote it, I suppose it goes."

"And the interview, too," rasped McQuiggan.

"It's usual," said Ellis to Hal. "The tail with the hide: the soul with the body, when you're selling."

"But we're not selling interviews," said Hal uneasily.

"You're getting nearly a thousand dollars' worth of copy, and giving a bonus that don't cost you anything," said his father. "The papers have done it for me ever since I've been in business."

"I guess that's right, too," agreed Ellis.

"Why don't you take McQuiggan down to meet your Mr. Shearson, Hal?" suggested the Doctor. "I'll stay here and round out a couple of other ideas for his campaign."

Hal had risen from his desk when there was a light knock at the door and Milly Neal's bright head appeared.

"Hullo!" said Dr. Surtaine. "What's up? Anything wrong at the shop, Milly?"

The girl walked into the room and stood trimly at ease before the four men.

"No, Chief," said she. "I understood Mr. Surtaine wanted to see me."

"I?" said Hal blankly, pushing a chair toward her.

"Yes. Didn't you? They told me you left word for me in the city room, to see you when I came in again. Sometimes I send my copy, so I only just got the message."

"Miss Neal is 'Kitty the Cutie,'" explained McGuire Ellis.

"Looks it, too," observed L.P. McQuiggan jauntily, addressing the upper far corner of the room.

Miss Neal looked at him, met a knowing and conscious smile, looked right through the smile, and looked away again, all with the air of one who gazes out into nothingness.

"Guess I'll go look up this Shearson person," said Mr. McQuiggan, a trifle less jauntily. "See you all later."

"I'd no notion you were the writer of the Cutie paragraphs, Milly," said Dr. Surtaine. "They're lively stuff."

"Nobody has. I'm keeping it dark. It's only a try-out. You *did* send for me, didn't you?" she added, turning to Hal.

"Yes. What I had in mind to say to you—that is, to the author—the writer of the paragraphs," stumbled Hal, "is that they're a little too—too—"

"Too flip?" queried his father. "That's what makes 'em go."

"If they could be done in a manner not quite so undignified," suggested the editor-in-chief.

Color rose in the girl's smooth cheek. "You think they're vulgar," she charged.

"That's rather too harsh a word," he protested.

"You do! I can see it." She flushed an angry red. "I'd rather stop altogether than have you think that."

"Don't be young," put in McGuire Ellis, with vigor. "Kitty has caught on. It's a good feature. The paper can't afford to drop it."

"That's right," supplemented Dr. Surtaine. "People are beginning to talk about those items. They read 'em. I read 'em myself. They've got the go, the pep. They're different. But, Milly, I didn't even know you could write."

"Neither did I," said the girl staidly, "till I got to putting down some of the things I heard the girls say, and stringing them together with nonsense of my own. One evening I showed some of it to Mr. Veltman, and he took it here and had it printed."

"I was going to suggest, Mr. Surtaine," said McGuire Ellis formally, "that we put Miss Kitty on the five-dollar-a-column basis and make her an every-other-day editorial page feature. I think the stuff's worth it."

"We can give it a trial," said his principal, a little dubiously, "since you think so well of it."

"Then, Milly, I suppose you'll be quitting the shop to become a full-fledged writer," remarked Dr. Surtaine.

"No, indeed, Chief." The girl smiled at him with that frank friendliness which Hal had noted as informing every relationship between Dr. Surtaine and the employees of the Certina plant. "I'll stick. The regular pay envelope looks good to me. And I can do this work after hours."

"How would it be if I was to put you on half-time, Milly?" suggested her employer. "You can keep your department going by being there in the mornings and have your afternoons for the writing."

The girl thanked him demurely but with genuine gratitude.

"Then we'll look for your copy here on alternate days," said Hal. "And I think I'll give you a desk. As this develops into an editorial feature I shall want to keep an eye on it and to be in touch with you. Perhaps I could make suggestions sometimes."

She rose, thanking him, and Hal held open the door for her. Once again he felt, with a strange sensation, her eyes take hold on his as she passed him.

"Pretty kid," observed Ellis. "Veltman is crazy about her, they say."

"*Good* kid, too," added Dr. Surtaine, emphasizing the adjective. "You might tell Veltman that, whoever he is."

"Tell him, yourself," retorted Ellis with entire good nature. "He isn't the sort to offer gratuitous information to."

Upon this advice, L.P. McQuiggan reëntered. "All fixed," said he, with evident satisfaction. "We went to the mat on rates, but Shearson agreed to give me some good reading notices. Now, I'll beat it. See you tonight, Andy?"

Dr. Surtaine nodded. "You owe me a commission, Boyee," said he, smiling at Hal as McQuiggan made his exit. "But I'll let you off this time. I guess it won't be the last business I bring in to you. Only, don't you and Ellis go looking every gift horse too hard in the teeth. You might get bit."

"Shut your eyes and swallow it and ask no questions, if it's good, eh, Doctor?" said McGuire Ellis. "That's the motto for your practice."

"Right you are, my boy. And it's the motto of sound business. What is business?" he continued, soaring aloft upon the wings of a Pæan of Policy. "Why, business is a deal between you and me in which I give you my goods and a pleasant word, and you give me your dollar and a polite reply. Some folks always want to know where the dollar came from. Not me! I'm satisfied to know that its coming to me. Money has wings, and if you throw stones at it, it'll fly away fast. And you want to remember," he concluded with the fervor of honest conviction, "that a newspaper can't be quite right, any more than a man can, unless it makes its own living. Well, I'm not going to preach any more. So long, boys."

"What do you think of it, Mr. Surtaine?" inquired McGuire Ellis, after the lecturer had gone his way. "Pretty sound sense, eh?"

"I wonder just what you mean by that, Ellis. Not what you say, certainly."

But Ellis only laughed and turned to his "flimsy."

Meantime the editor of the "Clarion" was being quietly but persistently beset by another sermonizer, less cocksure of text than the Sweet Singer of Policy, but more subtle in influence. This was Miss Esmé Elliot. Already, the half-jocular partnership undertaken at the outset of their acquaintance had developed into a real, if somewhat indeterminate connection. Esmé found her new acquaintance interesting both for himself and for his career. Her set in general considered the ripening friendship merely "another of Esmé's flirtations," and variously prophesied the dénouement. To the girl's own mind it was not a flirtation at all. She was (she assured herself) genuinely absorbed in the development of a new mission in which she aspired to be influential. That she already exercised a strong sway of personality over Hal Surtaine, she realized. Indeed, in the superb confidence of her charm, she would have been astonished had it been otherwise. Just where her interest in the newly adventured professional field ended, and in Harrington Surtaine, the man, began, she would have been puzzled to say. Kathleen Pierce had bluntly questioned her on the subject.

"Yes, of course I like him," said Esmé frankly. "He's interesting and he's a gentleman, and he has a certain force about him, and he's"—she paused, groping for a characterization—"he's unexpected."

"What gets me," said Kathleen, in her easy slang, "is that he never pulls any knighthood-in-flower stuff, yet you somehow feel it's there. Know what I mean? There's a scrapper behind that nice-boy smile."

"He hasn't scrapped with me, yet, Kathie," smiled the beauty.

"Don't let him," advised the other. "It mightn't be safe. Still, I suppose you understand him by now, down to the ground."

"Indeed I do not. Didn't I tell you he was unexpected? He has an uncomfortable trick," complained Miss Elliot, "just when everything is smooth and lovely, of suddenly leveling those gray-blue eyes of his at you, like two pistols. 'Throw up your hands and tell me what you really mean!' One doesn't always want to tell what one really means."

"Bet you have to with him, sooner or later," returned her friend.

This conversation took place at the Vanes' *al fresco* tea, to which Hal came for a few minutes, late in the afternoon of his father's visit with McQuiggan, mainly in the hope of seeing Esmé Elliot. Within five minutes after his arrival, Worthington society was frowning, or smiling, according as it was masculine or feminine, at their backs, as they strolled away toward the garden. Miss Esmé was feeling a bit petulant, perhaps because of Kathie Pierce's final taunt.

"I think you aren't living up to our partnership," she accused.

"Is it a partnership, where one party is absolute slave to the other's slightest wish?" he smiled.

"There! That is exactly it. You treat me like a child."

"I don't think of you as a child, I assure you."

"You listen to all I say with pretended deference, and smile and—and go your own way with inevitable motion."

"Wherein have I failed in my allegiance?" asked Hal, courteously concerned. "Haven't we published everything about all the charities that you're interested in?"

"Oh, yes. So far as that goes. But the paper itself doesn't seem to change any. It's got the same tone it always had."

"What's wrong with its tone?" The eyes were leveled at her now.

"Speaking frankly, it's tawdry. It's lurid. It's—well, yellow."

"A matter of method. You're really more interested, then, in the way we present news than in the news we present."

"I don't know anything about news, itself. But I don't see why a newspaper run by a gentleman shouldn't be in good taste."

"Nor do I. Except that those things take time. I suppose I've got to get in touch with my staff before I can reform their way of writing the paper."

"Haven't you done that yet?"

"I simply haven't had time."

"Then I'll make you a nice present of a very valuable suggestion. Give a luncheon to your employees, and invite all the editors and reporters. Make a little speech to them and tell them what you intend to do, and get them to talk it over and express opinions. That's the way to get things done. I do it with my mission class. And, by the way, don't make it a grand banquet at one of the big hotels. Have it in some place where the men are used to eating. They'll feel more at home and you'll get more out of them."

"Will you come?"

"No. But you shall come up to the house and report fully on it."

Had Miss Esmé Elliot, experimentalist in human motives, foreseen to what purpose her ingenious suggestion was to work out, she might well have retracted her complaint of lack of real influence; for this casual conversation was the genesis of the Talk-it-Over Breakfast, an institution which potently affected the future of the "Clarion" and its young owner.

CHAPTER XI

THE INITIATE

Within a month after Hal's acquisition of the "Clarion," Dr. Surtaine had become a daily caller at the office. "Just to talk things over," was his explanation of these incursions, which Hal always welcomed, no matter how busy he might be. Advice was generally the form which the visitor's talk took; sometimes warning; not infrequently suggestions of greater or less value. Always his counsel was for peace and policy.

"Keep in with the business element, Boyee. Remember all the time that Worthington is a business city, the liveliest little business city between New York and Chicago. Business made it. Business runs it. Business is going to keep on running it. Anybody who works on a different principle, I don't care whether it's in politics or journalism or the pulpit, is going to get hurt. I don't deny you've braced up the 'Clarion.' People are beginning to talk about it already. But the best men, the moneyed men, are holding off. They aren't sure of you yet. Sometimes I'm not sure myself. Every now and then the paper takes a stand I don't like. It goes too far. You've put ginger into it. I have to admit that. And ginger's a good thing, but sugar catches more flies."

The notion of a breakfast to the staff met with the Doctor's instant approval.

"That's the idea!" said he "I'll come to it, myself. Lay down your general scheme and policy to 'em. Get 'em in sympathy with it. If any of 'em aren't in sympathy with it, get rid of those. Kickers never did any business any good. You'll get plenty of kicks from outside. Then, when the office gets used to your way of doing things, you can quit wasting so much time on the news and editorial end."

"But that's what makes the paper, Dad."

"Get over that idea. You hire men to get out the paper. Let 'em earn their pay while you watch the door where the dollars come in. Advertising, my son: that's the point to work at. In a way I'm sorry you let Sterne out."

The ex-editor had left, a fortnight before, on a basis agreeable to himself and Hal, and McGuire Ellis had taken over his duties.

"Certainly you had no reason to like Sterne, Dad."

"For all that, he knew his job. Everything Sterne did had a dollar somewhere in the background. Even his blackmailing game. He worked with the business office, and he took his orders on that basis. Now if you had some man whom you could turn over this news end to while you're building up a sound advertising policy—"

"How about McGuire Ellis?"

Dr. Surtaine glanced over to the window corner where the associate editor was somnambulantly fighting a fly for the privilege of continuing a nap.

"Too much of a theorist: too much of a knocker."

"He's taught me what little I know about this business," said Hal. "Hi! Wake up, Ellis. Do you know you've got to make a speech in an hour? This is the day of the Formal Feed."

"Hoong!" grunted Ellis, arousing himself. "Speech? I can't make a speech. Make it yourself."

"I'm going to."

"What are you going to talk about?"

"Well, I might borrow your text and preach them a sermon on honesty in journalism. Seriously, I think the whole paper has degenerated to low ideals, and if I put it to them straight, that every man of them, reporter, copy-reader, or editor, has got to measure up to an absolutely straight standard of honesty—"

"They'll throw the tableware at you," said McGuire Ellis quietly: "at least they ought to, if they don't."

The two Surtaines stared at him in surprise.

"Who are you," continued the journalist, "to talk standards of honesty in journalism to those boys?"

"He's their boss: that's all he is," said Dr. Surtaine weightily.

"Let him set the example, then, jack the paper up where it belongs, and there'll be no difficulty with the men who write it."

"But, Mac, you've been hammering at me about the crookedness of journalism in Worthington from the first."

"All right. Crookedness there is. Where does it come from? From the men in control, mostly. Let me tell you something, you two: there's hardly a reporter in this city who isn't more honest than the paper he works for."

"Hifalutin nonsense," said Dr. Surtaine.

"From your point of view. You're an outsider. It's outsiders that make the newspaper game as bad as it is. Look at 'em in this town. Who owns the 'Banner'? A political boss. Who owns the 'News'? A brewer. The 'Star'? A promoter, and a pretty scaly one at that. The 'Observer' belongs body and soul to an advertising agency, and the 'Telegraph' is controlled by the banks. And one and all of 'em take their orders from the Dry Goods Union, which means Elias M. Pierce, because they live on its advertising."

"Why not? That's business," said Dr. Surtaine.

"Are we talking about business? I thought it was standards. What do those men know about the ethics of journalism? If you put the thing up to him, like as not E.M. Pierce would tell you that an ethic is something a doctor gives you to make you sleep."

"How about the 'Clarion,' Mac?" said Hal, smiling. "It's run by an outsider, too, isn't it?"

"That's what I want to know." There was no answering smile on Ellis's somber and earnest face. "I've thought there was hope for you. You've had no sound business training, thank God, so your sense of decency may not have been spoiled."

"You don't seem to think much of business standards," said the Doctor tolerantly.

"Not a great deal. I've bumped into 'em too hard. Not so long ago I was publisher of a paying daily in an Eastern city. The directors were all high-class business men, and the chairman of the board was one of those philanthropist-charity-donator-pillar-of-the-church chaps with a permanent crease of high respectability down his front. Well, one day there turned up a double murder in the den of one of these venereal quacks that infest every city. It set me on the trail, and I had my best reporter get up a series about that gang of vampires. Naturally that necessitated throwing out their ads. The advertising manager put up a howl, and we took the thing to the board of directors. In those days I had all my enthusiasm on tap. I had an array of facts, too, and I went at that board like a revivalist, telling 'em just the kind of devil-work the 'men's specialists' did. At the finish I sat down feeling pretty good. Nobody said anything for quite a while. Then the chairman dropped the pencil he'd been puttering with, and said, in a kind of purry voice: 'Gentlemen: I thought Mr. Ellis's job on this paper was to make it pay dividends, and not to censor the morals of the community.'"

"And, by crikey, he was right!" cried Dr. Surtaine.

"From the business point of view."

"Oh, you theorists! You theorists!" Dr. Surtaine threw out his hands in a gesture of pleasant despair. "You want to run the world like a Sunday-school class."

"Instead of like a three-card-monte game."

"With your lofty notions, Ellis, how did you ever come to work on a sheet like the 'Clarion'?"

"A man's got to eat. When I walked out of that directors' meeting I walked out of my job and into a saloon; and from that saloon I walked into a good many other saloons. Luckily for me, booze knocked me out early. I broke down, went West, got my health and some sense back again, drifted to this town, found an opening on the 'Clarion,' and took it, to make a living."

"You won't continue to do that," advised Dr. Surtaine bluntly, "if you keep on trying to reform your bosses."

"But what makes me sick," continued Ellis, disregarding this hint, "is to have people assume that newspaper men are a lot of semi-crooks and shysters. What does the petty grafting that a few reporters do—and, mind you, there's mighty little of it done—amount to, compared with the rottenness of a paper run by my church-going reformer with the business standards?"

A call from the business office took Hal away. At once Ellis turned to the older man.

"Are you going to run the paper, Doc?"

"No: no, my boy. Hal owns it, on his own money."

"Because if you are, I quit."

"That's no way to talk," said the magnate, aggrieved. "There isn't a man in Worthington treats his employees better or gets along with 'em smoother than me."

"That's right, too, I guess. Only I don't happen to want to be your employee."

"You're frank, at least, Mr. Ellis."

"Why not? I've laid my cards on the table. You know me for what I am, a disgruntled dreamer. I know you for what you are, a hard-headed business man. We don't have to quarrel about it. Tell you what I'll do: I'll match you, horse-and-horse, for the soul of your boy."

"You're a queer Dick, Ellis."

"Don't want to match? Then I suppose I've got to fight you for him," sighed the editor.

The big man laughed whole-heartedly. "Not a chance, my friend! Not a chance on earth. I don't believe even a woman could come between Hal and me, let alone a man."

"*Or* a principle?"

"Ah—ah! Dealing in abstractions again. Look out for this fellow, Boyee," he called jovially as Hal came back to his desk. "He'll make your paper the official organ of the Muckrakers' Union."

"I'll watch him," promised Hal. "Meantime I'll take your advice about my speech, Mac, and blue-pencil the how-to-be-good stuff."

"Now you're talking! I'll tell you, Boss: why not get some of the fellows to speak up. You might learn a few things about your own paper that would interest you."

"Good idea! But, Mac, I wish you wouldn't call me 'Boss.' It makes me feel absurdly young."

"All right, Hal," returned Ellis, with a grin. "But you've still got some youngness to overcome, you know."

An hour later, looking down the long luncheon table, the editor-owner felt his own inexperience more poignantly. With a very few exceptions, these men, his employees, were his seniors in years. More than that, he thought to see in the faces an air of capability, of assurance, of preparedness, a sort of work-worthiness like the seaworthiness of a vessel which has passed the high test of wind and wave. And to him, untried, unformed, ignorant, the light amateur, all this human mechanism must look for guidance. Humility clouded him at the recollection of the spirit in which he had taken on the responsibility so vividly personified before him, a spirit of headlong wrath and revenge, and he came fervently to a realization and a resolve. He saw himself as part of a close-knit whole; he visioned, sharply, the Institution, complex, delicate, almost infinitely powerful for good or evil, not alone to those who composed it, but to the community to which it bore so subtle a relationship. And he resolved, with a determination that partook of the nature of prayer and yet was more than prayer, to give himself loyally, unsparingly, devotedly to the common task. In this spirit he rose, at the close of the luncheon, to speak.

No newspaper reported the maiden speech of Mr. Harrington Surtaine to the staff of the Worthington "Clarion." Newspapers are reticent about their own affairs. In this case it is rather a pity, for the effort is said to have been an eminently successful one. Estimated by its effect, it certainly was, for it materialized with quite spiritistic suddenness, from out the murk of uncertainty and suspicion, the form and substance of a new *esprit de corps*, among the "Clarion" men, and established the system of Talk-it-Over Breakfasts which made a close-knit, jealously guarded corporation and club out of the staff. Free of all ostentation or self-assertiveness was Hal's talk; simple, and, above all virtues, brief. He didn't tell his employees what he expected of them. He told them what they might expect of him. The frankness of his manner, the self-respecting modesty of his attitude toward an audience of more experienced subordinates, his shining faith and belief in the profession which he had adopted; all this eked out by his ease of address and his dominant physical charm, won them from the first. Only at the close did he venture upon an assertion of his own ideas or theories.

"It is the Sydney 'Bulletin,' I think, which preserves as its motto the proposition that every man has at least one good story in him. I have been studying newspaper files since I took this job,—all the files of all the papers I could get,—and I'm almost ready to believe that much news which the papers publish has got realer facts up its sleeve: that the news is only the shadow of the facts. I'd like to get at the Why of the day's news. Do you remember Sherlock Holmes's 'commonplace' divorce suit, where the real cause was that the husband used to remove his front teeth and hurl 'em at the wife whenever her breakfast-table conversation wasn't sprightly enough to suit him? Once out of a hundred times, I suppose, the everyday processes of our courts hide something picturesque or perhaps important in the background. Any paper that could get and present that sort of news would liven up its columns a good deal. And it would strike a new note in Worthington. I'll give you a motto for the 'Clarion,' gentlemen: 'The Facts Behind the News.' And now I've said my say, and I want to hear from you."

Here for the first time Hal struck a false note. Newspaper men, as a class, abhor public speaking. So much are they compelled to hear from "those bores who prate intolerably over dinner tables," that they regard the man who speaks when he isn't manifestly obliged to, as an enemy to the public weal, and are themselves most loath thus to add to the sum of human suffering. Merely by way of saving the situation, Wayne, the city editor, arose and said a few words complimentary to the new owner. He was followed by the head copy-reader in the same strain. Two of the older sub-editors perpetrated some meaningless but well-meant remarks, and the current of events bade fair to end in complete stagnation, when from out of the ruck, midway of the table, there rose the fringed and candid head of one William S. Marchmont, the railroad and markets reporter.

Marchmont was an elderly man, of a journalistic type fast disappearing. There is little room in the latter-day pressure of newspaper life for the man who works on "booze." But though a steady drinker, and occasionally an unsteady one, Marchmont had his value. He was an expert in his specialty. He had a wide acquaintance, and he seldom became unprofessionally drunk in working hours. To offset the unwonted strain of rising before noon, however, he had fortified himself for this occasion by several cocktails which were manifest in his beaming smile and his expansive flourish in welcoming Mr. Surtaine to the goodly fellowship of the pen.

"Very good, all that about the facts behind the news," he said genially. "Very instructive and—and illuminating. But what I wanta ask you is this: We fellows who have to *write* the facts behind the news; where do we get off?"

"I don't understand you," said Hal.

"Lemme explain. Last week we had an accident on the Mid-and-Mud. Engineer ran by his signals. Rear end collision. Seven people killed. Coroner's inquest put all the blame on the engineer. Engineer wasn't tending to his duty. That's news, isn't it, Mr. Surtaine?"

"Undoubtedly."

"Yes: but here's the facts. That engineer had been kept on duty forty-eight hours with only five hours off. He was asleep when he ran past the block and killed those people."

"Is he telling the truth, Mac?" asked Hal in a swift aside to Ellis.

"If he says so, it's right," replied Ellis.

"What do you call that?" pursued the speaker.

"Murder. I call it murder." Max Veltman, who sat just beyond the speaker, half rose from his chair. "The men who run the road ought to be tried for murder."

"Oh, *you* can call it that, all right, in one of your Socialist meetings," returned the reporter genially. "But I can't."

"Why can't you?" demanded Hal.

"The railroad people would shut down on news to the 'Clarion.' I couldn't get a word out of them on anything. What good's a reporter who can't get news? You'd fire me in a week."

"Can you prove the facts?"

"I can."

"Write it for tomorrow's paper. I'll see that you don't lose your place."

Marchmont sat down, blinking. Again there was silence around the table, but this time it was electric, with the sense of flashes to come. The slow drawl of Lindsay, the theater reporter, seemed anti-climatic as he spoke up, slouched deep in his seat.

"How much do you know of dramatic criticism in this town, Mr. Surtaine?"

"Nothing."

"Maybe, then, you'll be pained to learn that we're a set of liars—I might even go further—myself among the number. There hasn't been honest dramatic criticism written in Worthington for years."

"That is hard to believe, Mr. Lindsay."

"Not if you understand the situation. Suppose I roast a show like 'The Nymph in the Nightie' that played here last week. It's vapid and silly, and rotten with suggestiveness. I wouldn't let my kid sister go within gunshot of it. But I've got to tell everybody else's kid sister, through our columns, that it's a delightful and enlivening *mélange* of high class fun and frolic. To be sure, I can praise a fine performance like 'Kindling' or 'The Servant in the House,' but I've got to give just as clean a bill of health to a gutter-and-brothel farce. Otherwise, the high-minded gentlemen that run our theaters will cut off my tickets."

"Buy them at the box-office," said Hal.

"No use. They wouldn't let me in. The courts have killed honest criticism by deciding that a manager can keep a critic out on any pretext or without any. Besides, there's the advertising. We'd lose that."

"Speaking of advertising,"—now it was Lynch, a young reporter who had risen from being an office boy,—"I guess it spoils some pretty good stories from the down-town district. Look at that accident at Scheffer and Mintz's; worth three columns of anybody's space. Tank on the roof broke, and drowned out a couple of hundred customers. Panic, and broken bones, and all kinds of things. How much did we give it? One stick! And we didn't name the place: just called it 'a Washington Street store.' There were facts behind *that* news, all right. But I guess Mr. Shearson wouldn't have been pleased if we'd printed 'em."

In fact, Shearson, the advertising manager, looked far from pleased at the mention.

"If you think a one-day story would pay for the loss of five thousand a year in advertising, you've got another guess, young man," he growled.

"He's right, there," said Dr. Surtaine, on one side of Hal; and from the other, McGuire Ellis chirped:—

"Things are beginning to open up, all right, Mr. Editor."

Two aspirants were now vying for the floor, the winner being the political reporter for the paper.

"Would you like to hear some facts about the news we don't print?" he asked.

"Go ahead," replied Hal. "You have the floor."

"You recall a big suffrage meeting here recently, at which Mrs. Barkerly from London spoke. Well, the chairman of that meeting didn't get a line of his speech in the papers: didn't even get his name mentioned. Do you know why?"

"I can't even imagine," said Hal.

"Because he's the Socialist candidate for Governor of this State. He's black-balled from publication in every newspaper here."

"By whom?" inquired Hal.

"By the hinted wish of the Chamber of Commerce. They're so afraid of the Socialist movement that they daren't even admit it's alive."

"Not at all!" Dr. Surtaine's rotund bass boomed out the denial. "There are some movements that it's wisest to disregard. They'll die of themselves. Socialism is a destructive force. Why should the papers help spread it by noticing it in their columns?"

"Well, I'm no Socialist," said the political reporter, "but I'm a newspaper man, and I say it's news when a Socialist does a thing just as much as when any one else does it. Yet if I tried to print it, they'd give me the laugh on the copy-desk."

"It's a fact that we're all tied down on the news in this town," corroborated Wayne; "what between the Chamber of Commerce and the Dry Goods Union and the theaters and the other steady advertisers. You must have noticed, Mr. Surtaine, that if there's a shoplifting case or anything of that kind you never see the name of the store in print. It's always 'A State Street Department Store' or 'A Warburton Avenue Shop.' Ask Ellis if that isn't so."

"Correct," said Ellis.

"Why shouldn't it be so?" cried Shearson. "You fellows make me tired. You're always thinking of the news and never of the advertising. Who is it pays your salaries, do you think? The men who advertise in the 'Clarion.'"

"Hear! Hear!" from Dr. Surtaine.

"And what earthly good does it do to print stuff like those shoplifting cases? Where's the harm in protecting the store?"

"I'll tell you where," said Ellis. "That McBurney girl case. They got the wrong girl, and, to cover themselves, they tried to railroad her. It was a clear case. Every paper in town had the facts. Yet they gave that girl the reputation of a thief and never printed a correction for fear of letting in the store for a damage suit."

"Did the 'Clarion' do that?" asked Hal.

"Yes."

"Get me a full report of the facts."

"What are you going to do?" asked Shearson.

"Print them."

"Oh, my Lord!" groaned Shearson.

The circle was now drawing in and the talk became brisker, more detailed, more intimate. To his overwhelming amazement Hal learned some of the major facts of that subterranean journalistic history which never gets into print; the ugly story of the blackmail of a President of the United States by a patent medicine concern (Dr. Surtaine verified this with a nod); the inside facts of the failure of an important senatorial investigation which came to nothing because of the drunken debauchery of the chief senatorial investigator; the dreadful details of the death of a leading merchant in a great Eastern city, which were so glossed over by the local press that few of his fellow citizens ever had an inkling of the truth; the obtainable and morally provable facts of the conspiracy on the part of a mighty financier which had plunged a nation into panic; these and many other strange narratives of the news, known to every old newspaper man, which made the neophyte's head whirl. Then, in a pause, a young voice said:

"Well, to bring the subject up to date, what about the deaths in the Rookeries?"

"Shut up," said Wayne sharply.

There followed a general murmur of question and answer. "What about the Rookeries?"—"Don't know."—"They say the death-rate is a terror."—"Are they concealing it at the City Hall?"—"No; Merritt can't find out."—"Bet Tip O'Farrell can."—"Oh, he's in on the game."—"Just another fake, I guess."

In vain Hal strove to catch a clue from the confused voices. He had made a note of it for future inquiry, when some one called out: "Mac Ellis hasn't said anything yet." The others caught it up. "Speech from Mac!"—"Don't let him out."—"If you can't speak, sing a song."—"Play a tune on the *bazoo*."—"Hike him up there, somebody."—"Silence for the MacGuire!!"

"I've never made a speech in my life," said Ellis, glowering about him, "and you fellows know it. But last night I read this in Plutarch: 'Themistocles said that he certainly could not make use of any stringed instrument; could only, were a small and obscure city put into his hands, make it great and glorious.'"

Ellis paused, lifting one hand. "Fellows," he said, and he turned sharply to face Hal Surtaine, "I don't know how the devil old Themistocles ever could do it—unless he owned a newspaper!"

Silence followed, and then a quick acclaiming shout, as they grasped the implicit challenge of the corollary. Then again silence, tense with curiosity. No doubt of what they awaited. Their expectancy drew Hal to his feet.

"I had intended to speak but once," he said, in a constrained voice, "but I've learned more here this afternoon—more than—than I could have thought—" He broke off and threw up his hand. "I'm no newspaper man," he cried. "I'm only an amateur, a freshman at this business. But one thing I believe; it's the business of a newspaper to give the news without fear or favor, and that's what the 'Clarion' is going to do from this day. On that platform I'll stand by any man who'll stand by me. Will you help?"

The answer rose and rang like a cheer. The gathering broke into little, excited, chattering groups, sure symptom of the success of a meeting. Much conjecture was expressed and not a little cynicism. "Compared to us Ishmael would be a society favorite if Surtaine carries this through," said one. "It means suspension in six months," prophesied Shearson. But most of the men were excitedly enthusiastic. Your newspaper man is by nature a romantic; otherwise he would not choose the most adventurous of callings. And the fighting tone of the new boss stimulated in them the spirit of chance and change.

Slowly and reluctantly they drifted away to the day's task. At the close Hal sat, thoughtful and spent, in a far corner when Ellis walked heavily over to him. The associate editor gazed down at his bemused principal for a time. From his pocket he drew the thick blue pencil of his craft, and with it tapped Hal thrice on the shoulder.

"Rise up, Sir Newspaper Man," he pronounced solemnly. "I hereby dub thee Knight-Editor."

CHAPTER XII

THE THIN EDGE

Across the fresh and dainty breakfast table, Dr. Miles Elliot surveyed his even more fresh and dainty niece and ward with an expression of sternest disapproval. Not that it affected in any perceptible degree that attractive young person's healthy appetite. It was the habit of the two to breakfast together early, while their elderly widowed cousin, who played the part of Feminine Propriety in the household in a highly self-effacing and satisfactory manner, took her tea and toast in her own rooms. It was further Dr. Elliot's custom to begin the day by reprehending everything (so far as he could find it out) which Miss Esmé had done, said, or thought in the previous twenty-four hours. This, as he frequently observed to her, was designed to give her a suitably humble attitude toward the scheme of creation, but didn't.

"Out all night again?" he growled.

"Pretty nearly," said Esmé cheerfully, setting a very even row of very white teeth into an apple.

"Humph! What was it this time?"

"A dinner-dance at the Norris's."

"Have a good time?"

"Beautiful! My frock was pretty. And I was pretty. And everybody was nice to me. And I wish it were going to happen right over again tonight."

"Whom did you dance with mostly?"

"Anybody that asked me."

"Dare say. How many new victims?" he demanded.

"Don't be a silly Guardy. I'm not a man-eating tiger or tigress, or the Great American Puma—or pumess. Don't you think 'pumess' is a nice lady-word, Guardy?"

"Did you dance with Will Douglas?" catechised the grizzled doctor, declining to be shunted off on a philological discussion. Next to acting as legal major domo to E.M. Pierce, Douglas's most important function in life was apparently to fetch and carry for the reigning belle of Worthington. His devotion to Esmé Elliot had become stock gossip of the town, since three seasons previous.

"Almost half as often as he asked me," said the girl. "That was eight times, I think."

"Nice boy, Will."

"Boy!" There was a world of expressiveness in the monosyllable.

"Not a day over forty," observed the uncle. "And you are twenty-two. Not that you look it"—judicially—"like thirty-five, after all this dissipation."

Esmé rose from her seat, walked with great dignity past her guardian, and suddenly whirling, pounced upon his ear.

"Do I? Do I?" she cried. "Do I look thirty-five? Quick! Take it back."

"Ouch! Oh! No. Not more'n thirty. Oo! All right; twenty-five, then. Fifteen! Three!!!"

She kissed the assaulted ear, and pirouetted over to the broad window-seat, looking in her simple morning gown like a school-girl.

"Wonder how you do it," grumbled Dr. Elliot. "Up all night roistering like a sophomore—"

"I was in bed at three."

"Down next morning, fresh as a—a—"

"Rose," she supplied tritely.

"—cake o' soap," concluded her uncle. "Now, as for you and Will Douglas, as between Will's forty—"

"Marked down from forty-five," she interjected.

"And your twenty-two—"

"Looking like thirty-something."

"Never mind," said Dr. Elliot in martyred tones. "*I* don't want to finish *any* sentence. Why should I? Got a niece to do it for me."

"Nobody wants you to finish that one. You're a matchmaking old maid," declared Esmé, wrinkling her delicate nose at him, "and if you're ever put up for our sewing-circle I shall blackball you. Gossip!"

"Oh, if I wanted to gossip, I'd begin to hint about the name of Surtaine."

The girl's color did not change. "As other people have evidently been doing to you."

"A little. Did you dance with him last night?"

"He wasn't there. He's working very hard on his newspaper."

"You seem to know a good deal about it."

"Naturally, since I've bought into the paper myself. I believe that's the proper business phrase, isn't it?"

"Bought in? What do you mean? You haven't been making investments without my advice?"

"Don't worry, Guardy, dear. It isn't strictly a business transaction. I've been—ahem—establishing a sphere of influence."

"Over Harrington Surtaine?"

"Over his newspaper."

"Look here, Esmé! How serious is this Surtaine matter?" Dr. Elliot's tone had a distinct suggestion of concern.

"For me? Not serious at all."

"But for him?"

"How can I tell? Isn't it likely to be serious for any of the unprotected young of your species when a Great American Pumess gets after him?" she queried demurely.

"But you can't know him very well. He's been here only a few weeks, hasn't he?"

"More than a month. And from the first he's gone everywhere."

"That's quite unusual for your set, isn't it? I thought you rather prided yourselves on being careful about outsiders."

"No one's an outsider whom Jinny Willard vouches for. Besides every one likes Hal Surtaine for himself."

"You among the number?"

"Yes, indeed," she responded frankly. "He's attractive. And he seems older and more—well—interesting than most of the boys of my set."

"And that appeals to you?"

"Yes: it does. I get awfully bored with the just-out-of-college chatter of the boys. I want to see the wheels go round, Guardy. Real wheels, that make up real machinery and get real things done. I'm not quite an *ingénue*, you know."

"Thirty-five, thirty, twenty-five, fifteen, three," murmured her uncle, rubbing his ear. "And does young Surtaine give you inside glimpses of the machinery of his business?"

"Sometimes. He doesn't know very much about it himself, yet."

"It's a pretty dirty business, Honey. And, I'm afraid, he's a pretty bad breed."

"The father *is* rather impossible, isn't he?" she said, laughing. "But they say he's very kindly, and well-meaning, and public-spirited, and that kind of thing."

"He's a scoundrelly old quack. It's a bad inheritance for the boy. Where are you off to this morning?"

"To the 'Clarion' office."

"What! Well, but, see here, dear, does Cousin Clarice approve of that sort of thing?"

"Wholly," Esmé assured him, dimpling. "It's on behalf of the Recreation Club. That's the Reverend Norman Hale's club for working-girls, you know. We're going to give a play. And, as I'm on the Press Committee, it's quite proper for me to go to the newspapers and get things printed."

"Humph!" grunted Dr. Elliot. "Well: good hunting—Pumess."

After the girl had gone, he sat thinking. He knew well the swift intimacies, frank and clean and fine, which spring up in the small, close-knit social circles of a city like Worthington. And he knew, too, and trusted and respected the judgment of Mrs. Festus Willard, whose friendship was tantamount to a certificate of character and eligibility. As against that, he set the unforgotten picture of the itinerant quack, vending his poison across the countryside, playing on desperate fears and tragic hopes, coining his dollars from the grimmest of false dies; and now that same quack,—powerful, rich, generous, popular, master of the good things of life,—still draining out his millions from the populace, through just such deadly swindling as that which had been lighted up by the flaring exploitation of the oil torches fifteen years before. Could any good come from such a stock? He decided to talk it out with Esmé, sure that her fastidiousness would turn away from the ugly truth.

Meantime, the girl was making a toilet of vast and artful simplicity wherewith to enrapture the eye of the beholder. The first profound effect thereof was wrought upon Reginald Currier, alias "Bim," some fifteen minutes later, at the outer portals of the "Clarion" office.

"Hoojer wanter—" he began, and then glanced up. Almost as swiftly as had aforetime risen under Hal's irate and athletic impulsion, the redoubtable Bim was lifted from his seat by the power of Miss Elliot's glance. "Gee!" he murmured.

The Great American Pumess, looking much more like a very innocent, soft, and demurely playful kitten, accepted this ingenuous tribute to her charms with a smile. "Good-morning," she said. "Is Mr. Surtaine in?"

"Same t'you," responded the courteous Mr. Currier. "Sure he is. Walk this way, maddim!"

They found the editor at his desk. His absorbed expression brightened as he jumped up to greet his visitor.

"You!" he cried.

Esmé let her hand rest in his and her glance linger in his eyes, perhaps just a little longer than might have comported with safety in one less adept.

"How is the paper going?" she inquired, taking the chair which he pulled out for her.

"Completely to the dogs," said Hal.

"No! Why I thought—"

"You haven't given any advice to the editor for six whole days," he complained. "How can you expect an institution to run, bereft of its presiding genius? Is it your notion of a fair partnership to stay away and let your fellow toilers wither on the bough? I only wonder that the presses haven't stopped."

"Would this help at all?" The visitor produced from her shopping-bag the written announcement of the Recreation Club play.

"Undoubtedly it will save the day. Lost Atlantis will thrill to hear, and deep-sea cables bear the good news to unborn generations. What is it?"

She frowned upon his levity. "It is an interesting item, a *very* interesting item of news," she said impressively.

"Bring one in every day," he directed: "in person. We can't trust the mails in matters of such vital import." And scrawling across the copy a single hasty word in pencil, he thrust it into a wire box.

"What's that you've written on it?"

"The mystic word 'Must.'"

"Does it mean that it must be printed?"

"Precisely, O Fountain of Intuition. It is one of the proud privileges which an editor-in-chief has. Otherwise he does exactly what the city desk or the advertising manager or the head proof-reader or the fourth assistant office boy tells him. That's because he's new to his job and everybody in the place knows it."

"Yet I don't think it would be easy for any one to make you do a thing you really didn't want to do," she observed, regarding him thoughtfully.

"When you lift your eyebrows like that—"

"I thought you weren't to make pretty speeches to me in business hours," she reproached him.

"Such a stern and rock-bound partner! Very well. How does the paper suit your tastes?"

"You've got an awfully funny society column."

"We strive to amuse. But I thought only people outside of society ever read society columns—except to see if their names were there."

"I read *all* the paper," she answered severely. "And I'd like to know who Mrs. Wolf Tone Maher is."

"Ring up 'Information,'" he suggested.

"Don't be flippant. Also Mr. and Mrs. B. Kirschofer, and Miss Amelia Sproule. All of which give teas in the society columns of the 'Clarion.' *Or* dances. *Or* dinners. And I notice they're always sandwiched in between the Willards or the Vanes or the Ellisons or the Pierces, or some of our own crowd. I'm curious."

"So am I. Let's ask Wayne."

Accordingly the city editor was summoned and duly presented to Miss Elliot. But when she put the question to him, he looked uncomfortable. Like a good city editor, however, he defended his subordinate.

"It isn't the society reporter's fault," he said. "He knows those people don't belong."

"How do they get in there, then?" asked Hal.

"Mr. Shearson's orders."

"Is Mr. Shearson the society editor?" asked Esmé.

"No. He's the advertising manager."

"Forgive my stupidity, but what has the advertising manager to do with social news?"

"A big heap lot," explained Wayne. "It's the most important feature of the paper to him. Wolf Tone Maher is general manager of the Bee Hive Department Store. We get all their advertising, and when Mrs. Maher wants to see her name along with the 'swells,' as she would say, Mr. Shearson is glad to oblige. B. Kirschofer is senior partner in the firm of Kirschofer & Kraus, of the Bargain Emporium. Miss Sproule is the daughter of Alexander Sproule, proprietor of the Agony Parlors, three floors up."

"Agony Parlors?" queried the visitor.

"Painless dentistry," explained Wayne. "Mr. Shearson handles all that matter and sends it down to us."

"Marked 'Must,' I suppose," remarked Miss Elliot, not without malice. "So the mystic 'Must' is not exclusively a chief-editorial prerogative?"

The editor-in-chief looked annoyed, thereby satisfying his visitor's momentary ambition. "Hereafter, Mr. Wayne, all copy indorsed 'Must' is to be referred to me," he directed.

"That kills the 'Must' thing," commented the city editor cheerfully. "What about 'Must not'?"

"Another complication," laughed Esmé. "I fear I'm peering into the dark and secret places of journalism."

"For example, a story came in last night that was a hummer," said Wayne; "about E.M. Pierce's daughter running down an apple-cart in her sixty-horse-power car, and scattering dago, fruit, and all to the four winds of Heaven. Robbins saw it, and he's the best reporter we have for really funny stuff."

"Kathleen drives that car like a demon out on a spree," said Esmé. "But of course you wouldn't print anything unpleasant about it."

"Why not?" asked Wayne.

"Well, she belongs to our crowd,—Mr. Surtaine's friends, I mean,—and it was accidental, I suppose, and so long as the man wasn't hurt—"

"Only a sprained shoulder."

"—and I'm sure Agnes would be more than willing to pay for the damage."

"Oh, yes. She asked the worth of his stock and then doubled it, gave him the money, and drove off with her mud guards coquettishly festooned with grapes. That's what made it such a good story."

"But, Mr. Wayne"—Esmé's eyes were turned up to his pleadingly: "those things are funny to tell. But they're so vulgar, in the paper. Think, if it were your sister."

"If my sister went tearing through crowded streets at forty miles an hour, I'd have her examined for homicidal mania. That Pierce girl will kill some one yet. Even then, I suppose we won't print a word of it."

"What would stop us?" asked Hal.

"The fear of Elias M. Pierce. His 'Must not' is what kills this story."

"Let me see it."

"Oh, it isn't visible. But every editor in town knows too much to offend the President of the Consolidated Employers' Organization, let alone his practical control of the Dry Goods Union."

"You were at the staff breakfast yesterday, I believe, Mr. Wayne."

"What? Yes; of course I was."

"And you heard what I said?"

"Yes. But you can't do that sort of thing all at once," replied the city editor uneasily.

"We certainly never shall do it without making a beginning. Please hold the Pierce story until you hear from me."

"Tell me all about the breakfast," commanded Esmé, as the door closed upon Wayne.

Briefly Hal reported the exchange of ideas between himself and his staff, skeletonizing his own speech.

"Splendid!" she cried. "And isn't it exciting! I love a good fight. What fun you'll have. Oh, the luxury of saying exactly what you think! Even I can't do that."

"What limits are there to the boundless privileges of royalty?" asked Hal, smiling.

"Conventions. For instance, I'd love to tell you just how fine I think all this is that you're doing, and just how much I like and admire you. We've come to be real friends, haven't we? And, you see, I can be of some actual help. The breakfast was my suggestion, wasn't it? So you owe me something for that. Are you properly grateful?"

"Try me."

"Then, august and terrible sovereign, spare the life of my little friend Kathie."

Hal drew back a bit. "I'm afraid you don't realize the situation."

The Great American Pumess shot forth a little paw—such a soft, shapely, hesitant, dainty, appealing little paw—and laid it on Hal's hand.

"Please," she said.

"But, Esmé,"—he began. It was the first time he had used that intimacy with her. Her eyes dropped.

"We're partners, aren't we?" she said.

"Of course."

"Then you won't let them print it!"

"If Miss Pierce goes rampaging around the streets—"

"Please. For me,—partner."

"One would have to be more than human, to say no to you," he returned, laughing a little unsteadily. "You're corrupting my upright professional sense of duty."

"It can't be a duty to hold a friend up to ridicule, just for a little accident."

"I'm not so sure," said Hal, again. "However, for the sake of our partnership, and if you'll promise to come again soon to tell us how to run the paper—"

"I knew you'd be kind!" There was just the faintest pressure of the delicate paw, before it was withdrawn. The Great American Pumess was feeling the thrill of power over men and events. "I think I like the newspaper business. But I've got to be at my other trade now."

"What trade is that?"

"Didn't you know I was a little sister of the poor? When you've lost all your money and are ill, I'll come and lay my cooling hand on your fevered brow and bring wine jelly to your tenement."

"Aren't you afraid of contagious diseases?" he asked anxiously. "Such places are always full of them."

"Oh, they placard for contagion. It's safe enough. And I'm really interested. It's my only excuse to myself for living."

"If bringing happiness wherever you go isn't enough—"

"No! No!" She smiled up into his eyes. "This is still a business visit. But you may take me to my car."

On his way back Hal stopped to tell Wayne that perhaps the Pierce story wasn't worth running, after all. Unease of conscience disturbed his work for a time thereafter. He appeased it by the excuse that it was no threat or pressure from without which had influenced his action. He had killed the item out of consideration for the friend of his friend. What did it matter, anyway, a bit of news like that? Who was harmed by leaving it out? As yet he was too little the journalist to comprehend that the influences which corrupt the news are likely to be dangerous in proportion as they are subtle.

Wayne understood better, and smiled with a cynical wryness of mouth upon McGuire Ellis, who, having passed Hal and Esmé on the stairs, had lingered at the city desk and heard the editor-in-chief's half-hearted order.

"Still worrying about Dr. Surtaine's influence over the paper?" asked the city editor, after Hal's departure.

"Yes," said Ellis.

"Don't."

"Why not?"

"Did you happen to notice about the prettiest thing that ever used eyes for weapons, in the hall?"

"Something of that description."

"Let me present you, in advance, to Miss Esmé Elliot, the new boss of our new boss," said Wayne, with a flourish.

"God save the Irish!" said McGuire Ellis.

CHAPTER XIII

NEW BLOOD

Echoes of the Talk-it-Over Breakfast rang briskly in the "Clarion" office. It was suggested to Hal that the success of the function warranted its being established as a regular feature of the shop. Later this was done. One of the participants, however, was very ill-pleased with the morning's entertainment. Dr. Surtaine saw, in retrospect and in prospect, his son being led astray into various radical and harebrained vagaries of journalism. None of those at the breakfast had foreseen more clearly than the wise and sharpened quack what serious difficulties beset the course which Hal had laid out for himself.

Trouble was what Dr. Surtaine hated above all things. Whatever taste for the adventurous he may have possessed had been sated by his career as an itinerant. Now he asked only to be allowed to hatch his golden dollars peacefully, afar from all harsh winds of controversy. That his own son should feel a more stirring ambition left him clucking, a bewildered hen on the brink of perilous waters.

But he clucked cunningly. And before he undertook his appeal to bring the errant one back to shore he gave himself two days to think it over. To this extent Dr. Surtaine had become a partisan of the new enterprise; that he, too, previsioned an ideal newspaper, a newspaper which, day by day, should uphold and defend the Best Interests of the Community, and, as an inevitable corollary, nourish itself on their bounty. By the Best Interests of the Community—he visualized the phrase in large print, as a creed for any journal—Dr. Surtaine meant, of course, business in the great sense. Gloriously looming in the future of his fancy was the day when the "Clarion" should develop into the perfect newspaper, the fine flower of journalism, an organ in which every item of news, every line of editorial, every word of advertisement, should subserve the one vital purpose, Business; should aid in some manner, direct or indirect, in making a dollar for the "Clarion's" patrons and a dime for the "Clarion's" till. But how to introduce these noble and fortifying ideals into the mind of that flighty young bird, Hal?

Dr. Surtaine, after studying the problem, decided to employ the instance of the Mid-State and Great Muddy River Railroad as the entering wedge of his argument. Hal owned a considerable block of stock, earning the handsome dividend of eight per cent. Under attacks possibly leading to adverse legislation, this return might well be reduced and Hal's own income suffer a shrinkage. Therefore, in the interests of all concerned, Hal ought to keep his hands off the subject. Could anything be clearer?

Obviously not, the senior Surtaine thought, and so laid it before the junior, one morning as they were walking down town together. Hal admitted the assault upon the Mid-and-Mud; defended it, even; added that there would be another phase of it presently in the way of an attempt on the part of the paper to force a better passenger service for Worthington. Dr. Surtaine confessed a melancholious inability to see what the devil business it was of Hal's.

"It isn't I that's making the fight, Dad. It's the 'Clarion.'"

"The same thing."

"Not at all the same thing. Something very much bigger than I or any other one man. I found that out at the breakfast."

That breakfast! Socialistic, anarchistic, anti-Christian, were the climactic adjectives employed by Dr. Surtaine to signify his disapproval of the occasion.

"Sorry you didn't like it, Dad. You heard nothing but plain facts."

"Plain slush! Just look at this railroad accident article broad-mindedly, Boyee. You own some Mid-and-Mud stock."

"Thanks to you, Dad."

"Paying eight per cent. How long will it go on paying that if the newspapers keep stirring up trouble for it? Anti-railroad sentiment is fostered by just such stuff as the 'Clarion' printed. What if the engineer *was* worked overtime? He got paid for it."

"And seven people got killed for it. I understand the legislature is going to ask why, mainly because of our story and editorial."

"There you are! Sicking a pack of demagogues onto the Mid-and-Mud. How can it make profits and pay your dividends if that kind of thing keeps up?"

"I don't know that I need dividends earned by slaughtering people," said Hal slowly.

"Maybe you don't need the dividends, but there's plenty of people that do, people that depend on 'em. Widows and orphans, too."

"Oh, that widow-and-orphan dummy!" cried Hal. "What would the poor, struggling railroads ever do without it to hide behind!"

"You talk like Ellis," reproved his father. "Boyee, I don't want you to get too much under his influence. He's an impractical will-o'-the-wisp chaser. Just like all the writing fellows."

By this time they had reached the "Clarion" Building.

"Come in, Dad," invited Hal, "and we'll talk to Ellis about Old Home Week. He's with you there, anyway."

"Oh, he's all right aside from his fanatical notions," said the other as they mounted the stairs.

The associate editor nodded his greetings from above a pile of left-over copy.

"Old Home Week?" he queried. "Let's see, when does it come?"

"In less than six months. It isn't too early to give it a start, is it?" asked Hal Surtaine.

"No. It's news any time, now."

"More than that," said Dr. Surtaine. "It's advertising. I can turn every ad that goes out to the 'Clarion.'"

"Last year we got only the pickings," remarked Ellis.

"Last year your owner wasn't the son of the committee's chairman."

"By the way, Dad, I'll have to resign that secretaryship. Every minute of my spare time I'm going to put in around this office."

"I guess you're right. But I'm sorry to lose you."

"Think how much more I can do for the celebration with this paper than I could as secretary."

"Right, again."

"Some one at the breakfast," observed Hal, "mentioned the Rookeries, and Wayne shut him up. What are the Rookeries? I've been trying to remember to ask."

The other two looked at each other with raised eyebrows. As well might one have asked, "What is the City Hall?" in Worthington. Ellis was the one to answer.

"Hell's hole and contamination. The worst nest of tenements in the State. Two blocks of 'em, owned by our best citizens. Run by a political pull. So there's no touching 'em."

"What's up there now; more murders?" asked the Doctor.

"Somebody'll be calling it that if it goes much further," replied the newspaper man. "I don't know what the official *alias* of the trouble is. If you want details, get Wayne."

In response to a telephone call the city editor presented his lank form and bearded face at the door of the sanctum. "The Rookeries deaths?" he said. "Oh, malaria—for convenience."

"Malaria?" repeated Dr. Surtaine. "Why, there aren't any mosquitoes in that locality now."

"So the health officer, Dr. Merritt, says. But the certificates keep coming in. He's pretty worried. There have been over twenty cases in No. 7 and No. 9 alone. Three deaths in the last two days."

"Is it some sort of epidemic starting?" asked Hal. "That would be news, wouldn't it?"

At the word "epidemic," Dr. Surtaine had risen, and now came forward flapping his hand like a seal.

"The kind of news that never ought to get into print," he exclaimed. "That's the sort of thing that hurts a whole city."

"So does an epidemic if it gets a fair start," suggested Ellis.

"Epidemic! Epidemic!" cried the Doctor. "Ten years ago they started a scare about smallpox in those same Rookeries. The smallpox didn't amount to shucks. But look what the sensationalism did to us. It choked off Old Home Week, and lost us hundreds of thousands of dollars."

"I was a cub on the 'News' then," said Wayne. "And I remember there were a lot of deaths from chicken-pox that year. I didn't suppose people—that is, grown people—died of chicken-pox very often: not more often, say, than they die of malaria where there are no mosquitoes."

"Suspicion is one thing. Fact is another," said Dr. Surtaine decisively. "Hal, I hope you aren't going to take up with this nonsense, and risk the success of the Centennial Old Home Week."

"I can't see what good we should be doing," said the new editor.

"It's big news, if it's true," suggested Wayne, rather wistfully. "Suppression of a real epidemic."

"Ghost-tales and goblin-shine," laughed the big doctor, recovering his good humor. "Who's the physician down there?"

"Dr. De Vito, an Italian. Nobody else can get into the Rookeries to see a case. O'Farrell's the agent, and he sees to that."

"Tip O'Farrell, the labor politician? I know him. And I know De Vito well. In fact, he does part-time work in the Certina plant. I'll tell you what, Hal. I'll just make a little expert investigation of my own down there, and report to you."

"The 'Clarion's' Special Commissioner, Dr. L. André Surtaine," said Ellis sonorously.

"No publicity, boys. This is a secret commission. And here's your chance right now to make the 'Clarion' useful to the committee, Hal, by keeping all scare-stuff out of the paper."

"If it really does amount to anything, wouldn't it be better," said Hal, "to establish a quarantine and go in there and stamp the thing out? We've plenty of time before Old Home Week."

"No; no!" cried the Doctor. "Think of the publicity that would mean. It would be a year before the fear of it would die out. Every other city that's jealous of Worthington would make capital of it and thousands of people whose money we want would be scared away."

Ellis drew Wayne aside. "What does Dr. Merritt really think? Smallpox?"

"No. The place has been too well vaccinated. It might be scarlet fever, or diphtheria, or even meningitis. Merritt wants to go in there and open it up, but the Mayor won't let him. He doesn't dare take the responsibility without any newspaper backing. And none of the other papers dares tackle the ownership of the Rookeries."

"Then we ought to. A good, rousing sensation of that sort is just what the paper needs."

"We won't get it. There's too many ropes on the Boy Boss. First the girl and now the old man."

"Wait and see. He's got good stuff in him and he's being educated every day. Give him time."

"Mr. Wayne, I'd like to see the health office reports," called Hal, and the two went out.

Selecting one of his pet cigars, Dr. Surtaine advanced upon McGuire Ellis, extending it. "Mac, you're a good fellow at bottom," he said persuasively.

"What's the price," asked Ellis, "of the cigar and the compliment together? In other words, what do you want of me?"

"Keep your hands off the boy."

"Didn't I offer fair and square to match you for his soul? You insisted on fight."

"If you'd just let him alone," pursued the quack, "he'd come around right side up with care. He's sound and sensible at bottom. He's got a lot of me in him. But you keep feeding him up on your yellow journal ideas. What'll they ever get him? Trouble; nothing but trouble. Even if you should make a sort of success of the paper with your wild sensationalism it wouldn't be any real good to Hal. It wouldn't get him anywhere with the real people. It'd be a sheet he'd always have to be a little ashamed of. I tell you what, Mac, in order to respect himself a man has got to respect his business."

"Just so," said McGuire Ellis. "Do you respect your business, Doc?"

"Do I!! It makes half a million a year clear profit."

The associate editor turned to his work whistling softly.

CHAPTER XIV
THE ROOKERIES

Two conspicuous ornaments of Worthington's upper world visited Worthington's underworld on a hot, misty morning of early June. Both were there on business, Dr. L. André Surtaine in the fulfillment of his agreement with his son—the exact purpose of the visit, by the way, would have inspired Harrington Surtaine with unpleasant surprise, could he have known it; and Miss Esmé Elliot on a tour of inspection for the Visiting Nurses' Association, of which she was an energetic official. Whatever faults or foibles might be ascribed to Miss Elliot, she was no faddist. That which she undertook to do, she did thoroughly and well; and for practical hygiene she possessed an inborn liking and aptitude, far more so than, for example, her fortuitous fellow slummer of the morning, Dr. Surtaine, whom she encountered at the corner where the Rookeries begin. The eminent savant removed his hat with a fine flourish, further reflected in his language as he said:—

"What does Beauty so far afield?"

"Thank you, if you mean me," said Esmé demurely.

"Do you see something else around here that answers the description?"

"No: I certainly don't," she replied, letting her eyes wander along the street where Sadler's Shacks rose in grime and gauntness to offend the clean skies. "I am going over there to see some sick people."

"Ah! Charity as well as Beauty; the perfect combination."

The Doctor's pomposity always amused Esmé. "And what does Science so far from its placid haunts?" she mocked. "Are you scattering the blessings of Certina amongst a grateful proletariat?"

"Not exactly. I'm down here on some other business."

"Well, I won't keep you from it, Dr. Surtaine. Good-bye."

The swinging doors of a saloon opened almost upon her, and a short, broad-shouldered foreigner, in a ruffled-up silk hat, bumped into her lightly and apologized. He jogged up to Dr. Surtaine.

"Hello, De Vito," said Dr. Surtaine.

"At the service of my distinguish' confrère," said the squat Italian. "Am I require at the factory?"

"No. I've come to look into this sickness. Where is it?"

"The opposite eemediate block."

Dr. Surtaine eyed with disfavor the festering tenement indicated. "New cases?"

"Two, only."

"Who's treating them?"

"I am in charge. Mr. O'Farrell employs my services: so the pipple have not to pay anything. All the time which I am not at the Certina factory, I am here."

"Just so. And no other doctor gets in?"

"There is no call. They are quite satisfied."

"And is the Board of Health satisfied?"

The employee shrugged his shoulders and spread his hands. "How is it you Americans say? 'What he does not know cannot hurt somebody.'"

"Is O'Farrell agent for all these barracks?" Dr. Surtaine inquired as they walked up the street.

"All. Many persons own, but Mr. O'Farrell is boss of all. This Number 4, Mr. Gibbs owns. He is of the great department store. You know. A ver' fine man, Mr. Gibbs."

"A very fine fool," retorted the Doctor, "to let himself get mixed up with such rotten property. Why, it's a reflection on all us men of standing."

"Nobody knows he is owner. And it pays twelve per cent," said the Italian mildly. He paused at the door. "Do we go in?" he asked.

An acrid-soft odor as of primordial slime subtly intruded upon the sensory nerves of the visitor. The place breathed out decay; the decay of humanity, of cleanliness, of the honest decencies of life turned foul. Something lethal exhaled from that dim doorway. There was a stab of pestilence, reaching for the brain. But the old charlatan was no coward.

"Show me the cases," he said.

For an hour he moved through the black, stenchful passageways, up and down ramshackle stairs, from human warren to human warren, pausing here to question, there to peer and sniff and poke with an exploring cane. Out on the street again he drew full, heaving breath.

"O'Farrell's got to clean up. That's all there is to that," he said decisively.

"The Doctor thinks?" queried the little physician.

Dr. Surtaine shook his head. "I don't know. But I'm sure of one thing. There's three of them ought to be gotten out at once. The third-floor woman, and that brother and sister in the basement."

"And the German family at the top?"

Dr. Surtaine tapped his chest significantly. "Sure to be plenty of that in this kind of hole. Nothing to do but let 'em die." He did not mention that he had left a twenty-dollar bill and a word of cheer with the gasping consumptive and his wife. Outside of the line of business Dr. Surtaine's charities were silent. "How many of the *other* cases have you had here?"

"Eleven. Seven deaths. Four I take away."

"And what is your diagnosis, Doctor?" inquired the old quack professionally of the younger ignoramus.

Again De Vito shrugged. "For public, malignant malaria. How you call it? Pernicious. For me, I do' know. Maybe—" he leaned forward and spoke a low word.

"Meningitis?" repeated the other. "Possibly. I've never seen much of the infectious kind. What are you giving for it?"

"Certina, mostly."

Dr. Surtaine looked at him sharply, but the Italian's face was innocent of any sardonic expression.

"As well that as anything," muttered its proprietor. "By the way, you might get testimonials from any of 'em that get well. Can you find O'Farrell?"

"Yes, sir."

"Tell him I want to see him at my office at two o'clock."

"Ver' good. What do you think it is, Doctor?"

Dr. Surtaine waved a profound hand. "Very obscure. Demands consideration. But get those cases out of the city. There's no occasion to risk the Board of Health seeing them."

At the corner Dr. Surtaine again met Miss Elliot and stopped her. "My dear young lady, ought you to be risking your safety in such places as these?"

"No one ever interferes. My badge protects me."

"But there's so much sickness."

"That is what brings me," she smiled.

"It might be contagious. In fact, I have reason to believe that there is—er—measles in this block."

"I've had it, thank you. May I give you a lift in my car?"

"No, thank you. But I think you should consult your uncle before coming here again."

"The entire Surtaine family seems set upon barring me from the Rookeries. I wonder why."

With which parting shot she left him. Going home, he bathed and changed into his customary garb of smooth black, to which his rotund placidity of bearing imparted an indescribably silky finish. His discarded clothes he put, with his own hands, into an old grip, sprinkled them plenteously with a powerful disinfectant, and left orders that they be destroyed. It was a phase of Dr. Surtaine's courage that he never took useless risks, either with his own life, or (outside of business) with the lives of others.

Having lunched, he went to his office where he found O'Farrell waiting. The politician greeted him with a mixture of deference and familiarity. At one stage of their acquaintance familiarity had predominated, when having put through a petty but particularly rancid steal for the benefit of the Certina business, O'Farrell had become inspired with effusiveness to the extent of addressing his patron as "Doc." He never made that particular error again. Yet, to the credit of Dr. Surtaine's tact and knowledge of character be it said, O'Farrell was still the older man's loyal though more humble friend, after the incident. Today he was plainly apprehensive.

"Them other cases the same thing?" he asked.

"Yes, O'Farrell."

"What is it?"

"That I can't tell you."

"You went in and saw 'em?"

Dr. Surtaine nodded.

"By God, I wouldn't do it," declared O'Farrell, shivering. "I wouldn't go in there, not to collect the rent! It's catching, ain't it?"

"In all probability it is a contagious or zymotic disease."

The politician shook his head, much impressed, as it was intended he should be.

"Cleaning-up time for you, I guess, O'Farrell," pursued the other.

"All right, if you say so. But I won't have any Board o' Health snitches bossing it. They'd want to pull the whole row down."

"Exactly what ought to be done."

"What! And it averagin' better'n ten per cent," cried the agent in so scandalized a tone that the Doctor could not but smile.

"How have you managed to keep them out, thus far?"

"Haven't. There's been a couple of inspectors around, but I stalled 'em off. And we got the sick cases out right from under 'em."

"Dr. Merritt is a hard man to handle if he once gets started."

"He's got his hands full. The papers have been poundin' him because his milk regulations have put up the price. Persecution of the dairymen, they call it. Well, persecution of an honest property owner—with a pull—won't look pretty for Mr. Health Officer if he don't find nothing there. And the papers'll back me."

"Ellis of the 'Clarion' has his eye on the place."

"You can square that through your boy, can't you?"

The Doctor had his own private doubts, but didn't express them. "Leave it to me," he said. "Get some disinfectants and clean up. Your owners can stand the bill—at ten per cent. Much obliged for coming in, O'Farrell."

As the politician went out an office girl entered and announced:

"There's a man out in the reception hall, Doctor, waiting to see you. He's asleep with his elbow on the stand."

"Wake him up and ask him for his berth-check, Alice," said Dr. Surtaine, "and if he says his name is Ellis, send him in."

Ellis it was who entered and dropped into the chair pushed forward by his host.

"Glad to see you, my boy," Dr. Surtaine greeted him. "I thought you were going to send a reporter."

"Ordinarily we would have sent one. But I'm pretty well interested in this myself. I expected to hear from you long ago."

"Busy, my boy, busy. It's only been a week since I undertook the investigation. And these things take time."

"Apparently. What's the result?"

"Nothing." The quack spread his hands abroad in a blank gesture. "False alarm. Couple of cases of typhoid and some severe tonsillitis, that looked like diphtheria."

"People die of tonsillitis, do they?"

"Sometimes."

"And are buried?"

"Naturally."

"What in?"

"Why, in coffins, I suppose."

"Then why were these bodies buried in quicklime?"

"What bodies?"

"Last week's lot."

"You mean in Canadaga County? O'Farrell said nothing about quicklime."

"That's what I mean. Apparently O'Farrell *did* say something about more corpses smuggled out last week."

"Mr. Ellis," said the Doctor, annoyed at his slip, "I am not on the witness stand."

"Dr. Surtaine," returned the other in the same tone, "when you undertake an investigation for the 'Clarion,' you are one of my reporters and I expect a full and frank report from you."

"Bull's-eye for you, my boy. You win. They did run those cases out. Before we're through with it they'll probably run more out. You see, the Health Bureau has got it in for O'Farrell, and if they knew there was anything up there, they'd raise a regular row and queer things generally."

"What *is* up?"

"Honestly, I don't know."

"Nor even suspect?"

"Well, it might be scarlet fever. Or, perhaps diphtheria. You see strange types sometimes."

"If it's either, failure to report is against the law."

"Technically, yes. But we've got it fixed to clean things up. The people will be looked after. There's no real danger of its spreading much. And you know how it is. The Rookeries have got a bad name, anyway. Anything starting there is sure to be exaggerated. Why, look at that chicken-pox epidemic a few years ago."

"I understand nobody who had been vaccinated got any of the chicken-pox, as you call it."

"That's as may be. What did it amount to, anyway? Nothing. Yet it almost ruined Old Home Week."

"Naturally you don't want the Centennial Home Week endangered. But we don't want the health of the city endangered."

"'We.' Who's we?"

"Well, the 'Clarion.'"

"Don't work the guardian-of-the-people game on me, my boy. And don't worry about the city's health. If this starts to spread we'll take measures."

By no means satisfied with this interview, McGuire Ellis left the Certina plant, and almost ran into Dr. Elliot, whom he hailed, for he had the faculty of knowing everybody.

"Not doing any doctoring nowadays, are you?"

"No," retorted the other. "Doing any sickening, yourself?"

Ellis grinned. "It's despairing weariness that makes me look this way. I'm up against a tougher job than old Diogenes. I'm looking for an honest doctor."

"You fish in muddy waters," commented his acquaintance, glancing up at the Certina Building.

"There's something very wrong down in the Twelfth Ward."

"Not going in for reform politics, are you?"

"This isn't political. Some kind of disease has broken out in O'Farrell's Rookeries."

"Delirium tremens," suggested Dr. Elliot.

"Yes: that's a funny joke," returned the other, unmoved; "but did you ever hear of any one sneaking D-T cases across the county line at night to a pest-house run by a political friend of O'Farrell's?"

"Can't say I have."

"Or burying the dead in quicklime?"

"Quicklime? What's this, 'Clarion' sensationalism?"

"Don't be young. I'm telling you. Quicklime. Canadaga County."

Not only had Dr. Elliot served his country in the navy, but he had done duty in that efficient fighting force, which reaps less honor and follows a more noble, self-sacrificing and courageous ideal than any army or navy, the United

States Public Health Service. Under that banner he had fought famines, panic, and pestilence, from the stricken lumber-camps of the North, to the pent-in, quarantined bayous of the South; and now, at the hint of danger, there came a battle-glint into his sharp eyes.

"Tell me what you know."

"Now you're talking!" said the newspaper man. "It's little enough. But we've got it straight that they've been covering up some disease for weeks."

"What do the certificates call it?"

"Malaria and septic something, I believe."

"Septicæmia hemorrhagica?"

"That's it."

"An alias. That's what they called bubonic plague in San Francisco and yellow fever in Texas in the old days of concealment."

"It couldn't be either of those, could it?"

"No. But it might be any reportable disease: diphtheria, smallpox, any of 'em. Even that hardly explains the quicklime."

"Could you look into it for us; for the 'Clarion'?"

"I? Work for the 'Clarion'?"

"Why not?"

"I don't like your paper."

"But you'd be doing a public service."

"Possibly. How do I know you'd print what I discovered—supposing I discovered anything?"

"We're publishing an honest paper, nowadays."

"*Are* you? Got this morning's?"

Like all good newspaper men, McGuire Ellis habitually went armed with a copy of his own paper. He produced it from his coat pocket.

"Honest, eh?" muttered the physician grimly as he twisted the "Clarion" inside out. "Honest! Well, not to go any farther, what about this for honesty?"

Top of column, "next to reading," as its contract specified, the lure of the Neverfail Company stood forth, bold and black. "Boon to Troubled Womanhood" was the heading. Dr. Elliot read, with slow emphasis, the lying half-promises, the specious pretenses of the company's "Relief Pills." "No Case too Obstinate": "Suppression from Whatever Cause": "Thousands of Women have Cause to Bless this Sovereign Remedy": "Saved from Desperation."

"No doubt what that means, is there?" queried the reader.

"It seems pretty plain."

"What do you mean, then, by telling me you run an honest paper when you carry an abortion advertisement every day?"

"Will that medicine cause abortion?"

"Certainly it won't cause abortion!"

"Well, then."

"Can't you see that makes it all the worse, in a way? It promises to bring on abortion. It encourages any fool girl who otherwise might be withheld from vice by fear of consequences. It puts a weapon of argument into the hands of every rake and ruiner; 'If you get into trouble, this stuff will fix you all right.' How many suicides do you suppose your 'Boon to Womanhood' and its kind of hellishness causes in a year, thanks to the help of your honest journalism?"

"When I said we were honest, I wasn't thinking of the advertising."

"But I am. Can you be honest on one page and a crook on another? Can you bang the big drum of righteousness in one column and promise falsely in the next to commit murder? Ellis, why does the 'Clarion' carry such stuff as that?"

"Do you really want to know?"

"Well, you're asking me to help your sheet," the ex-surgeon reminded him.

"Because Dr. L. André Surtaine *is* the Neverfail Company."

"Oh," said the other. "And I suppose Dr. L. André Surtaine *is* the 'Clarion,' also. Well, I don't choose to be associated with that honorable and high-minded polecat, thank you."

"Don't be too sure about the 'Clarion.' Harrington Surtaine isn't his father."

"The same rotten breed."

"Plus another strain. Where it comes from I don't know, but there's something in the boy that may work out to big ends."

Dr. Miles Elliot was an abrupt sort of person, as men of independent lives and thought are prone to be. "Look here, Ellis," he said: "are you trying to be honest, yourself? Now, don't answer till you've counted three."

"One—two—three," said McGuire Ellis solemnly. "I'm honestly trying to put the 'Clarion' on the level. That's what you really want to know, I suppose."

"Against all the weight of influence of Dr. Surtaine?"

"Bless you; he doesn't half realize he's a crook. Thinks he's a pretty fine sort of chap. The worst of it is, he *is*, too, in some ways."

"Good to his family, I suppose, in the intervals of distributing poison and lies."

"He's all wrapped up in the boy. Which is going to make it all the harder."

"Make what all the harder?"

"Prying 'em apart."

"Have you set yourself that little job?"

"Since we're speaking out in meeting, I have."

"Good. Why are you speaking out in meeting to me, particularly?"

"On the theory that you may have reason for being interested in Mr. Harrington Surtaine."

"Don't know him."

"Your niece does."

"Just how does that concern this discussion?"

"What business is it of mine, you mean. Well, Dr. Elliot, I'm pretty much interested in trying to make a real newspaper out of the 'Clarion.' My notion of a real newspaper is a decent, clean newspaper. If I can get my young boss to back me up, we'll have a try at my theory. To do this, I'll use any fair means. And if Miss Elliot's influence is going to be on my side, I'm glad to play it off against Dr. Surtaine's."

"Look here, Ellis, I don't like this association of my niece's name with young Surtaine."

"All right. I'll drop it, if you object. Maybe I'm wrong. I don't know Miss Elliot, anyway. But sooner or later there's coming one big fight in the 'Clarion' office, and it's going to open two pairs of eyes. Old Doc Surtaine is going to discover his son. Hal Surtaine is going to find out about the old man. Neither of 'em is going to be awfully pleased. And in that ruction the fate of the Neverfail Company's ad is going to be decided and with it the fate and character of the 'Clarion.' Now, Dr. Elliot, my cards are on the table. Will you help me in the Rookeries matter?"

"What do you want me to do?"

"Go cautiously, and find out what that disease is."

"I'll go there tomorrow."

"They won't let you in."

"Won't they?" Dr. Elliot's jaw set.

"Don't risk it. Some of O'Farrell's thugs will pick a fight with you and the whole thing will be botched."

"How about getting a United States Public Health Surgeon down here?"

"Fine! Can you do it?"

"I think so. It will take time, though."

"That can't be helped. I'll look you up in a few days."

"All right. And, Ellis, if I can help in the other thing—the clean-up—I'm your man."

Meantime from his office Dr. Surtaine had, after several attempts, succeeded in getting the Medical Office of Canadaga County on the telephone.

"Hello! That you, Doctor Simons?—Seen O'Farrell?—Yes; you ought to get in touch with him right away—Three more cases going over to you.—Oh, they're there, are they? You're isolating them, aren't you?—Pest-house? That's all right.— All bills will be paid—liberally. You understand?—What are you calling it? Diphtheria?—Good enough for the present.—Ever see infectious meningitis? I thought it might be that, maybe—No? What do you think, then?—*What*! Good God, man! It can't be! Such a thing has never been heard of in this part of the country— What?—Yes: you're right. We can't talk over the 'phone. Come over tomorrow. Good-bye."

Putting up the receiver, Dr. Surtaine turned to his desk and sat immersed in thought. Presently he shook his head. He scratched a few notes on a pad, tore off the sheet and thrust it into the small safe at his elbow. Proof of a half-page Certina display beckoned him in buoyant, promissory type to his favorite task. He glanced at the safe. Once again he shook his head, this time more decisively, took the scribbled paper out and tore it into shreds. Turning to the proof he bent over it, striking out a word here, amending there, jotting in a printer's direction on the margin; losing himself in the major interest.

The "special investigator" of the "Clarion" was committing the unpardonable sin of journalism. He was throwing his paper down.

CHAPTER XV

JUGGERNAUT

Misfortunes never come singly—to the reckless. The first mischance breeds the second, apparently by ill luck, but in reality through the influence of irritant nerves. Thus descended Nemesis upon Miss Kathleen Pierce. Not that Miss Pierce was of a misgiving temperament: she had too calm and superb a conviction of her own incontrovertible privilege in every department of life for that. But Esmé Elliot had given her a hint of her narrow escape from the "Clarion," and she was angry. To the Pierce type of disposition, anger is a spur. Kathleen's large green car increased its accustomed twenty-miles-an-hour pace, from which the police of the business section thoughtfully averted their faces, to something nearer twenty-five. Three days after the wreck of the apple cart, she got results.

Harrington Surtaine was crossing diagonally to the "Clarion" office when the moan of a siren warned him for his life, and he jumped back from the Pierce juggernaut. As it swept by he saw Kathleen at the wheel. Beside her sat her twelve-year-old brother. A miscellaneous array of small luggage was heaped behind them.

"Never mind the speed laws," murmured Hal softly. "*Sauve qui peut.* There, by Heavens, she's done it!"

The car had swerved at the corner, but not quite quickly enough. There was a snort of the horn, a scream that gritted on the ear like the clamor of tortured metals, and a huddle of black and white was flung almost at Hal's feet. Equally quick with him, a middle-aged man, evidently of the prosperous working-classes, helped him to pick the woman up. She was a trained nurse. The white band on her uniform was splotched with blood. She groaned once and lapsed, inert, in their arms.

"Help me get her to the automobile," said Hal. "This is a hospital case."

"What automobile?" said the other.

Hal glanced up the street. He saw the green car turning a corner, a full block away.

"She didn't even stop," he muttered, in a paralysis of surprise.

"Stop?" said the other. "Her? That's E.M. Pierce's she-whelp. True to the breed. She don't care no more for a workin'-woman's life than her father does for a workin'-man's."

A policeman hurried up, glanced at the woman and sent in an ambulance call.

"I want your name," said Hal to the stranger.

"What for?"

"Publication now. Later, prosecution. I'm the editor of the 'Clarion.'"

The man took off his hat and scratched his head. "Leave me out of it," he said.

"You won't help me to get justice for this woman?'" cried Hal.

"What can you do to E.M. Pierce's girl in this town?" retorted the man fiercely. "Don't he own the town?"

"He doesn't own the 'Clarion.'"

"Let the 'Clarion' go up against him, then. I daresn't."

"You'll never get him," said a voice close to Hal's ear. It was Veltman, the foreman of the 'Clarion' composing-room. "He's a street-car employee. It's as much as his job is worth to go up against Pierce."

They were pressed back, as the clanging ambulance arrived with its white-coated commander.

"No; not dead," he said. "Help me get her in."

This being accomplished, Hal hurried up to the city room of the paper. He remembered the pile of suit-cases in the Pierce car, and made his deductions.

"Send a reporter to the Union Station to find Kathleen Pierce. She's in a green touring-car. She's just run down a trained nurse. Have him interview her; ask her why she didn't turn back after she struck the woman; whether she doesn't know the law. Find out if she's going to the hospital. Get her estimate of how fast she was going. We'll print anything she says. Then he's to go to St. James Hospital, and ask about the nurse. I'll give him the details of the accident."

News of a certain kind, of the kind important to the inner machinery of a newspaper, spreads swiftly inside an office. Within an hour, Shearson, the advertising manager, was at his chief's desk.

"About that story of Miss Pierce running over the trained nurse," he began.

"What is your suggestion?" asked Hal curiously.

"E.M. Pierce is a power in this town, and out of it. He's the real head of the Retail Dry Goods Union. He's a director in the Security Power Products Company. He's the big boss of the National Consolidated Employers' Association. He practically runs the Retail Dry Goods Union. Gibbs, of the Boston Store, is his brother-in-law, and the girl's uncle. Mr. Pierce has got a hand in pretty much everything in Worthington. And he's a bad man in a fight."

"So I have heard."

"If we print this story—"

"We're going to print the story, Mr. Shearson."

"It's full of dynamite."

"It was a brutal thing. If she hadn't driven right on—"

"But she's only a kid."

"The more reason why she shouldn't be driving a car."

"Why have you got it in for her, Mr. Surtaine?" ventured the other.

"I haven't got it in for her. But we've let her off once. And this is too flagrant a case."

"It means a loss of thousands of dollars in advertising, just as like as not."

"That can't be helped."

Shearson did the only thing he could think of in so unheard-of an emergency. He went out to call up the office of E.M. Pierce.

Left to his own thoughts, the editor-in-chief reconstructed the scene of the outrage. None too strong did that term seem to him. The incredible callousness of the daughter of millions, speeding away without a backward glance at the huddled form in the gutter, set a flame of wrath to heating his brain. He built up a few stinging headlines, and selected one which he set aside. "GIRL PLAYS JUGGERNAUT. ELIAS M. PIERCE'S DAUGHTER SERIOUSLY INJURES NURSE AND LEAVES HER LYING IN GUTTER." Not long after he had concluded,

McGuire Ellis entered, slumped into his chair, and eyed his employer from under bent brows.

"Got a grip on your temper?" he asked presently.

"What's the occasion?" countered Hal.

"I think you're going to have an interview with Elias M. Pierce."

"Where and when?"

"In his office. As soon as you can get there."

"I think not."

"Not?" repeated Ellis, conning the other with his curious air.

"Why should I go to Elias M. Pierce's office?"

"Because he's sent for you."

"Don't be absurd, Mac."

"And don't *you* be young. In all Worthington there aren't ten men that don't jump when Elias M. Pierce crooks his finger. Who are you, to join that noble company of martyrs?" Achieving no nibble on this bait, the speaker continued: "Jerry Saunders has been keeping Wayne's telephone on the buzz, ordering the story stopped."

"Who is Jerry Saunders?"

"Pierce's man, and master of our fates. So he thinks, anyway. In other words, general factotum of the Boston Store. Wayne told him the matter was in your hands. All storm signals set, and E.M.'s secretary telephoning that the Great Man wants to see you at once. *Don't* you think it would be safer to go?"

Mr. Harrington Surtaine swung full around on his chair, looked at his assistant with that set and level gaze of which Esmé Elliot had aforetime complained, and turned back again. A profound chuckle sounded from behind him.

"This'll be a shock to Mr. Pierce," said Ellis. "I'll break it diplomatically to his secretary." And thus was the manner of the Celt's diplomacy. "Hello,—Mr. Pierce's secretary?—Tell Mr. Pierce—get this *verbatim*, please,—that Mr. Harrington Surtaine is busy at present, but will try to find time to see him here—*here*, mind you, at the 'Clarion' office, at 4.30 this afternoon—What? Oh, yes; you understood, all right. Don't be young.—What? Do *not* sputter into the 'phone.—Just give him the message.—No; Mr. Surtaine will not speak with you.—Nor with Mr. Pierce. He's busy.—*Good*-bye."

"Two hours leeway before the storm," said Hal. "Why deliberately stir him up, Mac?"

"No one ever saw Pierce lose his temper. I've a curiosity in that direction. Besides, he'll be easier to handle, mad. Do you know Pierce?"

"I've lunched with him, and been there to the house to dinner once or twice. Wish I hadn't."

"Let me give you a little outline of him. Elias M. is the hard-shell New England type. He was brought up in the fear of God and the Poor-House. God was a good way off, I guess; but there stood the Poor-House on the hill, where you couldn't help but see it. The way of salvation from it was through the dollar. Elias M. worked hard for his first dollar, and for his millionth. He's still working hard. He still finds the fear of God useful: he puts it into everybody that goes up against his game. The fear of the Poor-House is with him yet, though he doesn't realize it. It's the mainspring of his religion. There's nothing so mean as fear; and Elias M.'s fear is back of all his meanness, his despotism in business, his tyranny as an employer. I tell you, Boss, if you ever saw a hellion in a cutaway coat, Elias M. Pierce is it, and you're going to smell sulphur when he gets here. Better let him do the talking, by the way."

Prompt to the minute, Elias M. Pierce arrived. With him came William Douglas, his personal counsel. Having risen to greet them, Hal stood leaning against his desk, after they were seated. The lawyer disposed himself on the far edge of his chair, as if fearing that a more comfortable pose might commit him to something. Mr. Pierce sat solid and square, a static force neatly buttoned into a creaseless suit. His face was immobile, but under the heavy lids the eyes smouldered, dully. The tone of his voice was lifelessly level: yet with an immanent menace.

"I do not make appointments outside my own office—" he began, looking straight ahead of him.

Mindful of Ellis's advice, Hal stood silent, in an attitude of courteous attention.

"But this is a case of saving time. My visit has to do with the accident of which you know."

Whether or not Hal knew was undeterminable from sign or speech of his.

"It was wholly the injured woman's fault," pursued Mr. Pierce, and turned a slow, challenging eye upon Hal.

Over his shoulder the editor-in-chief caught sight of McGuire Ellis laying finger on lip, and following up this admonition by a gesture of arms and hands as of one who pays out line to a fish. Douglas fidgeted on his desperate edge.

"You sent a reporter to interview my daughter. He was impertinent. He should be discharged."

Still Mr. Pierce was firing into silence. Something rattled and flopped in a chute at his elbow. He turned, irritably. That Mr. Pierce's attention should have been diverted even for a moment by this was sufficient evidence that he was disconcerted by the immobility of the foe. But his glance quickly reverted and with added weight. Heavily he stared, then delivered his ultimatum.

"The 'Clarion' will print nothing about the accident."

The editor of the "Clarion" smiled. At sight of that smile some demon-artist in faces blocked in with lightning swiftness parallel lines of wrath at right angles to the corners of the Pierce mouth. Through the lips shone a thin glint of white.

"You find me amusing?" Men had found Elias M. Pierce implacable, formidable, inscrutable, even amenable, in some circumstances, with a conscious and godlike condescension; but no opponent had ever smiled at his commands as this stripling of journalism was doing.

Still there was no reply. In his chair McGuire Ellis leaned back with an expression of beatitude. The lawyer, shrewd enough to understand that his principal was being baited, now took a hand.

"You may rely on Mr. Pierce to have the woman suitably cared for."

Now the editorial smile turned upon William Douglas. It was gentle, but unsatisfying.

"*And* the reporter will be discharged at once," continued Elias M. Pierce, exactly as if Douglas had not spoken at all.

"Mr. Ellis," said Hal, "will you 'phone Mr. Wayne to send up the man who covered the Pierce story?"

The summoned reporter entered the room. He was a youth named Denton, one year out of college, eager and high-spirited, an enthusiast of his profession, loving it for its adventurousness and its sense of responsibility and power. These are the qualities that make the real newspaper man. They die soon, and that is why there are no good, old reporters. Elias M. Pierce turned upon him like a ponderous machine of vengeance.

"What have you to say for yourself?" he demanded.

Up under Denton's fair skin ran a flush of pink. "Who are you?" he blurted.

"You are speaking to Mr. Elias M. Pierce," said Douglas hastily.

Six weeks before, young Denton would perhaps have moderated his attitude in the interests of his job. But now through the sensitive organism of the newspaper office had passed the new vigor; the feeling of independence and of the higher responsibility to the facts of the news only. The men believed that they would be upheld within their own rights and those of the paper. Harrington Surtaine's standards had been not only absorbed: they had been magnified and clarified by minds more expert than his own. Subconsciously, Denton felt that his employer was back of him, must be back of him in any question of professional honor.

"What I've got to say, I've said in writing."

"Show it to me." The insolence of the command was quite unconscious.

The reporter turned to Hal.

"Mr. Denton," said Hal, "did Miss Pierce explain why she didn't return after running the nurse down?"

"She said she was in a hurry: that she had a train to catch."

"Did you ask her if she was exceeding the speed limit?"

"She was not," interjected Elias M. Pierce.

"She said she didn't know; that nobody ever paid any attention to speed laws."

"What about her license?"

"I asked her and she said it was none of my business."

"Quite right," approved Mr. Pierce curtly.

"Tell the desk to run the interview *verbatim*, under a separate head. Will the nurse die?"

Mr. Pierce snorted contemptuously. "Die! She's hardly hurt."

"Dislocated shoulder, two ribs broken, and scalp wounds. She'll get well," said the reporter.

"Now, see here, Surtaine," said Douglas smoothly, "be reasonable. It won't do the 'Clarion' any good to print a lot of yellow sensationalism about this. There are half a dozen witnesses who say it was the nurse's fault."

"We have evidence on the other side."

"From whom?"

"Max Veltman, of our composing-room."

"Veltman? Veltman?" repeated Elias M. Pierce, who possessed a wonderful memory for men and events. "He's that anarchist fellow. Hates every man with a dollar. Stirred up the labor troubles two years ago. I told my men to smash his head if they ever caught him within two blocks of our place."

"Speaking of anarchy," said McGuire Ellis softly.

"A prejudiced witness; one of your own employees," pointed out the lawyer.

"I wouldn't believe him under oath," said Pierce.

"Perhaps you wouldn't believe me, either. I saw the whole thing myself," said Hal quietly.

"And you intend to print it?" demanded Pierce.

"It's news. The 'Clarion's' business is to print the news."

"Then there remains only to warn you," said Douglas, "that you will be held to full liability for anything you may publish, civil *and* criminal."

"Take that down, Mr. Denton," said Hal.

"I've got it," said the reporter.

"That isn't all." Elias M. Pierce rose and his eyes were wells of somber fury. "You print that story—one word of it—and I'll smash your paper."

"Take that down, Mr. Denton." Hal's voice was even.

"I've got it," said Denton in the same tone.

"You don't know what I am in this city." Every word of the great man's voice rang with the ruthless arrogance of his power. "I can make or mar any man or any business. I've fought the demagogues of labor and driven 'em out of town. I've fought the demagogues of politics and killed them off. And you think with your little spewing demagoguery of newspaper filth, you can override me? You think because you've got your father's quack millions behind you, that you can stand up to me?"

"Take that down, Mr. Denton."

"I've got it."

"Then take this, too," cried Elias M. Pierce, losing all control, under the quiet remorselessness of this goading: "people like my daughter and me aren't at the mercy of scum like you. We've got rights that aren't responsible to every little petty law. By God, I've made and unmade judges in this town: and I'll show you what the law can do before I'm through with you. I'll gut your damned paper."

"Not missing anything, are you, Mr. Denton?"

"I've got it all."

Throughout, Douglas, with a strained face, had been plucking at his principal's arm. Now Elias M. Pierce turned to him.

"Go to Judge Ransome," he said sharply, "and get an injunction against the 'Clarion.'"

McGuire Ellis sauntered over. "I wouldn't," he drawled.

"I'm not asking your advice."

"And I'm not looking for gratitude. But just let me suggest this: Ransome may be one of the judges you brag of owning. But if he grants an injunction I'll advise Mr. Surtaine to publish a spread on the front page, stating that we have the facts, that we're enjoined from printing them at present, but that now or a year from now we'll tell the whole story in every phase. With that hanging over him, I don't believe Judge Ransome will care to issue any fake injunction."

"There's such a thing as contempt of court," warned Douglas.

"Making and unmaking judges, for example?" suggested Ellis.

"Just one final word to you." The Pierce face was thrust close to Hal's. "You keep your hands off my daughter if you expect to live in this town."

"My one regret for Miss Pierce is that she is your daughter," retorted Hal. "You have given me the material for a leading editorial in tomorrow's issue. I recommend you to buy the paper."

The other glared at him speechless.

"It will be called," said Hal, "'A Study in Heredity.' Good-day."

And he gave the retiring magnate a full view of his back as he sat down to write it.

CHAPTER XVI
THE STRATEGIST

"**N**ever write with a hot pen." Thus runs one of McGuire Ellis's golden rules of journalism. Had his employer better comprehended, in those early days, the Ellisonian philosophy, perhaps the "Heredity" editorial might never have appeared. Now, as it lay before him in proof, it seemed but the natural expression of a righteous wrath.

"Neither Kathleen Pierce nor her father can claim exemption or consideration in this instance," Hal had written, in what he chose to consider his most telling passage. "Were it the girl's first offense of temerity, allowance might be made. But the city streets have long been the more perilous because of her defiance of the rights of others. Here she runs true to type. She is her father's own daughter. In the light of his character and career, of his use of the bludgeon in business, of his resort to foul means when fair would not serve, of his brutal disregard of human rights in order that his own power might be enhanced, of his ruthless and crushing tyranny, not alone toward his employees, but toward all labor in its struggle for better conditions, we can but regard the girl who left her victim crushed and senseless in the gutter and sped on because, in the words of her own bravado, she 'had a train to catch,' as a striking example of the influence of heredity. If the law which she so contemptuously brushed aside is to be aborted by the influence and position of her family, the precept will be a bitter and dangerous one. Much arrant nonsense is vented concerning the 'class-hatred' stirred up by any criticism of the rich. One such instance as the running-down of Miss Cleary bears within it far more than the extremest demagoguery the potentialities of an unleashed hate. It is a lesson in lawlessness."

Still in the afterglow of composition, Hal, tinkering lightly with the proofs, felt a hand on his shoulder.

"Well, Boy-ee," said the voice of Dr. Surtaine.

"Hello, father," returned Hal. "Sit down. What's up?"

"I've just had a message from E.M. Pierce."

"Did you obey a royal command and go to his office?"

"No."

"Neither did I."

"With you it's different. You're a younger man. And Elias M. Pierce is the most powerful—um—er—well, *as* powerful as any man in Worthington."

"Outside of this office, possibly."

"Don't you be foolish, Boy-ee. You can't fight him."

"Nor do I want to," said Hal, a little chilled, nevertheless, by the gravity of the paternal tone. "But when he comes in here and dictates what the 'Clarion' shall and shall not print—"

"About his own daughter."

"News, father. It's news."

"News is what you print. If you don't print it, it isn't news. Isn't that right? Well, then!"

"Not quite. News is what happens. If no paper published this, it would be current by word of mouth just the same. A hundred people saw it."

"Anyway, tone your article down, won't you, Boy-ee?"

"I'm afraid I can't, Dad."

"Of course you can. Here, let me see it."

McGuire Ellis looked up sharply, his face wrinkled into an anxious query. It relaxed when Hal handed the editorial proof to the Doctor, saying, "Look at this, instead."

Dr. Surtaine read slowly and carefully. "Do you know what you're doing?" he said, replacing the strip of paper.

"I think so."

"That editorial will line up every important business man in Worthington against you."

"I don't see why it should."

"Because they'll see that none of 'em are safe if a newspaper can do that sort of thing. It's never been done here. The papers have always respected men of position, and their business and their families, too. Worthington won't stand for that sort of thing."

"It's true, isn't it?"

"All the more harm if it is," retorted Dr. Surtaine, thus codifying the sum and essence of the outsider's creed of journalism. "Do you know what they'll call you if you print that? They'll call you an anarchist."

"Will they?"

"Ask Ellis."

"Probably," agreed the journalist.

"Every friend and business associate of Pierce's will be down on you."

"The whole angry hive of capital and privilege," confirmed Ellis.

"You see," cried the pleader; "you can't print it. Publishing an article about Kathleen Pierce will be bad enough, but it's nothing to what this other roast would be. One would make Pierce hate you as long as he lives. The other will make the whole Business Interests of the city your enemy. How can you live without business?"

"Business isn't as rotten as that," averred Hal. "If it is, I'm going to fight it."

"Fight business!" It was almost a groan. "Tell him, Ellis, what a serious thing this is. You agree with me in that, don't you?"

"Entirely."

"And that the 'Clarion' can't afford to touch the thing at all? You're with me there, too, aren't you?"

"Absolutely not."

"You're going to stand by and see my boy turn traitor to his class?"

"Damn his class," said McGuire Ellis, in mild, conversational tones.

"As much as you like," agreed the other, "in talk. But when it comes to print, remember, it's our class that's got the money."

"Wouldn't it be a refreshing change," suggested Ellis, "to have one paper in Worthington that money won't buy?"

"All very well, if you were strong enough." The wily old charlatan shifted his ground. "Wait until you've built up to it. Then, when you've got the public, you can afford to be independent."

"Get your price and then reform. Is that the idea, Father?" said Hal.

"Boy-ee, I don't know what's come over you lately. Journalism seems to have got into your blood."

"Blame Ellis. He's been my preceptor."

"Both of you have got your lesson to learn."

"Well, I've learned one," asserted Hal: "that it's the business of a newspaper to print the news."

"There's only one sound business principle, success. When it costs you more to print a thing than not to print it, it's bad business to print it."

"I'm sorry, Dad, but the 'Clarion' is going to carry this tomorrow."

"In case you're nervous about Mr. Pierce," put in McGuire Ellis with Machiavellian innuendo, "I can pass it on to him that you're in no way responsible for the 'Clarion's' policy."

"Me, afraid of Elias M. Pierce?" Our Leading Citizen's prickly vanity was up in arms at once. "I'll match him or fight him dollar for dollar, as long as my weasel-skin lasts. No, sir: if Hal's going to fight, I'll stick by him as long as there's a dollar in the till."

"It's mighty good of you, Dad, and I know you'd do it. But I've made up my mind to win out or lose out on the capital you gave me. And I won't take a cent more."

"That's business, too, son. I like that. But I hate to see you lose. By publishing your editorial you're committing your paper absolutely to a policy, and a fatal one. Well, I won't argue any more. But I haven't given up yet."

"Well, that's over," said Hal, as his father departed, gently smoothing down his silk hat. "And I hope that ends it."

"Do you?" McGuire Ellis raised a tuneful baritone in song:—

"'You may think you've got 'em going,' said the bar-keep to the bum. 'But cheer up And beer up. The worst is yet to come!'

"Unless my estimate of E.M. Pierce is wrong," he continued, "you'll begin to hear from the other newspapers soon."

So it proved. Advertising managers called up and talked interminably over the telephone. Editors-in-chief wrote polite notes. One fellow proprietor called. By all the canons of editorial courtesy they exhorted Mr. Surtaine to hold his hand from the contemplated sacrilege against their friend and patron, Elias M. Pierce. Equally polite, Mr. Surtaine replied that the "Clarion" would print the news. How much of the news would he print? All the news, now and forever, one and inseparable, or words to that effect. Painfully and protestingly the noble fellowship of the free and untrammeled press pointed out that if the "Clarion" insisted on informing the public, they too, in self-defense, must supply something in the way of information to cover themselves, loth though they were so to do. But the burden of sin and vengeance would rest upon the paper which forced them into such a course. Still patient, Hal found refuge in truism: to wit, that what his fellow editors chose to do was wholly and specifically their business. From the corollary, he courteously refrained.

Meantime, the object of Editor Surtaine's scathing had not been idle. To the indignant journalist, Miss Kathleen Pierce had appeared a brutal and hardened scion of wealth and injustice. This was hardly a just view. Careless she was, and unmindful of standards; but not cruel. In this instance, panic, not callousness, had been the mainspring of her apparent cruelty. She was badly scared; and when her angry father told her what she might expect at the hands of a "yellow news-paper," she became still more badly scared. In this frame of mind she fled for refuge to Miss Esmé Elliot.

"I didn't mean to run over her," she wailed. "You know I didn't, Esmé. She ran out just like a m-m-mouse, and I felt the car hit her, and then she was all crumpled up in the gutter. Oh, I was so frightened! I wanted to go back, but I was afraid, and Phil began to cry and say we'd killed her, and I lost my head and put on speed. I didn't mean to, Esmé!"

"Of course you didn't, dear. Who says you did?"

"The newspaper is going to say so. That awful reporter! He caught me at the station and asked me a lot of questions. I just shook my head and wouldn't say a word," lied the frightened girl. "But they're going to print an awful interview with me, father says. He's furious at me."

"In what paper, Kathie?"

"The 'Clarion.' Father says the other papers won't publish anything about it, but he can't stop the 'Clarion.'"

"I can," said Miss Esmé Elliot confidently.

The heiress to the Pierce millions lifted her woe-begone face. "You?" she cried incredulously. "How?"

"I've got a pull," said Esmé, dimpling.

A light broke in upon her suppliant. "Of course! Hal Surtaine! But father has been to see him and he won't promise a thing. I don't see what he's got against me."

"Don't worry, dear. Perhaps your father doesn't understand how to go about it."

"No," said the other thoughtfully. "Father would try to bully and threaten. He tried to bully me!" Miss Pierce stamped a well-shod foot in memory of her manifold wrongs. Then feminine curiosity interposed a check. "Esmé! Are you engaged to Hal Surtaine?"

"No, indeed!" The girl's laughter rang silvery and true.

"Are you going to be?"

"I'm not going to be engaged to anybody. Not for a long time, anyway. Life is too good as it is."

"Is he in love with you?" persisted Kathleen.

Esmé lifted up a very clear and sweet mezzo-soprano in a mocking lilt of song:—

"How should my heart know What love may be?"

The visitor regarded her admiringly. "Of course he is. What man wouldn't be! And you've seen a lot of him lately, haven't you?"

"I'm helping him run his paper—with good advice."

"Oh-h-h!" Miss Pierce's soft mouth and big eyes formed three circles. "And you're going to advise him—"

"I'm going to advise him ver-ree earnestly not to say a word about you in the paper, if you'll promise never, never to do it again."

The other clasped her in a bear-hug. "You duck! I'll just crawl through the streets after this. You watch me! The police will have to call time on me to make sure I'm not obstructing the traffic. But, Esmé—"

"Well?"

Kathleen caught her hand and snuggled it up to her childishly. "How often do you see Hal Surtaine?"

"You ought to know. There's something going on every evening now. And he goes everywhere."

"Yes: but outside of that?"

Esmé laughed. "How hard you're working to make a romance that isn't there. I go to his office once in a while, just to see the wheels go 'round."

"And are you going to the office now?"

"No," said Esmé, after consideration. "Hal Surtaine is coming here. This evening."

"You have an appointment with him?"

"Not yet. I'll telephone him."

"Father telephoned him, but he wouldn't come to see father. So father had to go to see him."

"Mahomet! Well, I'm the mountain in this case. Go in peace, my child." Esmé patted the other's head with an absurd and delightful affectation of maternalism. "And look in the 'Clarion' tomorrow with a clear assurance. You shan't find your name there—unless in the Social Doings column. Good-bye, dear."

Having thus engaged her honor, the advisor to the editor sat her down to plan. At the conclusion of a period of silent thought, she sent a telephone message which made the heart of young Mr. Surtaine accelerate its pace perceptibly. Was he too busy to come up to Greenvale, Dr. Elliot's place, at 8.30 sharp?

Busy he certainly was, but not too busy to obey any behest of his partner.

That was very nice of him. It would take but a few minutes.

As many minutes as she could use, she might have, or hours.

Then he was to consider himself gratefully thanked and profoundly curtsied to, over the wire. By the way, if he had a galley proof of anything that had been written about Kathleen Pierce's motor accident, would he bring that along? And didn't he think it quite professional of her to remember all about galleys and things?

Highly professional and clever (albeit in a somewhat altered tone, not unnoted by the acute listener). Yes, he would bring the proof. At 8.30, then, sharp.

"The new boss of our new boss," Wayne had styled the charming interloper, on the occasion of her first visit to the "Clarion" office. Had she heard, Esmé would have approved. More, she would have believed, though not without misgivings. Well she knew that she had not yet proved her power over her partner. Many and various as were the men upon whom, in the assay of her golden charm, she had exercised the arts of coquetry, this test was on a larger scale. This was the potential conquest of an institution. Could she make a newspaper change its hue, as she could make men change color, with the power of a word or the incitement of a glance? The very dubiety of the issue gave a new zest to the game.

Behold, now, Miss Esmé Elliot, snarer of men's eyes and hearts, sharpening her wits and weapons for the fray; aye, even preparing her pitfall. Cunningly she made a bower of one end of the broad living-room at Greenvale with great sprays of apple blossoms from the orchard, ravishing untold spoilage of her mother and forerunner, Eve, for the bedecking of the quiet, cozy nook. Pink was ever her color; the hue of the flushing of spring, of the rising blood in the cheek of maidenhood, and the tenderest of the fruit-blooms was not more downy-soft of tint than the face it bent to brush. At the close of the task, a heavy voice startled her.

"What's all this about?"

"Uncle Guardy! You mustn't, you really mustn't come in on tiptoe that way."

"Stamped like an elephant," asserted Dr. Elliot. "But you were so immersed in your floral designs—What kind of a play is it?"

She turned upon him the sparkle of golden lights in wine-brown eyes. "It's a fairy bower. I'm going to do a bewitchment."

"Upon what victim?"

"Upon a newspaper. I'm going to be a fairy godmother sort of witch and save my foster-child by—by arointing something out of print."

"Doing *what*?"

"Arointing it. Don't you know, you say, 'Aroint thee, witch,' when you want to get rid of her? Well, if a witch can be arointed, why shouldn't she aroint other things?"

"All very well, if you understand the process. Do you?"

"Of course. It's done 'with woven paces and with waving arms.' 'Beware, beware; her flashing eyes, her float—'"

"Stop it! You shall not make a poetry cocktail out of Tennyson and Coleridge, and jam it down my throat; or I'll aroint myself. Besides, you're not a witch, at all. I know you for all your big cap, and your cloak, and the basket on your arm. 'Grandmother, what makes your teeth so white?'"

"No, no. I'm not that kind of a beastie, at all. Wrong guess, Guardy."

"Yet there's a gleam of the hunt about you. Is it, oh, is it, the Great American Pumess that I have the honor to address?"

She made him a sweeping bow. "In a good cause."

"About which I shall doubtless hear tomorrow?"

"Don't I always confess my good actions?"

"At what hour does the victim's dying shriek rend the quivering air?"

"Mr. Surtaine is due here at half past eight."

"Humph! Young Surtaine, eh? Shy bird, if it has taken all this time to bring him down. Well, run and dress. It's after five and that gives you less than three hours for prinking up, counting dinner in."

Whatever time and effort may have gone to the making of the Great American Pumess's toilet, Hal thought, as he came down the long room to where she stood embowered in pink, that he had never beheld anything so freshly lovely. She gave him a warm and yielding hand in welcome, and drew away a bit, surveying him up and down with friendly eyes.

"You're looking unusually smart tonight," she approved. "London clothes don't set so well on many Americans. But your tie is askew. Wait. Let me do it."

With deft fingers she twitched and patted the bow into submission. The touch of intimacy represented the key in which she had chosen to pitch her play. Sinking back into a cushioned corner of the settee, she curled up cozily, and motioned him to a chair.

"Draw it around," she directed. "I want you where you can't get away, for I'm going to cast a spell over you."

"*Going* to?" The accent on the first word was stronger than the reply necessitated.

"Do many people ask favors of an editor?"

"More than enough."

"And is the editor often kind and obliging?"

"That depends on the favor."

"Not a little bit on the asker?"

"Naturally, that, too."

"Your tone isn't very encouraging." She searched his face with her limpid, lingering regard. "Did you bring the proofs?"

"Yes."

Still holding his eyes to hers, she stretched out her hand to receive the strip of print, "Do you think I'd better read it?"

"No."

"Then I will."

Studying her face, as she read, Hal saw it change from gay to grave, saw her quiver and wince with a swiftly indrawn breath, and straightened his spine to what he knew was coming.

"Oh, it's cruel," she said in a low tone, letting the paper fall on her knee.

"It's true," said Hal.

"Oh, no! Even if it were, it ought not to be published."

"Why?"

"Because—" The girl hesitated.

"Because she's one of us?"

"No. Yes. It has something to do with my feeling, I suppose. Why, you've been a guest at her house."

"Suppose I have. The 'Clarion' hasn't."

"Isn't that rather a fine distinction?"

"On the contrary. Personally, I might refrain from saying anything about it. Journalistically, how can I? It's the business of the 'Clarion' to give the news. More than that: it's the honor of the 'Clarion.'"

"But what possible good will it do?"

"If it did no other good, it would warn other reckless drivers."

"Let the police look to that. It's their business."

"You know that the police dare do nothing to the daughter of Elias M. Pierce. See here, Partner,"—Hal's tone grew gentle,—"don't you recall, in that long talk we had about the paper, one afternoon, how you backed me up when I told you what I meant to do in the way of making the 'Clarion' honest and clean and strong enough to be straight in its attitude toward the public? Why, you've been the inspiration of all that I've been trying to do. I thought that was the true Esmé. Wasn't it? Was I wrong? You're not going back on me, now?"

"But she's so young," pleaded Esmé, shifting her ground before this attack. "She doesn't think. She's never had to think. Your article makes her look a—a murderess. It isn't fair. It isn't true, really. If you could have seen her here, so frightened, so broken. She cried in my arms. I told her it shouldn't be printed. I promised."

Here was the Great American Pumess at bay, and suddenly splendid in her attitude of protectiveness. In that moment, she had all but broken Hal's resolution. He rose and walked over to the window, to clear his thought of the overpowering appeal of her loveliness.

"How can I—" he began, coming back: but paused because she was holding out to him the proof. Across it, in pencil, was written, "Must not," and the initials, E.S.M.E.

"Kill it," she urged softly.

"And my honesty with it."

"Oh, no. It can't be so fatal, to be kind for once. Let her off, poor child." Hal stood irresolute.

"If it were I?" she insisted softly.

"If it were you, would you ask it?"

"I shouldn't have to. I'd trust you."

The sweetness of it shook him. But he still spoke steadily.

"Others trust me, now. The men in the office. Trust me to be honest."

Again she felt the solid wall of character blocking her design, and within herself raged and marveled, and more deeply, admired. Resentment was uppermost, however. Find a way through that barrier she must and would. Whatever scruples may have been aroused by his appeal to her she banished. No integer of the impressionable sex had ever yet won from her such a battle. None ever should: and assuredly not this one. The Great American Pumess was now all feline.

She leaned forward to him. "You promised."

"I?"

"Have you forgotten?"

"I have never forgotten one word that has passed between us since I first saw you."

"Ah; but when was that?"

"Seven weeks ago today, at the station."

"Fifteen years ago this summer," she corrected. "You *have* forgotten," She laughed gayly at the amazement in his face. "And the promise." Up went a pink-tipped finger in admonition. "Listen and be ashamed, O faithless knight. 'Little girl, little girl: I'd do anything in the world for you, little girl. Anything in the world, if ever you asked me.' Think, and remember. Have you a scar on your left shoulder?"

The effort of recollection dimmed Hal's face. "Wait! I'm beginning to see. The light of the torches across the square, and the man with the knife.—Then darkness.—was unconscious, wasn't I?—Then the fairy child with the soft eyes, looking down at me. Little girl, little girl, it was you! That is why I seemed to remember, that day at the station, before I knew you."

"Yes," she said, smiling up at him.

"How wonderful! And you remembered. How more than wonderful!"

"Yes, I remembered." It was no part of her plan—quite relentless, now—to tell him that her uncle had recounted to her the events of that far-distant night, and that she had been holding them in reserve for some hitherto undetermined purpose of coquetry. So she spoke the lie without a tremor. What he would say next, she almost knew. Nor did he disappoint her expectation.

"And so you've come back into my life after all these years!"

"You haven't taken back your proof." She slipped it into his hand. "What have you done with my subscription-flower?"

"The arbutus? It stands always on my desk."

"Do you see the rest of it anywhere?"

Her eyes rested on a tiny vase set in a hanging window-box of flowers, and holding a brown and withered wisp. "I tend those flowers myself," she continued. "And I leave the dead arbutus there to remind me of the responsibilities of journalism—and of the hold I have over the incorruptible editor."

"Does it weigh upon you?" He answered the tender laughter in her eyes.

"Only the uncertainty of it."

"Do you realize how strong it is, Esmé?"

"Not so strong, apparently, as certain foolish scruples." A soft color rose in her face, as she half-buried it in a great mass of apple blossom. From the mass she chose a spray, and set it in the bosom of her dress, then got to her feet and moved slowly toward him. "You're not wearing my colors tonight." This was directed to the white rose in his buttonhole. He took it out and tossed it into the fireplace.

"Pink's the only wear," declared the girl gayly. With delicate fingers she detached a little luxuriant twig of the bloom from her breast, and set it in the place where the rose had been. Her face was close to his. He could feel her hands above his heart.

"Please," she breathed.

"What?" He was playing for time and reason.

"For Kathleen Pierce. Please."

His hand closed over hers. "You are bribing me."

If she said it again, she knew that he would kiss her. So she spoke, with lifted face and eyes of uttermost supplication. "For me. Please."

Men had kissed Esmé Elliot before; for she had played every turn of the game of coquetry. Some she had laughed to scorn and dismissed; some she had sweetly rebuked, and held to their adoring fealty. She had known the kiss of headlong passion, of love's humility, of desperation, even of hot anger; but none had ever visited her lips twice. The game, for her, was ended with the surrender and the avowal; and she protected herself the more easily in that her pulses had never been stirred to more than the thrill of triumph.

In Hal Surtaine's arms she was playing for another stake. So intent had she been upon her purpose that the guerdon of the modern Venus Victrix, the declaration of the lover, was held in the background of her mind. For a swift, bewildering moment, she felt his lips upon hers, the gentlest, the tenderest pressure, instantly relaxed: then the sudden knowledge of him for what he was, a loyal and chivalrous gentleman thus beguiled, burned her with a withering and intolerable shame. Simultaneously she felt her heart go out to him as never yet had it gone to any man, and in that secret shock to her maidenhood, the coquette in her waned and the woman waxed.

She drew back, quivering, aghast. With all the force of this new and tumultuous emotion, she hoped for her own defeat: yearned over him that he should refuse that for which she had unworthily pressed. Yet, such is the perversity of that strange struggle against the great surrender, that she gathered every power of her sex to gain the dreaded victory. By an effort she commanded her voice, releasing herself from his arms.

"Wait. Don't speak to me for a minute," she said hoarsely.

"But I must speak, now,—dear, dearest."

"Am—am I that to you?" The feline in her caught desperately at the opportunity.

"Always. From the first."

"But—you forgot."

"Let me atone with the rest of my life for that treason." He laughed happily.

"You keep your promise, then, to the little girl?" At her feet lay the galley proof. Birdlike she darted down upon it, seized, and tore it half across. "No: you do it," she commanded, thrusting it into his hand.

No longer was he master of himself. The kiss had undermined him. "Must I?" he said.

Victorious and aghast, she yet smiled into his face. "I knew I could believe in you," she cried. "You're a true knight, after all. I declare you my Knight-Editor. No well-equipped journalistic partnership should be without one."

Perhaps had the phrase been different, Hal might have yielded. So narrow a margin of chance divides the paths of honor and dishonor, to mortals groping dimly through the human maze. But the words were an echo to wake memory. Rugged, harsh, and fine the face of McGuire Ellis rose before Hal. He heard the rough voice, with its undertone of affection beneath the jocularity of the rather feeble pun, and it called him back like a trumpet summons to the loyalty which he had promised to the men of the "Clarion." He slipped the half-torn paper into his pocket.

"I can't do it, Esmé."

"You—can't—do—it?"

"No." Finality was in the monosyllable.

She looked into his leveled and quiet eyes, and knew that she had lost. And the demon of perversity, raging, stung her to its purposes.

"After this, you tell me that you can't, you won't?"

"Dearest! You're not going to let it make a difference in our love for each other."

"*Our* love! You go far, and fast."

"Do I go too far, since you have let me kiss you?"

"I didn't," she cried.

"Then you meant nothing by it?"

She shrugged her shoulders. "You are trying to take advantage of a position which you forced," she said coldly.

"Let me understand this clearly." He had turned white. "You let me make love to you, in order to entrap me and save your friend. Is that it?"

No reply came from her other than what he could read in compressed lips and smouldering eyes.

"So that is the kind of woman you are." There were both wonder and distress in his voice. "That is the kind of woman for whose promise to be my wife I would have given the heart out of my body."

At this the tumult and catastrophe of her emotion fused into a white hot, illogical anger against this man who was suffering, and by his suffering made her suffer.

"Your wife? Yours?" She smiled hatefully. "The wife of the son of a quack? You do yourself too much honor, Hal Surtaine."

"I fear that I did you too much honor," he replied quietly.

Suffocation pressed upon her throat as she saw him go to the door. For a moment the wild desire to hold him, to justify herself, to explain, even to ask forgiveness, seized her. Bitterly she fought it down, and so stood, with wide eyes and smiling lips. At the door he turned to look, with a glance less of appeal than of incredulity that she, so lovely, so alluring, so desirable beyond all the world, a creature of springtime and promise embowered amidst the springtime and promise of the apple-bloom, could be such as her speech and action proclaimed her.

Hal carried from her house, like a barbed arrow, the memory of that still and desperate smile.

CHAPTER XVII

REPRISALS

Working on an empty heart is almost as severe a strain as the less poetic process of working on an empty stomach. On the morning after the failure of Esmé's strategy and the wrecking of Hal's hopes, the young editor went to his office with a languid but bitter distaste for its demands. The first item in the late afternoon mail stung him to a fitter spirit, as a sharp blow will spur to his best efforts a courageous boxer. This was a packet, containing the crumbled fragments of a spray of arbutus, and a note in handwriting now stirringly familiar.

> I have read your editorial. From a man dishonest enough to print deliberate lies and cowardly enough to attack a woman, it is just such an answer as I might have expected.
>
> ELEANOR S.M. ELLIOT.

At first the reference to the editorial bewildered Hal. Then he remembered. Esmé had known nothing of the editorial until she read it in the paper. She had inferred that he wrote it after leaving her, thus revenging himself upon her by further scarification of the friend for whom she had pleaded. To the charge of deliberate mendacity he had no specific clue, not knowing that Kathleen Pierce had denied the authenticity of the interview. He mused somberly upon the venomed injustice of womankind. The note and its symbol of withered sweetness he buried in his waste-basket. If he could but discard as readily the vision of a face, strangely lovely in its anger and chagrin, and wearing that set and desperate smile! Well, there was but one answer to her note. That was to make the "Clarion" all that she would have it not be!

No phantoms of lost loveliness came between McGuire Ellis and his satisfaction over the Pierce *coup*. Characteristically, however, he presented the disadvantageous as well as the favorable aspects of the matter to his employer.

"Some paper this morning!" he began. "The town is humming like a hive."

"Over the Pierce story?" asked Hal.

"Nothing else talked of. We were sold out before nine this morning."

"Selling papers is our line of business," observed the owner-editor.

"You won't think so when you hear Shad Shearson. He's an avalanche of woe, waiting to sweep down upon you."

"What's his trouble? The department store advertising?"

"The Boston Store advertising is gone. Others are threatening to follow. Pierce has called a meeting of the Publications Committee of the Dry Goods Union. Discipline is in the air, Boss. Have you seen the evening papers?"

"Yes."

"What did you think of their stories of the accident?"

"I seemed to notice a suspicious similarity."

"You can bet every one of those stories came straight from E.M. Pierce's own office. You'll see, they'll be the same in tomorrow morning's papers. Now that we've opened up, they all have to cover the news, so they've thoughtfully sent around to inquire what Elias M. would like to have printed."

"From what they say," remarked Hal flippantly, "the nurse ought to be arrested for trying to bump a sixty-horsepower car out of the roadway."

"We strive to please, in the local newspaper shops."

Ellis turned to answer the buzzing telephone. "Get on your life preserver," he advised his principal. "Shearson's coming up to weep all over you."

The advertising manager entered, his plump cheeks sagging into lugubrious and reproachful lines, speaking witnesses to a sentiment not wholly unjustifiable in his case. To see circulation steadily going up and advertising as steadily going down, is an irritant experience to the official responsible for the main income of a daily paper, advertising revenue.

"Advertisers have some rights," he boomed, in his heavy voice.

"Including that of homicide?" asked Hal.

"Let the law take care of that. It ain't our affair."

"Would it be our affair if Pierce didn't control advertising?"

Shearson's fat hands went to his fat neck in a gesture of desperation. "That's different," he cried. "I can't seem to make you see my point. Why looka here, Mr. Surtaine. Who pays for the running of a newspaper? The advertisers. Where do your profits come from? Advertising. There never was a paper could last six months on circulation alone. It's the ads. that keep every paper going. Well, then: how's a paper going to live that turns against its own support? Tell me that. If you were running a business, and a big buyer came in, would you roast him and knock his methods, and criticize his family, and then expect to sell him a bill of goods? Or would you take him out to the theater and feed him a fat cigar, and treat him the best you know how? You might have your own private opinion of him—"

"A newspaper doesn't deal in private opinions," put in Hal.

"Well, it can keep 'em private for its own good, can't it? How many readers care whether E.M. Pierce's daughter ran over a woman or not? What difference does it make to them? They'd be just as well satisfied to read about the latest kick-up in Mexico, or the scandal at Washington, or Mrs. Whoopdoodle's Newport dinner to the troupe of educated fleas. But it makes a lot of difference to E.M. Pierce, and he can make it a lot of difference to us. So long as he pays us good money, he's got a right to expect us to look out for his interests."

"So have our readers who pay us good money, Mr. Shearson."

"What are their interests?" asked the advertising manager, staring.

"To get the news straight. You've given me your theory of journalism; now let me give you mine. As I look at it, there's a contract of honor between a newspaper and its subscribers. Tacitly the newspaper says to the subscriber, 'For two cents a day, I agree to furnish you with the news of your town, state, nation, and the outside world, selected to the best of my ability, and presented without fear or favor.' On this basis, if the newspaper fakes its news, if it distorts facts, or if it suppresses them, it is playing false with its subscribers. It is sanding its sugar, and selling shoddy for all-wool. Isn't that true?"

"Every newspaper does it," grumbled Shearson. "And the public knows it."

"Doubted. The public knows that newspapers make mistakes and do a lot of exaggerating and sensationalizing. But you once get it into their heads that a certain newspaper is concealing and suppressing news, and see how long that paper will last. The circulation will drop and the very men like Pierce will be the first to withdraw their advertising patronage. Your keen advertiser doesn't waste time fishing in dead pools. So even as a matter of policy the straight way may be the best, in the long run. Whether it is or not, get this firmly into your mind, Mr. Shearson. From now on the first consideration of the 'Clarion' will be news and not advertising."

"Then, good-*night* 'Clarion,'" pronounced Shearson with entire solemnity.

"Is that your resignation, Mr. Shearson?"

"Do you want me to quit?"

"No; I don't. I believe you're an efficient man, if you can adjust yourself to new conditions. Do you think you can?"

"Well, I ain't much on the high-brow stuff, Mr. Surtaine, but I can take orders, I guess. I'm used to the old 'Clarion,' and I kinda like you, even if we don't agree. Maybe this virtuous jag'll get us some business for what it loses us. But, say, Mr. Surtaine, you ain't going to get virtuous in your advertising columns, too, are you?"

"I hadn't considered it," said Hal. "One of these days I'll look into it."

"For God's sake, don't!" pleaded Shearson, with such a shaken flabbiness of vehemence that both Hal and Ellis laughed, though the former felt an uneasy puzzlement.

The article and editorial on the Pierce accident had appeared in a Thursday's "Clarion." In their issues of the following day, the other morning papers dealt with the subject most delicately. The "Banner" published, without obvious occasion, a long and rather fulsome editorial on E.M. Pierce as a model of high-minded commercial emprise and an exemplar for youth: also, on the same page in its "Pointed Paragraphs," the following, with a point quite too palpably aimed:—

"It is said, on plausible if not direct authority, that one of our morning contemporaries will appropriately alter its motto to read, 'With Malice toward All: with Charity for None.'"

But it remained for that evening's "Telegram" to bring up the heavy guns. From its first edition these headlines stood out, black and bold:—

E.M. PIERCE DEFENDS DAUGHTER

MAGNATE INCENSED AT UNJUST ATTACKS
WILL PUSH CASE AGAINST HER
TRADUCERS TO A FINISH

There followed an interview in which the great man announced his intention of bringing both civil and criminal action for libel against the "Clarion." McGuire Ellis frowned savagely at the sheet.

"Dirty skunk!" he growled.

"Meaning our friend Pierce?" queried Hal.

"No. Meaning Parker, and the whole 'Telegram' outfit."

"Why?"

"Because they printed that interview."

"What's wrong with it? It's news."

"Don't be positively infantile, Boss. Newspapers don't print libel actions brought against other newspapers. It's unprofessional. It's unethical. It isn't straight."

"No: I don't see that at all," decided Hal, after some consideration. "That amounts simply to this, that the newspapers are in a combination to discourage libel actions, by suppressing all mention of them."

"Certainly. Why not? Libel suits are generally holdups."

"I think the 'Telegram' is right. Whatever Pierce says is news, and interesting news."

"You bet Parker would never have carried that if his holding corporation wasn't a heavy borrower in the Pierce banks."

"Maybe not. But I think we'll carry it."

"In the 'Clarion'?" almost shouted Ellis.

"Certainly. Let's have Wayne send a reporter around to Pierce. If Pierce won't give us an interview, we'll reprint the 'Telegram's,' with credit."

"We'd be cutting our own throats, and playing Pierce's game. Besides, stuff about ourselves isn't news."

Hal's inexperience had this virtue, that it was free of the besetting and prejudicial superstitions of the craft of print. "If it's interesting, it's the 'Clarion' kind of news."

Ellis, about to protest further, met the younger man's level gaze, and swallowed hard.

"All right," he said. "I'll tell Wayne."

So the "Clarion" violated another tradition of newspaperdom, to the amused contempt of its rivals, who were, however, possibly not quite so amused or so contemptuous as they appeared editorially to be. Also it followed up the interview with an explicit statement of its own intentions in the matter, which were not precisely music to the savage breast of E.M. Pierce.

Evidences of that formidable person's hostilities became increasingly manifest from day to day. One morning a fire marshal dropped casually in upon the "Clarion" office, looked the premises over, and called the owner's attention to several minor and unsuspected violations of the law, the adjustment of which would involve no small inconvenience and several hundred dollars outlay. By a curious coincidence, later in the day, a factory inspector happened around,—a newspaper office being, legally, within the definition of a factory,—and served a summons on McGuire Ellis as publisher, for permitting smoking in the city room. From time immemorial every edition of every newspaper in the United States of America has evolved out of rolling clouds of tobacco smoke: but the "Clarion" alone, apparently, had come within the purview of the law. Subsequently, Hal learned, to his amusement, that all the other newspaper offices were placarded with notices of the law in Yiddish, so that none might be unduly disturbed thereby! To give point to the discrimination, down on the street, a zealous policeman arrested one of the "Clarion's" bulk-paper handlers for obstructing the sidewalk.

"Pierce's political pull is certainly working," observed Ellis, "but it's coarse work."

Finer was to come. Two libel suits mushroomed into view in as many days, provoked, as it were, out of conscious nothing; unimportant but harassing: one, brought by a ne'er-do-well who had broken a leg while engaged in a drunken prank months before, the other the outcome of a paragraph on a little, semi-fraudulent charity.

"I'll bet that eminent legal light, Mr. William Douglas, could tell something about these," said Ellis, "though his name doesn't appeal on the papers."

"We'll print these, too,—and we'll tell the reason for them," said Hal.

But on this last point his assistant dissuaded him. The efficient argument was that it would look like whining, and the one thing which a newspaper must not do was to lament its own ill-treatment.

On top of the libel suits came a letter from the Midland National Bank, stating with perfect courtesy that, under its present organization, a complicated account like that of the "Clarion" was inconvenient to handle; wherefore the bank was reluctantly obliged to request its withdrawal.

"Bottling us up financially," remarked Ellis. "I expected this, before."

"There are other banks than the Midland that'll be glad of our business," replied Hal.

"Probably not."

"No? Then they're curious institutions."

"There isn't one of 'em in which Elias M. Pierce isn't a controlling factor. Ask your father."

On the following day when Dr. Surtaine, who had been out of town for several days, dropped in at the office, Hal had a memorandum ready on the point. The old quack eased himself into a chair with his fine air of ample leisure, creating for himself a fragrant halo of cigar smoke.

"Well, Boyee." The tone was a mingling of warm affection and semi-humorous reproach. "You went and did it to Elias M., didn't you?"

"Yes, sir. We went and did it."

The Doctor shook his head, looking at the other through narrowing eyes. "And it's worrying you. You're not looking right."

"Oh, I'm well enough: a little sleeplessness, that's all."

He did not deem it necessary to tell his father that upon his white nights the unforgettable face of Esmé Elliot had gleamed persistently from out the darkness, banishing rest.

"Suppose you let me do some of the worrying, Boyee."

"Haven't you enough troubles in your own business, Dad?" smiled Hal.

"Machinery, son. Automatic, at that. Runs itself and turns out the dollars, regular, for breakfast. Very different from the newspaper game."

"I *should* like your advice."

"On the take-it-or-leave-it principle, I suppose," answered Dr. Surtaine, with entire good humor. "In the Pierce matter you left it. How do you like the results?"

"Not very much."

Dr. Surtaine spread out upturned hands, in dumb, oracular illustration of his own sagacity.

"But I'd do the same thing over again if it came up for decision."

"That's exactly what you mustn't do, Hal. Banging around the shop like that, cracking people on the knuckles may give you a temporary feeling of power and importance" (Hal flushed boyishly), "but it don't pay. Now, if I get you out of this scrape, I want you to go more carefully."

"How are you going to get me out of it?"

"Square it with E.M. Pierce. He's a good friend of mine."

"Do you really like Mr. Pierce, Dad?"

"Hm! Ah—er—well, Boyee, as for that, that's another tail on a cat. In a business way, I meant."

"In a business way he's trying to be a pretty efficient enemy of mine. How would you like it if he undertook to interfere with Certina?"

By perceptible inches Dr. Surtaine's chest rounded in slow expansion. "Legislatures and government bureaus have tried that. They never got away with it yet. Elias Pierce is a pretty big man in this town, but I guess he knows enough to keep hands and tongue off me."

"If not off your line of business," amended Ellis. "Did you see his interview in the 'Telegram'?"

He tossed over a copy of the paper folded to a column wherein Mr. Pierce, with more temper than tact, had possessed himself of his adversary's editorial text, "Heredity," and proceeded to perform a variant thereon.

"If this young whippersnapper," Mr. Pierce had said, "this fledgling thug of journalism, had stopped to think of the source of his unearned money, perhaps he wouldn't talk so glibly about heredity."

Thence the interview pursued a course of indirect reflection upon the matter and method of the patent medicine trade, as exemplified in Certina and its allied industries. The top button of Dr. Surtaine's glossy morning coat, as he read, seemed in danger of flying off into infinite space. His powerful hands opened and closed slowly. Leaning forward he reached for the telephone, but checked himself.

"Mr. Pierce seems to have let go both barrels at once," he said with a strong effort of control.

"Pretty little exhibition of temper, isn't it?" said Hal, smiling.

"Temper's expensive. Perhaps we'll teach Elias M. Pierce that lesson before we're through. You remember it, too, next time you start in on a muckraking jag."

"Our muckraking, as you call it, isn't a question of temper, Dad," said Hal earnestly. "It's a question of policy. What the 'Clarion' is doing, is done because we're trying to be a newspaper. We've got to stick to that. I've given my word."

"Who to?"

"To the men on the staff."

"What's more," put in McGuire Ellis, turning at the door on his way out to see a caller, "the fellows have got hold of the idea. That's what gives the 'Clarion' the go it's got. We're all rowing one stroke."

"And the captain can't very well quit in mid-race." Hal took up the other's metaphor, as the door closed behind him. "So you see, Dad, I've got to see it through, no matter what it costs me."

The father's rich voice dropped to a murmur. "Hasn't it cost you something more than money, already, Boyee? I understand Miss Esmé is a pretty warm friend of Pierce's girl."

Hal winced.

"All right, Boyee. I don't want to pry. But lots of things come quietly to the old man's ear. You've got a right to your secrets."

"It isn't any secret, Dad. In fact, it isn't anything any more," said Hal, smiling wanly. "Yes, the price was pretty high. I don't think any other will ever be so high."

Dr. Surtaine heaved his bulk out of the chair and laid a heavy arm across his son's shoulder.

"Boyee, you and I don't agree on a lot of things. We're going to keep on not agreeing about a lot of things. You think I'm an old fogy with low-brow standards. I think you've got a touch of that prevalent disease of youth, fool-in-the-head. But, I guess, as father and son, pal and pal, we're pretty well suited,—eh?"

"Yes," said Hal. There was that in the monosyllable which wholly contented the older man.

"Go ahead with your 'Clarion,' Boyee. Blow your fool head off. Deave us all deaf. Play any tune you want, and pay yourself for your piping. I won't interfere—any more'n I can help, being an old meddler by taste. Blood's thicker than water, they say. I guess it's thicker than printer's ink, too. Remember this, right or wrong, win or lose, Boyee, I'm with you."

CHAPTER XVIII
MILLY

All Hal's days now seemed filled with Pierce. Pierce's friends, dependents, employees, associates wrote in, denouncing the "Clarion," canceling subscriptions, withdrawing advertisements. Pierce's club, the Huron, compelled the abandonment of Mr. Harrington Surtaine's candidacy. Pierce's clergyman bewailed the low and vindictive tone of modern journalism. The Pierce newspapers kept harassing the "Clarion"; the Pierce banks evinced their financial disapproval; the Pierce lawyers diligently sought new causes of offense against the foe; while Pierce's mayor persecuted the newspaper office with further petty enforcements and exactions. Pierce's daughter, however, fled the town. With her went Miss Esmé Elliot. According to the society columns, including that of the "Clarion," they were bound for a restful voyage on the Pierce yacht.

From time to time Editor Surtaine retaliated upon the foe, employing the news of the slow progress of Miss Cleary, the nurse, to maintain interest in the topic. Protests invariably followed, sometimes from sources which puzzled the "Clarion." One of the protestants was Hugh Merritt, the young health officer of the city, who expressed his views to McGuire Ellis one day.

"No," Ellis reported to his employer, on the interview, "he didn't exactly ask that we let up entirely. But he seemed to think we were going too strong. I couldn't quite get his reasons, except that he thought it was a terrible thing for the Pierce girl, and she so young. Queer thing from Merritt. They don't make 'em any straighter than he is."

Alone of the lot of protests, that of Mrs. Festus Willard gained a response from Hal.

"You're treating her very harshly, Hal."

"We're giving the facts, Lady Jinny."

"*Are* they the facts? *All* the facts?"

"So far as human eyes could see them."

"Men's eyes don't see very far where a woman is concerned. She's very young and headstrong, and, Hal, she hasn't had much chance, you know. She's Elias Pierce's daughter."

"Thus having every chance, one would suppose."

"Every chance of having everything. Very little chance of being anything."

There was a pause. Then: "Very well, Hal, I know I can trust you to do what you believe right, at least. That's a good deal. Festus tells me to let you alone. He says that you must fight your own fight in your own way. That's the whole principle of salvation in Festus's creed."

"Not a bad one," said Hal. "I'm not particularly liking to do this, you know, Lady Jinny."

"So I can understand. Have you heard anything from Esmé Elliot since she left?"

"No."

"You mustn't drop out of the set, Hal," said the little woman anxiously.

"You've made good so quickly. And our crowd doesn't take up with the first comer, you know."

Since Esmé Elliot had passed out of his life, as he told himself, Hal found no incentive to social amusements. Hence he scarcely noticed a slow but widening ostracism which shut him out from house after house, under the pressure of the Pierce influence. But Mrs. Festus Willard had perceived and resented it. That any one for whom she had stood sponsor should fail socially in Worthington was both irritating and incredible to her. Hence she made more of Hal than she might otherwise have found time to do, and he was much with her and Festus Willard, deriving, on the one hand, recreation and amusement from her sparkling *camaraderie*, and on the other, support and encouragement from her husband's strong, outspoken, and ruggedly honest common sense. Neither of them fully approved of his attack on Kathleen Pierce, whom they understood better than he did. But they both—and more particularly Festus Willard—appreciated the courage and honor of the "Clarion's" new standards.

Except for an occasional dinner at their house, and a more frequent hour late in the afternoon or early in the evening, with one or both of them, Hal saw almost nothing of the people into whose social environment he had so readily slipped. Because of his exclusion, there prospered the more naturally a casual but swiftly developing intimacy which had sprung up between himself and Milly Neal.

It began with her coming to Hal for his counsel about her copy. From the first she assumed an attitude of unquestioning confidence in his wisdom and taste. This flattered the pedagogue which is inherent in all of us. He was wise enough to see promptly that he must be delicately careful in his criticism, since here he was dealing out not opinion, but gospel. Poised and self-confident the girl was in her attitude toward herself: the natural consequence of early success and responsibility. But about her writing she exhibited an almost morbid timidity lest it be thought "vulgar" or "common" by the editor-in-chief; and once McGuire Ellis felt called upon to warn Hal that he was "taking all the gimp out of the 'Kitty the Cutie' stuff by trying to sewing-circularize it." Of literature the girl knew scarcely anything; but she had an eager ambition for better standards, and one day asked Hal to advise her in her reading.

Not without misgivings he tried her with Stevenson's "Virginibus Puerisque" and was delighted with the swiftness and eagerness of her appreciation. Then he introduced her by careful selection to the poets, beginning with Tennyson, through Wordsworth, to Browning, and thence to the golden-voiced singers of the sonnet, and all of it she drank in with a wistful and wondering delight. Soon her visits came to be of almost daily occurrence. She would dart in of an evening, to claim or return a book, and sit perched on the corner of the big work-table, like a little, flashing, friendly bird; always exquisitely neat, always vividly pretty and vividly alive. Sometimes the talk wandered from the status of instructor and instructed, and touched upon the progress of the "Clarion," the view which Milly's little world took of it, possible ways of making it more interesting to the women readers to whom the "Cutie" column was supposed to cater particularly. More than once the more personal note was touched, and the girl spoke of her coming to the Certina factory, a raw slip of a country creature tied up in calico, and of Dr. Surtaine's kindness and watchfulness over her.

"He wanted to do well by me because of the old man—my father, I mean," she caught herself up, blushing. "They knew each other when I was a kid."

"Where?" asked Hal.

"Oh, out east of here," she answered evasively.

Again she said to him once, "What I like about the 'Clarion' is that it's trying to do something for *folks*. That's all the religion I could ever get into my head: that human beings are mostly worth treating decently. That counts for more than all your laws and rules and church regulations. I don't like rules much," she added, twinkling up at him. "I always want to kick 'em over, just as I always want to break through the police lines at a fire."

"But rules and police lines are necessary for keeping life orderly," said Hal.

"I suppose so. But I don't know that I like things too orderly. My teacher called me a lawless little demon, once, and I guess I still am. Suppose I should break all the rules of the office? Would you fire me?" And before he could answer she was up and had flashed away.

As the intimacy grew, Hal found himself looking forward to these swift-winged little visits. They made a welcome break in the detailed drudgery; added to the day a glint of color, bright like the ripple of half-hidden flame that crowned Milly's head. Once Veltman, intruding on their talk, had glared blackly and, withdrawing, had waited for the girl in the hallway outside from whence, as she left, Hal could hear the foreman's deep voice in anger and her clear replies tauntingly stimulating his chagrin.

Having neglected the Willards for several days, Hal received a telephone message, about a month after Esmé Elliot's departure, asking him to stop in. He found Mrs. Willard waiting him in the conservatory. His old friend looked up as he entered, with a smile which did not hide the trouble in her eyes.

"Aren't you a lily-of-the-field!" admired the visitor, contemplating her green and white costume.

"It's the Vanes' dance. Not going?"

"Not asked. Besides, I'm a workingman these days."

"So one might infer from your neglect of your friends. Hal, I've had a letter from Esmé Elliot."

"Any message?" he asked lightly, but with startled blood.

There was no answering lightness in her tones. "Yes. One I hate to give. Hal, she's engaged herself to Will Douglas. It must have been by letter, for she wasn't engaged when she left. 'Tell Hal Surtaine' she says in her letter to me."

"Thank you, Lady Jinny," said Hal.

The diminutive lady looked at him and then looked away, and suddenly a righteous flush rose on her cheeks.

"I'm fond of Esmé," she declared. "One can't help but be. She compels it. But where men are concerned she seems to have no sense of her power to hurt. I could *kill* her for making me her messenger. Hal, boy," she rose, slipping an arm through his caressingly, "I do hope you're not badly hurt."

"I'll get over it, Lady Jinny. There's the job, you know."

He started for the office. Then, abruptly, as he went, "the job" seemed purposeless. Unrealized, hope had still persisted in his heart—the hope that, by some possible turn of circumstance, the shattered ideal of Esmé Elliot would be revivified. The blighting of his love for her had been no more bitter, perhaps less so, than the realization which she had compelled in him of her lightness and unworthiness. Still, he had wanted her, longed for her, hoped for her. Now that hope was gone. There seemed nothing left to work for, no adequate good beyond the striving. He looked with dulled vision out upon blank days. With a sudden weakening of fiber he turned into a hotel and telephoned McGuire Ellis that he wouldn't be at the office that evening. To the other's anxious query was he ill, he replied that he was tired out and was going home to bed.

Meantime, far across the map at a famous Florida hostelry, the Great American Pumess, in the first flush and pride of her engagement which all commentators agree upon as characteristic of maidenhood's vital resolution, lay curled up in a little fluffy coil of misery and tears, repeating between sobs, "I hate him! I *hate* him!" Meaning her *fiancé*, Mr. William Douglas, with whom her mind and emotions should properly have been concerned? Not so, perspicacious reader. Meaning Mr. Harrington Surtaine.

Upon *his* small portion of the map, that gentleman wooed sleep in vain for hours. Presently he arose from his tossed bed, dressed quietly, slipped out of the big door and walked with long, swinging steps down to the "Clarion" Building. There it stood, a plexus of energies, in the midst of darkness and sleep. Eye-like, its windows peered vigilantly out into the city. A door opened to emit a voice that bawled across the way some profane demand for haste in the delivery of "that grub"; and through the shaft of light Hal could see brisk figures moving, and hear the roar and thrill of the press sealing its irrevocable message.

Again he felt, with a pride so profound that its roots struck down into the depths of humility, his own responsibility to all that straining life and energy and endeavor. He, the small atom, alone in the night, *was* the "Clarion." Those men, the fighting fellowship of the office, were rushing and toiling and coordinating their powers to carry out some ideal still dimly inchoate in his brain. What mattered his little pangs? There was a man's test to meet, and the man within him stretched spiritual muscles for the trial.

"If I could only be sure what's right," he said within himself, voicing the doubt of every high-minded adventurer upon unbeaten paths. Sharply, and, as it seemed to him, incongruously, he wondered that he had never learned to pray; not knowing that, in the unfinished phrase he had uttered true prayer. A chill breeze swept down upon him. Looking up into the jeweled heavens he recalled from the far distance of memory, the prayer of a great and simple soul,—

"Make thou my spirit pure and clear
As are the frosty skies."

Hal set out for home, ready now for a few hours' sleep. At a blind corner he all but collided with a man and a woman, walking at high speed. The woman half turned, flinging him a quick and silvery "Good-evening." It was Milly Neal. The man with her was Max Veltman.

CHAPTER XIX

DONNYBROOK

Worthington began to find the "Clarion" amusing. It blared a new note. Common matter of everyday acceptance which no other paper in town had ever considered as news, became, when trumpeted from between the rampant roosters, vital with interest. And whithersoever it directed the public attention, some highly respectable private privilege winced and snarled. Worthington did not particularly love the "Clarion" for the enemies it made. But it read it.

Now, a newspaper makes its enemies overnight. Friends take months or years in the making. Hence the "Clarion," whilst rapidly broadening its circle of readers, owed its success to the curiosity rather than to the confidence which it inspired. Meantime the effect upon its advertising income was disastrous. If credence could be placed in the lamenting Shearson, wherever it attacked an abuse, whether by denunciation or ridicule, it lost an advertiser. Moreover the public, not yet ready to credit any journal with honest intentions, was inclined to regard the "Clarion" as "a chronic kicker." The "Banner's" gibing suggestion of a reversal of the editorial motto between the triumphant birds to read "With malice toward all," stuck.

But there were compensations. The blatant cocks had occasional opportunity for crowing. With no small justification did they shrill their triumph over the Midland & Big Muddy Railroad. The "Mid and Mud" had declared war upon the "Clarion," following the paper's statement of the true cause of the Walkersville wreck, as suggested by Marchmont, the reporter, at the breakfast. Marchmont himself had been banished from the railroad offices. All sources of regular news were closed to him. Therefore, backed by the "Clarion," he proceeded to open up a line of irregular news which stirred the town. For years the "Mid and Mud" had given to Worthington a passenger service so bad that no community less enslaved to a *laissez-faire* policy would have endured it. Through trains drifted in anywhere from one to four hours late. Local trains, drawn by wheezy, tin-pot locomotives of outworn pattern, arrived and departed with such casualness as to render schedules a joke, and not infrequently "bogged down" between stations until some antediluvian engine could be resuscitated and sent out to the rescue. The day coaches were of the old, dangerous, wooden type. The Pullman service was utterly unreliable, and the station in which the traveling populace of Worthington spent much of its time, a draft-ridden barn. Yet Worthington suffered all this because it was accustomed to it and lacked any means of making protest vocal.

Then the "Clarion" started in publishing its "Yesterday's Time-Table of the Midland & Big Muddy R.R. Co." to this general effect:

Day Express

Due . . . . 10.00 A.M.
Arrived. . . . . 11.43 A.M.
Late . . . . .1 hour 43 min.

Noon Local

Due . . . . 12.00 A.M.
Arrived . . . . 2.10 P.M.
Late . . . . .2 hrs. 10 min.

Sunrise Limited

Due . . . . 3.00 P.M.
Arrived . . . . 3.27 P.M.
Late . . . . .0 hrs. 27 min.

And so on. From time to time there would appear, underneath, a special item, of which the following is an example:

"The Eastern States Through Express of the Midland & Big Muddy Railroad arrived and departed on time yesterday. When asked for an explanation of this phenomenon, the officials declined to be interviewed."

Against this "persecution," the "Mid and Mud" authorities at first maintained a sullen silence. The "Clarion" then went into statistics. It gave the number of passengers arriving and departing on each delayed train, estimated the value of their time, and constructed tables of the money value of time lost in this way to the city of Worthington, per day, per month, and per year. The figures were not the less inspiring of thought, for being highly amusing.

People began to take an interest. They brought or sent in personal experiences. A commercial traveler, on the 7.50 train (arriving at 10.01, that day), having lost a big order through missing an appointment, told the "Clarion" about it. A contractor's agent, gazing from the windows of the stalled "Limited" out upon "fresh woods and pastures new" twenty miles short of Worthington, what time he should have been at a committee meeting of the Council, forfeited a $10,000 contract and rushed violently into "Clarion" print, breathing slaughter and law-suits. Judge Abner Halloway and family, arriving at the New York pier in a speeding taxi from the Eastern Express (five hours late out of Worthington), just in time to see the Lusitania take his forwarded baggage for a pleasant outing in Europe, hired a stenographer (male) to tell the "Clarion" what he thought of the matter, in words of seven syllables. Professor Beeton Trachs, the globe-trotting lecturer, who arrived via the "M. and M." for an eight o'clock appearance, at 9.54, gave the "Clarion" an interview proper to the occasion of having to abjure a $200 guaranty, wherein the mildest and most judicial opinion expressed by Professor Trachs was that crawling through a tropical jungle on all fours was speed, and being hurtled down a mountain on the bosom of a landslide, comfort, compared to travel on the "Mid and Mud."

All these and many similar experiences, the "Clarion" published in its "News of the M. and M." column. It headed them, "Stories of Survivors." For six weeks the railroad endured the proddings of ridicule. Then the Fourth Vice-President of the road appeared in Mr. Harrington Surtaine's sanctum. He was bland and hinted at advertising. Two weeks later the Third Vice-President arrived. He was vague and hinted at reprisals. The Second Vice-President presented himself within ten days thereafter, departed after five unsatisfactory minutes, and reported at headquarters, with every symptom of an elderly gentleman suffering from shock, that young Mr. Surtaine had seemed bored. The First Vice-President then arrived on a special train.

"What do you want, anyway?" he asked.

"Decent passenger service for Worthington," said the editor. "Just what I've told every other species *and* number of Vice-President on your list."

"You get it," said the First Vice-President.

Thus was afforded another example of that super-efficiency which, we are assured, marks the caste of the American railroad as superior to all others, and which consists in sending four men and spending several weeks to do what one could do better in a single day. In the course of a few weeks the Midland & Big Muddy did bring its service up to a reasonable standard, and the owner of the "Clarion" savored his first pleasant proof of the power of the press.

Vastly less important, but swifter and more definite in results and more popular in effect, was the "Clarion's" anti-hat-check campaign. The Stickler, Worthington's newest hotel, had established a coat-room with the usual corps of girl-bandits, waiting to strip every patron of his outer garments before admitting him to the restaurant, and returning them only upon the blackmail of a tip. All the other good restaurants had followed suit. Worthington resented it, as it resented most innovations; but endured the imposition, for lack of solidarity, until the "Clarion" took up the subject in a series of paragraphs.

"Do you think," blandly inquired the editorial roosters, "that when you tip the hat-check girl she gets the tip? She doesn't. It goes to a man who rents from the restaurant the privilege of bullying you out of a dime or a quarter. The girl holds you up, because if she doesn't extort fifteen dollars a week, she loses her job and her own munificent wages of seven dollars. The 'Clarion' takes pleasure in announcing a series of portraits of the high-minded pirates of finance whom you support in luxury, when you 'give up' to the check-girl. Our first portrait, ladies and gentlemen, is that of Mr. Abe Hotzenmuller, race-track bookmaker and whiskey agent, who, in the intervals of these more reputable occupations, extracts alms from the patrons of the Hotel Stickler."

Next in line was "Shirty" MacDonough, a minor politician, "appropriately framed in silver dimes," as the "Clarion" put it. He was followed by Eddie Perkins, proprietor of a dubious resort on Mail Street. By this time coat-room franchises had suffered a severe depreciation. They dropped almost to zero when the newspaper, having clinched the lesson home with its "Photo-graft Gallery of Leading Dime-Hunters," exhorted its readers: "If you think you need your change as much as these men do, watch for the coupon in tomorrow's 'Clarion,' and Stick it in Your Hat." The coupon was as follows:

I READ THE CLARION. I WILL NOT GIVE ONE CENT IN TIPS TO ANY COAT-ROOM GRAFTER. WHAT ARE YOU GOING TO DO ABOUT IT?

The enterprise hit upon the psychological moment. Every check-room bristled with hats proclaiming defiance, and, incidentally, advertising the "Clarion." The "cut-out coupon" ran for three weeks. In one month the Stickler check-room, last to surrender, gave up the ghost, and Mr. Hotzenmuller sued the proprietor for his money back!

Over the theatrical managers the paper's victory was decisive in this, that it established honest dramatic criticism in Worthington. But only at a high cost. Not a line of theater advertising appeared in the columns after the editorial announcement of independence. Press tickets were cut off. The "Clarion's" dramatic reporter was turned back from the gate of the various theaters, after paying for admittance. Nevertheless, the "Clarion" continued to publish frank criticism of current drama, through a carefully guarded secret arrangement with the critic of the "Evening News." About this time a famous star, opening a three days' engagement, got into difficulties with the scene-shifters' union over an unjust demand for extra payment, refused to be blackmailed, and canceled the second performance. One paper only gave the facts, and that was the "Clarion," generally regarded as the defender and mouthpiece of the laboring as against the capitalistic interests. Great was the wrath of the unions. Boycott was threatened; even a strike in the office. In response, the editorial page announced briefly that its policy of giving the news accurately and commenting upon it freely exempted no man or organization. The trouble soon died out, but, while making new enemies amongst the rabid organization men, strengthened the "Clarion's" growing repute for independence. One of the most violent objectors was Max Veltman, whose protest, delivered to Hal and McGuire Ellis, was so vehement that he was advised curtly and emphatically to confine his activities and opinions to his own department.

"Look out for that fellow," advised Ellis, as the foreman went away fuming. "He hates you."

"Only his fanaticism," said Hal.

"More than that. It's personal. I think," added the associate editor after some hesitancy, "it's 'Kitty the Cutie.' He's jealous, Hal. And I think he's right. That girl's getting too much interested in you."

Hal flushed sharply. "Nonsense!" he said, and the subject lapsed.

Meantime the manager of the Ralston Opera House, where the labor trouble had occurred, made tentative proffer of peace in the form of sending in the theater advertising again. Hal promptly refused to accept it, by way of an object-lesson, despite the almost tearful protest of his own business office. This blow almost killed Shearson.

In fact, the unfortunate advertising manager now lived in an atmosphere of Stygian gloom. Two of the most extensive purchasers of newspaper space, the Boston Store and the Triangle Store, had canceled their contracts immediately after the attack on the Pierces, through a "joker" clause inserted to afford such an opportunity. All the other department stores threatened to follow suit when the "Clarion" took up the cause of the Consumers' League.

Mrs. Festus Willard was president of the organization, which had been practically moribund since its inception, for the sufficient reason that no mention of its activities, designs, or purposed reforms could gain admission to any newspaper in Worthington. The Retail Union saw to that through its all-potent Publication Committee. Perceiving the crescent emancipation of the "Clarion," Mrs. Willard, after due consultation with her husband, appealed to Hal. Would he help the League to obtain certain reforms? Specifically, seats for shopgirls, and extra pay for extra work, as during Old Home Week, when the stores kept open until 10 P.M.? Hal agreed, and, in the face of the dismalest forecasts from Shearson, prepared several editorials. Moreover, "Kitty the Cutie" took up the campaign in her column, and her series of "Lunch-Time Chats," with their slangy, pungent, workaday flavor, presented the case of the overworked saleswomen in a way to stir the dullest sympathies. The event fully justified Shearson in his rôle of Cassandra. Half of the remaining stores represented in the Retail Union notified the "Clarion" of the withdrawal of their advertising. Thus some twelve hundred dollars a week of income vanished. Moreover, the Union, it was hinted, would probably blacklist the "Clarion" officially. And the shop-folk gained nothing by the campaign. The merchants were strong enough to defeat the League and its sole backer at every point. This was one of the "Clarion's" failures.

Coincident with the ebb of the store advertising occurred a lapse in circulation, inexplicable to the staff until an analysis indicated that the women readers were losing interest. It was young Mr. Surtaine who solved the mystery, by a flash of that newspaper instinct with which Ellis had early credited him.

"Department store advertising is news," he decided, in a talk with Ellis and Shearson.

"How can advertising be news?" objected the manager.

"Anything that interests the public is news, on the authority of no less an expert than Mr. McGuire Ellis. Shopping is the main interest in life of thousands of women. They read the papers to find out where the bargains are. Watch 'em on the cars any morning and you'll see them studying the ads. The information in those ads. is what they most want. Now that we don't give it to them, they are dropping the paper. So we've got to give it to them."

"Now you're talking," cried Shearson. "Cut out this Consumers' League slush and I'll get the stores back."

"We'll cut out nothing. But we'll put in something. We'll print news of the department stores as news, not as advertising."

"Well, if that ain't the limit!" lamented Shearson. "If you give 'em advertising matter free, how can you ever expect 'em to pay for it?"

"We're not giving it to the stores. We're giving it to our readers."

"In which case," remarked McGuire Ellis with a grin, "we can afford to furnish the real facts."

"Exactly," said Hal.

From this talk developed a unique department in the "Clarion." An expert woman shopper collected the facts and presented them daily under the caption, "Where to Find Real Bargains," and with the prefatory note, "No paid matter is accepted for this column." The expert had an allowance for purchasing, where necessary, and the utmost freedom of opinion was granted her. Thus, in the midst of a series of items, such as—"The Boston Store is offering a special sale of linens at advantageous prices"; "The necktie sale at the Emporium contains some good bargains"; and "Scheffler and Mintz's 'furniture week' is worth attention, particularly in the rocking-chair and dining-set lines"—might appear some such information as this: "In the special bargain sale of ribbons at the Emporium the prices are slightly higher than the same lines sold for last week, on the regular counter"; or, "The heavily advertised antique rug collection at the Triangle is mostly fraudulent. With a dozen exceptions the rugs are modern and of poor quality"; or, "The Boston Shop's special sale of rain coats are mostly damaged goods. Accept none without guarantee."

Never before had mercantile Worthington known anything like this. Something not unlike panic was created in commercial circles. Lawyers were hopefully consulted, but ascertained in the first stages of investigation, that wherever a charge of fraud was brought, the "Clarion" office actually had the goods, by purchase. All this was costly to the "Clarion." But it added nearly four thousand solid circulation, of the buying class, a class of the highest value to any advertiser. Only with difficulty and by exercise of pressure on the part of E.M. Pierce, were the weaker members among the withdrawing advertisers dissuaded from resuming their patronage of the "Clarion."

"I wouldn't have thought it possible," said the dictator, angrily, to his associates. "The thing is getting dangerous. The damned paper is out for the truth."

"And the public is finding it out," supplemented Gibbs, his brother-in-law.

"Wait till my libel suit comes on," said Pierce grimly. "I don't believe young Mr. Surtaine will have enough money left to indulge in the luxury of muckraking, after that."

"Won't the old man back him up?"

"Tells me that the boy is playing a lone hand," said Pierce with satisfaction.

Herein he spoke the fact. While the "Clarion's" various campaigns were still in mid-career, Dr. Surtaine had made his final appeal to his son in vain, ringing one last change upon his Pæan of Policy.

"What good does it all do you or anybody else? You're stirring up muck, and you're getting the only thing you ever get by that kind of activity, a bad smell." He paused for his effect; then delivered himself of a characteristically vigorous and gross aphorism:

"Boyee, you can't sell a stink, in this town."

"Perhaps I can help to get rid of it," said Hal.

"Not you! Nobody thanks you for your pains. They take notice for a while, because their noses compel 'em to. Then they forget. What thanks does the public give a newspaper? But the man you've roasted—he's after you, all the time. A sore toe doesn't forget. Look at Pierce."

"Pierce has bothered me," confessed Hal. "He's shut me off from the banks. None of them will loan the 'Clarion' a cent. I have to go out of town for my money."

"Can you blame him? I'd have done the same if he'd roasted you as you roasted his girl."

"News, Dad," said Hal wearily. "It was news."

"Let's not go over that again. You'll stick to your policy, I suppose, till it ruins you. About finances, by the way, where do you stand?"

"Stand?" repeated Hal. "I wish we did. We slip. Downhill; and pretty fast."

"Why wouldn't you? Fighting your own advertisers."

"Some advertising has come in, though. Mostly from out of town."

"Foreign proprietary," said Dr. Surtaine, using the technical term for patent-medicine advertising from out of town, "isn't it? I've been doing a little missionary work among my friends in the trade, Hal; persuaded them to give the 'Clarion' a try-out. The best of it is, they're getting results."

"They ought to. Do you know we're putting on circulation at the rate of nearly a thousand a week?"

"Expensive, though, isn't it?"

"Pretty bad. The paper costs a lot more to get out. We've enlarged our staff. Now we need a new press. There's thirty-odd thousand dollars, in one lump."

"How long can you go on at this rate?"

"Without any more advertising?"

"You certainly aren't gaining, by your present policy."

"Well, I can stick it out through the year. By that time the advertising will be coming in. It's *got* to come to the paper that has the circulation, Dad."

"Hum!" droned the big doctor, dubiously. "Have you reckoned the Pierce libel suits in?"

"He can't win them."

"Can't he? I don't know. He intends to try. And he feels pretty cocky about it. E.M. Pierce has something up his sleeve, Boyee."

"That would be a body-blow. But he can't win," repeated Hal. "Why, I saw the whole thing myself."

"Just the same you ought to have the best libel lawyer you can get from New York. All the good local men are tied up with Pierce or afraid of him."

"Can't afford it."

To this point the big man had been leading up. "I've been thinking over this Pierce matter, Hal, and I've made up my mind. Pierce is getting to think he's the whole thing around here. He's bullied this town all his life, just as he's bullied his employees until they hate him like poison. But now he's gone up against the wrong game. Roast Certina, will he? The pup! Why, if he'd ever run his factories or his store or his Consolidated Employees' Organization one hundredth part as decently as I've run our business, he wouldn't have to stay in nights for fear some one might sneak a knife into him out of the dark."

This was something less than just to Elias M. Pierce, who, whatever his other faults, had never been a fearful man.

"Libel, eh?" continued the genius of Certina, quietly but formidably. "We'll teach him a few things about libel, before he's through. Here's my proposition, Boyee. You can fight Pierce, but you can't fight all Worthington. Every enemy you make for the 'Clarion' becomes an ally of Pierce. Quit all these other campaigns. Stop roasting the business men and advertisers. Drop your attack on the Mid and Mud: you've got 'em licked, anyway. Let up on the street railway: I notice you're taking a fall out of them on their overcrowding. Treat the theaters decently: they're entitled to a fair chance for their money. Cut out this Consumers' League foolishness (I'm surprised at Milly Neal—the way she's lost her head over that). Make friends instead of foes. And go after Elias M. Pierce, to the finish. Do this, and I'll back you with the whole Certina income. Come on, now, Boyee. Be sensible."

Hal's reply came without hesitation. "I'm sorry, Dad: but I can't do it. I've told you I'd stand or fall on what you've already given me. If I can't pull through on that, I can't pull through at all. Let's understand each other once and for all, Dad. I've got to try this thing out to the end. And I won't ask or take one cent from you or any one else, win or lose."

"All right, Boyee," returned his father sorrowfully. "You're wrong, dead wrong. But I like your nerve. Only, let me tell you this. You think you're going to keep on printing the news and the whole news and all that sort of thing. I tell you, it can't be done."

"Why can't it be done?"

"Because, sooner or later, you'll bump up against your own interests so hard that you'll have to quit."

"I don't see that at all, sir."

"No, you don't. But one of these days something in the news line will come up that'll hit you right between the eyes, if ever it gets into print. Then see what you'll do."

"I'll print it."

"No, you won't, Boyee. Human nature ain't built that way. You'll smother it, and be glad you've got the power to."

"Dad, you believe I'm honest, don't you?"

"Too blamed honest in some ways."

"But you'd take my word?"

"Oh, that! Yes. For anything."

"Then I put my honor on this. If ever the time comes that I have to suppress legitimate news to protect or aid my own interests, I'll own up I'm beaten: I'll quit fighting, and I'll make the 'Clarion' a very sucking dove of journalism. Is that plain?"

"Shake, Boyee. You've bought a horse. Just the same, I hate to let up on Pierce. Sure you won't let me hire a New York lawyer for the libel suit?"

"No. Thank you just as much, Dad. That's a 'Clarion' fight, and the 'Clarion's' money has got to back it."

It was the gist of this decision which, some days later, had reached E.M. Pierce, and caused him such satisfaction. With the "Clarion" depending upon its own resources, unbacked by the great reserve wealth of Certina's proprietor, he confidently expected to wreck it and force its suspension by an overwhelming verdict of damages. For, as Dr. Surtaine had surmised, he held a card up his sleeve.

CHAPTER XX
THE LESSER TEMPTING

Seven days of the week did Mr. Harrington Surtaine labor, without by any means doing all his work. For to the toil which goes to the making of many newspapers there is no end; only ever a fresh beginning. Had he brought to the enterprise a less eager appetite for the changeful adventure of it, the unremitting demand must soon have dulled his spirit. Abounding vitality he possessed, but even this flagged at times. One soft spring Sunday, while the various campaigns of the newspaper were still in mid-conflict, he decided to treat himself to a day off. So, after a luxurious morning in bed, he embarked in his runabout for an exploration around the adjacent country.

Having filled his lungs with two hours of swift air, he lunched, none too delicately, at a village fifty miles distant, and, on coming out of the hotel, was warned by a sky shaded from blue to the murkiest gray, into having the top of his car put up. The rain chased him for thirty miles and whelmed him in a wild swirl at the thirty-first. Driving through this with some caution, he saw ahead of him a woman's figure, as supple as a willow withe, as gallant as a ship, beating through the fury of the elements. Hal slowed down, debating whether to offer conveyance, when he caught a glint of ruddy waves beneath the drenched hat, and the next instant he was out and looking into the flushed face and dancing eyes of Milly Neal.

"What on earth are you doing here?" he cried.

"Can't you see?" she retorted merrily. "I'm a fish."

"You need to be. Get in. You're soaked to the skin," he continued, dismayed, as she began to shiver under the wrappings he drew around her. "Never mind. I'll have you home in a few minutes."

But the demon of mischance was abroad in the storm. Before they had covered half a mile the rear tire went. Milly was now shaking dismally, for all her brave attempts to conceal it. A few rods away a sign announced "Markby's Road-House." Concerned solely to get the girl into a warm and dry place, Hal turned in, bundled her out, ordered a private room with a fireplace, and induced the proprietor's wife by the persuasions of a ten-dollar bill to provide a change of clothing for the outer, and hot drinks for the inner, woman.

Half an hour later when he had affixed a new tire to the wheel, he and Milly sat, warmed and comforted before blazing logs, waiting for her clothes to dry out.

"I know I look a fright," she mourned. "That Mrs. Markby must buy her dresses by the pound."

She gazed at him comically from above a quaint and nondescript garment, to which she had given a certain daintiness with a cleverly placed ribbon or two and an adroit use of pins. Privately, Hal considered that she looked delightfully pretty, with her provocative eyes and the deep gleam of red in her hair like flame seen through smoke.

"Do you often go out wading, ten miles from home?" he asked.

"Not very. I was running away."

"I didn't see any one in pursuit."

"They knew too much." Her firm little chin set rather grimly. "Do you want to hear about it?"

"Yes. I'm curious," confessed Hal.

"I went to lunch with another girl and a couple of drummers, out at Callender's Pond Hotel. She said she knew the men and they were all right. They weren't. They got too fresh altogether. So I told Florence she could do as she pleased, but I was for home and the trolley. I guess I could have made it with a life-preserver," she laughed.

Hal was surprisedly conscious of a rasp of anger within him. "You ought not to put yourself into such a position," he declared.

She threw him a covert glance from the corner of her sparkling eyes. "Oh, I guess I can take care of myself," she decided calmly. "I always have. When fresh drummers begin to talk private dining-room and cold bottles, I spread my little wings and flit."

"To another private room," mocked Hal. "Aren't you afraid?"

"With you? You're different." There sounded in her voice the purring note of utter content which is the subtlest because the most unconscious flattery of womankind.

A silence fell between them. Hal stared into the fire.

"Are you warm enough?" he asked presently.

"Yes."

"Do you want something to eat? Or drink? What did you have to drink?" he added, glancing at the empty glass on the table.

"Certina."

"Certina?" he queried, uncertain at first whether she was joking. "How could you get Certina here?"

"Why not? They keep it at all these places. There's quite a bar-trade in it."

"Is that so?" said Hal, with a vague feeling of disturbance of ideas. "Which job do you like best: the Certina or the newspaper, Miss Neal?"

"My other boss calls me Milly," she suggested.

"Very well,—Milly, then."

"Oh, I'm for the office. It's more exciting, a lot."

"Your stuff," said Hal, in the language of the cult, "is catching on."

"You don't like it, though," she countered quickly.

"Yes, I do. Much better than I did, anyway. But the point is that it's a success. Editorially I *have* to like it."

"I'd rather you liked it personally."

"Some of it I do. The 'Lunch-Time Chats'—"

"And some of it you think is vulgar."

"One has to suit one's style to the matter," propounded Hal. "'Kitty the Cutie' isn't supposed to be a college professor."

"I hate to have you think me vulgar," she insisted.

"Oh, come!" he protested; "that isn't fair. I don't think *you* vulgar, Milly."

"I like to have you call me Milly," she said.

"It seems quite natural to," he answered lightly.

"I've thought sometimes I'd like to try my hand at a regular news story," she went on, in a changed tone. "I think I've got one, if I could only do it right; one of those facts-behind-the-news stories that you talked to us about. Do you remember meeting me with Max Veltman the other night?"

"Yes."

"Did you think it was queer?"

"A little."

"A girl I used to know back in the country tried to kill herself. She wrote me a letter, but it didn't get to me till after midnight, so I called up Max and got him to go with me down to the Rookeries district where she lives. Poor little Maggie! She got caught in one of those sewing-girl traps."

"Some kind of machinery?"

"Machinery? You don't know much about what goes on in your town, do you?"

"Not as much as an editor ought to know—which is everything."

"I'll bring you Maggie's letter. That tells it better than I can. And I want to write it up, too. Let me write it up for the paper." She leaned forward and her eyes besought him. "I want to prove I can do something besides being a vulgar little 'Kitty the Cutie.'"

"Oh, my dear," he said, half paternally, but only half, "I'm sorry I hurt you with that word."

"You didn't mean to." Her smile forgave him. "Maggie's story means another fight for the paper. Can we stand another?"

He warmed to the possessive "we." "So you know about our warfare," he said.

"More than you think, perhaps. The books you gave me aren't the only things I study. I study the 'Clarion,' too."

"Why?" he asked, interested.

"Because it's yours." She looked at him straightly now. "Can you pull it through, Boss?"

"I think so. I hope so."

"We've lost a lot of ads. I can reckon that up, because I had some experience in the advertising department of the Certina shop, and I know rates." She pursed her lips with a dainty effect of careful computation. "Somewhere about four thousand a week out, isn't it?"

"Four thousand, three hundred and seventy in store business last week."

The talk settled down and confined itself to the financial and editorial policies of the paper, Milly asking a hundred eager and shrewd questions, now and again proffering some tentative counsel or caution. Impersonal though it seemed, through it Hal felt a growing tensity of intercourse; a sense of pregnant and perilous intimacy drawing them together.

"Since you're taking such an interest, I might get you to help Mr. Ellis run the paper when I go away," he suggested jocularly.

"You're not going away?" The query came in a sort of gasp.

"Next week."

"For long?" Her hand, as if in protest against the dreaded answer, went out to the arm of his chair. His own met and covered it reassuringly.

"Not very. It's the new press."

"We're going to have a new press?"

"Hadn't you heard? You seem to know so much about the office. We're going to build up the basement and set the press just inside the front wall and then cut a big window through so that the world and his wife can see the 'Clarion' in the very act of making them better."

Both fell silent. Their hands still clung. Their eyes were fixed upon the fire. Suddenly a log, half-consumed, crashed down, sending abroad a shower of sparks. The girl darted swiftly up to stamp out a tiny flame at her feet. Standing, she half turned toward Hal.

"Where are you going?" she asked.

"To New York."

"Take me with you."

So quietly had the crisis come that he scarcely realized it. For a measured space of heart-beats he gazed into the fireplace. As he stared, she slipped to the arm of his chair. He felt the alluring warmth of her body against his shoulder. Then he would have turned to search her eyes, but, divining him, she denied, pressing her cheek close against his own.

"No; no! Don't look at me," she breathed.

"You don't know what you mean," he whispered.

"I do! I'm not a child. Take me with you."

"It means ruin for you."

"Ruin! That's a word! Words don't frighten me."

"They do me. They're the most terrible things in the world."

She laughed at that. "Is it the word you're afraid of, or is it me?" she challenged. "I'm not asking you anything. I don't want you to marry me. Oh!" she cried with a sinking break of the voice, "do you think I'm *bad*?"

Freeing himself, he caught her face between his hands.

"Are you—have you been 'bad,' as you call it?"

"I don't blame you for asking—after what I've said. But I haven't."

"And now?"

"Now, I care. I never cared before. It was that, I suppose, kept me straight. Don't you care for me—a little, Hal?"

He rose and strode to the window. When he turned from his long look out into the burgeoning spring she was standing silent, expectant. Like stone she stood as he came back, but her arms went up to receive him. Her lips melted into his, and the fire of her face flashed through every vein.

"And afterward?" he said hoarsely.

There was triumph in her answering laughter, passion-shaken though it was.

"Then you'll take me with you."

"But afterward?" he repeated.

Lingeringly she released herself. "Let that take care of itself. I don't care for afterward. We're free, you and I. What's to hinder us from doing as we please? Who's going to be any the worse for it? Oh, I told you I was lawless. It's the Hardscrabbler blood in me, I guess."

Deep in Hal's memory a response to that name stirred.

"Somewhere," he said, "I have run across a Hardscrabbler before."

"Me. But you've forgotten."

"Have I? Let me see. It was in the old days when Dad and I were traveling. You were the child with the wonderful red hair, the night I was hurt. *Were* you?"

"And next day I tried to bite you because you wanted to play with a prettier little girl in beautiful clothes."

Esmé! The electric spark of thought leaped the long space of years from the child, Esmé, to the girl, in the vain love of whom he had eaten his heart hollow. For the moment, passion for the vivid woman-creature before him had dulled that profounder feeling almost to obliteration. Perhaps—so the thought came to him—he might find forgetfulness, anodyne in Milly Neal's arms. But what of Milly, taken on such poor terms?

The bitter love within him gave answer. Not loyalty to Esmé Elliot whom he knew unworthy, but to Milly herself, bound him to honor and restraint; so strangely does the human soul make its dim and perilous way through the maze of motives. Even though the girl, now questing his face with puzzled, frightened eyes, asked nothing but to belong to him; demanded no bond of fealty or troth, held him free as she held herself free, content with the immediate happiness of a relation that, must end in sorrow for one or the other, yet he could not take what she so prodigally, so gallantly proffered, with the image of another woman smiling through his every thought. That, indeed, were to be unworthy, not of Esmé, not of himself, but of Milly.

He made a step toward her, and her glad hands went out to him again. Very gently he took them; very gently he bent and kissed her cheek.

"That's for good-bye," he said. The voice in which he spoke seemed alien to his ears, so calm it was, so at variance with his inner turmoil.

"You won't take me with you?"

"No."

"You promised."

"I know." He was not concerned now with verbal differentiations. Truly, he had promised, wordlessly though it had been. "But I can't."

"You don't care?" she said piteously.

"I care very much. If I cared less—"

"There's some other woman."

"Yes."

Flame leaped in her eyes. "I hope she poisons your life."

"I hope I haven't poisoned yours," he returned, lamely enough.

"Oh, I'll manage to live on," she gibed. "I guess there are other men in the world besides you."

"Don't make it too hard, Milly."

"You're pitying me! Don't you dare pity me!" A sob rose, and burst from her. Then abruptly she seized command over herself. "What does it all matter?" she said. "Go away now and let me change my clothes."

"Are they dry?"

"I don't care whether they're dry or not. I don't care what becomes of me now." All the sullen revolt of generations of lawlessness was vocal in her words. "You wait and see!"

Somehow Hal got out of the room, his mind awhirl, to await her downstairs. In a few moments she came, and with eyes somberly averted got into the runabout without a word. As they swung into the road, they met McGuire Ellis and Wayne, who bowed with a look of irrepressible surprise. During the ride homeward Hal made several essays at conversation. But the girl sat frozen in a white silence. Only when they pulled up at her door did she speak.

"I'm going to try to forget this," she said in a dry, hard voice. "You do the same. I won't quit my job unless you want me to."

"Don't," said Hal.

"But you won't be bothered with seeing me any more. I'll send you Maggie Breen's letter and the story. I guess I understand a little better now how she felt when she took the poison."

With that rankling in his brain, Hal Surtaine sat and pondered in his private study at home. His musings arraigned before him for judgment and contrast the two women who had so stormily wrought upon his new life. Esmé Elliot had played with his love, had exploited it, made of it a tinsel ornament for vanity, sought, through it, to corrupt him from the hard-won honor of his calling. She had given him her lips for a lure; she had played, soul and body, the petty cheat with a high and ennobling passion. Yet, because she played within the rules by the world's measure, there was no stain upon her honor. By that same measure, what of Milly Neal? In her was no trickery of sex; only the ungrudging, wide-armed offer of all her womanhood, reckless of aught else but love. Debating within himself the phrase, "an honest woman," Hal laughed aloud. His laughter lacked much of being mirthful, and something of being just. For he had reckoned two daughters of Eve by the same standard, which is perhaps the oldest and most disastrous error hereditary to all the sons of Adam.

CHAPTER XXI

THE POWER OF PRINT

Hal paid thirty-two thousand dollars for the new press. It was a delicate giant of mechanism, able not only to act, but also to think with stupendous accuracy and swiftness; lacking only articulate speech to be wholly superhuman. But in signing the check for it, Hal, for the first time in his luxurious life experienced a financial qualm. Always before there had been an inexhaustible source wherefrom to draw. Now that he had issued his declaration of pecuniary independence, he began to appreciate the perishable nature of money. He came back from his week's journey to New York feeling distinctly poorer.

Moreover there was an uncomfortable paradox connected with his purchase. That he should be put to so severe an expenditure merely for the purpose of incurring an increased current expense, struck him as a rather sardonic joke. Yet so it was. Circulation does not mean direct profit to a newspaper. On the contrary, it implies loss in many cases. For some weeks it had been costing the "Clarion," to print the extra papers necessitated by the increased demand, more than the money received from their sale. Until the status of the journal should justify a higher advertising charge, every added paper sold would involve a loss. True, an augmented circulation logically commands a higher advertising rate; it is thus that a newspaper reaps its harvest; and soon Hal hoped to be able to raise his advertising rate from fifteen to twenty-five cents a line. At that return his books would show a profit on a normal volume of advertising. Meantime he performed an act of involuntary philanthropy with every increase of issue, Nevertheless, Hal felt for his mechanical giant something of the new-toy thrill. To him it was a symbol of productive power. It made appeal to his imagination, typifying the reborn "Clarion." He saw it as a master-loom weaving fresh patterns, day by day, into the fabric of the city's life and thought. That all might view the process, he had it mounted high from the basement, behind a broad plate-glass show window set in the front wall, a highly unstrategic position, as McGuire Ellis pointed out.

"Suppose," said he, "a horse runs wild and makes a dive through that window? Or a couple of bums get shooting at each other, and a stray bullet comes whiffling through the glass and catches young Mr. Press in his delikit insides. We're out of business for a week, maybe, mending him up."

Shearson, however, was in favor of it. It suggested prosperity and aroused public interest. On Hal's return from New York, the fat and melancholious advertising manager had exhibited a somewhat mollified pessimism.

"The Boston Store is coming back," he visited Hal's sanctum to announce.

"Why, that's John M. Gibbs's store, isn't it?"

"Sure."

"And he's E.M. Pierce's brother-in-law. I thought he'd stick by his family in fighting the 'Clarion.'"

"Family is all right, but Grinder Gibbs is for business first and everything else afterwards. Our rates look good to him, with the circulation we're showing.

And he knows we bring results. He's been using us on the quiet for a little side issue of his own."

"What's that?"

"Some sewing-girls' employment thing. It's in the 'Classified' department. Don't amount to much; but it's proved to him that the 'Clarion' ad does the business. I've been on his trail for two weeks. So the store starts in Sunday with half-pages. They say Pierce is crazy mad."

"No wonder."

"The best of it is that now the Retail Union won't fight us, as a body, for taking up the Consumers' League fight. They can't very well, with their second biggest store using the 'Clarion's' columns."

McGuire Ellis, too, was feeling quite cheerful over the matter.

"It shows that you can be independent and get away with it," he declared, "if you get out an interesting enough paper. By the way, that's a hot little story 'Kitty the Cutie' turned in on the Breen girl's suicide."

"It was only attempted suicide, wasn't it?"

"The first time. She had a second trial at it day before yesterday and turned the trick. You'll find Neal's copy on your desk. I held it for you."

From out of a waiting heap of mail, proof, and manuscript, Hal selected the sheets covered with Milly Neal's neat business chirography. She had written her account briefly and with restraint, building her "story" around the girl's letter. It set forth the tragedy of a petty swindle.

The scheme was as simple as it was cruel. A concern calling itself "The Sewing Aid Association" advertised for sewing-women, offering from ten to fifteen dollars a week to workers; experience not necessary. Maggie Breen answered the advertisement. The manager explained to her that the job was making children's underclothing from pattern. She would be required to come daily to the factory and sew on a machine which she would purchase from the company, the price, thirty dollars, being reckoned as her first three weeks' wages. To all this, duly set forth in a specious contract, the girl affixed her signature.

She was set to work at once. The labor was hard, the forewoman a driver, but ten dollars a week is good pay. Hoping for a possible raise Maggie turned out more garments than any of her fellow workers. For two weeks and a half all went well. In another few days the machine would be paid for, the money would begin to come in, and Maggie would get a really square meal, which she had come to long for with a persistent and severe hankering. Then the trap was sprung. Maggie's work was found "unsatisfactory." She was summarily discharged. In vain did she protest. She would try again; she would do better. No use; "the house" found her garments unmarketable. Sorrowfully she asked for her money. No money was due her. Again she protested. The manager thrust a copy of her contract under her nose and turned her into the street. Thus the "Sewing Aid Association" had realized upon fifteen days' labor for which they had not paid one cent, and the "installment" sewing-machine was ready for its next victim. This is a very pleasant and profitable policy and is in use, in one form or another, in nearly every American city. Proof of which the sufficiently discerning eye may find in the advertising columns of many of our leading newspapers and magazines.

To Maggie Breen it was small consolation that she was but one of many.

Even her simple mind grasped the "joker" in the contract. She tore up that precious document, went home, reflected that she was rather hungry and likely to be hungrier, quite wretched and likely to be wretcheder; and so made a decoction of sulphur matches and drank it. An ambulance surgeon disobligingly arrived in time to save her life for once; but the second time she borrowed some carbolic acid, which is more expeditious than any ambulance surgeon.

This was the story which "Kitty the Cutie," while sticking close to the facts, had contrived to inform with a woman's wrath and a woman's pity. Reading it, Hal took fire. He determined to back it up with an editorial. But first he would look into the matter for himself. With this end in view he set out for Number 65 Sperry Street, where Maggie Breen's younger sister and bedridden mother lived. It was his maiden essay at reporting.

Sperry Street shocked Hal. He could not have conceived that a carefully regulated and well-kept city such as Worthington (he knew it, be it remembered, chiefly from above the wheels of an automobile) would permit such a slum to exist. On either side of the street, gaunt wooden barracks, fire-traps at a glance, reared themselves five rackety stories upward, for the length of a block. Across intersecting Grant Street the sky-line dropped a few yards, showing ragged through the metal cornice and sickly brick chimneys of a tenement row only a degree less forbidding than the first. The street itself was a mere refuse patch smeared out over bumpy cobbles. The visitor entered the tenement at 65, between reeking barrels which had waited overlong for the garbage cart.

He was received without question, as a reporter for the "Clarion." At first Sadie Breen, anæmic, hopeless-eyed, timorous, was reluctant to speak. But the mother proved Hal's ally.

"Let 'im put it in the paper," she exhorted. "Maybe it'll keep some other girl away from them sharks."

"Why didn't your sister sue the company?" asked Hal.

"Where'd we get the money for a lawyer?" whined Sadie.

"It's no use, anyway," said Mrs. Breen. "They've tried it in Municipal Court. The sharks always wins. Somebody ought to shoot that manager," she added fiercely.

"Yes; that's great to say," jeered Sadie, in a whine. "But look what happened to that Mason girl from Hoppers Hollow. She hit at him with a pair of scissors, an' they sent her up for a year."

"Better that than Cissy Green's way. You know what become of her. Went on the street," explained Mrs. Breen to Hal.

They poured out story after story of poor women entrapped by one or another of those lures which wring the final drop of blood from the bleakest poverty. In the midst of the recital there was a knock at the door, and a tall young man in black entered. He at once introduced himself to Hal as the Reverend Norman Hale, and went into conference with the two women about a place for Sadie. This being settled, Hal's mission was explained to him.

"A reporter?" said the Reverend Norman. "I wish the papers *would* take this thing up. A little publicity would kill it off, I believe."

"Won't the courts do anything?"

"They can't. I've talked to the judge. The concern's contract is water-tight."

The two young men went down together through the black hallways, and stood talking at the outer door.

"How do people live in places like this?" exclaimed Hal.

"Not very successfully. The death-rate is pretty high. Particularly of late. There's what a friend of mine around the corner—he happens to be a barkeeper, by the way—calls a lively trade in funerals around here."

"Is your church in this district?"

"My club is. People call it a mission, but I don't like the word. It's got too much the flavor of reaching down from above to dispense condescending charity."

"Charity certainly seems to be needed here."

"Help and decent fairness are needed; not charity. What's your paper, by the way?"

"The 'Clarion.'"

"Oh!" said the other, in an altered tone. "I shouldn't suppose that the 'Clarion' would go in much for any kind of reform."

"Do you read it?"

"No. But I know Dr. Surtaine."

"Dr. Surtaine doesn't own the 'Clarion.' I do."

"You're Harrington Surtaine? I thought I had seen you somewhere before. But you said you were a reporter."

"Pardon me, I didn't. Mrs. Breen said that. However, it's true; I'm doing a bit of reporting on this case. And I'm going to do some writing on it before I'm through."

"As for Dr. Surtaine—" began the young clergyman, then checked himself, pondering.

What further he might have had to say was cut off by a startling occurrence. A door on the floor above opened; there was a swift patter of feet, and then from overhead, a long-drawn, terrible cry. Immediately a young girl, her shawl drawn about her face, ran from the darkness into the half-light of the lower hall and would have passed between them but that Norman Hale caught her by the arm.

"Lemme go! Lemme go!" she shrieked, pawing at him.

"Quiet," he bade her. "What is it, Emily?"

"Oh, Mr. Hale!" she cried, recognizing him and clutching at his shoulder. "Don't let it get me!"

"Nothing's going to hurt you. Tell me about it."

"It's the Death," she shuddered.

The man's face changed. "Here?" he said. "In this block?"

"Don't you go," she besought. "Don't you go, Mr. Hale. You'll get it."

"Where is it? Answer me at once."

"First-floor front," sobbed the girl. "Mrs. Schwarz."

"Don't wait for me," said the minister to Hal. "In fact you'd better leave the place. Good-day."

Thus abruptly discarded from consideration, Hal turned to the fugitive.

"Is some one dead?"

"Not yet."

"Dying, then?"

"As good as. It's the Death," said the girl with a strong shudder.

"You said that before. What do you mean by the Death?"

"Don't keep me here talkin'," she shivered. "I wanta go home."

Hal walked along with her, wondering. "I wish you would tell me," he said gently.

"All I know is, they never get well."

"What sort of sickness is it?"

"Search me." The petty slang made a grim medium for the uncertainty of terror which it sought to express. "They've had it over in the Rookeries since winter. There ain't no name for it. They just call it the Death."

"The Rookeries?" said Hal, caught by the word. "Where are they?"

"Don't you know the Rookeries?" The girl pointed to the long double row of grisly wooden edifices down the street. "Them's Sadler's Shacks on this side, and Tammany Barracks on the other. They go all the way around the block."

"You say the sickness has been in there?"

"Yes. Now it's broken out an' we'll all get it an' die," she wailed.

A little, squat, dark man hurried past them. He nodded, but did not pause.

"I know him," said Hal. "Who is he?"

"Doc De Vito. He tends to all the cases. But it's no good. They all die."

"You keep your head," advised Hal. "Don't be scared. And wash your hands and face thoroughly as soon as you get home."

"A lot o' good that'll do against the Death," she said scornfully, and left him.

Back at the office, Hal, settling down to write his editorial, put the matter of the Rookeries temporarily out of mind, but made a note to question his father about it.

Milly Neal's article, touched up and amplified by Hal's pen, appeared the following morning. The editorial was to be a follow-up in the next day's paper. Coming down early to put the finishing touches to this, Hal found the article torn out and pasted on a sheet of paper. Across the top of the paper was written in pencil:

"*Clipped from the Clarion; a Deadly Parallel.*"

The penciled legend ran across the sheet to include, under its caption a second excerpt, also in "Clarion" print, but of the advertisement style:

WANTED—Sewing-girls for simple machine work. Experience not necessary.
$10 to $15 a week guaranteed. Apply in person at 14 Manning Street.
THE SEWING AID ASSOCIATION.

Below, in the same hand writing was the query:

"*What's your percentage of the blood-money, Mr. Harrington Surtaine?*"

Hal threw it over to Ellis. "Whose writing is that?" he asked. "It looks familiar to me."

"Max Veltman's," said Ellis. He took in the meaning of it. "The insolent whelp!" he said.

"Insolent? Yes; he's that. But the worst of it is, I'm afraid he's right." And he telephoned for Shearson.

The advertising manager came up, puffing.

Hal held out the clipping to him.

"How long has that been running?"

"On and off for six months."

"Throw it out."

"Throw it out!" repeated the other bitterly. "That's easy enough said."

"And easily enough done."

"It's out already. Taken out by early notice this morning."

"That's all right, then."

"*Is* it all right!" boomed Shearson. "*Is* it! You won't think so when you hear the rest of it."

"Try me."

"Do you know *who* the Sewing Aid Association is?"

"No."

"It's John M. Gibbs! That's who it is!"

"Yell louder, Shearson. It may save you from apoplexy," advised McGuire Ellis with tender solicitude.

"And we lose every line of the Boston Store advertising, that I worked so hard to get back."

"That'll hurt," allowed Ellis.

"Hurt! It draws blood, that does. That Sewing Aid Association is Gibbs's scheme to supply the children's department of his store. Why couldn't you find out who you were hitting, Mr. Surtaine?" demanded Shearson pathetically, "before you went and mucksed everything up this way? See what comes of all this reform guff."

"Are you sure that John M. Gibbs is back of that sewing-girl ad?"

"Sure? Didn't he call me up this morning and raise the devil?"

"Thank you, Mr. Shearson. That's all."

To his editorial galley-proof Hal added two lines.

"What's that, Mr. Surtaine?" asked the advertising manager curiously.

"That's outside of your department. But since you ask, I'll tell you. It's an editorial on the kind of swindle that causes tragedies like Maggie Breen's. And the sentence which I have just added, thanks to you, is this:

"'The proprietor of this scheme which drives penniless women to the street or to suicide is John M. Gibbs, principal owner of the Boston Store.'"

Words failed Shearson; also motive power, almost. For reckonable seconds he stood stricken. Then slowly he got under way and rolled through the door. Once, on the stairs, they heard from him a protracted rumbling groan. "Ruin," was the one distinguishable word.

It left an echo in Hal's brain, an echo which rang hollowly amongst misgivings.

"*Is* it ruin to try and run a newspaper without taking a percentage of that kind of profits, Mac?" he asked.

"Well, a newspaper can't be too squeamish about its ads." was the cautious answer.

"Do all newspapers carry that kind of stuff?"

"Not quite. Most of them, though. They need the money."

"What's the matter with business in this town? Everything seems to be rotten."

Ellis took refuge in a proverb. "Business is business," he stated succinctly.

"And it's as bad everywhere as here? This is all new to me, you know. I rather expected to find every concern as decently and humanly run as Certina."

One swift, suspicious glance Ellis cast upon his superior, but Hal's face was candor itself. "Well, no," he admitted. "Perhaps it isn't as bad in some cities. The trouble here is that all the papers are terrorized or bribed into silence. Until we began hitting out with our little shillalah, nobody had ever dared venture a peep of disapproval. So, business got to thinking it could do as it pleased. You can't really blame business much. Immunity from criticism isn't ever good for the well-known human race."

Hal took the matter of the "Sewing Aid" swindle home with him for consideration. Hitherto he had considered advertising only as it affected or influenced news. Now he began to see it in another light, as a factor in itself of immense moral moment and responsibility. It was dimly outlined to his conscience that, as a partner in the profit, he became also a partner in the enterprise. Thus he faced the question of the honesty or dishonesty of the advertising in his paper. And this is a question fraught with financial portent for the honorable journalist.

CHAPTER XXII

PATRIOTS

Worthington's Old Home Week is a gay, gaudy, and profitable institution. During the six days of its course the city habitually maintains the atmosphere of a three-ringed circus, the bustle of a county fair, and the business ethics of the Bowery. Allured by widespread advertising and encouraged by special rates on the railroads, the countryside for a radius of one hundred miles pours its inhabitants into the local metropolis, their pockets filled with greased dollars. Upon them Worthington lavishes its left-over and shelf-cluttering merchandise, at fifty per cent more than its value, amidst general rejoicings. As Festus Willard once put it, "There is a sound of revelry by night and larceny by day." But then Mr. Willard, being a manufacturer and not a retailer, lacks the subtler sympathy which makes lovely the spirit of Old Home hospitality.

This year the celebration was to outdo itself. Because of the centennial feature, no less a person than the President of the United States, who had spent a year of his boyhood at a local school, was pledged to attend. In itself this meant a record crowd. Crops had been good locally and the toil-worn agriculturist had surplus money wherewith to purchase phonographs, gold teeth, crayon enlargements of self and family, home instruction outfits for hand-painting sofa cushions, and similar prime necessities of farm life. To transform his static savings into dynamic assets for itself was Worthington's basic purpose in holding its gala week. And now this beneficent plan was threatened by one individual, and he young, inexperienced, and a new Worthingtonian, Mr. Harrington Surtaine. This unforeseen cloud upon the horizon of peace, prosperity, and happiness rose into the ken of Dr. Surtaine the day after the appearance of the sewing-girl editorial.

Dr. Surtaine hadn't liked that editorial. With his customary air of long-suffering good nature he had told Hal so over his home-made apple pie and rich milk, at the cheap and clean little luncheon place which he patronized. Hal had no defense or excuse to offer. Indeed, his reference to the topic was of the most casual order and was immediately followed by this disconcerting question:

"What about the Rookeries epidemic, Dad?"

"Epidemic? There's no epidemic, Boyee."

"Well, there's something. People are dying down there faster than they ought to. It's spread beyond the Rookeries now."

This was no news to the big doctor. But it was news to him that Hal knew it.

"How do you know?" he asked.

"I've been down there and ran right upon it."

The father's affection and alarm outleapt his caution at this. "You better keep away from there, Boyee," he warned anxiously.

"If there's no epidemic, why should I keep away?"

"There's always a lot of infection down in those tenements," said Dr. Surtaine lamely.

"Dad, when you made your report for the 'Clarion' did you tell us all you knew?"

"All except some medical technicalities," said the Doctor, who never told a lie when a half-lie would serve.

"I've just had a talk with the health officer, Dr. Merritt."

"Merritt's an alarmist."

"He's alarmed this time, certainly."

"What does he think it is?"

"It?" said Hal, a trifle maliciously. "The epidemic?"

"Epidemic's a big word. The sickness."

"How can he tell? He's had no chance to see the cases. They still mysteriously disappear before he can get to them. By the way, your Dr. De Vito seems to have a hand in that."

"Hal, I wish you'd get over your trick of seeing a mystery in everything," said his father with a mild and tempered melancholy. "It's a queer slant to your brain."

"There's a queer slant to this business of the Rookeries somewhere, but I don't think it's in my brain. Merritt says the Mayor is holding him off, and he believes that Tip O'Farrell, agent for the Rookeries, has got the Mayor's ear. He wants to force the issue by quarantining the whole locality."

"And advertise to the world that there's some sort of contagion there!" cried Dr. Surtaine in dismay.

"Well, if there is—"

"Think of Old Home Week," adjured his father.

"The whole thing would be stamped out long before then."

"But not the panic and the fear of it. Hal, I do hope you aren't going to take this up in the 'Clarion.'"

"Not at present. There isn't enough to go on. But we're going to watch, and if things get any worse I intend to do something. So much I've promised Merritt."

The result of this conversation was that Dr. Surtaine called a special meeting of the Committee on Arrangements for Old Home Week. In conformity with the laws of its genus, the committee was made up of the representative business men of the city, with a clergyman or two for compliment to the Church, and most of the newspaper owners or editors, to enlist the "services of the press."

Its chairman was thoroughly typical of the mental and ethical attitude of the committee. He felt comfortably assured that as he thought upon any question of local public import, so would they think. Nevertheless, he didn't intend to tell them all he knew. Such was not the purpose of the meeting. Its real purpose, not to put too fine a point on it, was to intimidate the newspapers, lest, if the "Clarion" broke the politic silence, others might follow; and, as a secondary step, to furnish funds for the handling of the Rookeries situation. Since Dr. Surtaine designed to reveal as little as possible to his colleagues, he naturally began his speech with the statement that he would be perfectly frank with them.

"There's more sickness than there ought to be in the Rookeries district," he proceeded. "It isn't dangerous, but it may prove obstinate. Some sort of malarious affection, apparently. Perhaps it may be necessary to do some cleaning up down there. In that case, money may be needed."

"How much?" somebody asked.

"Five thousand dollars ought to do it."

"That's a considerable sum," another pointed out.

"And this is a serious matter," retorted the chairman. "Many of us remember the disastrous effect that rumors of smallpox had on Old Home Week, some years back. We can't afford to have anything of that sort this time. An epidemic scare might ruin the whole show."

Now, an epidemic to these hard-headed business men was something that kept people away from their stores. And the rumor of an epidemic might accomplish that as thoroughly as the epidemic itself. Therefore, without questioning too far, they were quite willing to spend money to avert such disaster. The sum suggested was voted into the hands of a committee of three to be appointed by the chair.

"In the mean time," continued Dr. Surtaine, "I think we should go on record to the effect that any newspaper which shall publish or any individual who shall circulate any report calculated to inspire distrust or alarm is hostile to the best interests of the city."

"Well, what newspaper is likely to do that?" demanded Leroy Vane, of the "Banner."

"If it's any it'll be the 'Clarion,'" growled Colonel Parker, editor of the "Telegram."

"The newspaper business in this town is going to the dogs since the 'Clarion' changed hands," said Carney Ford, of the "Press," savagely. "Nobody can tell what they're going to do next over there. They're keeping the decent papers on the jump all the time, with their yellowness and scarehead muckraking."

"A big sensational story about an epidemic would be great meat for the 'Clarion,'" said Vane. "What does it care for the best interests of the town?"

"As an editor," observed Dr. Surtaine blandly, "my son don't appear to be over-popular with his confrères."

"Why should he be?" cried Parker. "He's forever publishing stuff that we've always let alone. Then the public wants to know why we don't get the news. Get it? Of course we get it. But we don't always want to print it. There's such a thing as a gentleman's understanding in the newspaper business."

"So I've heard," replied the chairman. "Well, gentlemen, the boy's young. Give him time."

"I'll give him six months, not longer, to go on the way he's been going," said John M. Gibbs, with a vicious snap of his teeth.

"Does the 'Clarion' really intend to publish anything about an epidemic?" asked Stickler, of the Hotel Stickler.

"Nothing is decided yet, so far as I know. But I may safely say that there's a probability of their getting up some kind of a sensational story."

"Can't you control your own son?" asked some one bluntly.

"Understand this, if you please, gentlemen. Over the Worthington 'Clarion' I have no control whatsoever."

"Well, there's where the danger lies," said Vane. "If the 'Clarion' comes out with a big story, the rest of us have got to publish something to save our face."

"What's to be done, then?" cried Stickler. "This means a big loss to the hotel business."

"To all of us," amended the chairman. "My suggestion is that our special committee be empowered to wait upon the editor of the 'Clarion' and talk the matter over with him."

Embodied in the form of a motion this was passed, and the chair appointed as that committee three merchants, all of whom were members of the Publication Committee of the Retail Union; and, as such, exercised the most powerful advertising control in Worthington. Dr. Surtaine still pinned his hopes to the dollar and its editorial potency.

Unofficially and privately these men invited to go with them to the "Clarion" office Elias M. Pierce, who had not been at the meeting. At first he angrily refused. He wished to meet that young whelp Surtaine nowhere but in a court of law, he announced. But after Bertram Hollenbeck, of the Emporium, the chairman of the subcommittee, had outlined his plan, Pierce took a night to think it over, and in the morning accepted the invitation with a grim smile.

Forewarned by his father, who had begged that he consider carefully and with due regard to his own future the proposals to be set before him, Hal was ready to receive the deputation in form. Pierce's presence surprised him. He greeted all four men with equally punctilious politeness, however, and gave courteous attention while Hollenbeck spoke for his colleagues. The merchant explained the purpose of the visit; set forth the importance to the city of the centennial Old Home Week, and urged the inadvisability of any sensationalism which might alarm the public.

"We have sufficient assurance that there's nothing dangerous in the present situation," he said.

"I haven't," said Hal. "If I had, there would be nothing further to be said. The 'Clarion' is not seeking to manufacture a sensation."

"What is the 'Clarion' seeking to do?" asked Stensland, another of the committee.

"Discover and print the news."

"Well, it isn't news until it's printed," Hollenbeck pointed out comfortably. "And what's the use of printing that sort of thing, anyway? It does a lot of people a lot of harm; but I don't see how it can possibly do any one any good."

"Oh, put things straight," said Stensland. "Here, Mr. Editor; you've stirred up a lot of trouble and lost a lot of advertising by it. Now, you start an epidemic scare and kill off the biggest retail business of the year, and you won't find an advertiser in town to stand by you. Is that plain?"

"Plain coercion," said Hal.

"Call it what you like," began the apostle of frankness, when Hollenbeck cut in on him.

"No use getting excited," he said. "Let's hear Mr. Surtaine's views. What do you think ought to be done about the Rookeries?"

In anticipation of some such question Hal had been in consultation with Dr. Elliot and the health officer that morning.

"Open up the Rookeries to the health authorities and to private physicians other than Dr. De Vito. Call Tip O'Farrell's blockade off. Clean out and disinfect the tenements. If necessary, quarantine every building that's suspected."

"Why, what do you think the disease is?" cried Hollenbeck, taken aback by the positiveness of Hal's speech.

"Do *you* tell *me*. You've come here to give directions."

"Something in the nature of malaria," said Hollenbeck, recovering himself. "So there's no call for extreme measures. The Old Home Week Committee will look after the cleaning-up. As for quarantine, that would be a confession. And we want to do the thing as quietly as possible."

"You've come to the wrong shop to buy quiet," said Hal mildly.

"Now listen to *me*." Elias M. Pierce sat forward in his chair and fixed his stony gaze on Hal's face. "This is what you'll do with the 'Clarion.' You'll agree here and now to print nothing about this alleged epidemic."

Hal turned upon him a silent but benign regard. The recollection of that contained smile lent an acid edge to the magnate's next speech.

"You will further promise," continued Pierce, "to quit all your muckraking of the business interests and business men of this town."

Still Hal smiled.

"And you will publish tomorrow a full retraction of the article about my daughter and an ample apology for the attack upon me."

The editorial expression did not change.

"On those conditions," Pierce concluded, "I will withdraw the criminal proceedings against you, but not the civil suit. The indictment will be handed down tomorrow."

"I'm ready for it."

"Are you ready for this? We have two unbiased witnesses—unbiased, mind you—who will swear that the accident was Miss Cleary's own fault. And—" there was the hint of an evil smile on the thin lips, as they released the final words very slowly—"and Miss Cleary's own affidavit to that effect."

For the moment the words seemed a jumble to Hal. Meaning, dire and disastrous, informed them, as he repeated them to himself. Providentially his telephone rang, giving him an excuse to go out. He hurried over to McGuire Ellis.

"I'm afraid it's right, Boss," said the associate editor, after hearing Hal's report.

"But how can it be? I saw the whole thing."

"E.M. Pierce is rich. The nurse is poor. That is, she has been poor. Lately I've had a man keeping tabs on her. Since leaving the hospital, she's moved into an expensive flat, and has splurged out into good clothes. Whence the wherewithal?"

"Bribery!"

"Without a doubt."

"Then Pierce has got us."

"It looks so," admitted Ellis sorrowfully.

"But we can't give in," groaned Hal. "It means the end of the 'Clarion.' What is there to do?"

"Play for time," advised the other. "Go back there with a stiff upper lip and tell 'em you won't be bulldozed or hurried. Then we'll have a council."

"Suppose they demand an answer."

"Refuse. See here, Hal. I know Pierce. He'd never give up his revenge, for any good he could do to the cause of the city by holding off the 'Clarion' on this Old Home Week business if there weren't something else. Pierce isn't built that way. That bargain offer is mighty suspicious. There's a weak spot in his case somewhere. Hold him off, and we'll hunt for it."

None could have guessed, from the young editor's bearing, on his return, that he knew himself to be facing a crucial situation. With the utmost nonchalance he insisted that he must have time for consideration. Influenced by Pierce, who was sure he had Hal beaten, the committee insisted on an immediate reply to their ultimatum.

"You go up against this bunch," advised Stensland, "and it's dollars to doughnuts the receiver'll have your 'Clarion' inside of six months."

Hal leaned indolently against the door. "Speaking of dollars and doughnuts," he said, "I'd like to tell you gentlemen a little story. You all know who Babson is, the biggest stock-market advertiser in the country. Well, Babson's vanity is to be a great man outside of his own line. He owns a big country place down East, near the old town of Singatuck; one of the oldest towns on the coast. Babson is as new as Singatuck is old. The people didn't care much about his patronizing ways. Nevertheless, he kept doing things to 'brace the town up,' as he put it. The town needed it. It was about bankrupt. The fire department was a joke, the waterworks a farce, and the town hall a ruin. Babson thought this gave him a chance to put his name on the map. So he said to his local factotum, 'You go down to the meeting of the selectmen next week, shake a bagful of dollars in front of those old doughnuts, and make 'em this proposition: I'll give five thousand dollars to the fire department, establish a water system, rebuild the town hall, pay off the town debt and put ten thousand dollars into the treasury if they'll change the name of the town from Singatuck to Babson.'

"The factotum went to the meeting and presented the proposition. Now Singatuck is proud of its age and character with a local pride that is quite beyond the Babson dollars or the Babson type of imagination. His proposition aroused no debate. There was a long silence. Then an old moss-farmer who hadn't had money enough to buy himself a new tooth for twenty years arose and said: 'I move you, Mister Chairman, that this body thank Mr. Babson kindly for his offer and tell him to go to hell.'

"The motion was carried unanimously, and the meeting proceeded to the consideration of other business. I cite this, gentlemen, merely as evidence that the disparity between the dollar and the doughnut isn't as great as some suppose."

The third member of the committee, who had thus far spoken no word, peered curiously at Hal from above a hooked nose. He was Mintz, of Sheffler and Mintz.

"Do I get you righd?" he observed mildly; "you're telling us to go where the selectmen sent Misder Babson."

"Plumb," replied Hal, with his most amiable expression. "So far as any immediate decision is concerned."

"Less ged oud," said Mr. Mintz to his colleagues. They got out. Mintz was last to go. He came over to Hal.

"I lyg your story," he said. "I lyg to see a feller stand up for his bizniz against the vorlt. I'm a Jew. I hope you lose—but—goot luck!"

He held out his hand. Hal took it. "Mr. Mintz, I'm glad to know you," said he earnestly.

Nothing now remained for the committee to do but to expend their allotted fund to the best purpose. Their notion of the proper method was typically commercial. They thought to buy off an epidemic. Many times this has been tried. Never yet has it succeeded. It embodies one of the most dangerous of popular hygienic fallacies, that the dollar can overtake and swallow the germ.

CHAPTER XXIII

CREEPING FLAME

For sheer uncertainty an epidemic is comparable only to fire on shipboard. The wisest expert can but guess at the time or place of its catastrophic explosion. It may thrust forth here and there a tongue of threat, only to subside and smoulder again. Sometimes it "sulks" for so protracted a period that danger seems to be over. Then, without warning, comes swift disaster with panic in its train.

But one man in all Worthington knew, early, the true nature of the disease which quietly crept among the Rookeries licking up human life, and he was well trained in keeping his own counsel. In this crisis, whatever Dr. Surtaine may have lacked in scrupulosity of method, his intentions were good. He honestly believed that he was doing well by his city in veiling the nature of the contagion. Scientifically he knew little about it save in the most general way; and his happy optimism bolstered the belief that if only secrecy could be preserved and the fair repute of the city for sound health saved, the trouble would presently die out of itself. He looked to his committee to manage the secrecy. Unfortunately this particular form of trouble hasn't the habit of dying out quietly and of itself. It has to be fought and slain in the open.

As Dr. Surtaine's committee hadn't the faintest notion of how to handle their five-thousand-dollar appropriation, they naturally consulted the Honorable Tip O'Farrell, agent for and boss of the Rookeries. And as the Honorable Tip had a very definite and even eager notion of what might be done with that amount of ready cash, he naturally volunteered to handle the fund to the best advantage, which seemed quite reasonable, since he was familiar with the situation. Therefore the disposition of the money was left to him. Do not, however, oh high-minded and honorable reader, be too ready to suppose that this was the end of the five thousand dollars, so far as the Rookeries are concerned. Politicians of the O'Farrell type may not be meticulous on points of finance. But they are quite likely to be human. Tip O'Farrell had seen recently more misery than even his toughened sensibilities could uncomplainingly endure. Some of the fund may have gone into the disburser's pocket. A much greater portion of it, I am prepared to affirm, was distributed in those intimate and effective forms of beneficence which, skillfully enough managed, almost lose the taint of charity. O'Farrell was tactful and he knew his people. Many cases over which organized philanthropy would have blundered sorely, were handled with a discretion little short of inspired. Much wretchedness was relieved; much suffering and perhaps some lives saved.

The main issue, nevertheless, was untouched. The epidemic continued to spread beneath the surface of silence. O'Farrell wasn't interested in that side of it. He didn't even know what was the matter. What money he expended on that phase of the difficulty was laid out in perfecting his system of guards, so that unauthorized doctors couldn't get in, or unauthorized news leak out. Also he continued to carry on an irregular but costly traffic in dead bodies. Meantime, the Special Committee of the Old Home Week Organization, thus comfortably relieved of responsibility and the appropriation, could now devote itself single-mindedly to worrying over the "Clarion."

According to Elias M. Pierce, no mean judge of men, there was nothing to worry about in that direction. That snake, he considered, was scotched. It might take time for said snake, who was a young snake with a head full of poison (his uncomplimentary metaphor referred, I need hardly state, to Mr. Harrington Surtaine), to come to his serpentine senses; but in the end he must realize that he was caught. The committee wasn't so smugly satisfied. Time was going on and there was no word, one way or the other, from the "Clarion" office.

Inside that office more was stirring than the head of it knew about. On a warmish day, McGuire Ellis, seated at his open window, had permitted the bland air of early June to lull him to a nap, which was rudely interrupted by the intrusion of a harsh point amongst his waistcoat buttons. Stumbling hastily to his feet he confronted Dr. Miles Elliot.

"Wassamatter?" he demanded, in the thick tones of interrupted sleep. "What are you poking me in the ribs for?"

"McBurney's point," observed the visitor agreeably. "Now, if you had appendicitis, you'd have yelped. You haven't got appendicitis."

"Much obliged," grumped Mr. Ellis. "Couldn't you tell me that without a cane?"

"I spoke to you twice, but all you replied was 'Hoong!' As I speak only the Mandarin dialect of Chinese—"

"Sit down," said Ellis, "and tell me what you're doing in this den of vice and crime."

"Vice and crime is correct," confirmed the physician. "You're still curing cancer, consumption, corns, colds, and cramps in print, for blood money. I've come to report."

McGuire Ellis stared. "What on?"

"The Rookeries epidemic."

"Quick work," the journalist congratulated him sarcastically. "The assignment is only a little over two months old."

"Well, I might have guessed, any time in those two months, but I wanted to make certain."

"*Are* you certain?"

"Reasonably."

"What is it?"

"Typhus."

"What's that? Something like typhoid?"

"It bears about the same relation to typhoid," said the Doctor, eyeing the other with solemnity, "as housemaid's knee does to sunstroke."

"Well, don't get funny with me. I don't appreciate it. Is it very serious?"

"Not more so than cholera," answered the Doctor gravely.

"Hey! Then why aren't we all dead?"

"Because it doesn't spread so rapidly. Not at first, anyway."

"How does it spread? Come on! Open up!"

"Probably by vermin. It's rare in this country. There was a small epidemic in New York in the early nineties. It was discovered early and confined to one tenement. There were sixty-three people in the tenement when they clapped on the quarantine. Thirty-two of 'em came out feet first. The only outside case was a reporter who got in and wrote a descriptive article. He died a week later."

"Sounds as if this little affair of the Rookeries might be some story."

"It is. There may have been fifty deaths to date; or maybe a hundred. We don't know."

Ellis sat back in his chair with a bump. "Who's 'we'?"

"Dr. Merritt and myself."

"The Health Bureau is on, then. What's Merritt going to do about it?"

"What can he do?"

"Give out the whole thing, and quarantine the district."

"The Mayor will remove him the instant he opens his mouth, and kill any quarantine. Merritt will be discredited in all the papers—unless the 'Clarion' backs him. Will it?"

Ellis dropped his head in his hand. "I don't know," he said finally.

"Not running an honest paper this week?" sneered the physician lightly. "By the way, where's Young Hopeful?"

"See here, Dr. Elliot," said Ellis. "You're a good old scout. If you hadn't poked me in the stomach I believe I'd tell you something."

"Try it," encouraged the other.

"All right. Here it is. They've put it up to Hal Surtaine pretty stiff, this gang of perfectly honorable business men, leading citizens, pillars of the church, porch-climbers, and pickpockets who run the city. I guess you know who I mean."

Dr. Elliot permitted himself a reserved grin.

"All right. They've got him in a clove hitch. At least it looks so. And one of the conditions for letting up on him is that he suppresses all news of the epidemic. Then they'll have the 'Clarion' right where they've got every other local paper."

"Nice town, Worthington," observed Dr. Elliot, with easy but apparently irrelevant affability.

But McGuire Ellis went red. "It's easy enough for you to sit there and be righteous," he said. "But get this straight. If the young Boss plays straight and tells 'em all to go to hell, it'll be a close call of life or death for the paper."

"And if he doesn't?"

"Easy going. Advertising'll roll in on us. Money'll come so fast we can't dodge it. Are you so blame sure what *you'd* do in those conditions?"

"Mac," said the brusque physician, for the first time using the familiar name: "between man and man, now: *what* about the boy?"

From the ancient loyalty of his race sprang McGuire Ellis's swift word, "My hand in the fire for any that loves him."

"But—stanch, do you think?" persisted the other.

"I hope it."

"Well, I wish it was you owned the 'Clarion.'"

"Do you, now? I don't. How do *I* know what I'd do?"

"Human lives, Mac: human lives, on this issue."

"Who else knows it's typhus, Doc?"

"Nobody but Merritt and me. You bound me in confidence, you know."

"Good man!"

"There's one other ought to know, though."

"Who's that?"

"Norman Hale."

"The Reverend Norman's all right. We could do with a few more ministers like him around the place. But why, in particular, should he know?"

"For one thing, he suspects, anyway. Then, he's down in the slums there most of the time, and he could help us. Besides, he's got some rights of safety himself. He's out in the reception room now, under guard of that man-eating office boy of yours."

"All right, if you say so."

Accordingly the Reverend Norman Hale was summoned, sworn to confidence, and informed. He received the news with a quiver of his long, gaunt features. "I was afraid it was something like that," he said. "What's to be done?"

"I'll tell you my plan," said Ellis, who had been doing some rapid thinking. "I'll put the best man in the office on the story, and give him a week on it if necessary. How soon is the epidemic likely to break, Doctor?"

"God knows," said the physician gravely.

"Well, we'll hurry him as much as we can. Our reporter will work independently. No one else on the staff will know what he's doing. I'll expect you two and Dr. Merritt to give him every help. I'll handle the story myself, at this end. And I'll see that it's set up in type by our foreman, whom I can trust to keep quiet. Therefore, only six people will know about it. I think we can keep the secret. Then, when I've got it all in shape, two pages of it, maybe, with all the facts, I'll pull a proof and hit the Boss right between the eyes with it. That'll fetch him, I *think*."

The others signified their approval. "But can't we do something in the mean time?" asked Dr. Elliot. "A little cleaning-up, maybe? Who owns that pest-hole?"

"Any number of people," said the clergyman. "It's very complicated, what with ground leases, agencies, and trusteeships. I dare say some of the owners don't even know that the property belongs to them."

"One of the things we might find out," said Ellis. "Might be interesting to publish."

"I'll send you a full statement of what I got about the burials in Canadaga County," promised Dr. Elliot. "Coming along, Mr. Hale?"

"No. I want to speak to Mr. Ellis about another matter." The clergyman waited until the physician had left and then said, "It's about Milly Neal."

"Well, what about her?"

"I thought you could tell me. Or perhaps Mr. Surtaine."

Remembering that encounter outside of the road house weeks before, Ellis experienced a throb of misgiving.

"Why Mr. Surtaine?" he demanded.

"Because he's her employer."

Ellis gazed hard at the young minister. He met a straight and clear regard which reassured him.

"He isn't, now," said he.

"She's left?"

"Yes."

"That's bad," worried the clergyman, half to himself.

"Bad for the paper. 'Kitty the Cutie' was a feature."

"Why did she leave?"

"Just quit. Sent in word about ten days ago that she was through. No explanation."

"Mr. Ellis, I'm interested in Milly Neal," said the minister, after some hesitation. "She's helped me quite a bit with our club down here. There's a lot in that girl. But there's a queer, un-get-at-able streak, too. Do you know a man named Veltman?"

"Max? Yes. He's foreman of our composing-room."

"She's been with him a great deal lately."

"Why not? They're old friends. No harm in Veltman."

"He's a married man."

"That so! I never knew that. Well, 'Kitty the Cutie' ought to be keen enough to take care of herself."

"There's the difficulty. She doesn't seem to want to take care of herself. She's lost interest in the club. For a time she was drinking heavily at some of the all-night places. And this news of her quitting here is worst of all. She seemed so enthusiastic about the work."

"Her job's open for her if she wants to come back."

"Good! I'm glad to hear that. It gives me something to work on."

"By the way," said McGuire Ellis, "how do you like the paper?" Sooner or later he put this question to every one with whom he came in contact. What he found out in this way helped to make him the journalistic expert he was.

"Pretty well," hesitated the other.

"What's wrong with it?" inquired Ellis.

"Well, frankly, some of your advertising."

"We're the most independent paper in this town on advertising," stated Ellis with conviction.

"I know you dropped the Sewing Aid Society advertisement," admitted Hale. "But you've got others as bad. Yes, worse."

"Show 'em to me."

Leaning forward to the paper on Ellis's desk, the visitor indicated the "copy" of Relief Pills. Ellis's brow puckered.

"You're the second man to kick on that," he said. "The other was a doctor."

"It's a bad business, Mr. Ellis. It's the devil's own work. Isn't it hard enough for girls to keep straight, with all the temptations around them, without promising them immunity from the natural results of immorality?"

"Those pills won't do the trick," blurted Ellis.

"They won't?" cried the other in surprise.

"So doctors tell me."

"Then the promise is all the worse," said the clergyman hotly, "for being a lie."

"Well, I have troubles enough over the news part of the paper, without censoring the ads. When an advertiser tries to control news or editorial policy, I step in. Otherwise, I keep out. There's my platform."

Hale nodded. "Let me know how I can help on the epidemic matter," said he, and took his leave.

"The trouble with really good people," mused McGuire Ellis, "is that they always expect other people to be as good as they are. And *that's* expensive," sighed the philosopher, turning back to his desk.

While Ellis and his specially detailed reporter were working out the story of the Rookeries epidemic in the light of Dr. Elliot's information, Hal Surtaine, floundering blindly, sought a solution to his problem, which was the problem of his newspaper. Indeed, it meant, as far as he could judge, the end of the "Clarion" in a few months, should he decide to defy Elias M. Pierce. Against the testimony of the injured nurse, he could scarcely hope to defend the libel suits successfully. Even though the assessed damages were not heavy enough to wreck him, the loss of prestige incident to defeat would be disastrous. Moreover, there was the chance of imprisonment or a heavy fine on the criminal charge. Furthermore, if he decided to print the account of the epidemic (always supposing that he could discover what it really was), practically every local advertiser would desert him in high dudgeon over the consequent ruin of the centennial celebration. Was it better to publish an honest paper for the few months and die fighting, or compromise for the sake of life, and do what good he might through the agency of a bound, controlled, and tremulous journalistic policy?

For the first time, now that the crisis was upon him, he realized to the full how profoundly the "Clarion" had become part of his life. At the outset, only the tool of a casual though fascinating profession, later, the lever of an expanding and increasing power, the paper had insensibly intertwined with every fiber of his ambition. To a degree that startled him he had come to think, feel, and hope in terms of this thought-machine which he owned, which owned him. It had taken on for him a character; his own, yet more than his own and greater. For it spoke, not of his spirit alone, but with a composite voice; sometimes confused, inarticulate, only semi-expressive; again as with the tongues of prophecy. His ship was beginning to find herself; to evolve, from the anarchic clamor of loose effort, a harmony and a personality.

With the thought came a warm glow of loyalty to his fellow workers; to the men who, knowing more than he knew, had yet accepted his ideals so eagerly and stood to them so loyally; to the spirit that had flashed to meet his own at that first "Talk-It-Over" breakfast, and had never since flagged; to Ellis, the harsh, dogged, uncouth evangel, preaching his strange mission of honor; to Wayne, patient, silent, laborious, dependable; to young Denton, a "gentleman unafraid," facing the threats of E.M. Pierce; even to portly Shearson, struggling against such dismal odds for *his* poor little principle of journalism—to make the paper pay. How could he, their leader, recant his doctrine before these men?

Yet—and the qualifying thought dashed cold upon his enthusiasm—what did the alternative imply for them? The almost certain loss of their places. To be thrown into the street, a whole officeful of them, seeking jobs which didn't exist, on the collapse of the "Clarion." Could he do that to them? Did he not, at least, owe them a living? Some had come to the "Clarion" from other papers, even from other cities, attracted by its enterprise, by its "ginger," by the rumor of a fresh and higher standard in journalism. What of them? For himself he had only reputation, ethical standard, the intangible matter of existence to consider. For them it might be hunger and want. Here, indeed, was a conflicting ideal.

His mind reverted to the things he had been able to get done, in the few months of his editorial tenure; the success of some of his campaigns, the educational effect of them even where they had failed of their definite object, as had the fight for the Consumers' League. One article had put the chief gambler of the city on the defensive to an extent which seriously crippled his business. Another had killed forever the vilest den in town, a saloon back-room where vicious women gathered in young boys and taught them to snuff cocaine, and had led to an anti-cocaine ordinance, which the saloon element, who instinctively resented any species of "reform" as a threat against business, opposed. Whereupon, Hal, in an editorial on the prohibition movement, had tartly pointed out that where the saloons were openly vaunting themselves disdainful of public decency, the public was in immediate process of wiping out the saloons. Which citation of fact caused a cold chill to permeate the spines of the liquor interests, and led the large, sleek leader of that clan to make a surpassingly polite and friendly call upon Hal, who, rather to his surprise, found that he liked the man very much. They had parted, indeed, on hearty terms and the understanding that there would be no further objection to the "coke-law" from the saloon keepers. There wasn't. The liquor men kept faith.

Though aiming at independence in politics, the "Clarion" had been drawn into a number of local political fights, and more than once had gone wrong in advocating an apparently useful measure only to find itself serving some hidden politician's selfish ends. These same politicians, Hal came in time to learn, were not all bad, even the worst of them. The toughest and crookedest of the grafting aldermen felt a genuine interest and pride in his vice-sodden ward, and when the "Clarion" had helped to abate a notorious nuisance there, dropped in to see the editor.

"Mr. Surtaine," said he, chewing his cigar with some violence, "you and me ain't got much in common. You think I'm a grafter, and I think you're a lily-finger. But I came to thank you just the same for helping us out over there."

"Glad to help you out when I can," said Hal, with his disarming smile: "or to fight you when I have to."

"Shake," said the heeler. "I guess we'll average down into pretty good enemies. Lemme know whenever I can do you a turn."

Then there was the electric light fight. Since the memory of man Worthington had paid the most exorbitant gas rate in the State. The "Clarion" set out to inquire why. So insistent was its thirst for information that the "Banner" and the "Telegram" took up the cudgels for the public-spirited corporation which paid ten per cent dividends by overcharging the local public. Thereupon the "Clarion" pointed out that the president of the gas company was the second largest stockholder in the "Telegram," and that the local editorial writer of the "Banner" derived, for some unexplained reason, a small but steady income in the form of salary, from the gas company. This exposure was regarded as distinctly "not clubby" by the newspaper fraternity in general: but the public rather enjoyed it, and made such a fuss over it that a legislative investigation was ordered. Meantime, by one of those curious by-products of the journalistic output, the local university preserved to itself the services of its popular professor of political economy, who was about to be discharged for *lèse majesté*, in that he had held up as an unsavory instance of corporate control, the Worthington Gas Company, several of whose considerable stockholders were members of the institution's board of trustees. The "Clarion" made loud and lamentable noises about this, and the board reconsidered hastily. Louder and much more lamentable were the noises made by the president of the university, the Reverend Dr. Knight, a little brother of one of the richest and greatest of the national corporations, in denunciation of the "Clarion": so much so, indeed, that they were published abroad, thereby giving the paper much extensive free advertising.

Pleasant memories, these, to Hal. Not always pleasant, perhaps, but at least vividly interesting, the widely varying types with whom his profession had brought him into contact: McGuire Ellis, "Tip" O'Farrell, the Reverend Norman Hale, Dr. Merritt, Elias M.—

The mechanism of thought checked with a wrench. Pierce had it in his power to put an end to all this. He must purchase the right to continue, and at Pierce's own price. But was the price so severe? After all, he could contrive to do much; to carry on many of his causes; to help build up a better and cleaner Worthington; to preserve a moiety of his power, at the sacrifice of part of his independence; and at the same time his paper would make money, be successful, take its place among the recognized business enterprises of the town. As for the Rookeries epidemic upon which all this turned, what did he really know of it, anyway? Very likely it had been exaggerated. Probably it would die out of itself. If lives were endangered, that was the common chance of a slum.

Then, of a sudden, memory struck at his heart with the thrust of a more vital, more personal, dread. For one day, wandering about in the stricken territory, he had seen Esmé Elliot entering a tenement doorway.

CHAPTER XXIV
A FAILURE IN TACTICS

Miss Eleanor Stanley Maxwell Elliot, home from her wanderings, stretched her hammock and herself in it between two trees in a rose-sweet nook at Greenvale, and gave herself up to a reckoning of assets and liabilities. Decidedly the balance was on the wrong side. Miss Esmé could not dodge the unseemly conclusion that she was far from pleased with herself. This was perhaps a salutary frame of mind, but not a pleasant one. If possible, she was even less pleased with the world in which she lived. And this was neither salutary nor pleasant. Furthermore, it was unique in her experience. Hitherto she had been accustomed to a universe made to her order and conducted on much the same principle. Now it no longer ran with oiled smoothness.

Her trip on the Pierce yacht had been much less restful than she had anticipated. For this she blamed that sturdy knight of the law, Mr. William Douglas. Mr. Douglas's offense was that he had inveigled her into an engagement. (I am employing her own term descriptive of the transaction.) It was a crime of brief duration and swift penalty. The relation had endured just four weeks. Possibly its tenure of life might have been longer had not the young-middle-aged lawyer accepted, quite naturally, an invitation to join the cruise of the Pierce family and *his fiancée*. The lawyer's super-respectful attitude toward his principal client disgusted Esmé. She called it servile.

For contrast she had the memory of another who had not been servile, even to his dearest hope. There were more personal contrasts of memory, too; subtler, more poignant, that flushed in her blood and made the mere presence of her lover repellent to her. The status became unbearable. Esmé ended it. In plain English, she jilted the highly eligible Mr. William Douglas. To herself she made the defense that he was not what she had thought, that he had changed. This was unjust. He had not changed in the least; he probably never would change from being the private-secretary type of lawyer. Toward her, in his time of trial, he behaved not ill. Justifiably, he protested against her decision. Finding her immovable, he accepted the prevailing Worthingtonian theory of Miss Elliot's royal prerogative as regards the male sex, and returned, miserably enough, to his home and his practice.

Another difficulty had arisen to make distasteful the Pierce hospitality. Kathleen Pierce, in a fit of depression foreign to her usually blithe and easy-going nature, had become confidential and had blurted out certain truths which threw a new and, to Esmé, disconcerting light upon the episode of the motor accident. In her first appeal to Esmé, it now appeared, the girl had been decidedly less than frank. Therefore, in her own judgment of Hal and the "Clarion," Esmé had been decidedly less than just. In her resentment, Esmé had almost quarreled with her friend. Common honesty, she pointed out, required a statement to Harrington Surtaine upon the point. Would Kathleen write such a letter? No! Kathleen would not. In fact, Kathleen would be d-a-m-n-e-d, darned, if she would. Very well; then it remained only (this rather loftily) for Esmé herself to explain to Mr.

Surtaine. Later, she decided to explain by word of mouth. This would involve her return to Worthington, which she had come to long for. She had become sensible of a species of homesickness.

In some ill-defined way Harrington Surtaine was involved in that nostalgia. Not that she had any desire to see him! But she felt a certain justifiable curiosity—she was satisfied that it was justifiable—to know what he was doing with the "Clarion," since her established sphere of influence had ceased to be influential. Was he really as unyielding in other tests of principle as he had shown himself with her? Already she had altered her attitude to the extent of admitting that it *was* principle, even though mistaken. Esmé had been subscribing to the "Clarion," and studying it; also she had written, withal rather guardedly, to sundry people who might throw light on the subject; to her uncle, to Dr. Hugh Merritt, her old and loyal friend largely by virtue of being one of the few young men of the place who never had been in love with her (he had other preoccupations), to young Denton the reporter, who was a sort of cousin, and to Mrs. Festus Willard, who, alone of the correspondents, suspected the underlying motive. From these sundry informants she garnered diverse opinions; the sum and substance of which was that, on the whole, Hal was fighting the good fight and with some success. Thereupon Esmé hated him harder than before—and with considerably more difficulty.

On a late May day she had slipped quietly back into Worthington. That small portion of the populace which constituted Worthington society was ready to welcome her joyously. But she had no wish to be joyously welcomed. She didn't feel particularly joyous, herself. And society meant going to places where she would undoubtedly meet Will Douglas and would probably not meet Hal Surtaine. Esmé confessed to herself that Douglas was rather on her conscience, a fact which, in itself, marked some change of nature in the Great American Pumess. She decided that society was a bore. For refuge she turned to her interest in the slums, where the Reverend Norman Hale, for whom she had a healthy, honest respect and liking, was, so she learned, finding his hands rather more than full. Always an enthusiast in her pursuits, she now threw herself into this to the total exclusion of all other interests.

To herself she explained this on the theory that she needed something to occupy her mind. Something *else* she really meant, for Mr. Harrington Surtaine was now occupying it to an inexcusable extent. She wished very much to see Harrington Surtaine, and, for the first time in her life, she feared what she wished. What she had so loftily announced to Kathleen Pierce as her unalterable determination toward the editor of the "Clarion" wasn't as easy to perform as to promise. Yet, the explanation of the partial error, into which the self-excusatory Miss Pierce had led her, was certainly due him, according to her notions of fair play. If she sent for him to come, he would, she shrewdly judged, decline. The alternative was to beard him in his office. In the strengthening and self-revealing solitude of her garden, this glowing summer day, Esmé sat trying to make up her mind. A daring brown thrasher, his wings a fair match for the ruddy-golden glow in the girl's eyes, hopped into her haunt, and twittered his counsel of courage.

"I'll do it NOW," said Esmé, and the bird, with a triumphant chirp of congratulation, swooped off to tell the news to the world of wings and flowers.

To the consequent interview there was no witness. So it may best be chronicled in the report made by the interviewer to her friend Mrs. Festus Willard, who, in the cool seclusion of her sewing-room, was overwhelmed by a rush of Esmé to the heart, as she put it. Not having been apprised of Miss Elliot's conflicting emotions since her departure, Mrs. Willard's mind was as a page blank for impressions when her visitor burst in upon her, pirouetted around the room, appropriated the softest corner of the divan, and announced spiritedly:

"You needn't ask me where I've been, for I won't tell you; or what I've been doing, for it's my own affair; anyway, you wouldn't be interested. And if you insist on knowing, I've been revisiting the pale glimpses of the moon—at three o'clock P.M."

"What do you mean, moon?" inquired Mrs. Willard, unconsciously falling into a pit of slang.

"The moon we all cry for and don't get. In this case a haughty young editor."

"You've been to see Hal Surtaine," deduced Mrs. Willard.

"You have guessed it—with considerable aid and assistance."

"What for?"

"On a matter of journalistic import," said Miss Elliot solemnly.

"But you don't cry for Hal Surtaine," objected her friend, reverting to the lunar metaphor.

"Don't I? I'd have cried—I'd have burst into a perfect storm of tears—for him—or you—or anybody who so much as pointed a finger at me, I was so scared."

"Scared? You! I don't believe it."

"I don't believe it myself—now," confessed Esmé, candidly. "But it felt most extremely like it at the time."

"You know I don't at all approve of—"

"Of me. I know you don't, Jinny. Neither does he."

"What did you do to him?"

"Me? I cooed at him like a dove of peace.

"But he was very stiff and proud He said, 'You needn't talk so loud,'" chanted Miss Esmé mellifluously.

"He didn't!"

"Well, if he didn't, he meant it. He wanted to know what the big, big D-e-v, dev, I was doing there, anyway."

"Norrie Elliot! Tell me the truth."

"Very well," said Miss Elliot, aggrieved. "*You* report the conversation, then, since you won't accept my version."

"If you would give me a start—"

"Just what he wouldn't do for me," interrupted Esmé. "I went in there to explain something and he pointed the finger of scorn at me and accused me of frequenting low and disreputable localities."

"Norrie!"

"Well," replied the girl brazenly, "he said he'd seen me about the Rookeries district; and if that isn't a low—"

"Had he?"

"Nothing more probable, though I didn't happen to see him there."

"What were you doing there?"

"Precisely what he wanted to know. He said it rather as if he owned the place. So I explained in words of one syllable that I went there to pick edelweiss from the fire escapes. Jinny, dear, you don't know how hard it is to crowd 'edelweiss' into one syllable until you've tried. It splutters."

"So do you," said the indignant Mrs. Willard. "You do worse; you gibber. If you weren't just the prettiest thing that Heaven ever made, some one would have slain you long ago for your sins."

"Pretty, yourself," retorted Esmé. "My real charm lies in my rigid adherence to the spirit of truth. Your young friend Mr. Surtaine scorned my floral jest. He indicated that I ought not to be about the tenements. He said there was a great deal of sickness there. That was why I was there, I explained politely. Then he said that the sickness might be contagious, and he muttered something about an epidemic and then looked as if he wished he hadn't."

"I've heard some talk of sickness in the Rookeries. Ought you to be going there?" asked the other anxiously.

"Mr. Surtaine thinks not. Quite severely. And in elderly tones. Naturally I asked him what kind of an epidemic it was. He said he didn't know, but he was sure the place was dangerous, and he was surprised that Uncle Guardy hadn't warned me. Uncle Guardy *had*, but I don't do everything I'm warned about. So then I asked young Mr. Editor why, as he knew there was a dangerous epidemic about, he should warn little me privately instead of warning the big public, publicly."

"Meddlesome child! Can you never learn to keep your hands off?"

"I was spurring him to his editorial duties."

"But he was very proud and stiff ... He said that he would tell me, if—"

lilted Miss Esmé, rising to do a *pas seul* upon the Willards' priceless Anatolian rug.

"Sit down," commanded her hostess. "If—what?"

"If nothing. Just if. That's the end of the song. Don't you know your Lewis Carroll?

"I sent a message to the fish, I told them, 'This is what I wish.' The little fishes of the sea, They sent an answer—"

"I don't want to know about the fish," disclaimed Mrs. Willard vehemently. "I want to know what happened between you and Hal Surtaine."

"And you the Vice-President of the Poetry Club!" reproached Esmé. "Very well. He was very proud and—Oh, I said that before. But he really was, this time. He said, 'Our last discussion of the policy of the "Clarion" closed that topic between us.' Somebody called him away before I could think of anything mean and superior enough to answer, and when he came back—always supposing he isn't still hiding in the cellar—I was no longer present."

"Then you didn't give him the message you went for."

"No. Didn't I say I was scared?"

Mrs. Willard excused herself, ostensibly to speak to a maid; in reality to speak to a telephone. On her return she made a frontal attack:—

"Norrie, what made you break your engagement to Will Douglas?"

"Why? Don't you approve?"

"Did you break it for the same reason that drove you into it?"

"What reason do you think drove me into it?"

"Hal Surtaine."

"He didn't!" she denied furiously.

"And you didn't break it because of him?"

"No! I broke it because I don't want to get married," cried the girl in a rush of words. "Not to Will Douglas. Or to—to anybody. Why should I? I don't want to—I won't," she continued, half laughing, half sobbing, "go and have to bother about running a house and have a lot of babies and lose my pretty figure—and get fat—and dowdy—and slow-poky—and old. Look at Molly Vane: twins already. She's a horrible example. Why do people always have to have children—"

She stopped, abruptly, herself stricken at the stricken look in the other's face. "Oh, Jinny, darling Jinny," she gasped; "I forgot! Your baby. Your little, dead baby! I'm a fool; a poor little silly fool, chattering of realities that I know nothing about."

"You will know some day, my dear," said the other woman, smiling valiantly. "Don't deny the greatest reality of all, when it comes. Are you sure you're not denying it now?"

The sunbeams crept and sparkled, like light upon ruffled waters, across Esmé's obstinately shaken head.

"Perhaps you couldn't help hurting him. But be sure you aren't hurting yourself, too."

"That's the worst of it," said the girl, with one of her sudden accesses of sweet candor. "I needn't have hurt him at all. I was stupid." She paused in her revelation. "But he was stupider," she declared vindictively; "so it serves him right."

"How was he stupider?"

"He thought," said Esmé with sorrowful solemnity, "that I was just as bad as I seemed. He ought to have known me better."

The older woman bent and laid a cheek against the sunny hair. "And weren't you just as bad as you seemed?"

"Worse! Anyway, I'm afraid so," said the confessional voice, rather muffled in tone. "But I—I just got led into it. Oh, Jinny, I'm not awfully happy."

Mrs. Willard's head went up and she cocked an attentive ear, like an expectant robin. "Some one outside," said she. "I'll be back in a moment. You sit there and think it over."

Esmé curled back on the divan. A minute later she heard the curtains part at the end of the dim room, and glanced up with a smile, to face, not Jeannette Willard, but Hal Surtaine.

"You 'phoned for me, Lady Jinny," he began: and then, with a start, "Esmé! I—I didn't expect to find you here."

"Nor I to see you," she said, with a calmness that belied her beating heart. "Sit down, please. I have something to tell you. It's what I really came to the office to say."

"Yes?"

"About Kathleen Pierce."

Hal frowned. "Do you think there can be any use—"

"Please," she begged, with uplifted eyes of entreaty. "She—she didn't tell me the truth about that interview with your reporter. It was true; but she made me think it wasn't. She confessed to me, and she feels very badly. So do I. I believed that you had deliberately made that up, about her saying that she didn't turn back because she wanted to catch a train. I believed, too, that the editorial was written after our—our talk. I'm sorry."

Hal stood above her, looking rather stern, and a little old and worn, she thought.

"If that is an apology, it is accepted," he said with surface politeness.

To him she was, in that moment, a light-minded woman apologizing for the petty misdeed, and paying no heed to the graver wrong that she had done him. Jeannette Willard could have set him right in a word; could have shown him what the girl felt, unavowedly to herself but with underlying conviction, that for so great an offense no apology could suffice; nothing short of complete surrender. But Mrs. Willard was not there to help out. She was waiting hopefully, outside.

"And that is all?" he said, after a pause, with just a shade of contempt in his voice.

"All," she said lightly, "unless you choose to tell me how the 'Clarion' is getting on."

"As well as could be expected. We pay high for our principles. But thus far we've held to them. You should read the paper."

"I do."

"To expect your approval would be too much, I suppose."

"No. In many ways I like it. In fact, I think I'll renew my subscription."

It was innocently said, without thought of the old playful bargain between them, which had terminated with the mailing of the withered arbutus. But to Hal it seemed merely a brazen essay in coquetry; an attempt to reconstitute the former relation, for her amusement.

"The subscription lists are closed, on the old terms," he said crisply.

"Oh, you couldn't have thought I meant that!" she whispered; but he was already halfway down the room, on the echo of his "Good-afternoon, Miss Elliot."

As before, he turned at the door. And he carried with him, to muse over in the depths of his outraged heart once more, the mystery of that still and desperate smile. Any woman could have solved it for him. Any, except, possibly, Esmé Elliot.

"It didn't come out as I hoped, Festus," said the sorrowful little Mrs. Willard to her husband that evening. "I don't know that Hal will ever believe in her again. How can he be so—so stupidly unforgiving!"

"Always the man's fault, of course," said her big husband comfortably.

"No. She's to blame. But it's the fault of men in general that Norrie is what she is; the men of this town, I mean. No man has ever been a man with Norrie Elliot."

"What have they been?"

"Mice. It's a tradition of the place. They lie down in rows for her to trample on. So of course she tramples on them."

"Well, I never trampled on mice myself," observed Festus Willard. "It sounds like uncertain footing. But I'll bet you five pounds of your favorite candy against one of your very best kisses, that if she undertakes to make a footpath of Hal Surtaine she'll get her feet hurt."

"Or her heart," said his wife. "And, oh, Festus dear, it's such a real, warm, dear heart, under all the spoiled-childness of her."

CHAPTER XXV

STERN LOGIC

Between Dr. Surtaine and his son had risen a barrier built up of reticences. At the outset of their reunion, they had chattered like a pair of schoolboy friends, who, after long separation, must rehearse to each other the whole roster of experiences. The Doctor was an enthusiast of speech, glowingly loquacious above knife and fork, and the dinner hours were enlivened for his son by his fund of far-gathered business incidents and adventures, pointed with his crude but apt philosophy, and irradiated with his centripetal optimism. He possessed and was conscious of this prime virtue of talk, that he was never tiresome. Yet recently he had noted a restlessness verging to actual distaste on Hal's part, whenever he turned the conversation upon his favorite topic, the greatness of Certina and the commercial romance of the proprietary medicine business.

In his one close fellowship, the old quack cultivated even the minor and finer virtues. With Hal he was scrupulously tactful. If the boy found *his* business an irksome subject, he would talk about the boy's business. And he did, sounding the Pæan of Policy across the Surtaine mahogany in a hundred variations supported by a thousand instances. But here, also, Hal grew restive. He responded no more willingly to leads on journalism than to encomiums of Certina. Again the affectionate diplomat changed his ground. He dropped into the lighter personalities; chatted to Hal of his new friends, and was met halfway. But in secret he puzzled and grieved over the waning of frankness and freedom in their intercourse. Dinner, once eagerly looked forward to by both as the best hour of the day, was now something of an ordeal, a contact in which each must move warily, lest, all unknowing, he bruise the other.

Of the underlying truth of the situation Dr. Surtaine had no inkling. Had any one told him that his son dared neither speak nor hear unreservedly, lest the gathering suspicions about his father, against which he was fighting while denying to himself their very existence, should take form and substance of unescapable facts, the Doctor would have failed utterly of comprehension. He ascribed Hal's unease and preoccupation to a more definite cause. Sedulous in everything which concerned his "Boyee," he had learned something of the affair with Esmé Elliot, and had surmised distressfully how hard the blow had been: but what worried him much more were rumors connecting Hal's name with Milly Neal. Several people had seen the two on the day of the road-house adventure. Milly, with her vivid femininity was a natural mark for gossip. The mere fact that she had been in Hal's runabout was enough to set tongues wagging. Then, sometime thereafter, she had resigned her position in the "Clarion" office without giving any reason, so Dr. Surtaine understood. The whole matter looked ugly. Not that the charlatan would have been particularly shocked had Hal exhibited a certain laxity of morals in the matter of women. For this sort of offense Dr. Surtaine had an easy toleration, so long as it was kept decently under cover. But that his son should become entangled with one of his—Dr. Surtaine's—employees, a woman under the protection of his roof, even though it were but the factory roof—that, indeed, would be a shock to his feudal conception of business honor.

Such dismal considerations the Doctor had suppressed during an unusually uncomfortable dinner, on a hot and thunder-breeding evening when both of the Surtaines had painfully talked against time. Immediately after the meal, Hal, on pretext of beating the storm to the office, left. His father took his forebodings to the club and attempted to lose them along with several rubbers of absent-minded bridge. Meantime the woman for whom his loyalty was concerned as well as for his son, was stimulating a resolution with the slow poison of liquor around the corner from the "Clarion" office.

Nine P.M. is slack tide in a morning newspaper office. The afternoon news is cleared up; the night wires have not yet begun to buzz with outer-world tidings of importance; the reporters are still afield on the evening's assignments. As the champion short-distance sleeper of his craft, which distinction he claimed for himself without fear of successful contradiction, McGuire Ellis was wont to devote half an hour or more, beginning on the ninth stroke of the clock, to the cultivation of Morpheus. Intruders were not popular at that hour.

To respect for this habitude, Reginald Currier, known to mortals as Bim, Guardian of the Sacred Gates, had been rigorously educated. But Bim had a creed of his own which mollified the rigidity of specific standards, and one tenet thereof was the apothegm, "Once a 'Clarion' man, always a 'Clarion' man," the same applying to women. Therefore, when Milly Neal appeared at the gate at 9.05 in the evening, the Cerberus greeted her professionally with a "How goes it, Miss Cutie?" and passed her in without question. She went straight to the inner office.

"Hoong!" grunted McGuire Ellis, rubbing his eyes in a desperate endeavor to disentangle dreams from actualities. "What are *you* doing here?"

"I want to see Mr. Surtaine."

Something in the girl's aspect put Ellis on his guard. "What do you want to see him about?" he asked.

"I don't see any Examination Bureau license pinned to you, Ellis," she retorted hardily.

"The Boss is out."

"I don't believe it."

"All right," said McGuire Ellis equably. "I'm a liar."

"Then you're the proper man for a 'Clarion' job," came the savage retort.

"Come off, Kitty. Don't be young!"

"I want to see Hal Surtaine," she said with sullen insistence.

Shaking himself out of his chair, the associate editor started across the room to the telephone at Hal's desk, but halted sharply in front of the girl.

"You've been drinking," he said.

"What's it to you if I have?"

The man's hand fell on her shoulder. There was no familiarity in the act; only comradeship. Comradeship in the voice, also, and concern, as he said, "Cut it, Neal, cut it. There's nothing in it. You're too good stuff to throw yourself away on that."

"Don't you worry about me." She shook off his hand, and seated herself.

"Still working at the Certina joint?"

"No. I'm not working."

"See here, Neal: what made you quit us?"

The girl withheld speech back of tight-pressed lips.

"Oh, well, never mind that. The point is, we miss you. We miss the 'Cutie' column. It was good stuff. We want you back."

Still silence.

"And I guess you miss us. You liked the job, didn't you?"

The girl gazed past him with ashen eyes. "Oh, my God!" she said under her breath.

"Your job back and no questions asked," pursued Ellis, with an outer cheerfulness which cost him no small effort in the face of his growing conviction of some tragic issue pending.

Now she looked directly at him, and there was a flicker of flame in her regard.

"Do you know what a Hardscrabbler is, Ellis?" she asked.

The other rubbed his head in puzzlement. "I don't believe I do," he confessed.

"Then you won't understand when I tell you that I'm one and that I'd see your 'Clarion' blazing in hell before I'd take another cent of your money." The fire died from her face, and in her former tone of dulled stolidity she repeated, "I want to see Mr. Surtaine."

With every word uttered, McGuire Ellis's forebodings had grown darker. That Hal Surtaine, carried away by the girl's vividness and allure, might have involved himself in a *liaison* with her was credible enough. He recalled the episode of the road-house, on that stormy spring day. That Hal would have deserted her afterward, Ellis could not believe. And yet—and yet—why otherwise should she come with the marks of fierce misery in her face, demanding an interview at this time? On one point Ellis's mind was swiftly made up: she should not see Hal.

"Miss Neal," he said quietly, "you can sit there all night, but you can't see the Boss unless you tell me your errand."

The girl rose, slowly. "Oh, I guess you all stand together here," she said. "Well, remember: I gave him his chance to square himself."

When Hal came up from a visit to the new press half an hour later, Ellis had decided to say nothing of the call. Later, he must have it out with his employer, for the sake of both of them and of the "Clarion." But it was an ordeal which he was glad to postpone. Nothing more, he judged, was to be feared that night, from Milly Neal; he could safely sleep over the problem. Having a certain sufficient religion of his own, McGuire Ellis still believes that a merciful Heaven forgives us our sins; but, looking back on that evening's decision, he sometimes wonders whether it ever fully pardons our mistakes.

While he sat reading proof on the status of a flickering foreign war, the Hardscrabbler's daughter, in a quiet back room farther down the block, slowly sipped more gin; and gin is fire and fury to the Hardscrabbler blood.

At eleven o'clock that evening, Dr. Surtaine, returning to that massive hybrid of architecture which he called home, found Milly Neal waiting in his study.

"Well, Milly: what's up?" he asked, cheerfully enough in tone, but with a sinking heart.

"I want to know what you're going to do for me?"

"Something wrong?"

"You've got a right to know. I'm in trouble."

"What kind of trouble?"

"The kind you make money out of with your Relief Pills."

"Milly! Milly!" cried the quack, in honest distress. "I wouldn't have believed it of you."

"Yes: it's terrible, isn't it!" mocked the girl. "What are you going to do about it? It's up to you."

"Up to me?" queried the Doctor, bracing himself for what was coming.

"Don't you promise, with your Relief Pills to get women out of trouble?"

Dr. Surtaine's breath came a little easier. Perhaps she was not going to force the issue upon him by mentioning Hal. If this were diplomacy, he would play the game.

"Certainly not! Certainly not!" he protested with a scandalized air. "We've never made such a claim. It would be against the law."

"Look at this." She held up in her left hand a clipping, showing a line-cut of a smiling woman, over the caption "A Happy Lady"; and announcing in wide print, "Every form of suppression relieved. The most obstinate cases yield at once. Thousands of once desperate women bless the name of Relief Pills."

"I don't want to look at it," said the Doctor.

"No, I guess you don't! It's from the 'Clarion,' that clipping. And the Never-fail Company that makes the fake abortion pills is *you*."

"It doesn't mean—that. You've misread it."

"It *does* mean just that to every poor, silly fool of a girl that reads it. What else can it mean? 'The most obstinate cases'—"

"Don't! Don't!" There was a pause, then:

"Of course, you can't stay in the Certina factory after this."

A bitter access of mirth seized the girl. The sound of it

"rang cracked and thin, Like a fiend's laughter, heard in Hell, Far down."

"Of course!" she mocked. "The pious and holy Dr. Surtaine couldn't have an employee who went wrong. Not even though it was his lies that helped tempt her."

"Don't try to put it off on me. You are suffering for your own sin, my girl," accused the quack.

"I'll stand my share of it; the suffering and the disgrace, if there is any. But you've got to stand your share. You promised to get me out of this and I believed you."

"*I*! Promised to—"

"In plain print." She tossed the clipping at him with her left hand. The other she held in her lap, under a light wrap which she carried. "And I believed you. I thought you were square. Then when the pills didn't help, I went to a doctor, and he laughed and said they were nothing but sugar and flavoring. He wouldn't help me. He said no decent doctor would. *You* ain't a decent doctor. You're a lying devil. Are you going to help me out?"

"If you had come in a proper spirit—"

"That's enough. I've got my answer." She rose slowly to her feet. "After I found out what was wrong with me, I went home to my father. I didn't tell him about myself. But I told him I was quitting the Certina business. And he told me about my mother, how you sent her to her death. One word from me would have brought him here after you. *This* time he wouldn't have missed you. Then they'd have hung him, I suppose. That's why I held my tongue. You killed my mother, you and your quack medicines; and now you've done this to me." Her hand jerked up out of the wrap. "I don't see where you come in to live any longer," said Milly Neal deliberately.

Dr. Surtaine looked into the muzzle of a revolver.

There was a step on the soft rug outside, the curtain of the door to Dr. Surtaine's right parted, and Hal appeared. He carried a light stick.

"I thought I heard—" he began. Then, seeing the revolver, "What's this! Put that down!"

"Don't move, either of you," warned the girl. "I haven't said my say out. You're a fine-matched pair, you two! Him with his sugar-pills and you, Hal Surtaine, with your lying promises."

Lying promises! The phrase, thus used in the girl's mouth against the son, struck to the father's heart, confirming his dread. It *was* Hal, then. For the moment he forgot his instant peril, in his sorrow and shame.

"I don't know why I shouldn't kill you both," went on the half-crazed girl. "That'd even the score. Two Surtaines against two Neals, my mother and me."

The light of slaying was in her eyes, as she stiffened her arm. Just a fraction of an inch the arm swerved, for a streak of light was darting toward her. Hal had taken the only chance. He had flung his cane, whirling, in the hope of diverting her aim, and had followed it at a leap.

The two shots were almost instantaneous. At the second, the quack reeled back against the wall. The girl turned swiftly upon Hal, and as he seized her he felt the cold steel against his neck. The touch seemed to paralyze him. Strangely enough, the thought of death was summed up in a vast, regretful curiosity to know why all this was happening. Then the weapon fell.

"I can't kill *you*!" cried the girl, in a bursting sob, and fell, face down, upon the floor.

Hal, snatching up the revolver, ran to his father.

"I'm all right," declared the quack. "Only the shoulder. Just winged. Get me a drink from that decanter."

His son obeyed. With swift, careful hands he got the coat off the bulky-muscled arm, and saw, with a heart-lifting relief, that the bullet had hardly more than grazed the flesh. Meantime the girl had crawled, still sobbing, to a chair.

"Did I kill him?" she asked, covering her eyes against what she might see.

"No," said Hal.

"Listen," commanded Dr. Surtaine. "Some one's coming. Keep quiet." He walked steadily to the door and called out, "It's nothing. Just experimenting with a new pistol. Go back to your bed."

"Who was it?" asked Hal.

"The housekeeper. There's just one thing to do for the sake of all of us. This has *got* to be hushed up. I'm going out to telephone. Don't let her get away, Hal."

"Get away! Oh, my God!" breathed the girl.

Hal walked over to her, his heart wrung with pity.

"Why did you come here to kill my father, Milly?" he asked.

She stooped to pick up the "Happy Lady" clipping from the floor.

"That's why," she said.

"Good God!" said Hal. "Have you been taking that—those pills?"

"Taking 'em? Yes, and believing in 'em, till I found out it was all damned lies. And your fine and noble and honest 'Clarion' advertises the lies just as your fine and noble and honest father makes the pills. They're no good. Do you get that? And when I came here and told your father he'd got to help me out of my trouble, what do you think he told me? That I'd lost my job at the factory!"

"Who is the man, Milly?"

"What business is that of yours?"

"I'll go after him and see that he marries you if it takes—"

"Oh, he'd be only too glad to marry me if he could. He can't. Poor Max has got a wife somewhere—"

"Max? It's Veltman!" cried Hal. "The dirty scoundrel."

"Oh, don't blame Max," said the girl wearily. "It isn't his fault. After you threw me down"—Hal winced—"I started to run wild. It's the Hardscrabbler in me. I took to drinking and running around, and Max pulled me out of it, and I went to live with him. I didn't care. Nothing mattered, anyway. And I wasn't afraid of anything like this happening, because I thought the pills made it all safe."

Here Dr. Surtaine reappeared. "I've got a detective coming that I can trust."

"A detective?" cried Hal. "Oh, Dad—"

"You keep out of this," retorted his father, in a tone such as his son had never heard from him before. "I guess you've done enough. The question is"—he continued as regardless of Milly as if she had been deaf—"how to hush her up."

"You've had your chance to hush me up," said the girl sullenly.

"Any money within reason—"

"I don't want your money."

"Listen here, then. You tried to murder me. That's ten years in State's prison. Now, if ever I hear of you opening your mouth about this, I'll send you up. I guess that will keep you quiet. Now, then, what's your answer?"

"Give me a glass of whiskey, and I'll tell you."

Hal poured her out a glass. She passed a swift hand above it.

"Here's peace and quiet in the proprietary medicine business," she said, and drank. "I guess that'll—make—some—stir," she added, with an effect of carefully timing her words.

Her body lapsed quite gently back into the chair. The two men ran and bent over her as the glass tinkled and rolled on the floor. There was an acrid, bitter scent in the air. They lifted their heads, and their eyes met in a haggard realization. No longer was there any need of hushing up Milly Neal.

CHAPTER XXVI

THE PARTING

The doorbell buzzed.

"That's the detective," said Dr. Surtaine to Hal. "Stay here."

He wormed himself painfully into an overcoat which concealed his scarified shoulder, and went out. In a few moments he and the officer reappeared. The latter glanced at the body.

"Heart disease, you say?" he asked.

"Yes: valvular lesion."

"Better 'phone the coroner's office, eh?"

"Not necessary. I can give a certificate. The coroner will be all right," said Dr. Surtaine, with an assurance derived from the fact that a year before he had given that functionary five hundred dollars for not finding morphine in the stomach of a baby who had been dosed to death on the "Sure Soother" powders.

"That goes," agreed the detective. "What undertaker?"

"Any. And, Murtha, while you're at the 'phone, call up the 'Clarion' office and tell McGuire Ellis to come up here on the jump, will you?"

Left to themselves, with the body between them, father and son fell into a silence, instinct with the dread of estranging speech. Hal made the first effort.

"Your shoulder?" he said.

"Nothing," declared the Doctor. "Later on will do for that." He brooded for a time. "You can trust Ellis, can you?"

"Absolutely."

"It's the newspapers we have to look out for. Everything else is easy."

He conducted the detective, who had finished telephoning, into the library, set out drinks and cigars for him and returned. Nothing further was said until Ellis arrived. The associate editor's face, as he looked from the dead girl to Hal, was both sorrowful and stern. But he was there to act; not to judge or comment. He consulted his watch.

"Eleven forty-five," he said. "Better give out the story tonight."

"Why not wait till tomorrow?" asked Dr. Surtaine.

"The longer you wait, the more it will look like suppressing it."

"But we *want* to suppress it."

"Certainly," agreed Ellis. "I'm telling you the best way. Fix the story up for the 'Clarion' and the other papers will follow our lead."

"If we can arrange a story that they'll believe—" began Hal.

"Oh, they won't believe it! Not the kind of story we want to print. They aren't fools. But that won't make any difference."

"I should think it would be just the sort of possible scandal our enemies would catch at."

"You've still got a lot to learn about the newspaper game," replied his subordinate contemptuously. "One newspaper doesn't print a scandal about the owner of another. It's an unwritten law. They'll publish just what we tell 'em to—as we would if it was their dis—I mean misfortune. Come, now," he added, in a hard, businesslike voice, "what are we going to call the cause of death?"

"Miss Neal died of heart disease."

"Call it heart disease," confirmed the other. "Circumstances?"

This was a poser. Dr. Surtaine and Hal looked at each other and looked away again.

"How would this do?" suggested Ellis briskly. "Miss Neal came here to consult Dr. Surtaine on an emergency in her department at the factory, was taken ill while waiting, and was dead when he—No; that don't fit. If she died without medical attendance, the coroner would have to give a permit for removal. Died shortly after Dr. Surtaine's arrival in spite of his efforts to revive her; that's it!"

"Just about how it happened," said Dr. Surtaine gratefully.

"For publication. Now give me the real facts—under that overcoat of yours."

Dr. Surtaine started, and winced as the movement tweaked the raw nerves of his wound. "There's nothing else to tell," he said.

"You brought me here to lie for you," said the journalist. "All right, I'm ready. But if I'm to lie and not get caught at it, I must know the truth. Now, when I see a man wearing an overcoat over a painful arm, and discover what looks like a new bullet hole in the wall of the room, I think a dead body may mean something more than heart disease."

"I don't see—" began the charlatan.

But Hal cut him short. "For God's sake," he cried in a voice which seemed to gouge its way through his straining throat, "let's have done with lies for once." And he blurted out the whole story, eking out what he lacked in detail, by insistent questioning of his father.

When they came to the part about the Relief Pills, Ellis looked up with a bitter grin.

"Works out quite logically, doesn't it?" he observed. Then, walking over to the body, he looked down into the face, with a changed expression. "Poor little girl!" he muttered. "Poor little Kitty!" He whirled swiftly upon the Surtaines. "By God, *I'd* like to write her story!" he cried. The outburst was but momentary. Instantly he was his cool, capable self again.

"You've had experience in this sort of thing before, I suppose?" he inquired of Dr. Surtaine.

"Yes. No! Whaddye mean?" blustered the quack.

"Only that you'll know how to fix the police and the coroner."

"No call for any fixing."

"So all that I have to do is to handle the newspapers," pursued the other imperturbably. "All right. There'll be no more than a paragraph in any paper tomorrow. 'Working-Girl Drops Dead,' or something like that. You can sleep easy, gentlemen."

So obvious was the taunt that Hal stared at his friend, astounded. Upon the Doctor it made no impression.

"Say, Ellis. Do something for me, will you?" he requested. "Wire to Belford Couch, the Willard, Washington, to come on here by first train."

"Couch? Oh, that's Certina Charley, isn't it? Your professional fixer?"

"Never mind what he is. You'll be sure to do it, won't you?"

"No. Do it yourself," said Ellis curtly, and walked out without a good-night.

"Well, whaddye think of that!" spluttered Dr. Surtaine. "That fellow's getting the big-head."

Hal made no reply. He had dropped into a chair and now sat with his head between his hands. When he raised his face it was haggard as if with famine.

"Dad, I'm going away."

"Where?" demanded his father, startled.

"Anywhere, away from this house."

"No wonder you're shaken, Boyee," said the other soothingly. "We'll talk about it in the morning. After a night's rest—"

"In this house? I couldn't close my eyes for fear of what I'd see!"

"It's been a tough business. I'll give you a sleeping powder."

"No; I've got to think this out: this whole business of the Relief Pills."

Dr. Surtaine was instantly on the defensive. "Don't go getting any sentimental notions now, Hal. It's a perfectly legal business."

"So much the worse for the law, then."

"You talk like an anarchist!" returned his father, shocked. "Do you want to be better than the law?"

"If the law permits murder—I do," said Hal, very low.

Indignation rose up within Dr. Surtaine: not wholly unjustified, considering his belief that Hal was primarily responsible for the tragedy. "Are your hands so clean, then?" he asked significantly.

"God knows, they're not!" cried the son, with passion. "I didn't know. I didn't realize."

"Yet you turn on me—"

"Oh, Dad, I don't want to quarrel with you. All I know is, I can't stay in this house any more."

Dr. Surtaine pondered for a few minutes. Perhaps it was better that the boy should go for a time, until his conscience worked out a more satisfactory state of mind. His own conscience was clear. He was doing business within the limits set for him by the law and the Post Office authorities, which had once investigated the "Pills" and given them a clean bill. Milly Neal should not put the onus of her own recklessness and immorality upon him. Nevertheless, he was glad that Belford Couch was coming on; and, by the way, he must telephone a dispatch to him. Rising, he addressed his son.

"Where shall you go?"

"I don't know. Some hotel. The Dunstan."

"Very well. I'll see you at the office soon, I suppose. Good-night."

All Hal's world whirled about him as he saw his father leave the room. What seemed to him a monstrous manifestation of chance had overwhelmed and swept him from all moorings. But was it chance? Was it not, rather, as McGuire Ellis had suggested, the exemplification of an exact logic?

The closing of the door behind his father sent a current of air across the room in which a bit of paper on the floor wavered and turned. Hal picked it up. It was the clipping from the "Clarion"—his newspaper—which Milly Neal had brought as her justification. One line of print stood out, writhing as if in an uncontrollable access of diabolic glee: "Only $1 A Box: Satisfaction Guaranteed"; and above it the face of the Happy Lady, distorted by the crumpling of the paper, smirked up at him with a taunt. He thought to interpret that taunt in the words which Veltman had used, aforetime:—

"What's *your* percentage?"

CHAPTER XXVII
THE GREATER TEMPTING

Journalistic Worthington ran true to type in the Milly Neal affair. No newspaper published more than a paragraph about the "sudden death." Suicide was not even hinted at in print. But newspaperdom had its own opinion, magnified and colored by the processes of gossip, over which professional courtesy exercised no control. That the girl had killed herself was generally understood: that there had been a shooting, previous to her death, was also current. Eager report recalled and exaggerated the fact that she had been seen with Hal Surtaine at a dubious road-house some months previous. The popular "inside knowledge" of the tragedy was that Milly had gone to the Surtaine mansion to force Hal's hand, failing in which she had shot him, inflicting an inconsiderable wound, and then killed herself; and that Dr. Surtaine had thereupon turned his son out of the house. Hal's removal to the hotel served to bear out this surmise, and the Doctor's strategic effort to cover the situation by giving it out that his son's part of the mansion was being remodeled—even going to the lengths of actually setting a force of men to work there—failed to convince the gossips.

Between the two men, the situation was now most difficult. Quite instinctively Hal had fallen in with his father's theory that the primal necessity, after the tragedy, was to keep everything out of print. That by so doing he wholly subverted his own hard-won policy did not, in the stress of the crisis, occur to him. Later he realized it. Yet he could see no other course of action as having been possible to him. The mere plain facts of the case constituted an accusation against Dr. Surtaine, unthinkable for a son to publish against his father. And Hal still cozened himself into a belief in the quack's essential innocence, persuading his own reason that there was a blind side to the man which rendered it impossible for him to see through the legal into the ethical phases of the question. By this method he was saving his loyalty and affection. But so profound had been the shock that he could not, for a time, endure the constant companionship of former days. Consequently the frequent calls which Dr. Surtaine deemed it expedient to make for the sake of appearances, at Hal's hotel, resulted in painful, rambling, topic-shifting talks, devoid of any human touch other than the pitiful and thwarted affection of two personalities at hopeless odds. "Least said soonest mended" was a favorite aphorism of the experienced quack. But in this tangle it failed him. It was he who first touched on the poisoned theme.

"Look here, Boy-ee," said he, a week after the burial. "We're both scared to death of what each of us is thinking. Let's agree to forget this until you are ready to talk it out with me."

"What good will talk do?" said Hal drearily.

"None at present." His father sighed. He had hoped for a clean breast of it, a confession of the intrigue that should leave the way open to a readjustment of relations. "So let's put the whole thing aside."

"All right," agreed Hal listlessly. "I suppose you know," he added, "before we close the subject, that I've ordered the Relief Pills advertising out of the

'Clarion.'"

"You needn't have bothered. It won't be offered again."

Silence fell between them. "I've about decided to quit that line," the charlatan resumed with an obvious effort. "Not that it isn't strictly legal," he added, falling back upon his reserve defense. "But it's too troublesome. The copy is ticklish; I've had to write all those ads. myself. And, at that, there's some newspapers won't accept 'em and others that want to edit 'em. Belford Couch and I have been going over the whole matter. He's the diplomat of the concern. And we've about decided to sell out. Anyway," he added, brightening, "there ain't hardly money enough in a side-line like the Pills to pay for the trouble of running it separate."

If Dr. Surtaine had looked for explicit approval of his virtuous resolution, he was disappointed. Yet Hal experienced, or tried to believe that he experienced, a certain factitious glow of satisfaction at this proof that his father was ready to give up an evil thing even without being fully convinced of its wrongfulness. This helped the son to feel that, at least, his sacrifice had been made for a worthy affection. Still, he had no word to say except that he must get to the office. The Doctor left with gloom upon his handsome face.

With McGuire Ellis, Hal's association had become even more difficult than with the Doctor. Since his abrupt and unceremonious departure from the room of death, in the belief in Hal's guilt, Ellis had maintained a purely professional attitude toward his employer. For a time, in his wretchedness and turmoil of spirit, Hal had scarcely noticed Ellis's withdrawal of fellowship, vaguely attributing his silence to unexpressed sympathy. But later, when he broached the subject of Milly's death, he was met with a stony avoidance which inspired both astonishment and resentment. Sub-normal as he now was in nervous strength and tension, he shrank from having it out with Ellis. But he felt, for the first time in his life, forlorn and friendless.

On his part McGuire Ellis brooded over a deep anger. He was not a man to yield lightly of his best; but he had given to Hal, first a fine loyalty, and later, as they grew into closer association, a warm if rather reticent affection. For the rough idealist had found in his employer an idealism not always as clear and intelligent as his own, yet often higher and finer; and along with the professional protectiveness which he had assumed over the younger man's inexperience had come an honest admiration and far-reaching hopes. Now he saw in his chief one who had betrayed his cause through a weak and selfish indulgence. The clear-sighted journalist knew that the newspaper owner with a shameful secret binds his own power in the coils of that secret. And fatally in error as he was as to the nature of the entanglement in which Hal was involved, he foresaw the inevitable effect of the situation upon the "Clarion." Moreover, he was bitterly disappointed in Hal as a man. Had his superior "gone on the loose" and contracted a *liaison* with some woman of the outer world, Ellis would have passed over the abstract morality of the question. But to take advantage of a girl in his own employ, and then so cruelly to leave her to her fate,—there was rot at the heart of the man who could do that. The excision of the offending "Relief Pills" ad after the culmination of the tragedy, was simply a sop to hypocrisy.

Only once had Ellis made any reference to Milly's death. On the day of her funeral Max Veltman had disappeared, without notice. A week later he reported for duty, shaken and pallid.

"Do you want to take him back?" Ellis inquired of Hal.

Hal's first impulse was to say "No"; but he conquered it, remembering Milly Neal's pitiful generosity toward her lover.

"Where has he been?" he asked.

"Drunk, I guess."

"What do you think?"

"I think yes."

"All right, if he's sobered up. Tell him it mustn't happen again."

There was a gleam in McGuire Ellis's eye. "Suppose *you* tell him that it mustn't happen again. It would come with more force from you."

Hal whirled in his chair. "Mac, what's the matter with you?"

"Nothing. I was just thinking of 'Kitty the Cutie.'"

"What were you thinking of her?"

"Only that Max Veltman would have gone through hell-fire for her. And, from his looks, he's been through and had the heart burned out of him."

With that he resumed his proof-reading in a dogged silence.

To Hal's great relief Veltman kept out of his way. The man seemed dazed with misery, but did his work well enough. Rumors reached the office that he was striving to gain a refuge from his sufferings by giving all his leisure hours to work in the Rookeries district, under the direction of the Reverend Norman Hale. Ellis was of the opinion that his mind was somewhat affected, and that he would bear watching a bit; and was the more disturbed in that Veltman shared the secret of the great epidemic "spread," now practically completed for the "Clarion's" publishing or suppressing. Ellis held the belief that, now, Hal would order it suppressed. The man who had shirked his responsibility to Milly Neal could hardly be relied on for the stamina necessary to such an exploitation.

The time was at hand for the decision to be made. The two physicians, Elliot and Merritt, pressed for publication. Every day, they pointed out, not only meant a further risk of life, but also increased the impending danger of a general outburst which would find the city wholly unprepared. On the other hand, the journalists, Ellis and Wayne, held out for delay. They perceived the one weak point in their case, that neither a dead body nor a living patient had as yet come to the hands of the constituted authorities for diagnosis. The sole determination had been made on corpses carried across the line and now probably impossible of identification. The committee fund was doing its work of concealment effectually. But Fate tripped the strategy board at last, using the Reverend Norman Hale as its agent.

Since Milly Neal's death, the Reverend Norman had tried to find time to call on Hal Surtaine, and had failed. He wished to talk with him about Veltman. Three days after the funeral he had hauled the "Clarion's" foreman out of the gutter, stood between him and suicide for one savage night of struggle, and listened to the remorse of a haunted soul. Being a man and a brother, the Reverend Norman forbore blame or admonition; being a physician of the inner being, he devised work for the wreck in his slums, and had driven him relentlessly that he might find peace in the service of others. Slowly the man won back to sanity. One obsession persisted, however, disturbing to the clergyman. Veltman was willing to do penance himself, in any possible way, but he insisted that, since the

Surtaines shared his guilt, they, too, must make amends, before his dead mistress could rest in her grave. Apprised by Veltman of the whole wretched story, Hale secretly sympathized with this view of the Surtaines' responsibility. But he was concerned lest, in Veltman, it take some form of direct vengeance. When he learned that Veltman had returned to the "Clarion" composing-room to work, the minister, unable to spare time for a call from his almost sleepless activities, sent an urgent request to Hal to meet him at the Recreation Club. Hal being out, Ellis got the note, observed the "Immediate and Important" on the envelope, read the contents, and set out for the rendezvous.

He never got there. For at the corner of Sperry Street he was met by a messenger who knew him.

"The back room at McManey's," said the urchin. "He's in there, waitin'."

Ellis entered the place. At a table sat the Reverend Norman Hale, with an expression of radiant happiness on his gaunt face. The barkeeper, who, on his own initiative, had just brought in a steaming hot drink, stood watching him with unfeigned concern. Hale welcomed Ellis warmly, and drew a chair close for him.

"You sent for Mr. Surtaine," said Ellis.

"Did I?" asked the other vaguely. "I forget. It doesn't matter. Nothing matters, now. Ellis, I've found out the secret."

"What secret?"

"The great secret. The solution," replied the young minister, buoyantly. "All that is necessary is to get the bodies."

"Yes, of course," agreed the other, with rising uneasiness. "But they smuggle them out as fast—"

"They won't when I've told them. McGuire Ellis,"—he gripped his companion suddenly with fingers that clamped like a burning vise,—"*I can bring the dead back to life.*"

"Tell me about it. But take a swallow of this first." Ellis pushed the hot drink toward him. "You're cold."

"Nothing but excitement. The glory of it! All this suffering and grief and death—"

"Wait a minute. I want a drink myself."

He turned to the bartender. "Get an auto," he whispered. "Quick!"

"There's a rig outside," said the man. "I seen he was sick when he came in, so I sent for it."

"Good man!" said Ellis. "Telephone to Dr. Merritt at the Health Office to meet me instantly at the hospital. Tell him why. Now, Mr. Hale," he added, "come on. Let's get along. You can tell me on the way."

Still rapt with his vision the minister rose, and permitted himself to be guided to the carriage. Once inside he fell into a semi-stupor. Only at the hospital, where Dr. Merritt was waiting to see him safe within the isolation ward, did he come to his rightful senses, cool, and, as ever, thoughtful of everything but himself.

"You've got your chance for a diagnosis at last, Doctor," he whispered to the health officer.

Half an hour later, Dr. Merritt came out to the waiting journalist.

"Typhus," he said, with grievous exultation. "Unmistakably and officially typhus. We've got our case. Only, I wish to God it had been any of the rest of us."

"Will he die?" queried Ellis.

"God knows. I should say his chance was worse than even. He's worn out from overwork."

For assurance, Dr. Elliot was sent for and added his diagnosis. Ellis got authoritative interviews with both men, and the "Clarion's" great, potential sensation was now fully ripe for print. Denton the reporter had done the previous work well. His "story," leaded out and with subheads, ran flush to two pages of the paper, and every paragraph of it struck fire. It would, as Ellis said, set off a ton of dynamite beneath sleepy Worthington. That night Veltman "pulled" a proof, and Ellis stayed far into the morning, pasting up a dummy of the article for Hal's inspection and final judgment.

It was on Thursday that Norman Hale was taken to the hospital. Friday noon McGuire Ellis laid before his principal the carefully constructed dummy with the brief comment:

"There's the epidemic story."

Hal accepted and read it in silence. Once or twice he made a note. When he had finished, he turned to find Ellis's gaze fixed upon him.

"We ought to run it Monday," said Ellis. "We can round it all up by then."

Monday is the dead day of journalism, the day for which news articles which do not demand instant production are reserved, both to liven up a dull paper and because the sensation produced is greater. However, the sensation inevitable to the publishing of this article, as Hal instantly realized, would be enormous on any day.

"It's big stuff," said he, with a long breath.

Ellis nodded. "Shall I release it for Monday?"

"N-n-no," came the dubious reply.

"It's been held already for ten days."

"Then what does it matter if we hold it a little longer?"

"Human lives, maybe. Isn't that matter enough?"

"That's only a guess. I've got to have time on this," insisted Hal. "It's the most vital question of policy that the paper has had to face."

"Policy!" grunted Ellis savagely.

"Besides, I've given my word to the Chamber of Commerce Committee that we wouldn't publish any epidemic news without due warning to them."

"Then it's to be killed?"

"'Wait for orders' proof," said Hal stonily.

"I might have known," sneered Ellis, with an infinite depth of scorn, and went to bear the bitter message to Wayne.

While the "Clarion" policy trembled in the balance, Dr. Surtaine's Committee on Suppression was facing a new crisis brought about by the striking down of Norman Hale, of which they received early information. Should he die, as was believed probable, the news, whether or not the full facts got into print, would surely become a focus for the propagation of alarmist rumors. In their distress, the patriots of commerce paid a hasty visit to their chief, craving counsel. Having foreseen the possibility of some such contingency, Dr. Surtaine was ready with a plan. The committee would enlarge itself, call a meeting of the representative men of the town, organize an Emergency Health Committee of One

Hundred, and take the field against the onset of pernicious malaria. This show of fighting force would allay public alarm, a large fund would be raised, the newspapers would be kept in thorough subjection, and the disease could be wiped out without undue publicity or the imperiling of Old Home Week.

"What about the 'Clarion'?" inquired Hollenbeck, of the committee. "They're still holding off."

"Safe as your hat," Dr. Surtaine assured the questioner with a smile.

"At the meeting you told us you couldn't answer for your son's paper," Stensland recalled.

"I can now," said the confident quack. "Just you leave it to me."

He went direct to the "Clarion" office, revolving in his mind the impending interview. For the first time since the tragedy he anticipated a meeting with his son without embarrassment, for now he had a definite topic to talk about, difficult though it might be.

Finding Hal at the editorial desk he went direct to the point.

"Boy-ee, the epidemic is spreading."

"I know it."

"I'm going to take hold of the matter personally, from now on."

"In what way?"

"By organizing a committee of one hundred to cover the city and make a scientific campaign."

"Are you going to let people know that it's typhus?"

"Sh-sh-sh! So you know, do you? Well, the important thing now is to see that others don't find out. Don't even whisper the word. Malaria's our cue; pernicious malaria. What's the use of scaring every one to death? We'll call a public meeting for next week—"

"Publicity is the last thing you want, I should think."

"Semi-public, I should have said. The epidemic has gone so far that people are beginning to take notice. We've got to reassure them and the right kind of an Emergency Health Committee is the way to do it. Belford Couch is working up the meeting now. I've kept him over on purpose for it. He's the best little diplomat in the proprietary business. And Yours Truly will be elected Chairman of the Committee. It'll cost us a ten-thousand-dollar donation to the fund, but it's worth it to the business."

"To the business? I don't quite see how."

"Simple as a pin! When it's all over and we're ready to let the account of it get into print, Dr. Surtaine, proprietor of Certina, will be the principal figure in the campaign. What's that worth in advertising to the year's business? Not that I'm doing it for that. I'm doing it to save Old Home Week."

"With a little profit on the side."

Dr. Surtaine deemed it politic to ignore the tone of the commentary.

"Why not? Nobody's hurt by it. You'll be on the Central Committee, Boy-ee."

"No; I don't think so."

"Why not?"

"I think I'd better keep out of the movement, Dad."

"As you like. And you'll see that the 'Clarion' keeps out of it, too?"

"So that's it."

"Yes, Boy-ee: that's it. You can see, for yourself, that a newspaper sensation would ruin everything just now—and also ruin the paper that sprung it."

"So I heard from Elias M. Pierce sometime since."

"For once Pierce is right."

"Are you asking me to suppress the epidemic story?"

"To let us handle it our own way," substituted the Doctor. "We've got our campaign all figured out and ready to start. Do you know what the great danger is now?"

"Letting the infection go on without taking open measures to stop it."

"You're way wrong! Starting a panic that will scatter it all over the place is the real danger. Have you heard of a single case outside of the Rookeries district, so far?"

Hal strove to recall the death-list on the proof. "No," he admitted.

"You see! It's confined to one locality. Now, what happens if you turn loose a newspaper scare? Why, those poor, ignorant people will swarm out of the Rookeries and go anywhere to escape the quarantine that they know will come. You'll have an epidemic not localized, but general. The situation will be ten times as difficult and dangerous as it is now."

Struck with the plausibility of this reasoning, Hal hesitated. "That's up to the authorities," he said.

"The authorities!" cried the charlatan, in disdain. "What could they do? The damage would be done before they got ready to move. You see, we've got to handle this situation diplomatically. Look here, Boyee; what's the worst feature of an epidemic? Panic. You know the Bible parable. The seven plagues came to Egypt and ten thousand people died. The Grand Vizier said to the plagues, 'How many of my people have you slain?' The plagues said, 'A thousand.' 'What about the other nine thousand?' said the Grand Vizier. 'Not guilty!' said the plagues. 'They were slain by Fear.' Maybe it was in 'Paradise Lost' and not the Bible. But the lesson's the same. Panic is the killer."

"But the disease is increasing all the time," objected Hal. "Are we to sit still and—"

"Is it?" broke in the wily controversialist. "How do you account for this, then?" He drew from his pocket a printed leaflet. "Take a peek at those figures. Fewer deaths in the Rookeries this last week than in any week since March."

This was true. Not infrequently there comes an inexplicable subsidence of mortality in mid-epidemic. No competent hygienist is deceived into mistaking this phenomenon for an indication of the end. Not being a hygienist Hal was again impressed.

"The Health Bureau's own statistics," continued the argumentator, pushing his advantage. "With Dr. Merritt's signature at the bottom."

"Dr. Merritt says that the epidemic is being fostered by secrecy, suppression, and lying."

"All sentimentalism. Merritt would turn the city upside down if he had his way. Was it him that told you it was typhus?"

"No. We've got a two-page story in proof now, giving the whole facts of the epidemic."

"You can't publish it, Boy-ee," said his father firmly.

"Can't? That sounds like an order."

Adroitly Dr. Surtaine caught at the word. "An order drawn on your word of honor."

"If there's any question of honor to the 'Clarion,' it's to tell the truth plainly and take the consequences."

"Who said anything about the 'Clarion's' honor? This is between you and me."

"You'll have to speak more plainly," said Hal with a dawning dread.

"Boyee, I hate to do this, but I've got to, to save the city. You gave me your word that the day you had to suppress news for your own sake, you'd quit this Don Quixotic business and treat others as decently and considerately as you treated yourself."

"Go on," said Hal, in a half whisper.

"Well—Milly Neal." Dr. Surtaine wet his lips nervously. "You saved yourself there by keeping the story out of the papers. Of course you were right. You were dead right. You'd have been a fool to do anything else. But there you are. And there's your promise."

A nausea of the soul sickened Hal. That his father, whom he had so loved and honored, should make of the loyalty which had, at the cost of principle, protected the name of Surtaine against open disgrace, a tool wherewith to tear down his professional standards—it was like some incredible and malign jocosity of a devilish logic. Of what was going on in the quack's mind he had no inkling. He could not know that his father saw in the suppression of the suicide news, only a natural and successful effort on the part of Hal to conceal his own guilt in Milly's death. No more could Dr. Surtaine comprehend that it was the dreadful responsibility of the Surtaine quackery for which Hal had unhesitantly sacrificed the declared principle of the "Clarion." So they gazed darkly at each other across the chasm, each seeing his opponent in the blackest colors.

"You hold me to that?" demanded Hal, half choked.

"I have to, Boy-ee."

To Dr. Surtaine the issue which he had raised was but the distasteful means to a necessary end. To Hal it meant the final capitulation to the forces against which he had been fighting since his first enlightenment.

"I might as well sell the 'Clarion' now, and be done with it," he declared bitterly.

"Nonsense! If you stuck to this foolishness you'd have to sell it or lose it. You'd be ruined, both in influence and in money. How would you feel when Mac Ellis, and Wayne, and all the fellows that stuck by you found themselves out of a job because of your pig-headedness? And what harm are you doing by dropping the story, anyway? We've got this thing beaten, right now. It isn't spreading. It's dropping off. What'll the 'Clarion' look like when its great sensation peters out into thin air? But by that time the harm'll be done and the whole country will think we're a plague-stricken city. Don't do all that damage and spoil everything just for a false delusion, Boyee."

But Hal's mind was brooding on the fatal promise which he had so confidently made his father. One way out there was.

"Since it's a question of my word to you," he said, "I could still publish the truth about Milly Neal."

"No. You couldn't do that, Boyee," said his father in a tone, half sorrowful, half shamed.

"No. You're right. I couldn't—God help me!"

To proclaim his own father a moral criminal in his own paper was the one test which Hal lacked the power to meet. It was the world-old conflict between loyalty and principle—in which loyalty so often and so tragically wins the first combat.

After all, Hal forced himself to consider, he was not serving his public ill by this particular sacrifice of principle. The official mortality figures helped him to persuade himself that the typhus was indeed ebbing. For himself, as the price of silence, there was easy sailing under the flag of local patriotism, and with every success in prospect. Yet it was with sunken eyes that he turned to the tempter.

"All right," he said, with a half groan, "I give in. We won't print it."

Dr. Surtaine heaved a great sigh of relief. "That's horse sense!" he cried jovially. "Now, you go ahead on those lines and you'll make the 'Clarion' the best-paying proposition in Worthington. I'll drop a few hints where they'll do the most good, and you'll see the advertisers breaking their necks to come in. Journalism is no different from any other business, Boy-ee. Live and let live. Bear and forbear. There's the rule for you. The trouble with you, Boy-ee, has been that you've been trying to run a business on pink-tea principles."

"The trouble with me," said his son bitterly, "is that I've been trying to reform a city when I ought to have been reforming myself."

"Oh, you're all right, Boy-ee," his affectionate and admiring father reassured him. "You're just finding yourself. As for this reform—" And he was launched upon the second measure of the Pæan of Policy when Hal cut him short by ringing a bell and ordering the boy to send McGuire Ellis to him. Ellis came up from the city room.

"Kill the epidemic story, Mr. Ellis," he ordered.

Red passion surged up into Ellis's face.

"Kill—" he began, in a strangled voice.

"Kill it. You understand?" The associate editor's color receded. He looked with slow contempt from father to son.

"Oh, yes, I understand," he said. "Any other orders today?"

Hal made no reply. His father, divining that this was no time for further speech, took his departure. McGuire Ellis went out with black despair at his heart, a soldier betrayed by his captain. And the proprietor of the "Clarion," his feet now set in the path of success and profit, turned back to his work in sodden disenchantment, sighing as youth alone sighs, and as youth sighs only when it foregoes the dream of ideals which is its immortal birthright.

CHAPTER XXVIII
"WHOSE BREAD I EAT"

Having yielded, Hal proposed to take profit by his surrender. With a cynicism born of his bitter disappointment and self-contempt, he took a certain savage and painful satisfaction in stating the new policy editorially.

"As the 'Clarion' is going to be a journalistic prostitute," said he to his father, across the luncheon table, where they were consulting on details of the new policy, "I'm going to go after the business on that basis."

Dr. Surtaine was pained. Every effort of his own convenient logic he put forth to prove that, in this instance, the path of duty and of glory (financial) was one and the same. Hal refused the proffered gloss. "At least you and I can call things by their right names now," said he.

But however Hal might talk, what he wrote met his elder's unqualified approval, as it appeared in the proof sent him by his son. It was a cunningly worded leading editorial, headed "Standards," and it dealt appreciatively, not to say reverently, with the commercial greatness of Worthington. Business, the editor stated, might have to adjust itself to new conditions and opinions in Worthington as elsewhere, but nobody who understood the character of the city's leading men could doubt their good purpose or ability to effect the change with the least damage to material prosperity. Meantime the fitting attitude for the public was one not of criticism but of forbearance and assistance. This was equally true of journalism. The "Clarion" admitted seeing a new light. Constructive rather than destructive effort was called for. And so forth, and so on. No intelligent reader could have failed, reading it, to understand that the "Clarion" had hauled down its flag.

Yet the capitulation must not, for business reasons, be too obvious. Hal spent some toilful hours over the proof, inserting plausible phrases, covering his tracks with qualifying clauses, putting the best front on the shameful matter, with a sick but determined heart, and was about to send it up with the final "O.K." when he came out of his absorption to realize that some one was standing waiting, had been standing waiting, for some minutes at his elbow. He looked around and met the intent gaze of the foreman of the composing-room.

"What is it, Veltman?" he asked sharply.

"That epidemic story."

"Well? What about it?"

"Did you order it killed?"

"Certainly. Haven't you thrown it down?"

"No. It's still in type."

"Throw it down at once."

"Mr. Surtaine, have you thought what you are doing?"

"It is no part of your job to catechize me, Veltman."

"Between man and man." He stepped close to Hal, his face blazing with exaltation. "I must speak now or forever hold my peace."

"Speak fast, then."

"It's your last chance, this epidemic spread. Your last chance to save the 'Clarion' and yourself."

"That will do, Velt—"

"No, no! Listen to me. I didn't say a word when you kept Milly's suicide out of print."

"I should think not, indeed!" retorted Hal angrily.

"That's my shame. I ought to have seen that published if I had to set it up myself."

"Perhaps you're not aware, Veltman, that I know your part in the Neal affair."

"I'd have confessed to you, if you hadn't. But do you know your own? Yours and your father's?"

"Keep my father out of this!"

"Your own, then. Do you know that the money that bought this paper for you was coined out of the blood of deceived girls? Do you know that you and I are paid with the proceeds of the ad that led Milly Neal to her death? Do you know that?"

"And if I do, what then?" asked Hal, overborne by the man's conviction and vehemence.

"Tell it!" cried the other, beating his fist upon the desk until the blood oozed from the knuckles. "Tell it in print. Confess, man, and warn others!"

"Veltman, suppose we were to print that whole wretched story tomorrow, including the truth about your relations with her."

"Do it! Do it!" cried the other, choked with eagerness. "I'd thank you on my knees. Penance! Give me my chance to do penance! I'll make my own confession in writing. I'll write it in my own blood if need be."

"Steady, Veltman. Keep cool."

"You think I'm crazy? Perhaps I am. There's a fire at my brain since she died. I loved her, Mr. Surtaine."

"But you sacrificed her, Veltman," returned Hal in a gentler tone, for the man's face was livid with agony.

"Don't I know it! My God, don't I know it! But *you* can't escape the responsibility because of my sin. It was your paper that helped fool her. She believed in the paper, and in your father."

"The Relief Pills advertising is out. That much I'll tell you."

"Now that it's done its work. Not enough! You and I can't bring Milly back to life, Mr. Surtaine, but we can save other lives in peril. God has given you your chance, in this epidemic."

"How do you know about the epidemic?"

"Hasn't it taken Mr. Hale, the only friend I've got in the world? And won't it take its hundreds of other lives unless warning is given? Why doesn't the 'Clarion' speak out, Mr. Surtaine? *Why is that story ordered killed?*"

"Consideration of policy which—"

"Policy! Oh, my God! And the people dying! Harrington Surtaine,"—his eyes blazed into the other's with the flame of fanaticism,—"I tell you, if you don't accept this opportunity that the Lord gives you, you and your paper are damned. Do you know what it means to damn the soul of a paper? Why, man, there are people who believe in the 'Clarion' like gospel."

Hal got to his feet. "Veltman, I dare say you mean well. But you don't understand this."

"Don't I!" The face took on a sudden appalling savagery. "Don't I know you're bought and paid for! Sold out! That's what you've done. A bargain! A bargain! Pay my little price and I'll do your meanest bidding. I'd rather have hell burning at my heart as it burns now than what you've got rotting at yours, young Surtaine."

The tensity of Hal's restraint broke. With one powerful effort he sent the foreman whirling through the open door into the hall, slammed the door after him, and stood shaking. He heard and felt the jar of Veltman's body as it struck the wall, and slumped to the floor; then the slow limp of his retreating footsteps. With a seething brain he returned to his proof—and shuddered away from it. There was blood spattered over the print. Hurriedly he thrust it aside and rang for a fresh galley. But the red spots rose between his eyes and the work, like an accusation, like a prophecy. Of a sudden he beheld this great engine of print which had been, first, the caprice of his last flicker of irresponsible and headlong youth, then the very mould in which his eager and ambitious manhood was to form and fulfill itself—he beheld this vast mechanism blazingly illumined as with some inner fire, and now become a terrific genius, potent beyond the powers of humanity, working out the dire complications of men, and the tragic destruction of women. And he beheld himself, fast in its grip.

He thrust the proof into the tube, scrawled the "O.K." order on it for the morrow, and hurried away from the office as from a place accursed.

That night conscience struck at him once more, making a weapon of words from the book of a dead master. He had been reading "Beauchamp's Career"; and, seeking refuge from the torture of thought in its magic, he came upon the novelist-philosopher's damning indictment of modern journalism:

"And this Press, declaring itself independent, can hardly walk for fear of treading on an interest here, an interest there. It cannot have a conscience. It is a bad guide, a false guardian; its abject claim to be our national and popular interpreter—even that is hollow and a mockery. It is powerful only when subservient. An engine of money, appealing to the sensitiveness of money, it has no connection with the mind of the nation. And that it is not of, but apart from the people, may be seen when great crises come—in strong gales the power of the Press collapses; it wheezes like a pricked pigskin of a piper."

Hal flung the book from him. But its accusations pursued him through the gates of sleep, and poisoned his rest.

In the morning he had recovered his balance, and with it his dogged determination to see the matter through. He forced himself to read the leading editorial, finding spirit even to admire the dexterity with which he had held out the promise of good behavior to the business interests, whilst pretending to a sturdy independence. Shearson met him at the entrance to the building, beaming.

"That'll bring business," said the advertising manager. "I've had half a dozen telephones already about it."

"That's good," replied Hal half-heartedly.

"Yes, *sir*," pursued the advertising manager: "I can smell money in the air today. And, by the way, I've got a tip that, for a little mild apology, E.M. Pierce will withdraw both his suits."

"I'll think about it," promised Hal. He was rather surprised at the intensity of his own relief from the prospect of the court ordeal. At least, he was getting his price.

McGuire Ellis was, for once, not asleep, though there was no work on his desk when Hal entered the sanctum.

"Veltman's quit," was his greeting.

"I'm not surprised," said Hal.

"Then you've seen the editorial page this morning?"

"Yes. But what has that to do with Veltman's resignation?"

"Everything, I should think. Notice anything queer about the page?"

"No."

"Look it over again."

Hal took up the paper and scrutinized the sheet. "I don't see a thing wrong," he said.

"That lets me out," said Ellis grimly. "If you can't see it when you're told it's there, I guess I can't be blamed for not catching it in proof. Of course the last thing one notices is a stock line that's always been there unchanged. Look at the motto of the paper. Veltman must have chiseled out the old one, and set this in, himself, the last thing before we went to press. How do you like it? Looks to me to go pretty well with our leading editorial this morning."

There between the triumphal cocks, where formerly had flaunted the braggart boast of the old "Clarion," and more latterly had appeared the gentle legend of the martyred President, was spread in letters of shame to the eyes of the "Clarion's" owner, the cynic profession of the led captain, of the prostituted pen, of all those who have or shall sell mind and soul and honor for hire;—

"Whose Bread I Eat, his Song I Sing."

CHAPTER XXIX

CERTINA CHARLEY

Mr. Belford Couch was a man of note. You might search vainly for the name among the massed thousands of "Who's Who in America," or even in those biographical compilations which embalm one's fame and picture for a ten-dollar consideration. Shout the cognomen the length of Fifth Avenue, bellow it up Walnut and down Chestnut Street, lend it vocal currency along the Lake Shore Drive, toss it to the winds that storm in from the Golden Gate to assault Nob Hill, and no answering echo would you awake. But give to its illustrious bearer his familiar title; speak but the words "Certina Charley" within the precincts of the nation's capital and the very asphalt would find a viscid voice wherewith to acclaim the joke, while Senate would answer House, and Department reply to Bureau with the curses of the stung ones. For Mr. Belford Couch was least loved where most laughed at.

From the nature of his profession this arose. His was a singular career. He pursued the fleeting testimonial through the mazy symptoms of disease (largely imaginary) and cure (wholly mythical). To extract from the great and shining ones of political life commendations of Certina; to beguile statesmen who had never tasted that strange concoction into asseverating their faith in the nostrum's infallibility for any and all ailments; to persuade into fulsome print solemnly asinine Senators and unwarily flattered Congressmen—that was the touchstone of his living. Some the Demon Rum betrayed into his hands. Others he won by sheer personal persuasiveness, for he was a master of the suave plea. Again, political favors or "inside information" made those his debtors from whom he exacted and extracted the honor of their names for Dr. Surtaine's upholding. Blackmail, even, was hinted at. "What does it matter?" thought the deluded or oppressed victim. "Merely a line of meaningless indorsement to sign my name to." And within a fortnight advertising print, black and looming, would inform the reading populace of the whole country that "United States Senator Gull says of Certina: 'It is, in my opinion, unrivaled as a never-failing remedy for coughs and colds,'" with a picture, coarse-screen, libelously recognizable.

Certina Charley was not a testimonial-chaser alone. Had he been, Dr. Surtaine would not have retained him at a generous salary, but would have paid him, as others of his strange species are paid, by the piece; one hundred dollars for a Representative, two hundred and fifty dollars for a Senator, and as high as five hundred for a hero conspicuous in the popular eye. The special employee of Certina was a person of diverse information and judicious counsel. His chief had not incorrectly described him as the diplomat of the trade.

No small diplomacy had been required for the planning of the Emergency Committee scheme, the details of which Mr. Couch had worked out, himself. It was, as he boasted to Dr. Surtaine, "a clincher."

"Look out for the medicos," he had said to Dr. Surtaine in outlining his great idea. "They're mean to handle. You can always buy or bluff a newspaper, but a doctor is different. Some of 'em you can grease, but they're the scrubs. The real fellers won't touch money, and the worst of 'em just seem to love trouble. Merritt's that kind. But we can fix Merritt by raising twenty or thirty thousand dollars and handing it over to him to organize his campaign against the epidemic. From all I can learn, Merritt has got the goods as a health officer. He knows his business. There's no man in town could handle the thing better, unless it's you, Chief, and you don't want to mix up in the active part of it. Merritt'll be crazy to do it, too. That's where we'll have him roped. You say to him, 'Take this money and do the work, but do it on the quiet. That's the condition. If you can't keep our secret, we'll have you fired and get some man that can.' The Mayor will chuck him if the committee says so. But it won't be necessary, if I've got Merritt sized up. He wants to get into this fight so bad that he'll agree to almost anything. His assistants we can square.

"So much for the official end of it. But what about the run of the medical profession? If they go around diagnosing typhus, the news'll spread almost as fast as through the papers. So here's how we'll fix them. Recommend the City Council to pass an ordinance making it a misdemeanor punishable by fine, imprisonment, and revocation of license to practice, for a physician to make a diagnosis of any case as a pestilential disease. The Council will do it on the committee's say-so."

"Whew!" whistled the old charlatan. "That's going pretty strong, Bel. The doctors won't stand for that."

"Believe me, they will. It's been tried and it worked fine, on the Coast, when they had the plague there. That's where I got the notion: but the revocation of the license is my own scheme. That'll scare 'em out of their wits. You'll find they don't dare peep about typhus. Especially as there aren't a dozen doctors in town that ever saw a case of it."

"That's so," agreed his principal. "I guess you're right after all, Bel."

"Sure, am I! You say you've got the newspapers fixed."

"Sewed up tight."

"Keno! Our programme's complete. You and Mr. Pierce and the Mayor see Merritt and get him. Call the meeting for next week. Make some good-natured, diplomatic feller chairman. Send out the call to about three hundred of your solidest men. Then we'll elect you permanent chairman, you can pick your Emergency Committee, put the resolution about pest-diagnosis up to the City Council—and there you are. My job's done. I shall *not* be among those present."

"Done, and mighty well done, Bel. You'll be going back to Washington?"

"No, I guess I better stick around for a while—in case. Besides, I want a little rest."

Like so many persons of the artistic temperament, Certina Charley was subject to periods of relaxation. With him these assumed the phase of strong drink, evenly and rather thickly spread over several days. On the afternoon before the carefully planned meeting, ten days after Norman Hale was taken to the hospital, the diplomat of quackery, his shoulders eased of all responsibility, sat lunching early at the Hotel Dunston. His repast consisted of a sandwich and a small bottle of well-frappéd champagne. To him, lunching, came a drummer of the patent medicine trade; a blatant and boastful fellow, from whose methods the diplomat in Mr. Belford Couch revolted. Nevertheless, the newcomer was a forceful person, and when, over two ponies of brandy ordered by the luncher in the way of inevitable hospitality, he launched upon a criticism of some of the recent Certina legislative strategy as lacking vigor (a reproach by no means to be laid to the speaker's language), Mr. Couch's tenderest feelings were lacerated. With considerable dignity for one in his condition, he bade his guest go farther and fare worse, and in mitigation of the latter's Parthian taunt, "Kid-glove fussing, 'bo," called Heaven and earth and the whole café to witness that, abhorrent though self-trumpeting was to him, no man had ever handled more delicately a prickly proposition than he had handled the Certina legislative interests. Gazing about him for sympathy he espied the son of his chief passing between the tables, and hailed him.

Two casual meetings with Certina Charley had inspired in Hal a mildly amused curiosity. Therefore, he readily enough accepted an invitation to sit down, while declining a coincident one to have a drink, on the plea that he was going to work.

"Say," appealed Charley, "did you hear that cough-lozenge-peddling boob trying to tell me where to get off, in the proprietary game? Me!"

"Perhaps he didn't know who you are," suggested Hal tactfully.

"Perhaps he don't know the way from his hand to his face with a glass of booze, either," retorted the offended one, with elaborate sarcasm. "Everybody in the trade knows me. Sure you won't have a drink?"

"No, thank you."

"Don't drink much myself," announced the testimonial-chaser. "Just once in a while. Weak kidneys."

"That's a poor tribute from a Certina man."

"Oh, Certina's all right—for those that want it. The best doctor is none too good for me when I'm off my feed."

"Well, they call Certina 'the People's Doctor,'" said Hal, quoting an argument his father had employed.

"One of the Chief's catchwords. And ain't it a corker! He's the best old boy in the business, on the bunk."

"Just what do you mean by that?" asked Hal coldly.

But Certina Charley was in an expansive mood. It never occurred to him that the heir of the Certina millions was not in the Certina secrets: that he did not wholly understand the nature of his father's trade, and view it with the same jovial cynicism that inspired the old quack.

"Who's to match him?" he challenged argumentatively. "I tell you, they all go to school to him. There ain't one of our advertising tricks, from Old Lame-Boy down to the money-back guarantee, that the others haven't crabbed. Take that 'People's Doctor' racket. Schwarzman copied it for his Marovian Mixture. Vollmer ran his 'Poor Man's Physician' copy six months, on Marsh-Weed. 'Poor Man's Doctor'! It's pretty dear treatment, I tell you."

"Surely not," said Hal.

"Sure *is* it! What's a doctor's fee? Three dollars, probably."

"And Certina is a dollar a bottle. If one bottle cures—"

"Does *what*? Quit your jollying," laughed Certina Charley unsteadily.

"Cures the disease," said Hal, his suspicions beginning to congeal into a cold dread that the revelation which he had been unconfessedly avoiding for weeks past was about to be made.

"If it did, we'd go broke. Do you know how many bottles must be sold to any one patron before the profits begin to come in? Six! Count them, six."

"Nonsense! It can't cost so much to make as—"

"Make? Of course it don't. But what does it cost to advertise? You think I'm a little drink-taken, but I ain't. I'm giving you the straight figures. It costs just the return on six bottles to get Certina into Mr. E.Z. Mark's hands, and until he's paid his seventh dollar for his seventh bottle our profits don't come in. Advertising is expensive, these days."

"How many bottles does it take to cure?" asked Hal, clinging desperately to the word.

"Nix on the cure thing, 'bo. You don't have to put up any bluff with me. I'm on the inside, right down to the bottom."

"Very well. Maybe you know more than I do, then," said Hal, with a grim determination, now that matters had gone thus far, to accept this opportunity of knowledge, at whatever cost of disillusionment. "Go ahead. Open up."

"A real cure couldn't make office-rent," declared the expert with conviction. "What you want in the proprietary game is a jollier. Certina's that. The booze does it. You ought to see the farmers in a no-license district lick it up. Three or four bottles will give a guy a pretty strong hunch for it. And after the sixth bottle it's all velvet to us, except the nine cents for manufacture and delivery."

"But it must be some good or people wouldn't keep on buying it," pursued Hal desperately.

"You've got all the old stuff, haven't you! The good ol' stock arguments," said Certina Charley, giggling. "The Chief has taught you the lesson all right. Must be studyin' up to go before a legislative committee. Well, here's the straight of it. Folks keep on buying Certina for the kick there is in it. It's a bracer. And it's a repeater, the best repeater in the trade."

"But it must cure lots of them. Look at the testimonials. Surely they're genuine."

"So's a rhinestone genuine—as a rhinestone. The testimonials that ain't bought, or given as a favor, are from rubes who want to see their names in print."

"At least I suppose it isn't harmful," said Hal desperately.

"No more than any other good ol' booze. It won't hurt a well man. I used to soak up quite a bit of it myself till my doc gave me an option on dyin' of Bright's disease or quittin'."

"Bright's disease!" exclaimed Hal.

"Oh, yes, I know: we cure Bright's disease, don't we? Well, if there's anything worse for old George W. Bright's favorite ailment than raw alcohol, then my high-priced physizzian don't know his business."

"Let me get this straight," said Hal with a white face. "Do I understand that Certina—"

"Say, wassa matter?" broke in Certina Charley, in concern; "you look sick."

"Never mind me. You go on and tell me the truth about this thing."

"I guess I been talkin' too much," muttered Certina Charley, dismayed. He gulped down the last of his champagne with a tremulous hand. "This's my second bottle," he explained. "An' brandy in between. Say, I thought you knew all about the business."

"I know enough about it now so that I've got to know the rest."

"You—you won't gimme away to the Chief? I didn't mean to show up his game. I'm—I'm pretty strong for the old boy, myself."

"I won't give you away. Go on."

"Whaddye want to know, else?"

"Is there *anything* that Certina is good for?"

"Sure! Didn't I tell you? It's the finest bracer—"

"As a cure?"

"It's just as good as any other prup-proprietary."

"That isn't the question. You say it is harmful in Bright's disease."

"Why, looka here, Mr. Surtaine, you know yourself that booze is poison to any feller with kidney trouble. Rheumatism, too, for that matter. But they get the brace, and they think they're better, and that helps push the trade, too."

"And that's where my money came from," said Hal, half to himself.

"It's all in the trade," cried Certina Charley, summoning his powers to a defense. "There's lots that's worse. There's the cocaine dopes for catarrh; they'll send a well man straight to hell in six months. There's the baby dopes; and the G-U cures that keep the disease going when right treatment could cure it; and the methylene blue—"

"Stop it! Stop it!" cried Hal. "I've heard enough."

Alcohol, the juggler with men's thoughts, abruptly pressed upon a new center of ideation in Certina Charley's brain.

"D'you think I like it?" he sniveled, with lachrymose sentimentality. "I gotta make a living, haven't I? Here's you and me, two pretty decent young fellers, having to live on a fake. Well," he added with solacing philosophy, "if we didn't get it, somebody else would."

"Tell me one thing," said Hal, getting to his feet. "Does my father know all this that you've been telling me?"

"Does the Chief *know* it? *Does* he? Why, say, my boy, Ol' Doc Surtaine, he *wrote* the proprietary medicine business!"

Misgivings beset the optimistic soul of Certina Charley as his guest faded from his vision; faded and vanished without so much as a word of excuse or farewell. For once Hal had been forgetful of courtesy. Gazing after him his host addressed the hovering waiter:—

"Say, Bill, I guess I been talkin' too much with my face. Bring's another of those li'l bo'ls."

CHAPTER XXX

ILLUMINATION

Certina Charley, plus an indeterminate quantity of alcohol, had acted upon Hal's mind as a chemical precipitant. All the young man's hitherto suppressed or unacknowledged doubts of the Certina trade and its head were now violently crystallized. Hal hurried out of the hotel, the wrath in his heart for the deception so long wrought upon him chilled by a profounder feeling, a feeling of irreparable loss. He thought in that moment that his love for his father was dead. It was not. It was only his trust that was dying, and dying hard.

Since that day of his first visit to the Certina factory, Hal's standards had undergone an intrinsic but unconscious alteration. Brought up to the patent medicine trade, though at a distance, he thought of it, by habit, as on a par with other big businesses. One whose childhood is spent in a glue factory is not prone to be supersensitive to odors. So, to Harrington Surtaine, those ethical and moral difficulties which would have bulked huge to one of a different training, were merely inherent phases of a profitable business. Misgivings had indeed stirred, at first. For these he had chided himself, as for an over-polite revulsion from the necessary blatancy of a broadly advertised enterprise. More searching questions, as they arose within him, he had met with the counter-evidence of the internal humanism and fair-dealing of the Certina shop, and of the position of its beloved chief in the commercial world.

In the face of the Relief Pills exposure, Hal could no longer excuse his father on the ground that Dr. Surtaine honestly credited his medicines with impossible efficacies. Still, he had reasoned, the Doctor had been willing instantly to abandon this nostrum when the harm done by it was concretely brought home to him. Though this argument had fallen far short of reconciling Hal to the Surtaine standards, nevertheless it had served as a makeshift to justify in part his abandonment of the hard-won principles of the "Clarion," a surrender necessary for the saving of a loved and honored father in whose essential goodness he had still believed.

Now the edifice of his faith was in ruins. If Certina itself, if the tutelary genius of the House of Surtaine, were indeed but a monstrous quackery cynically accepted as such by those in the secret, what shred of defense remained to him who had so prospered by it? Through the wreckage of his pride, his loyalty, his affection, Hal saw, in place of the glowing and benign face of Dr. Surtaine, the simulacrum of Fraud, sleek and crafty, bloated fat with the blood of tragically hopeful dupes.

One great lesson of labor Hal had already learned, that work is an anodyne. From his interview with Certina Charley he made straight for the "Clarion" office. As he hurried up the stairs, the door of Shearson's room opened upon him, and there emerged therefrom a brick-red, agile man who greeted him with a hard cordiality.

"Your paper certainly turned the trick. I gotta hand it to you!"

"What trick?" asked Hal, not recognizing the stranger.

"Selling my stock. Streaky Mountain Copper Company. Don't you remember?"

Hal did remember now. It was L.P. McQuiggan.

"More of the same for me, *if* you please," continued the visitor. "I've just made the deal with Shearson. He's stuck me up on rates a little. That's all right, though. The 'Clarion' fetches the dough. I want to start the new campaign with an interview on our prospects. Is it O.K.?"

"Come up and see Mr. Ellis," said Hal.

Having led him to the editorial office, Hal sat down to work, but found no escape from his thoughts. There was but one thing to do: he must have it out at once with Dr. Surtaine. He telephoned the factory for an appointment. Sharp-eared McQuiggan caught the call.

"That my old pal, Andy?" said he. "Gimme a shot at him while you've got him on the wire, will you?"

Cheery, not to say chirpy, was the mining promoter's greeting projected into the transmitter which Hal turned over to him. Straightway, however, a change came o'er his blithe spirit.

"Something's biting the old geezer," he informed Hal and Ellis. "Seems to have a grouch. Says he's coming over, pronto—right quick."

Five minutes later, while Mr. McQuiggan was running over some proofs which he had brought with him, Dr. Surtaine walked into the office. There was about him a formidable smoothness, as of polished metal. He greeted his old friend with a nod and a cool "Back again, I see, Elpy."

"And doing business at the old stand," rejoined his friend. "Worthington's the place where the dollars grow, all right."

"Grow, *and* stay," said Dr. Surtaine.

"Meaning?" inquired McQuiggan solicitously.

"That you've over-medicated this field."

"Have I got any dollars away from you, Andy?"

"No. But you have from my people."

"Well, their money's as good to buy booze with as anybody else's, I reckon."

Dr. Surtaine had sat down, directly opposite the visitor, fronting him eye-to-eye. Nothing loath, McQuiggan accepted the challenge. His hard, brisk voice, with a sub-tone of the snarl, crossed the Doctor's strong, heavy utterance like a rapier engaging a battle-axe. Both assumed a suavity of manner felt to be just at the breaking point. The two spectators sat, surprised and expectant.

"I don't suppose," said Dr. Surtaine, after a pause, "there's any use trying to get you to refund."

"Still sticking out for the money-back-if-not-satisfied racket—in the other fellow's business, eh, Andy? Better practice it in your own."

"Hal,"—Dr. Surtaine turned to his son,—"has McQuiggan brought in a new batch of copy?"

"So I understand."

"The 'Clarion' mustn't run it."

"The hell it mustn't!" said McQuiggan.

"It's crooked," said the quack bluntly.

The promoter laughed. "A hot one, you are, to talk about crookedness."

"He's paying his advertising bills out of my people's pay envelopes!"

accused Dr. Surtaine.

"How's that, Doc?" asked Ellis.

"Why, when he was here before, he spent some time around the Certina plant and got acquainted with the department managers and a lot of the others, and damn me!" cried Dr. Surtaine, grinning in spite of his wrath, "if he didn't sting 'em all for stock."

"How do you know they're stung?" inquired Ellis.

"From an expert on the ground. I got anxious when I found my own people were in it, and had a man go out there from Phoenix. He reports that the Streaky Mountain hasn't got a thing but expectations and hardly that."

"Well, you didn't say there was anything more, did you?" inquired the bland McQuiggan.

"I? I didn't say?"

"Yes, *you*. You got up the ads."

"Well—well—well, of all the nerve!" cried Dr. Surtaine, grievously appealing to the universe at large. "I got 'em up! You gave me the material, didn't you?"

"Sure, did I. Hot stuff it was, too."

"Hot bunk! And to flim-flam my own people with it, too!"

"Anybody that works in your joint ought to be wise to the bunk game," suggested McQuiggan.

"I'll tell you one thing: you don't run any more of it in this town."

"Maybe I don't and then again maybe I do. It won't be as good as your copy, p'r'aps. But it'll get *some* coin, I reckon. Take a look," he taunted, and tossed his proofs to the other.

The quack broke forth at the first glance. "Look here! You claim fifty thousand tons of copper in sight."

"So there is."

"With a telescope, I suppose."

"Well, telescope's sight, ain't it? You wouldn't try to hear through one, would you?"

"And $200,000.00 worth, ready for milling," continued the critic.

"Printer's error in the decimal point," returned the other, with airy impudence. "Move it two to the left. Keno! There you have it: $2000.00."

"Very ingenious, Mr. McQuiggan," said Hal. "But you're practically admitting that your ads. are faked."

"Admittin' nothin'! I offer you the ads. and I've got the ready stuff to pay for 'em."

"And you think that is all that's necessary?"

"Sure do I!"

"Mr. McQuiggan," remarked Ellis, "has probably been reading our able editorial on the reformed and chastened policy of the 'Clarion.'"

Hal turned an angry red. "That doesn't commit us to accepting swindles."

"Don't it?" queried McQuiggan. "Since when did you get so pick-an'-choosy?"

"Straight advertising," announced Dr. Surtaine, "has been the unvarying policy of this paper since my son took it over."

"Straight!" vociferated McQuiggan. "*Straight?* Ladies and gents: the well-known Surtaine Family will now put on their screamin' farce entitled 'Honesty is the Best Policy.'"

"When you're through playing the clown—" began Hal.

"Straight advertising," pursued the other. "Did I really hear them sweet words in Andy Certain's voice? No! Say, somebody ring an alarm-clock on me. I can't wake up."

"I think we've heard enough from you, McQuiggan," warned Hal.

"Do you!" The promoter sprang from his chair and all the latent venom of his temper fumed and stung in the words he poured out. "Well, take another think. I've got some things to tell you, young feller. Don't you come the high-and-holy on me. You and your smooth, big, phony stuffed-shirt of a father."

"Here, you!" shouted the leading citizen thus injuriously designated, but the other's voice slashed through his protest like a blade through pulp.

"Certina! Ho-oh! Warranted to cure consumption, warts, heart-disease, softening of the brain, and the bloody pip! And what is it? Morphine and booze."

"You're a liar," thundered the outraged proprietor: "Ten thousand dollars to any one who can show a grain of morphine in it."

"Changed the formula, have you? Pure Food Law scared you out of the dope, eh? Well, even at that it's the same old bunk. What about your testimonials? Fake 'em, and forge 'em, and bribe and blackmail for 'em and then stand up to me and pull the pious plate-pusher stuff about being straight. Oh, my Gawd! It'd make a straddle-bug spit at the sun, to hear you. Why, I'm no saint, but the medical line was too strong for my stomach. I got out of it."

"Yes, you did, you dirty little dollar-snatcher! You got put of it into jail for peddling raw gin—."

"Don't you go raking up old muck with me, you rotten big poisoner!" roared McQuiggan: "or you'll get the hot end of it. How about that girl that went batty after taking Cert—"

"Wait a moment! Father! Please!" Hal broke in, aghast at this display. "We're not discussing the medical business. We're talking advertising. McQuiggan, yours is refused. We don't run that class of matter in the 'Clarion.'"

"No? Since when? You'd better consult an oculist, young Surtaine."

"If ever this paper carried such a glaring fake as your Streaky Mountain—"

"Stop right there! Stop! look! and listen!" He caught up the day's issue from the floor and flaunted it, riddling the flimsy surface with the stiffened finger of indictment. "Look at it! Look at this ad—and this—and this." The paper was rent with the vehemence of his indication. "Put my copy next to that, and it'd come to life and squirm to get away."

"Nothing there but what every paper takes," defended Ellis.

"Every paper'd be glad to take my stuff, too. Why, Streaky Mountain copy is the Holy Bible compared to what you've got here. Take a slant at this: 'Consumption Cured in Three Months.'—'Cancer Cured or your Money Back.'—Catarrh dopes, headache cures, germ-killers, baby-soothers, nerve-builders,—the whole stinkin' lot. Don't I know 'em! Either sugar pills that couldn't cure a belly-ache, or hell's-brew of morphine and booze. Certina ain't the worst of 'em, any more than it's the best. I may squeeze a few dollars out of easy boobs, but you, Andy Certain, you and your young whelp here, you're playin' the poor suckers for their lives. And then you're too lily-fingered to touch a mining proposition because there's a gamble in it!"

He crumpled the paper in his sinewy hands, hurled it to the floor, kicked it high over Dr. Surtaine's head, and stalking across to Hal's desk, slapped down his proofs on it with a violence that jarred the whole structure.

"You run that," he snarled, "or I'll hire the biggest hall in Worthington and tell the whole town what I've just been telling you."

His face, furrowed and threatening, was thrust down close to Hal's. Thus lowered, the eyes came level with a strip of print, pasted across the inner angle of the desk.

"'Whose Bread I Eat, his Song I Sing,'" he read. "What's that?"

"A motto," said McGuire Ellis. "The complete guide to correct journalistic conduct. Put there, lest we forget."

"H'm!" said McQuiggan, puzzled. "It's in the right place, all right, all right. Well, does my ad go?"

"No," said Hal. "But I'm much obliged to you, McQuiggan."

"You go to hell. What're you obliged to me for?" said the visitor suspiciously.

"For the truth. I think you've told it to me. Anyway you've made me tell it to myself."

"I guess I ain't told you much you don't know about your snide business."

"You have, though. Go ahead and hire your hall. But—take a look at tomorrow's 'Clarion' before you make your speech. Now, good-day to you."

McQuiggan, wondering and a little subdued by a certain quiet resolution in Hal's speech, went, beckoning Ellis after him for explication. Hal turned to his father.

"I don't suppose," he began haltingly, "that you could have told me all this yourself."

"What?" asked Dr. Surtaine, consciously on the defensive.

"About the medical ads."

"McQuiggan's a sore-head"—began the Doctor.

"But you might have told me about Certina, as I've been living on Certina money."

"There's nothing to tell." All the self-assurance had gone out of the quack's voice.

"Father, does Certina cure Bright's disease?"

"Cure? Why, Boyee, what *is* a cure?"

"Does it cure it?" insisted Hal.

"Sit down and cool off. You've let that skunk, McQuiggan, get you all excited."

"This began before McQuiggan."

"Then you've been talking to some jealous doctor-crank."

"For God's sake, Father, answer my plain question."

"Why, there's no such thing as an actual cure for Bright's disease."

"Don't you say in the advertisements that Certina will cure it?"

"Oh, advertisements!" returned the quack with an uneasy smile. "Nobody takes an advertisement for gospel."

"I'm answered. Will it cure diabetes?"

"No medicine will. No doctor can. They're incurable diseases. Certina will do as much—"

"Is it true that alcohol simply hastens the course of the disease?"

"Authorities differ," said the quack warily. "But as the disease is incurable—"

"Then it's all lies! Lies and murder!"

"You're excited, Boy-ee," said the charlatan with haggard forbearance. "Let me explain for a moment."

"Isn't it pretty late for explanations between you and me?"

"This is the gist of the proprietary trade," said the Doctor, picking his words carefully. "Most diseases cure themselves. Medicine isn't much good. Doctors don't know a great deal. Now, if a patent medicine braces a patient up and gives him courage, it does all that can be done. Then, the advertising inspires confidence in the cure and that's half the battle. There's a lot in Christian Science, and a lot in common between Christian Science and the proprietary business. Both work on the mind and help it to cure the body. But the proprietary trade throws in a few drugs to brace up the system, allay symptoms, and push along the good work. There you have Certina."

Hal shook his head in dogged misery. "It can't cure. You admit it can't cure. And it may kill, in the very cases where it promises to cure. How could you take money made that way?"

A flash of cynicism hardened the handsome old face. "Somebody's going to make a living off the great American sucker. If it wasn't us, it'd be somebody else." He paused, sighed, and in a phrase summed up and crystallized the whole philosophy of the medical quack: "Life's a cut-throat game, anyway."

"And we're living on the blood," said Hal. "It's a good thing," he added slowly, "that I didn't know you as you are before Milly Neal's death."

"Why so?"

"Because," cried the son fiercely, "I'd have published the whole truth of how she died and why, in the 'Clarion.'"

"It isn't too late yet," retorted Dr. Surtaine with pained dignity, "if you wish to strike at the father who hasn't been such a bad father to you. But would you have told the truth of your part in it?"

"My part in it?" repeated Hal, in dull puzzlement. "You mean the ad?"

"You know well enough what I mean. Boy-ee, Boy-ee,"—there was an edge of genuine agony in the sonorous voice,—"we've drawn far apart, you and I. Is all the wrong on my side? Can you judge me so harshly, with your own conscience to answer?"

"What I've got on my conscience you've put there. You've made me turn back on every principle I have. I've dishonored myself and my office for you. You've cost me the respect of the men I work with, and the faith of the best friend I've got in the world."

"The *best* friend, Boy-ee?" questioned the Doctor gently.

"The best friend: McGuire Ellis."

Hal's gaze met his father's. And what he saw there all but unmanned him. From the liquid depths of the old quack's eyes, big and soft like an animal's, there welled two great tears, to trickle slowly down the set face.

Hal turned and stumbled from the office.

Hardly knowing whither he went, he turned in at the first open door, which chanced to be Shearson's. There he sat until his self-control returned. As the aftermath of his anger there remained with him a grim determination. It was implicit in his voice, as he addressed Shearson, who walked in upon him.

"Cut out every line of medical from the paper."

"When?" gasped Shearson.

"Now. For tomorrow's paper."

"But, Mr. Surtaine—"

"Every—damned—line. And if any of it ever gets back, the man responsible loses his job."

"Yes, sir," said the cowed and amazed Shearson.

Hal returned to his sanctum, to find Ellis in his own place and Dr. Surtaine gone.

"Ellis, you put that motto on my desk."

"Yes."

"What for?"

"Lest we forget," repeated Ellis.

"Not much danger of that," replied his employer bitterly. "Now, I want you to take it down."

"Is that an order?"

"Would you obey it if it were?"

"No."

"You'd resign first?"

"Yes."

"Then I'll take it down myself."

With his letter-opener he pried the offensive strip loose, tore it across thrice, and scattered the pieces on the floor.

"Mr. Ellis," said he formally, "hereafter no medical advertising will be accepted for or published in the 'Clarion.' The same rule applies to fraudulent advertising of any kind. I wish you and the other members of the staff to act as censors for the advertising."

"Yes, sir," said McGuire Ellis.

He turned back to his desk, and sprawled his elbows on it. His head lapsed lower and lower until it attained the familiar posture of rest. But McGuire Ellis was not sleeping. He was thinking.

CHAPTER XXXI
THE VOICE OF THE PROPHET

Two hundred and fifty representative citizens, mostly of the business type, with a sprinkling of other occupations not including physicians, sat fanning themselves into a perspiration in the Chamber of Commerce assembly rooms, and wondering what on earth an Emergency Health Meeting might be. Congressman Brett Harkins, a respectable nonentity, who was presiding, had refrained from telling them: deliberately, it would appear, as his speech had dealt vaguely with the greatness of Worthington's material prosperity, now threatened—if one might credit his theory—by a combination of senseless panic and reckless tongues; and had concluded by stating that Mr. William Douglas, one of the leaders of our bar, as all the chairman's hearers well knew, would explain the situation and formulate a plan for the meeting's consideration.

Explanation, however, did not prove to be Mr. William Douglas's forte. Coached by that practiced diplomat, Certina Charley, he made a speech memorable chiefly for what it did not say. The one bright, definite gleam, amidst rolling columns of oratory, was the proposal that an Emergency Committee of One Hundred be appointed to cope with the situation, that the initial sum of twenty-five thousand dollars be pledged by subscription, and that their distinguished fellow citizen, Dr. L. André Surtaine, be permanent chairman of said committee, with power to appoint. Dr. Surtaine had generously offered to subscribe ten thousand dollars to the fund. (Loud and prolonged applause; the word "thousand" preceding the word "dollars" and itself preceded by any numeral from one to one million, inclusive, being invariably provocative of acclaim in a subscription meeting of representative citizens.) Mr. Douglas took pride in nominating that Midas of Medicine, Dr. Surtaine. (More and louder applause.) The Reverend Dr. Wales, of Dr. Surtaine's church, sonorously seconded the nomination. So did Hollis Myers, of the Security Power Products Company. So, a trifle grumpily, did Elias M. Pierce. Also Col. Parker, editor of the "Telegram," Aaron Scheffler, of Scheffler and Mintz, and Councilman Carlin. The presiding officer inquired with the bland indifference of the assured whether there were any further nominations. There were not. But turning in his second-row seat, Festus Willard, who was too important a figure commercially to leave out, though Dr. Surtaine had entertained doubts of his "soundness," demanded of McGuire Ellis, seated just behind him, what it was all about.

"Ask the chairman," suggested Ellis.

"I will," said Willard. He got up and did.

The Honorable Brett Harkins looked uncomfortable. He didn't really know what it was all about. Moreover, it had been intimated to him that he'd perhaps better not know. He cast an appealing glance at Douglas.

"That is not exactly the question before the meeting," began Douglas hastily.

"It is the question I asked," persisted Willard. "Before we elect Dr. Surtaine or any one else chairman of a committee with a fund to spend, I want to know what the committee is for."

"To cope with the health situation of the city."

"Very well. Now we're getting somewhere. Where's Dr. Merritt? I think we ought to hear from him on that point."

Murmurs of assent were heard about the room. Dr. Surtaine rose to his feet.

"If I may be pardoned for speaking to a motion of which I am a part," he said in his profound and mellow voice.

"I think I can throw light upon the situation. Quite a number of us have observed with uneasiness the increase of sickness in Worthington. Sensationalists have gone so far as to whisper that there is an epidemic. I have myself made a rigid investigation. More than this, my son, Mr. Harrington Surtaine, has placed the resources of the 'Clarion' staff at our disposal, and on the strength of both inquiries, I am prepared to assure this gathering that nothing like an epidemic exists."

"Well, I *am* damned!" was McGuire Ellis's astounded and none too low-voiced comment upon this bold perversion of the "Clarion" enterprise. Stretching upward from his seat he looked about for Hal. The young editor sat in a far corner, his regard somberly intent upon the speaker.

"Alarm there has undoubtedly been, and is," pursued Dr. Surtaine. "To find means to allay it is the purpose of the meeting. We must remove the cause. Both our morbidity and our mortality rate, though now retrograding, have been excessive for several weeks, especially in the Rookeries district. There has been a prevalence of malaria of a severe type, which, following last winter's epidemic of grip, has proven unusually fatal. Dr. Merritt believes that he can wipe out the disease quietly if a sufficient sum is put at his disposal."

This was not authoritative. Merritt had declined to commit himself, but Dr. Surtaine was making facts of his hopes.

"In this gathering it is hardly necessary for me to refer to the municipal importance of Old Home Week and to the damage to its prospects which would be occasioned by any suspicion of epidemic," continued the speaker. "Whatever may be the division of opinion as to methods, we are surely unanimous in wishing to protect the interests of the centennial celebration. And this can best be done through a committee of representative men, backing the constituted health authorities, without commotion or disturbance. Have I answered your doubts, Mr. Willard?" he concluded, turning a brow of benign inquiry upon that gentleman.

"Not wholly," said Festus Willard. "I've heard it stated on medical authority that there is some sort of plague in the Rookeries."

A murmur of inquiry rose. "Plague? What kind of plague?"—"Who says so?"—"Does he mean bubonic?"—"No doctor that knows his business—"—"They say doctors are shut out of the Rookeries."—"Order! Order!"

Through the confusion cleaved the edged voice of E.M. Pierce, directed to the chairman:

"Shut that off."

A score took the cue. "Question! Question!" they cried.

"Do I get an answer to my question?" persisted Willard.

"What is your question?" asked the harassed chairman.

"Is there a pestilence in the Rookeries? If so, what is its nature?"

"There is not," stated Dr. Surtaine from his seat. "Who ever says there is, is an enemy to our fair and healthy city."

This noble sentiment, delivered with all the impressiveness of which the old charlatan was master, roused a burst of applause. To its rhythm there stalked down the side aisle and out upon the rostrum the gaunt figure of the Reverend Norman Hale.

"Mr. Chairman," he said.

"How did that fellow get here?" Dr. Surtaine asked of Douglas.

"We invited all the ministers," was the low response. "I understood he was seriously ill."

"He is a trouble-maker. Tell Harkins not to let him talk."

Douglas spoke a word in the chairman's ear.

"There's a motion before the house—I mean the meeting," began Congressman Harkins, when the voice behind him cut in again, hollow and resonant:

"Mr. Chairman."

"Do you wish to speak to the question?" asked the chairman uncertainly.

"I do."

"No, no!" called Douglas. "Out of order. Question!"

Voices from the seats below supported him. But there were other calls for a hearing for the newcomer. Curiosity was his ally. The meeting anticipated a sensation. The chairman, lacking a gavel, hammered on the stand with a tumbler, and presently produced a modified silence, through which the voice of the Reverend Norman Hale could be heard saying that he wished but three minutes.

He stepped to the edge of the platform, and the men below noticed for the first time that he carried in his right hand a wreath of metal-mounted, withered flowers. There was no mistaking the nature of the wreath. It was such as is left lying above the dead for wind and rain to dissipate. Hale raised it slowly above his head. The silence in the hall became absolute.

"I brought these flowers from a girl's grave," said the Reverend Norman Hale. "The girl had sinned. Death was the wage of her sin. She died by her own hand. So her offense is punished. That account is closed."

"What has all this to do—" began the chairman; but he stopped, checked by a wave of sibilant remonstrance from the audience.

The speaker went on, with relentless simplicity, still holding the mortuary symbol aloft:—

"But there is another account not yet closed. The girl was deceived. Not by the father of her unborn child. That is a different guilt, to be reckoned with in God's own time. The deception for which she has paid with her life was not the deception of hot passion, but of cold greed. A man betrayed her, as he has betrayed thousands of other unfortunates, to put money into his own pockets. He promised her immunity. He said to her and to all women, in print, that she need not fear motherhood if she would buy his medicine. She believed the promise. She paid her dollar. And she found, too late, that it was a lie.

"So she went to the man. She knew him. And she determined either that he should help her or that she would be revenged on him. All this she told me in a note, to be opened in case of her death. He must have refused to help. He had not the criminal courage to produce the abortion which he falsely promised in his advertisements. What passed between them I do not know. But I believe that she attempted to kill him and failed. She attempted to kill herself and succeeded. The blood of Camilla Neal is on every cent of Dr. Surtaine's ten-thousand-dollar subscription."

He tossed the wreath aside. It rolled, clattering and clinking, and settled down at the feet of the Midas of Medicine who stared at it with a contorted face.

The meeting sat stricken into immovability. It seemed incredible that the tensity of the silence should not snap. Yet it held.

"I shall vote 'No' on the motion," said the Reverend Norman Hale, still with that quiet and appalling simplicity. "I came here from a hand-to-hand struggle with death to vote 'No.' I have strength for only a word more. The city is stricken with typhus. It is no time for concealment or evasion. We are at death-grips with a very dreadful plague. It has broken out of the Rookeries district. There are half a dozen new foci of infection. In the face of this, silence is deadly. If you elect Dr. Surtaine and adopt his plan, you commit yourself to an alliance with fraud and death. You deceive and betray the people who look to you for leadership. And there will be a terrible price to pay in human lives. I thank you for hearing me patiently."

No man spoke for long seconds after the young minister sat down, wavering a little as he walked to a chair at the rear. But through the representative citizenship of Worthington, in that place gathered, passed a quiver of sound, indeterminate, obscure, yet having all the passion of a quelled sob. Eyes furtively sought the face of Dr. Surtaine. But the master-quack remained frozen by the same bewilderment as his fellows. Perhaps alone in that crowd, Elias M. Pierce remained untouched emotionally. He rose, and his square granite face was cold as abstract reason. There was not even feeling enough in his voice to give the semblance of a sneer to his words as he said:

"All this is very well in its place, and doubtless does credit to the sentimental qualities of the speaker. But it is not evidence. It is an unsupported statement, part of which is admittedly conjecture. Allowing the alleged facts to be true, are we to hold a citizen of Dr. Surtaine's standing and repute responsible for the death of a woman caused by her own immorality? The woman whose death Mr. Hale has turned to such oratorical account was, I take it, a prostitute—"

"That is a damned lie!"

Hal Surtaine came down the aisle in long strides, speaking as he came.

"Milly Neal was my employee and my father's employee. If she went astray once, who are you to judge her? Who are any of us to judge her? I took part of that blood-money. The advertisement was in my paper, paid for with Surtaine money. What Mr. Hale says is the living truth. No man shall foul her memory in my hearing."

"And what was she to you? You haven't told us that yet?" There was a rancid sneer in Pierce's insinuation.

Hal turned from the aisle and went straight for him. A little man rose in his way. It was Mintz, who had given him the heartening word after the committee meeting. In his blind fury Hal struck him a staggering blow. But the little Jew was plucky. He closed with the younger man, and clinging to him panted out his good advice.

"Don'd fighd 'im, nod here. It's no good. Go to the pladform an' say your say. We'll hear you."

But it was impossible to hear any one now. Uproar broke loose. Men shouted, stormed, cursed; the meeting was become a rabble. Above the din could be distinguished at intervals the voice of the Honorable Brett Harkins, who, in frantic but not illogical reversion to the idea of a political convention, squalled for the services of the sergeant-at-arms. There was no sergeant-at-arms.

Mintz's pudgy but clogging arms could restrain an athlete of Hal's power only a brief moment; but in that moment sanity returned to the fury-heated brain.

"I beg your pardon, Mintz," he said; "you're quite right. I thank you for stopping me."

He returned to the aisle, pressing forward, with what purpose he could hardly have said, when he felt the sinewy grasp of McGuire Ellis on his shoulder.

"Tell 'em the whole thing," fiercely urged Ellis. "Be a man. Own up to the whole business, between you and the girl."

"I don't know what you mean!" cried Hal.

"Don't be young," groaned Ellis; "you've gone halfway. Clean it up. Then we can face the situation with the 'Clarion.' Tell 'em you were her lover."

"Milly's? I wasn't. It was Veltman."

"Good God of Mercy!"

"Did you think—"

"Yes;—Lord forgive me! Why didn't you tell me?"

"How could I tell you suspected—"

"All right! I know. We'll talk it out later. The big thing now is, what's the paper going to do about this meeting?"

"Print it."

Into Ellis's face flashed the fervor of the warrior who sees victory loom through the clouds of hopeless defeat.

"You mean that?"

"Every word of it. And run the epidemic spread—"

Before he could finish, Ellis was fighting his way to a telephone.

Hal met his father's eyes, and turned away with a heartsick sense that, in the one glance, had passed indictment, conviction, a hopeless acquiescence, and the dumb reproach of the trapped criminal against avenging justice. He turned and made for the nearest exit, conscious of only two emotions, a burning desire to be away from that place and a profound gladness that, without definite expression of the change, the bitter alienation of McGuire Ellis was past.

As Hal left, there arose, out of the turmoil, one clear voice of reason: the thundering baritone of Festus Willard moving an adjournment. It passed, and the gathering slowly dispersed. Avoiding the offered companionship of Congressman Harkins and Douglas, Dr. Surtaine took himself off by a side passage. At the end of it, alone, stood the Reverend Norman Hale, leaning against the sill of an open window. The old quack rushed upon him.

"Keep off!" warned the young minister, throwing himself into an attitude of defense.

"No, no," protested Dr. Surtaine: "don't think I meant *that*. I—I want to thank you."

"Thank *me*?" The minister put his hand to his head. "I don't understand."

"For leaving my boy out of it."

"Oh! That. I didn't see the necessity of dragging him in."

"That was kind. You handled me pretty rough. Well, I'm used to rough work. But the boy—look here, you knew all about this Milly Neal business, didn't you?"

"Yes."

"Maybe you could tell me," went on the old quack miserably. "I can understand Hal's getting into a—an affair with the girl—being kinda carried away and losing his head. What I can't get is his—his quittin' her when she was in trouble."

"I still don't understand," protested the minister. "My head isn't very good. I've been ill, you know."

"You let him off without telling his name tonight. And that made me think maybe he wasn't in wrong so far as I thought. Maybe there were—what-ye-call-'em?—mitigating circumstances. Were there?"

A light broke in upon the Reverend Norman Hale. "Did you think your son was Milly Neal's lover? He wasn't."

"Are you sure?" gasped the father.

"As sure as of my faith in Heaven."

The old man straightened up, drawing a breath so profound that it seemed to raise his stature.

"I wouldn't take a million dollars for that word," he declared.

"But your own part in this?" queried the other in wonderment. "I hated to have to say—"

"What does it matter?"

"You have no concern for yourself?" puzzled the minister.

"Oh, I'll come out on top. I always come out on top. What got to my heart was my boy. I thought he'd gone wrong. And now I know he hasn't."

The old charlatan's strong hand fell on his assailant's shoulder, then slipped down supportingly under his arm.

"You look pretty shaky," said he with winning solicitude. "Let me take you home in my car. It's waiting outside."

The Reverend Norman Hale accepted, marveling greatly over the complex miracle of the soul of man—who is formed in the image of his Maker.

CHAPTER XXXII

THE WARNING

Tradition of the "Clarion" office embalms "the evening the typhus story broke" as a nightmare out of which was born history. Chronologically, according to the veracious records of Bim the Guardian of Portals, the tumult began at exactly 10.47, with the arrival of Mr. McGuire Ellis, traveling up the staircase five steps at a jump and calling in a strangled voice for Wayne. That usually controlled journalist rushed out of an inner room in alarm, demanding to know whether New York City had been whelmed with a tidal wave or the King of England murdered in his bed, and in an instant was struggling in the grasp of his fellow editor.

"What's left of the epidemic spread?" demanded the new arrival breathlessly.

"The killed story?"

"What's left of it?" clamored Ellis, dancing all over his colleague's feet. "Can you find the copy? Notes? Anything?"

"Proofs," said Wayne. "I saved a set."

Ellis sat down in a chair and regarded his underling with an expression of stupefied benevolence.

"Wayne," he said, "you're a genius. You're the fine flower and perfect blossom of American journalism. I love you, Wayne. With passionate fervor, I love you. Now, *gitta move on*!!!" His voice soared and exploded. "We're going to run it tomorrow!"

"Tomorrow? How? It isn't up to date. Nobody's touched it since—"

"Bring it up to date! Fire every man in the office out on it. Tear the hide off the old paper and smear the story all over the front page. Haul in your eyes and *start*!"

The whirl of what ensued swamped even Bim's cynic and philosophic calm. Amidst a buzz of telephones and a mighty scurrying of messengers the staff of the "Clarion" was gathered into the fold, on a "drop-everything" emergency call, and instantly dispersed again to the hospitals, the homes of the health officials, the undertakers' establishments, the cemeteries, and all other possible sources of information. The composing-room seethed and clanged. Copy-readers yelled frantically through tubes, and received columns of proofs which, under the ruthless slaughter of their blue pencils, returned as "stickfuls," that room might be made for the great story. Cable news was slashed right and left. Telegraph "skeletons" waited in vain for their bones to be clothed with the flesh of print. The Home Advice Department sank with all on board, and the most popular sensational preacher in town, who had that evening made a stirring anti-suffrage speech full of the most unfailing jokes, fell out of the paper and broke his heart. The carnage in news was general and frightful. Two pages plus of a story that "breaks" after 10 P.M. calls for heroic measures.

At 10.53 Mr. Harrington Surtaine arrived, hardly less tempestuously than his predecessor. He did not even greet Bim as he passed through the gate, which was unusual; but went direct to Ellis.

"Can we do it, Mac?"

"The epidemic story? Yes. There was a proof saved."

"Good. Can you do the story of the meeting?"

Ellis hesitated. "All of it?"

"Every bit. Leave out nothing."

"Hadn't you better think it over?"

"I've thought."

"It'll hit the old—your father pretty hard."

"I can't help it."

A surge of human pity overswept Ellis's stimulated journalistic keenness. "You don't *have* to do this, Hal," he suggested. "No other paper—"

"I do have to do it," retorted the other. "And worse."

Ellis stared.

"I've got to print the story of Milly's death: the facts just as they happened. And I've got to write it myself."

The professional zest surged up again in McGuire Ellis. "My Lord!" he exclaimed. "*What a paper tomorrow's 'Clarion' will be!* But why? Why? Why the Neal story—now?"

"Because I can't print the epidemic spread unless I print the other. I've given my word. I told my father if ever I suppressed news for my own protection, I'd give up the fight and play the game like all the other papers. I've tried it. Mac, it isn't my game."

"No," replied his subordinate in a curious tone, "it isn't your game."

"You'll write the meeting?"

"Yes."

"Save out a column for my story."

Ellis returned to Wayne at the news desk. "Hell's broke loose at the Emergency Health meeting," he remarked, employing the conventional phrasing of his craft.

And Wayne, in the same language, inquired:

"How much?"

"Two columns. And a column from the Boss on another story."

"Whew!" whistled Wayne. "We *shall* have some paper."

From midnight until 2.30 in the morning the reporters on the great story dribbled in. Each, as he arrived, said a brief word to Wayne, got a curt direction, slumped into his seat, and silently wrote. It was all very methodical and quiet and orderly. A really big news event always is after the first disturbance of adjustment. Newspaper offices work smoothest when the tension is highest.

At 12.03 A.M. Bim received two flurried Aldermen and the head of a city department. At 12.35 he held spirited debate with the Deputy Commissioner of Health. Just as the clock struck one, two advertising managers, arriving neck and neck, merged their appeals in an ineffectual attempt to obtain information from the youthful Cerberus, which he loftily declined to furnish, as to the whereabouts of anyone with power to ban or bind, on the "Clarion." At 1.30 the Guardian of the Gate had the honor and pleasure of meeting, for the first time, his Honor the Mayor of the City. Finally, at 1.59 he "took a chance," as he would have put it, and, misliking the autocratic deportment of a messenger from E.M. Pierce, told that emissary that he could tell Mr. Pierce exactly where to go to—and go there himself. All the while, unmoved amidst protestation, appeal, and threat, the steady news-machine went on grinding out unsuppressible history for itself and its city.

Sharp to the regular hour, the presses clanged, and the building thrilled through its every joint to the pulse of print. Hal Surtaine rose from his desk and walked to the window. McGuire Ellis also rose, walked over and stood near him.

"Three pretty big beats tomorrow," he said awkwardly, at length.

"The Milly Neal story won't be a beat," replied Hal.

"No? How's that?"

"I've sent our proofs to all the other papers."

"Well, I'm—What's the idea?"

"We lied to them about the story in the first instance. They played fair, according to the rules, and took our lie. We can't beat 'em on our own story, now."

"Right you are. Bet none of 'em prints it, though." Wherein he was a true prophet.

There was a long, uneasy pause.

"Hal," said Ellis hesitantly.

"Well?"

"I'm a fool."

The white weariness of Hal's face lit up with a smile. "Why, Mac—" he began.

"A pin-head," persisted the other stubbornly. "A block of solid ivory from the collar up. I'm—I'm *young* in the head," he concluded, with supreme effort of self-condemnation.

"It's all right," said his chief, perfectly knowing what Ellis meant.

"Have I said enough?"

"Plenty."

"You didn't put Veltman in your story?"

"No. What was the good?"

"That's right, too."

"Good-night, Mac, I'm for the hotel."

"Good-night, Hal. See you in the morning."

"Yes. I'll be around early."

Ellis's eyes followed his chief out through the door. He returned to his desk and sat thinking. He saw, with pitiless clearness, the storm gathering over the "Clarion": the outburst of public hostility, the depletion of advertisers and subscribers, the official opposition closing avenues of information, the disastrous probabilities of the Pierce libel suits, now soon to be pushed; and his undaunted spirit of a crusader rose and lusted for the battle.

"They may lick us," he said to his paste-pot, the recipient of many a bitter confidence and thwarted hope in the past; "but we'll show 'em what a real newspaper is, for once. And"—his eyes sought the door through which Hal Surtaine had passed—"I've got this much out of it, anyway: I've helped a boy make himself a Man."

Ten thousand extra copies sped from the new and wonder-working press of the "Clarion" that night, to be absorbed, swallowed, engulfed by a mazed populace. In all the city there was perhaps not a man, woman, or child who, by the following evening, had not read or heard of the "Clarion's" exposure of the epidemic—except one. Max Veltman lay, senseless to all this, between stupor and a fevered delirium in which the spirit of Milly Neal called on him for delayed vengeance.

CHAPTER XXXIII

THE GOOD FIGHT

Earthquake or armed invasion could scarce have shocked staid Worthington more profoundly than did the "Clarion's" exposure. Of the facts there could be no reasonable doubt. The newspaper's figures were specific, and its map of infection showed no locality exempt. The city had wakened from an untroubled sleep to find itself poisoned.

As an immediate result of the journalistic tocsin, the forebodings of Dr. Surtaine and his associates as to the effects of publicity bade fair to be justified. Undeniably there was danger of the disease scattering, through the medium of runaways from the stricken houses. But the "Clarion" had its retort pat for the tribe of "I-told-you-so," admitting the prospect of some primary harm to save a great disaster later. More than one hundred lives, it pointed out, giving names and dates, had already been sacrificed to the shibboleth of secrecy; the whole city had been imperiled; the disease had set up its foci of infection in a score of places, and there were some three hundred cases, in all, known or suspected. One method only could cope with the situation: the fullest public information followed by radical hygienic measures.

Of information there was no lack. So tremendous a news feature could not be kept out of print by the other dailies, all of whom now admitted the presence of the pestilence, while insisting that its scope had been greatly exaggerated, and piously deprecating the "sensationalism" of their contemporary. Thus the city administration was forced to action. An appropriation was voted to the Health Bureau. Dr. Merritt, seizing his opportunity, organized a quarantine army, established a detention camp and isolation hospital, and descended upon the tenement districts, as terrible (to the imagination of the frantic inhabitants) as a malevolent god. The Emergency Health Committee, meantime, died and was forgotten overnight.

Something not unlike panic swept the Rookeries. Wild rumors passed from mouth to mouth, growing as they went. A military cordon, it was said, was to be cast about the whole ward and the people pent up inside to die. Refugees were to be shot on sight. The infected buildings were to be burned to the ground, and the tenants left homeless. The water-supply was to be poisoned, to get rid of the exposed—had already been poisoned, some said, and cited sudden mysterious deaths. Such savage imaginings of suspicion as could spring only from the ignorant fears of a populace beset by a secret and deadly pest, roused the district to a rat-like defiance. Such of the residents as were not home-bound by the authorities, growled in saloon back rooms and muttered in the streets. Hatred of the "Clarion" was the burden of their bitterness. Two of its reporters were mobbed in the hard-hit ward, the day after the publication of the first article.

Nor was the paper much better liked elsewhere. It was held responsible for all the troubles. Though the actuality of the quarantine fell far short of the expectant fears, still there was a mighty turmoil. Families were separated, fugitives were chased down and arrested, and close upon the heels of the primary harassment came the threat of economic complications, as factories and stores all over the city, for their own protection, dismissed employees known to live within the near range of the pestilence. In the minds of the sufferers from these measures and of their friends, the "Clarion" was an enemy to the public. But it was read with avid impatience, for Wayne, working on the principle that "it is news and not evil that stirs men," contrived to find some new sensational development for every issue. Do what the rival papers might, the "Clarion" had and held the windward course.

Representative Business, that Great Mogul of Worthington, was, of course, outraged by the publication. Hal Surtaine was an ill bird who had fouled his own nest. The wires had carried the epidemic news to every paper in the country, and Worthington was proclaimed "unclean" to the ears of all. The Old Home Week Committee on Arrangements held a hasty meeting to decide whether the celebration should be abandoned or postponed, but could come to no conclusion. Denunciation of the "Clarion" for its course was the sole point upon which all the speakers agreed. Also there was considerable incidental criticism of its editor, as an ingrate, for publishing the article on Milly Neal's death which reflected so severely upon Dr. Surtaine. As the paper had been bought with Dr. Surtaine's hard cash, the least Hal could have done, in decency, was to refrain from "roasting" the source of the money. Such was the general opinion. The representative business intellect of Worthington failed to consider that the article had been confined rigidly to a statement of facts, and that any moral or ethical inference must be purely a derivative of those facts as interpreted by the reader. Several of those present at the meeting declared vehemently that they would never again either advertise in or read the "Clarion." There was even talk of a boycott. One member was so incautious as to condole with Dr. Surtaine upon his son's disloyalty. The old quack's regard fell upon his tactless comforter, dull and heavy as lead.

"My son is my son," said he; "and what's between us is our own business. Now, as to Old Home Week, it'll be time enough to give up when we're licked." And, adroit opportunist that he was, he urged upon the meeting that they support the Health Bureau as the best hope of clearing up the situation.

Amongst the panic-stricken, meanwhile, moved and worked the volunteer forces of hygiene, led by the Reverend Norman Hale. Weakened and unfit though he was, he could not be kept from the battle-ground, notwithstanding that Dr. Merritt, fearing for his life, had threatened him with kidnaping and imprisonment in the hospital. At Hale's right hand were Esmé Elliot and Kathleen Pierce. There had been one scene at Greenvale approaching violence on Dr. Elliot's part and defiance on that of his niece when her guardian had flatly forbidden the continuance of her slum work. It had ended when the girl, creeping up under the guns of his angry eyes, had dropped her head on his shoulder, and said in unsteady tones:—

"I—I'm not a very happy Esmé, Uncle Guardy. If I don't have something to do—something real—I'll—I'll c-c-cry and get my pretty nose all red."

"Quit it!" cried the gruff doctor desperately. "What d'ye mean by acting that way! Go on. Do as you like. But if Merritt lets anything happen to you—"

"Nothing will happen, Guardy. I'll be careful," promised the girl.

"Well, I don't know whatever's come over you, lately," retorted her uncle, troubled.

"Neither do I," said Esmé.

She went forth and enlisted Kathleen Pierce, whose energetic and restless mind was ensnared at once by what she regarded as the romantic possibilities of the work, and the two gathered unto themselves half a dozen of the young males of the species, who readily volunteered, partly for love and loyalty to the chieftainesses of their clan, partly out of the blithe and adventurous spirit of youth, and of them formed an automobile corps, for scouting, messenger service, and emergency transportation, as auxiliary to Hale and Merritt; an enterprise which subsequently did yeoman work and taught several of the gilded youth something about the responsibilities of citizenship which they would never have learned in any other school.

Tip O'Farrell was another invaluable aide. He had one brief encounter, on enlistment, with the health officer.

"You ought to be in jail," said Dr. Merritt.

"What fer?" demanded O'Farrell.

"Smuggling out bodies without a permit."

"Ferget it," advised the politician. "I tried my way, an' it wasn't good enough. Now I'll try yours. You can't afford to jug me."

"Why can't I?"

"I'm too much use to you."

"So far you've been just the other thing."

"Ain't I tellin' you I'm through with that game? On the level! Doc, these poor boobs down here *know* me. They'll do as I tell 'em. Gimme a chance."

So O'Farrell, making his chance, did his work faithfully and well through the dismal weeks to follow. It takes all kinds of soldiers to fight an epidemic.

Those two sturdy volunteers, Miss Elliot and Miss Pierce, were driving slowly along the fringe of the Rookeries,—yes, slowly, notwithstanding that Kathleen Pierce was acting as her own chauffeur,—having just delivered a consignment of emergency nurses from a neighboring city to Dr. Merritt, when the car slowed down.

"Did you see that?" inquired Miss Pierce, indicating, with a jerk of her head, the general topography off to starboard.

"See what?" inquired her companion. "I didn't notice anything except a hokey-pokey seller, adding his mite to the infant mortality of the district."

"Esmé, you talk like nothing human lately!" accused her friend. "You're a—a—regular health leaflet! I meant that man going into the corner tenement. I believe it was Hal Surtaine."

"Was it?"

"And you needn't say, 'Was it?' in that lofty, superior tone, like an angel with a new halo, either," pursued her aggrieved friend. "You know it was. What do you suppose he's doing down here?"

"The epidemic is the 'Clarion's' special news. He spends quite a little time in this district, I believe."

"Oh, you believe! Then you've seen him lately?"

"Yes."

Miss Pierce stared rigidly in front of her and made a detour of magnificent distance to avoid a push-cart which wasn't in her way anyhow. "Esmé," she said,

"Yes?"

"Did you give me away to him?"

"No. He didn't give me an opportunity."

"Oh!" There was more silence. Then, "Esmé, I was pretty rotten about that, wasn't I?"

"Why, Kathie, I think you ought to have written to him."

"I meant to write and own up, no matter if I did tell you I wouldn't. But I kept putting it off. Esmé, did you notice how thin and worn he looks?"

The other winced. "He's had a great deal to worry him."

"Well, he hasn't got our lawsuit to worry him any more. That's off."

"Off?" A light flashed into Esmé's face. "Your father has dropped it?"

"Yes. He had to. I told him the accident was my fault, and if I was put on the stand I'd say so. I'm not so popular with Pop as I might be, just now. But, Esmé, I *didn't* mean to run away and leave her in the gutter. I got rattled, and Brother was crying and I lost my head."

"That will save the 'Clarion,'" said Esmé, with a deep breath.

Kathleen looked at her curiously, and then made a singular remark. "Yes; that's what I did it for."

"But what interest have you in saving the 'Clarion'?" demanded Esmé, bewildered.

"The failure of the 'Clarion' would be a disaster to the city," observed Miss Pierce in copy-book style.

"Kathie! You should make two jabs in the air with your forefinger when you quote. Otherwise you're a plagiarist. Let me see." Esmé pondered. "Hugh Merritt," she decided.

Kathleen kept her eyes steady ahead, but a flood of color rose in her face.

"I had an awful fight over it with him before—before I gave in," she said.

"Are you going to marry Hugh?" demanded Esmé bluntly.

The color deepened until even the velvety eyes seemed tinged with it. "I don't know. *He* isn't exactly popular with Pop, either."

Esmé reached over and gave her friend a surreptitious little hug, which might have cost a crossing pedestrian his life if he hadn't been a brisk dodger.

"Hugh Merritt is a *man*," said she in a low voice: "He's brave and he's straight and he's fine. And oh, Kathie, dearest, if a man of that kind loves you, don't you ever, ever let anything come between you."

"Hello!" said Kathleen in surprise. "That don't sound much like the Great American Man-eating Pumess of yore. There's been a big change in you since you sidetracked Will Douglas, Esmé. Did you really care? No, of course, you didn't," she answered herself. "He's a nice chap, but he isn't particularly brave or fine, I guess."

A light broke in upon her:

"Esmé! Is it, after all—"

"No, no, no, no, NO!" cried the victim of this highly feminine deduction, in panic. "It isn't any one."

"No, of course it isn't, dear. I didn't mean to tease you. Hello! what have we here?"

The car stopped with a jar on a side street, some distance from the quarantined section. Seated on the curb a woman was wailing over the stiffened form of a young child. The boy's teeth were clenched and his face darkly suffused.

"Convulsions," said Esmé.

The two girls were out of the car simultaneously. The agonized mother, an Italian, was deaf to Esmé's persuasions that the child be turned over to them.

"What shall we do?" she asked, turning to Kathleen in dismay. "I think he's dying, and I can't make the woman listen."

Something of her father's stern decisiveness of character was in Kathleen Pierce.

"Don't be a fool!" she said briskly to the mother, and she plucked the child away from her. "Start the car, Esmé."

The woman began to shriek. A crowd gathered. O'Farrell providentially appeared from around a corner. "Grab her, you," she directed O'Farrell.

The politician hesitated. "What's the game?" he began. Then he caught sight of Esmé. "Oh, it's you, Miss Elliot. Sure. Hi! Can it!" he shouted, fending off the distracted mother. "They'll take the kid to the hospital. See? You go along quiet, now."

Speeding beyond all laws, but under protection of their red cross, they all but ran down Dr. Merritt and stopped to take him in. He confirmed Esmé's diagnosis.

"It'll be touch and go whether we save him," said he.

Esmé carried the stricken child into the hospital ward. The two volunteers waited outside for word. In an hour it came. The boy would probably live, thanks to their promptitude.

"But you ought not to be picking up chance infants around the district," he protested. "It isn't safe."

"Oh, we belong to the St. Bernard tribe," retorted Miss Pierce. "We take 'em as we find 'em. Hugh, come and lunch with us."

The grayish young man looked at her wistfully. "Haven't time," he said.

"No: I didn't suppose you'd step aside from the thorny path, even to eat," she retorted; and Esmé, hearing the new tone under the flippant words, knew that all was well with the girl, and envied her with a great and gentle envy.

CHAPTER XXXIV

VOX POPULI

These were the days when Hal Surtaine worked with a sense of wild freedom from all personal bonds. He had definitely broken with his father. He had challenged every interest in Worthington from which there was anything to expect commercially. He had peremptorily banished Esmé Elliot from his heart and his hopes, though she still forced entrance to his thoughts and would not be denied, there, the precarious rights of an undesired guest. He was now simply and solely a journalist with a mind single to his purpose, to go down fighting the best fight there was in him. Defeat, he believed, was practically certain. He would make it a defeat of which no man need be ashamed.

The handling of the epidemic news, Hal left to his colleagues, devoting his own pen to a vigorous defense of the "Clarion's" position and assertion of its policy, in the editorial columns. Concealment and suppression, he pointed out, had been the chief factor in the disastrous spread of the contagion. Early recognition of the danger and a frank fighting policy would have saved most of the sacrificed lives. The blame lay, not with those who had disclosed the peril, but with those who had fostered it by secrecy; probing deeper into it, with those who had blocked such reform of housing and sanitation as would have checked a filth disease like typhus. In time this would be indicated more specifically. Tenements which netted twelve per cent to their owners and bred plagues, the "Clarion" observed editorially, were good private but poor public investments. Whereupon a number of highly regarded Christian citizens began to refer to the editor as an anarchist.

The "Clarion" principle of ascertaining "the facts behind the news" had led naturally to an inquiry into ownership of the Rookeries. Wayne had this specifically in charge and reported sensational results from the first.

"It'll be a corking follow-up feature," he said. "Later we can hitch it up to the Housing Reform Bill."

"Make a fifth page full spread of it for Monday."

"With pictures of the owners," suggested Wayne.

"Why not this way? Make a triple lay-out for each one. First, a picture of the tenement with the number of deaths and cases underneath. Then the half-tone of the owner. And, beyond, the picture of the house he lives in. That'll give contrast."

"Good!" said Wayne. "Fine and yellow."

By Sunday, four days after the opening story, all the material for the second big spread was ready except for one complication. Some involution of trusteeship in the case of two freeholds in Sadler's Shacks, at the heart of the Rookeries, had delayed access to the records. These two were Number 3 and Number 9 Sperry Street, the latter dubbed "the Pest-Egg" by the "Clarion," as being the tenement in which the pestilence was supposed to have originated. These two last clues, Wayne was sure, would be run down before evening. Already the net of publicity had dragged in, among other owners of the dangerous property, a high city official, an important merchant, a lady much given to blatant platform philanthropies, and the Reverend Dr. Wales's fashionable church. It was, indeed, a noble company of which the "Clarion" proposed to make martyrs on the morrow.

One man quite unconnected with any twelve per cent ownership, however, had sworn within his ravaged soul that there should be no morrow's "Clarion." Max Veltman, four days previously, had crawled home to his apartment after a visit to the drug store where he had purchased certain acids. With these he worked cunningly and with complete absorption in his pursuit, neither stirring out of his own place nor communicating with any fellow being. Consequently he knew nothing of the sensation which had convulsed Worthington, nor of the "Clarion's" change of policy. To his inflamed mind the Surtaine organ was a noxious thing, and Harrington Surtaine the guilty partner in the profits of Milly's death who had rejected the one chance to make amends.

Carrying a carefully wrapped bundle, he went forth into the streets on Sunday evening, and wandered into the Rookeries district. A red-necked man, standing on a barrel, was making a speech to a big crowd gathered at one of the corners. Dimly-heard, the word "Clarion" came to Veltman's ears.

"What's he saying?" he asked a neighbor.

"He's roastin' the —— 'Clarion,'" replied the man. "We ought to go up there an' tear the buildin' down."

To Veltman it seemed quite natural that popular rage should be directed toward the object of his hatred. He sat down weakly upon the curb and waited to see what would happen.

Another chance auditor of that speech did not wait. McGuire Ellis stayed just long enough to scent danger, and hurried back to the office.

"Trouble brewing down in the Rookeries," he told Hal.

"More than usual?"

"Different from the usual. There's a mob considering paying us a visit."

"The new press!" exclaimed Hal.

"Just what I was thinking. A rock or a bullet in its pretty little insides would cost money."

"We'd better notify Police Headquarters."

"I have. They gave me the laugh. Told me it was a pipe-dream. They're sore on us because of our attack on the department for dodging saloon law enforcement."

"I don't like this, Mac," said Hal. "What a fool I was to put the press in the most exposed place."

"Fortify it."

"With what?"

"The rolls."

Print-paper comes from the pulp-mills in huge cylinders, seven feet long by four in diameter. The highest-powered small arm could not send a bullet through the close-wrapped fabric. Ellis's plan offered perfect protection if there was enough material to build the fortification. The entire pressroom force was at once set to work, and in half an hour the delicate and costly mechanism was protected behind an impenetrable barrier which shut it off from view except at the south end. The supply of rolls had fallen a little short.

"Let 'em smash the window if they like," said Ellis. "Plate-glass insurance covers that. I wish we had something for that corner."

"With a couple of revolvers we could guard it from these windows," said Hal. "But where are we to get revolvers on a Sunday night?"

"Leave that to me," said Ellis, and went out.

Hal, standing at the open second-story window, surveyed the strategic possibilities of the situation. His outer office jutting out into a narrow L overlooked, from a broad window, the empty space of the street. From the front he could just see the press, behind its plate-glass. This was set back some ten feet from the sidewalk line proper, and marking the outer boundary stood a row of iron posts of old and dubious origin, formerly connected by chains. Hal had a wish that they were still so joined. They would have served, at least, as a hypothetical guard-line. The flagged and slightly depressed space between these and the front of the building, while actually of private ownership, had long been regarded as part of the thoroughfare. Overlooking it from the north end, opposite Hal's office, was another window, in the reference room. Any kind of gunnery from those vantage-spots would guard the press. But would the mere threat of firing suffice? That is what Hal wished to know. He had no desire to pump bullets into a close-packed crowd. On the other hand, he did not propose to let any mob ruin his property without a fight. His military reverie was interrupted by the entrance of Bim Currier, followed by Dr. Elliot.

"Why the fortification?" asked the latter.

"We've heard rumors of a mob attack."

"So've I. That's why I'm here. Want any help?"

"Why, you're very kind," began Hal dubiously; "but—"

"Rope off that space," cut in the brisk doctor, seizing, with a practiced eye, upon the natural advantage of the sentinel posts. "Got any rope?"

"Yes. There's some in the pressroom. It isn't very strong."

"No matter. Moral effect. Mobs always stop to think, at a line. I know. I've fought 'em before."

"This is very good of you, to come—"

"Not a bit of it. I noticed what the 'Clarion' did to its medical advertisers. I like your nerve. And I like a fight, in a good cause. Have 'em paint up some signs to put along the ropes. 'Danger.'—'Keep Out.'—'Trespassers Enter Here at their Peril'; and that sort of thing."

"I'll do it," said Hal, going to the telephone to give the orders.

While he was thus engaged, McGuire Ellis entered.

"Hello!" the physician greeted him. "What have you got there? Revolvers?"

"Count 'em; two," answered Ellis.

"Gimme one," said the visitor, helping himself to a long-barreled .45.

"Here! That's for Hal Surtaine," protested Ellis.

"Not by a jug-ful! He's too hot-headed. Besides, can he afford to be in it if there *should* be any serious trouble? Think of the paper!"

"You're right there," agreed Ellis, struck by the keen sense of this view. "If they could lay a killing at his door, even in self-defense—"

"Pre-cisely! Whereas, I don't intend to shoot unless I have to, and probably not then."

They explained the wisdom of this procedure to Hal, who reluctantly admitted it, agreeing to leave the weapons in the hands of Dr. Elliot and McGuire Ellis.

"Put Ellis here in this window. I'll hold the fort yonder." He pointed across the space to the reference room in the opposite L. "Nine times out of ten a mob don't really—" He stopped abruptly, his face stiffening with surprise, and some other emotion, which Hal for the moment failed to interpret. Following the direction of his glance, the two other men turned. Dr. Surtaine, suave and smiling, was advancing across the floor.

"Ellis, how are you? Good-evening, Dr. Elliot. Ah! Pistols?"

"Yes. Have one?" invited Ellis smoothly.

"I brought one with me." He tugged at his pocket, whence emerged a cheap and shiny weapon. Hal shuddered, recognizing it. It was the revolver which Milly Neal had carried.

"So you've heard?" asked Ellis.

"Ten minutes ago. I haven't any idea it will amount to much, but I thought I ought to be here in case of danger."

Dr. Elliot grunted. Ellis, suggesting that they take a look at the other defense, tactfully led him away, leaving father and son together. They had not seen each other since the Emergency Health Committee meeting. Something of the quack's glossy jauntiness faded out of his bearing as he turned to Hal.

"Boy-ee," he began diffidently, "there's been a pretty bad mistake."

"There's been worse than that," said Hal sadly.

"About Milly Neal. I thought—I thought it was you that got her into trouble."

"Why? For God's sake, why?"

"Don't be too hard on me," pleaded the other. "I'd heard about the road-house. And then, what she said to you. It all fitted in. Hale put me right. Boy-ee, I can sleep again, now that I know it wasn't you."

The implication caught at Hal's throat.

"Why, Dad," he said lamely, "if you'd only come to me and asked—"

"Somehow I couldn't. I was waiting for you to tell me." He slid his big hand over Hal's shoulder, and clutched him in a sudden, jerky squeeze, his face averted.

"Now, that's off our minds," he said, in a loud and hearty voice. "We can—"

"Wait a minute. Father, you saw the story in the 'Clarion,'—the story of Milly's death?"

"Yes, I saw that."

"Well?"

"I suppose you did what you thought was right, Boy-ee."

"I did what I had to do. I hated it."

"I'm glad to know that much, anyway."

"But I'd do it again, exactly the same."

The Doctor turned troubled eyes on his son. "Hasn't there been enough judging of each other between you and me, Boy-ee?" he asked sorrowfully.

In wretched uncertainty how to meet this appeal, Hal hesitated. He was saved from decision by the return of McGuire Ellis.

"No movement yet from the enemy's camp," he reported. "I just had a telephone from Hale's club."

"Perhaps they won't come, after all," surmised Hal.

"There's pretty hot talk going. Somebody's been helping along by serving free drinks."

"Now who could that be, I wonder?"

"Maybe some of our tenement-owning politician friends who aren't keen about having tomorrow's 'Clarion' appear."

"We ought to have a reporter down there, Mac."

"Denton's there. Well, as there's nothing doing, I'll tackle a little work." And seating himself at his desk beside the broad window Ellis proceeded to annihilate some telegraph copy, fresh off the wire. With the big tenement story spread, the morrow's paper would be straitened for space. Excusing himself to his father, Hal stepped into his private office—and recoiled in uttermost amazement. There, standing in the further doorway, lovely, palpitant, with the color flushing in her cheeks and the breath fluttering in her throat, stood Esmé Elliot.

"Oh!" she gasped, stretching out her hands to him. "I've tried so to get you by 'phone. There's a mob coming—"

"Yes, I know," said Hal gently. He led her to a chair. "We're ready for them."

"Are you? I'm so glad. I was afraid you wouldn't know in time."

"How did you find out?"

"I've been working with Mr. Hale down in the district. I heard rumors of it. Then I listened to what the people said, and I hurried here in my car to warn you. They're drunk, and mean trouble."

"That was good of you! I appreciate it."

"No. It was a debt. I owed it to the 'Clarion.' You've been—splendid about the typhus."

"Worthington doesn't look at it that way," returned Hal, with a rather grim smile.

"When they understand, they will."

"Perhaps. But, see here, you can't stay. There may be danger. It's awfully good of you to come. But you must get away."

She looked at him sidelong. In her coming she had been the new Esmé, the Esmé who was Norman Hale's most unselfish and unsparing worker, the Esmé who thought for others, all womanly. But, now that the strain had relaxed, she reverted, just a little, to her other self. It was, for the moment, the Great American Pumess who spoke:—

"Won't you even say you're glad to see me?"

"Glad!" The echo leaped to his lips and the fire to his eyes as the old unconquered longing and passion surged over him. "I don't think I've known what gladness is since that night at your house."

Her eyes faltered away from his. "I don't think I quite understand," she said weakly; then, with a change to quick resolution:—

"There is something I must tell you. You have a right to know it. It's about the paper. Will you come to see me tomorrow?"

"Yes. But go now. No! Wait!"

From without sounded a dull murmur pierced through with an occasional whoop, jubilant rather than threatening.

"Too late," said Hal quietly. "They're coming."

"I'm not afraid."

"But I am—for you. Stay in this room. If they should break into the building, go up those stairs and get to the roof. They won't come there."

He went into the outer room, closing the door behind him.

From both directions and down a side street as well the dwellers in the slums straggled into the open space in front of the "Clarion" office. To Hal they seemed casual, purposeless; rather prankish, too, like a lot of urchins out on a lark. Several bore improvised signs, uncomplimentary to the "Clarion." They seemed surprised when they encountered the rope barrier with its warning placards. There were mutterings and queries.

"No serious harm in them," opined Dr. Elliot, to whom Hal had gone to see whether he wanted anything. "Just mischief. A few rocks maybe, and then they'll go home. Look at old Mac."

Opposite them, at his brilliantly lighted window desk, sat McGuire Ellis, in full view of the crowd below, conscientiously blue-penciling telegraph copy.

"Hey, Mac!" yelled an acquaintance in the street. "Come down and have a drink."

The associate editor lifted his head. "Don't be young," he retorted. "Go home and sleep it off." And reverted to his task.

"What are we doin' here, anyway?" roared some thirster for information.

Nobody answered. But, thus recalled to a purpose, the mob pressed against the ropes.

"Ladies *and* gentlemen!" A great, rounded voice boomed out above them, drawing every eye to the farthermost window where stood Dr. Surtaine, his chest swelling with ready oratory.

"Hooray!" yelled the crowd. "Good Old Doc!"—"He pays the freight."—"Speech!"

"Say, Doc," bawled a waggish soul, "I gotta corn, marchin' up here. Will Certina cure it?"

And another burst into the final lines of a song then popular; in which he was joined by several of his fellows:

"Father, he drinks Seltzer. Redoes, like hell! (*Crescendo.*) He drinks Cer-tee-nah!"

"Ladies *and* gentlemen," boomed the wily charlatan. "Unaccustomed as I am to *extempore* speaking, I cannot let pass this opportunity to welcome you. We appreciate this testimonial of your regard for the 'Clarion.' We appreciate, also, that it is a warm night and a thirsty one. Therefore, I suggest that we all adjourn back to the Old Twelfth Ward, where, if the authorities will kindly look the other way, I shall be delighted to provide liquid refreshments for one and all in which to drink to the health and prosperity of an enlightened free press."

The crowd rose to him with laughter. "Good old Sport!"—"Mine's Certina."—"Come down and make good."—"Free booze, free speech, free press!"—"You're on, Doc! You're on."

"He's turned the trick," growled Dr. Elliot to Hal. "He's a smooth one!"

Indeed, the crowd wavered, with that peculiar swaying which presages a general movement. At the south end there was a particularly dense gathering, and there some minor struggle seemed to be in progress. Cries rose: "Let him through."—"What's he want?"

"It's Max Veltman," said Hal, catching sight of a wild, strained face. "What is he up to?"

The former "Clarion" man squirmed through the front rank and crawled slowly under the ropes. Above the murmur of confused tones, a voice of terror shrilled out:

"He's got a bomb."

The mass surged back from the spot. Veltman, moving forward upon the unprotected south end of the press, was fumbling at his pocket. "I'll fix your free and enlightened press," he screamed.

Dr. Elliot turned on Hal with an imperative question.

"Is it true, do you think? Will he do it? Quick!"

"Crazy," said Hal.

"God forgive me!" prayed the ex-navy man as his arm whipped up.

There were two quick reports. At the second, Veltman stopped, half turned, threw his arms widely outward, and vanished in a blinding glare, accompanied by a gigantic *snap!* as if a mountain of rock had been riven in twain.

To Hal it seemed that the universe had disintegrated in that concussion. Blackness surrounded him. He was on the floor, half crouching, and, to his surprise, unhurt. Groping his way to the window he leaned out above an appalling silence. It endured only a moment. Then rose the terrible clamor of a mob in panic-stricken flight, above an insistent undertone of groans, sobs, and prayers.

"I had to kill him," muttered Dr. Elliot's shaking voice at Hal's ear. "There was just the one chance before he could throw his bomb."

Every light in the building had gone out. Guiding himself by the light of matches, Hal hurried across to his den. He heard Esmé's voice before he could make her out, standing near the door. "Is any one hurt?"

Hal breathed a great sigh. "You're all right, then! We don't know how bad it is."

"An explosion?"

"Veltman threw a bomb. He's killed."

"Boy-ee!" called Dr. Surtaine.

"Here, Dad. You're safe?"

"Yes."

"Thank God! Careful with that match! The place is strewn with papers."

Men from below came hurrying in with candles, which are part of every newspaper's emergency equipment. They reported no serious injuries to the staff or the equipment. Although the plate-glass window had been shattered into a million fragments and the inner fortification toppled over, the precious press had miraculously escaped injury. But in a strewn circle, outside, lay rent corpses, and the wounded pitifully striving to crawl from that shambles.

With the steadiness which comes to nerves racked to the point of collapse, Hal made the rounds of the building. Two men in the pressroom were slightly hurt. Their fellows would look after them. Wayne, with his men, was already in the street, combining professional duty with first aid. The scattered and stricken mob had begun to sift back, only a subdued and curious crowd now. Then came the ambulances and the belated police, systematizing the work.

Quarter of an hour had passed when Dr. Surtaine, Esmé Elliot, her uncle—much surprised at finding her there—and Hal stood in the editorial office, hardly able yet to get their bearings.

"I shall give myself up to the authorities," decided Dr. Elliot. He was deadly pale, but of unshaken nerve.

"Why?" cried Hal. "It was no fault of yours."

"Rules of the game. Well, young man, you have a paper to get out for tomorrow, though the heavens fall. Good-night."

Hal gripped at his hand. "I don't know how to thank you—" he began.

"Don't try, then," was the gruff retort. "Where's Mac?"

He turned to McGuire Ellis's desk to bid that sturdy toiler good-night. There, dimly seen through the flickering candlelight, the undisputed Short-Distance Slumber Champion of the World sat, his head on his arms, in his familiar and favorite attitude of snatching a few moments' respite from a laborious existence.

"Will you *look* at *that!*" cried the physician in utmost amazement.

At the sight a wild surge of mirth overwhelmed Hal's hair-trigger nerves. He began to laugh, with strange, quick catchings of the breath: to laugh tumultuously, rackingly, unendurably.

"Stop it!" shouted Dr. Elliot, and smote him a sledge-blow between the shoulders.

For the moment the hysteria was jarred out of Hal. He gasped, gurgled, and took a step toward his assistant.

"Hey, Mac! Wake up! You've spilled your ink."

Before he could speak or move further, Esmé Elliot's arms were about him. Her face was close to his. He could feel the strong pressure of her breast against him as she forced him back.

"No, no!" she was pleading, in a swift half-whisper. "Don't go near him. Don't look. *Please* don't. Come away."

He set her aside. A candlelight flared high. From Ellis's desk trickled a little stream. Dr. Elliot was already bending over the slackened form.

"So it wasn't ink," said Hal slowly. "Is he dead, Dr. Elliot?"

"No," snapped the other. "Esmé, bandages! Quick! Your petticoat! That'll do. Get another candle. Dr. Surtaine, help me lift him. There! Surtaine, bring water. *Do you hear?* Hurry!"

When Hal returned, uncle and niece were working with silent deftness over Ellis, who lay on the floor. The wounded man opened his eyes upon his employer's agonized face.

"Did he get the press?" he gasped.

"Keep quiet," ordered the Doctor. "Don't speak."

"Did he get the press?" insisted Ellis obstinately.

"Mac! Mac!" half sobbed Hal, bending over him. "I thought you were dead." And his tears fell on the blood-streaked face.

"Don't be young," growled Ellis faintly. "Did—he—get—the—press?"

"No."

The wounded man's eyes closed. "All right," he murmured.

Up to the time that the ambulance surgeons came to carry Ellis away, Dr. Elliot was too busy with him even to be questioned. Only after the still burden had passed through the door did he turn to Hal.

"A piece of metal carried away half the back of his neck," he said. "And we let him sit there, bleeding his life away!"

"Is there any chance?" demanded Hal.

"I doubt if they'll get him to the hospital alive."

"The best man in Worthington!" said Hal passionately. "Oh!" He shook his clenched fists at the outer darkness. "I'll make somebody pay for this."

Esmé's hand fell upon his arm. "Do you want me to stay?" she asked.

"No. You must go home. It's been a terrible thing for you."

"I'll go to the hospital," she said, "and I'll 'phone you as soon as there is any news."

"Better come home with me, Hal," said his father gently.

The younger man turned with an involuntary motion toward the desk, still wet with his friend's blood.

"I'll stay on the job," he said.

Understanding, the father nodded his sympathy. "Yes; I guess that would have been Mac's way," said he.

Work pressing upon the editor from all sides came as a boon. The paper had to be made over for the catastrophe which, momentarily, overshadowed the typhus epidemic in importance. In hasty consultation, it was decided that the "special" on the ownership of the infected tenements should be set aside for a day, to make space. Hal had to make his own statement, not alone for the "Clarion," but for the other newspapers, whose representatives came seeking news and also—what both surprised and touched him—bearing messages of sympathy and congratulation, and offers of any help which they could extend from men to pressroom accommodations. Not until nearly two o'clock in the morning did Hal find time to draw breath over an early proof, which stated the casualties as seven killed outright, including Veltman who was literally torn to pieces, and twenty-two seriously wounded.

From his reading Hal was called to the 'phone. Esmé's voice came to him with a note of hope and happiness.

"Oh, Hal, they say there's a chance! Even a good chance! They've operated, and it isn't as bad as it looked at first. I'm so glad for you."

"Thank you," said Hal huskily. "And—bless you! You've been an angel tonight."

There was a pause: then, "You'll come to see me—when you can?"

"Tomorrow," said he. "No—today. I forgot."

They both laughed uncertainly, and bade each other good-night.

Hal stayed through until the last proof. In the hallway a heavy figure lifted itself from a chair in a corner as he came out.

"Dad!" exclaimed Hal.

"I thought I'd wait," said the charlatan wistfully.

No other word was necessary. "I'll be glad to be home again," said Hal. "You can lend me some pajamas?"

"They're laid out on your bed. Every night."

The two men passed down the stairs, arm in arm. At the door they paused. Through the building ran a low tremor, waxing to a steady thrill. The presses were throwing out to the world once again their irrevocable message of fact and fate.

CHAPTER XXXV

TEMPERED METAL

Monday's newspapers startled Hal Surtaine. Despite the sympathetic attitude expressed after the riot by the other newspaper men, he had not counted upon the unanimous vigor with which the local press took up the cudgels for the "Clarion." That potent and profound guild-fellowship of newspaperdom, which, when once aroused, overrides all individual rivalry and jealousy, had never before come into the young editor's experience.

To his fellow editors the issue was quite clear. Here was an attack, not upon one newspaper alone, but upon the principle of journalistic independence. Little as the "Banner," the "Press," the "Telegram," and their like had practiced independence of thought or writing, they could both admire and uphold it in another. Their support was as genuine as it was generous. The police department, and, indeed, the whole city administration of Worthington, came in for scathing and universal denunciation, in that they had failed to protect the "Clarion" against the mob's advance.

The evening papers got out special bulletins on McGuire Ellis. None too hopeful they were, for the fighting journalist, after a brief rally, had sunk into a condition where life was the merest flicker. Always a picturesque and well-liked personality, Ellis now became a species of popular hero. Sympathy centralized on him, and through him attached temporarily to the "Clarion" itself, which he now typified in the public imagination. His condition, indeed, was just so much sentimental capital to the paper, as the Honorable E.M. Pierce savagely put it to William Douglas. Nevertheless, the two called at the hospital to make polite inquiries, as did scores of their fellow leading citizens. Ellis, stricken down, was serving his employer well.

Not that Hal knew this, nor, had he known it, would have cared. Sick at heart, he waited about the hospital reception room for such meager hopes as the surgeons could give him, until an urgent summons compelled him to go to the office. Wayne had telephoned for him half a dozen times, finally leaving a message that he must see him on a point in the tenement-ownership story, to be run on the morrow.

Wayne, at the moment of Hal's arrival, was outside the rail talking to a visitor. On the copy-book beside his desk was stuck an illustration proof, inverted. Idly Hal turned it, and stood facing his final and worst ordeal of principle. The half-tone picture, lovely, suave, alluring, smiled up into his eyes from above its caption:—

"*Miss Esmé Elliot, Society Belle and Owner of No. 9 Sadler's Shacks, Known as the Pest-Egg.*"

"You've seen it," said Wayne's voice at his elbow.

"Yes."

"Well; it was that I wanted to ask you about."

"Ask it," said Hal, dry-lipped.

"I knew you were a—a friend of Miss Elliot's. We can kill it out yet. It—it isn't absolutely necessary to the story," he added, pityingly.

He turned and looked away from a face that had grown swiftly old under his eyes. In Hal's heart there was a choking rush of memories: the conquering loveliness of Esmé; her sweet and loyal womanliness and comradeship of the night before; the half-promise in her tones as she had bid him come to her; the warm pressure of her arms fending him from the sight of his friend's blood; and, far back, her voice saying so confidently, "I'd trust you," in answer to her own supposititious test as to what he would do if a news issue came up, involving her happiness.

Blotting these out came another picture, a swathed head, quiet upon a pillow. In that moment Hal knew that he was forever done with suppressions and evasions. Nevertheless, he intended to be as fair to Esmé as he would have been to any other person under attack.

"You're sure of the facts?" he asked Wayne.

"Certain."

"How long has she owned it?"

"Oh, years. It's one of those complicated trusteeships."

Hope sprang up in Hal's soul. "Perhaps she doesn't know about it."

"Isn't she morally bound to know? We've assumed moral responsibility in the other trusteeships. Of course, if you want to make a difference—" Wayne, again wholly the journalist, jealous for the standards of his craft, awaited his chief's decision.

"No. Have you sent a man to see her?"

"Yes. She's away."

"Away? Impossible!"

"That's what they said at the house. The reporter got the notion that there was something queer about her going. Scared out, perhaps."

Hal thought of the proud, frank eyes, and dismissed that hypothesis. Whatever Esmé's responsibility, he did not believe that she would shirk the onus of it.

"Dr. Elliot?" he enquired.

"Refused all information and told the reporter to go to the devil."

Hal sighed. "Run the story," he said.

"And the picture?"

"And the picture."

Going out he left directions with the telephone girl to try to get Miss Elliot and tell her that it would be impossible for him to call that day.

"She will understand when she sees the paper in the morning," he thought. "Or think she understands," he amended ruefully.

The telephone girl did not get Miss Elliot, for good and sufficient reasons, but succeeded in extracting a promise from the maiden cousin at Greenvale that the message would be transmitted.

Through the day and far into the night Hal worked unsparingly, finding time somehow to visit or call up the hospital every hour. At midnight they told him that Ellis was barely holding his own. Hal put the "Clarion" to bed that night, before going to the Surtaine mansion, hopeless of sleep, yet, nevertheless, so worn out that he sank into instant slumber as soon as he had drawn the sheets over him. On his way to the office in the morning, he ran full upon Dr. Elliot. For a moment Hal thought that the ex-officer meant to strike him with the cane which he raised. It sank.

"You miserable hound!" said Dr. Elliot.

Hal stood, silent.

"What have you to say for yourself?"

"Nothing."

"My niece came to your office to save your rag of a sheet. I shot down a poor crazy devil in your defense. And this is how you repay us."

Hal faced him, steadfast, wretched, determined upon only one thing: to endure whatever he might say or do.

"Do you know who's really responsible for that tenement? Answer me!"

"No."

"I! I! I!" shouted the infuriated man.

"You? The records show—"

"Damn the records, sir! The property was trusteed years ago. I should have looked after it, but I never even thought of its being what it is. And my niece didn't know till this morning that she owned it."

"Why didn't you say so to our reporter, then?" cried Hal eagerly. "Let us print a statement from you, from her—"

"In your sheet? If you so much as publish her name again—By Heavens, I wish it were the old days, I'd call you out and kill you."

"Dr. Elliot," said Hal quietly, "did you think I wanted to print that about Esmé?"

"Wanted to? Of course you wanted to. You didn't have to, did you?"

"Yes."

"What compelled you?" demanded the other.

"You won't understand, but I'll tell you. The 'Clarion' compelled me. It was news."

"News! To blackguard a young girl, ignorant of the very thing you've held her up to shame for! The power of the press! A power to smirch the names of decent people. And do you know where my girl is now, on this day when your sheet is smearing her name all over the town?" demanded the physician, his voice shaking with wrath and grief. "Do you know that—you who know everybody's business?"

Chill fear took hold upon Hal. "No," he said.

"In quarantine for typhus. Here! Keep off me!"

For Hal, stricken with his first experience of that black, descending mist which is just short of unconsciousness, had clutched at the other's shoulder to steady himself.

"Where?" he gasped.

"I won't tell you," retorted the Doctor viciously. "You might make another article out of that, of the kind you enjoy so much."

But this was too ghastly a joke. Hal straightened, and lifted his head to an eye-level with his denouncer. "Enjoy!" he said, in a low tone. "You may guess how much when I tell you that I've loved Esmé with every drop of my blood since the first time I ever spoke with her."

The Doctor's grim regard softened a little. "If I tell you, you won't publish it? Or give it away? Or try to communicate with her? I won't have her pestered."

"My word of honor."

"She's at the typhus hospital."

"And she's got typhus?" groaned Hal.

"No. Who said she had it? She's been exposed to it."

Hardly was the last word out of his mouth when he was alone. Hal had made a dash for a taxi. "Health Bureau," he cried.

By good fortune he found Dr. Merritt in.

"You've got Esmé Elliot at the typhus hospital," he said breathlessly.

"Yes. In the isolation ward."

"Why?"

"She's been exposed. She carried a child, in convulsions, into the hospital. The child developed typhus late Saturday night; must have been infected at the time. As soon as I knew, I sent for her, and she came like the brave girl she is, yesterday morning."

"Will she get the fever?"

"God forbid! Every precaution has been taken."

"Merritt, that's an awful place for a girl like Miss Elliot. Get her out."

"Don't ask me! I've got to treat all exposed cases alike."

"But, Merritt," pleaded Hal, "in this case an exception can't injure any one. She can be completely quarantined at home. You told Wayne you owed the 'Clarion' and me a big debt. I wouldn't ask it if it were anything else; but—"

"Would you do it yourself?" said the young health officer steadily. "Have you done it in your paper?"

"But this may be her life," argued the advocate desperately. "Think! If it were your sister, or—or the woman you cared for."

Dr. Merritt's fine mouth quivered and set. "Kathleen Pierce is quarantined with Esmé," he said quietly.

The pair looked each other through the eyes into the soul and knew one another for men.

"You're right, Merritt," said Hal. "I'm sorry I asked."

"I'll keep you posted," said the official, as his visitor turned away.

Meantime, Esmé had volunteered as an emergency nurse, and been gladly accepted. In the intervals of her new duties she had received from her distracted cousin, who had been calling up every half-hour to find out whether she "had it yet," Hal's message that he would not be able to see her that day, and, not having seen the "Clarion," was at a loss to understand it.

Chance, by all the truly romantic, is supposed to be a sort of matrimonial agency, concerned chiefly in bringing lovers together. In the rougher realm of actuality it operates quite as often, perhaps, to keep them apart. Certainly it was no friend to Esmé Elliot on this day. For when later she learned from her guardian of his attack upon Hal (though he took the liberty of editing out the *finale* of the encounter as he related it), she tried five separate times to reach Hal by 'phone, and each time Chance, the Frustrator, saw to it that Hal was engaged. The inference, to Esmé's perturbed heart, was obvious; he did not wish to speak to her. And to a woman of her spirit there was but one course. She would dismiss him from her mind. Which she did, every night, conscientiously, for many weary days.

CHAPTER XXXVI
THE VICTORY

Nation-wide sped the news, branding Worthington as a pest-ridden city. Every newspaper in the country had a conspicuous dispatch about it. The bulletin of the United States Public Health Service, as in duty bound, gave official and statistical currency to the town's misfortune. Other cities in the State threatened a quarantine against Worthington. Commercial travelers and buyers postponed their local visits. The hotel registers thinned out notably. Business drooped. For all of which the "Clarion" was vehemently blamed by those most concerned.

Conversely, the paper should have received part credit for the extremely vigorous campaign which the health authorities, under Dr. Merritt, set on foot at once. Using the "Clarion" exposure as a lever, the health officer pried open the Council-guarded city tills for an initial appropriation of ten thousand dollars, got a hasty ordinance passed penalizing, not the diagnosing of typhus, but failure to diagnose and report it,—not a man from the Surtaine army of suppression had the temerity to oppose the measure,—organized a medical inspection and detection corps, threw a contagion-proof quarantine about every infected building, hunted down and isolated the fugitives from the danger-points who had scattered at the first alarm, inspired the county medical society to an enthusiastic support, bullied the police into a state of reasonable efficiency, and with a combined volunteer and regular force faced the epidemic in military form. Not least conspicuous among the volunteers were Miss Esmé Elliot and Miss Kathleen Pierce, who had been released from quarantine quite as early as the law allowed, because of the need for them at the front.

"We could never have done our job without you," said Dr. Merritt to Hal, meeting him by chance one morning ten days after the publication of the "spread." "If the city is saved from a regular pestilence, it'll be the Clarion's' doing."

"That doesn't seem to be the opinion of the business men of the place," said Hal, with a rather dreary smile. He had just been going over with the lugubrious Shearson a batch of advertising cancellations.

"Oh, don't look for any credit from this town," retorted the health officer. "I'm practically ostracized, already, for my share in it."

"But are you beating it out?"

"God knows," answered the other. "I thought we'd traced all the foci of infection. But two new localities broke out today. That's the way an epidemic goes."

And that is the way the Worthington typhus went for more than a month. Throughout that month the "Clarion" was carrying on an anti-epidemic campaign of its own, with the slogan "Don't Give up Old Home Week." Wise strategy this, in a double sense. It rallied public effort for victory by a definite date, for the Committee on Arrangements, despite the arguments of the weak-kneed among its number, and largely by virtue of the militant optimism of its chairman, had decided to go on with the centennial celebration if the city could show a clean bill of health by August 30, thus giving six weeks' leeway.

Furthermore, it put the "Clarion" in the position of champion of the city's commercial interests and daily bade defiance to those who declared the paper an enemy and a traitor to business. In editorials, in interviews, in educational articles on hygiene and sanitation, in a course of free lectures covering the whole city and financed by the paper itself, the "Clarion" carried on the fight with unflagging zeal. Slowly it began to win back general confidence and much of the popularity which it had lost. One of its reporters in the course of his work contracted the fever and barely pulled through alive, thereby lending a flavor of possible martyrdom to the cause. McGuire Ellis's desperate fight for life also added to the romantic element which is so potent an asset with the sentimental American public. Business, however, still sulked. The defiance to its principles was too flagrant to be passed over. If the "Clarion" pulled through, the press would lose respect for the best interests and the vested privileges of commercial Worthington. Indeed, others of the papers, since the "Clarion's" declaration of independence, had exhibited a deplorable tendency to disregard hints hitherto having the authority of absolutism over them.

In withholding advertising patronage from the Surtaine daily, the business men were not only seeking reprisals, but also following a sound business principle. For according to information sedulously spread abroad, it was doubtful whether the "Clarion" would long survive. Elias M. Pierce's boast that he would put it out of business gained literal interpretation, as he had intended that it should. Contrary to his accustomed habit of reticence, he had sought occasion to inform his friends that he expected verdicts against the libeler of his daughter which would throw the concern into bankruptcy, and, perhaps, its proprietor into jail. No advertiser cares to put money into a publication which may fail next week. Hence, though the circulation of the "Clarion" went up pretty steadily, the advertising patronage did not keep pace. Hal found himself hard put to it, at times, to cling to his dogged hopes. But it was worth while fighting it out to the last dollar. So much he was assured of by the messages of praise and support which began to come in to him, not from "representative citizens," but from the earnest, thoughtful, and often obscure toilers and thinkers of the city: clergymen, physicians, laboring-men, working-women, sociological workers—his peers.

Then, too, there was the profound satisfaction of promised victory over the pest. For at the end of six weeks the battle was practically won; by what heroisms, at the cost of what sacrifices, through what disappointments, reversals, and setbacks, against the subtleties of what underground opposition of political influence and twelve per cent finance, is not to be set down here. The government publications tell, in their brief and pregnant records, this story of one of the most complete and brilliant victories in the history of American hygiene. My concern is with the story, not of the typhus epidemic, but of a man who fought for and surrendered and finally retrieved his own manhood and the honor of the paper which was his honor. His share, no small one, in the wiping-out of the pestilence was, to him, but part of the war for which he had enlisted.

But though the newspapers, with one joyous voice, were able to announce early in August, on the authority of the federal reports, "No new case in a week," the success of Old Home Week still swayed in the balance. Outside newspapers, which had not forgotten the scandal of the smallpox suppression years before, hinted that the record might not be as clear as it appeared. The President of the United States, they pointed out, who was to be the guest of honor and the chief feature of the celebration, would not be justified in going to a city over which any suspicion of pestilence still hovered. In fact, the success or failure of the event practically hung upon the Chief Executive's action. If, now, he decided to withdraw his acceptance, on whatever ground, the country would impute it to a justified caution, and would maintain against the city that intangible moral quarantine which is so disastrous to its victim. Throughout, Hal Surtaine in his editorial columns had vigorously maintained that the President would come. It was mostly "bluff." He had nothing but hope to build on.

Two more "clean" weeks passed. At the close of the second, Hal stopped one day at the hospital to see McGuire Ellis, who was finally convalescent and was to be discharged on the following week. At the door of Ellis's room he met Dr. Elliot. Somewhat embarrassed, he stepped aside. The physician stopped.

"Er—Surtaine," he said hesitantly.

"Well?"

"I've had time to think things over. And I've had some talks with Mac. I—I guess I was wrong."

"You were right enough from your point of view."

"Think so?" said the other, surprised.

"Yes. And I know I was right, from mine."

"Humph!" There was an uncomfortable pause. Then: "I called names. I apologize."

"That's all right, then," returned Hal heartily.

"Woof!" exhaled the physician. "That's off my chest. Now, I've got an item for you."

"For the 'Clarion'?"

"Yep. The President's coming."

"Coming? To Old Home Week?"

"To Old Home Week."

"An item! Great Cæsar! A spread! A splurge!! A blurb!!! Where did you get it?"

"From Washington. Just been there."

"Tell me all of it."

"Know Redding? He and I saw some tough service together in the old M.H.S. That's the United States Public Health Service now. Redding's the head of it; Surgeon-General. First-class man, every way. So I went to see him and told him we had to have the President, and why. He saw it in a minute. Knew all about the 'Clarion's' fight, too. He went to the White House and explained the whole business. The President said that a clean bill of health from the Service was good enough for him, and he'd come, sure. Here's his letter to the Surgeon-General. It goes out for publication tomorrow. There's a line in it speaking of the 'Clarion's' good work."

"Great Cæsar!" said Hal again, rather weakly.

"Does that square accounts between us?"

"More! A hundred times more! That's the biggest indorsement any paper in this town ever had. Old Home Week's safe. Did you tell Mac?"

"Yes. He's up there cursing now because they won't let him go to the office to plan out the article."

To the "Clarion," the presidential encomium was a tremendous boom professionally. Financially, however, it was of no immediate avail. It did not bring local advertising, and advertising was what the paper sorely needed. Still, it did call attention to the paper from outside. A few good contracts for "foreign" advertising, a department which had fallen off to almost nothing when Hal discarded all medical "copy," came in. With these, and a reasonable increase in local support which could be counted upon, now that commercial bitterness against the paper was somewhat mollified, Hal reckoned that he could pull through—if it were not for the Pierce suits. There was the crux of the situation. Nothing was being done about them. They had been postponed more than once, on motion of Pierce's counsel. Now they hung over Hal's head in a suspense fast becoming unbearable. At length he decided that, in fairness to his staff, he should warn them of the situation.

He chose, for the explanation, one of the Talk-It-Over Breakfasts, the first one which McGuire Ellis, released temporarily from the hospital for the occasion, had attended since his wound. He sat at Hal's right, still pale and thin, but with his look of bulldog obstinacy undiminished; enhanced, rather, by the fact that one ear had been sharpened to a canine pointedness by the missile which had so narrowly grazed his life. Ellis had been goaded to a pitch of high exasperation by the solicitude and attentions of his fellows. It was his emphatically expressed opinion that the whole gathering lay under a blight of superlative youthfulness. In his mind he exempted Hal, over whose silence and distraction he was secretly worried. The cause was explained when the chairman rose to close the meeting.

"There is something I have to say," he said. "I've put it off longer than I should. I may have to give up the 'Clarion.' It depends upon the outcome of the libel suits brought by E.M. Pierce. If, as we fear, Miss Cleary, the nurse who was run over, testifies for the prosecution, we can't win. Then it's only a question of the size of the damages. A big verdict would mean the ruin of the paper, I'm telling you this so that you may have time to look for new jobs."

There was a long silence. Then a melancholy, musing voice said: "Gee! That's tough! Just as the paper pulled off the Home Week stunt, too."

"How much of a verdict would bust us?" asked another.

"Twenty-five thousand dollars," said Hal, "together with lawyers' fees. I couldn't go on."

"Say, I know that old hen of a nurse," said one of the sporting writers, with entire seriousness. "Wonder if it'd do any good to marry her?"

A roar went up from the table at this, somewhat relieving the tension of the atmosphere.

Shearson, the advertising manager, lolling deep in his chair, spoke up diffidently, as soon as he could be heard:

"I ain't rich. But I've put a little wad aside. I could chip in three thou' if that'd help."

"I've got five hundred that isn't doing a stitch of work," declared Wainwright.

"Some of my relations have wads of money," suggested young Denton. "I wouldn't wonder if—"

"No, no, no!" cried Hal, in a shaken voice. "I know how well you fellows mean it. But—"

"As a loan," said Wainwright hopefully. "The paper's good enough security."

"*Not* good enough," replied Hal firmly. "I can't take it, boys. You—you're a mighty good lot, to offer. Now, about looking for other places—"

"All those that want to quit the 'Clarion,' stand up," shouted McGuire Ellis. Not a man moved.

"Unanimous," observed the convalescent. "I thought nobody'd rise to that. If anybody had," he added, "I'd have punched him in the eye."

The gathering adjourned in gloom.

"All this only makes it harder, Mac," said Hal to his right-hand man afterward. "They can't afford to stick till we sink."

"If a sailor can do it, I guess a newspaper man can," retorted the other resentfully. "I wish I could poison Pierce."

At dinner that night Hal found his father distrait. Since the younger man's return, the old relations had been resumed, though there were still, of necessity, difficult restraints and reservations in their talk. The "Clarion," however, had ceased to be one of the tabooed subjects. Since the publication of the President's letter and the saving of Old Home Week, Dr. Surtaine had become an avowed Clarionite. Also he kept in personal touch with the office. This evening, however, it was with an obvious effort that he asked how affairs were going. Hal answered listlessly that matters were going well enough.

"No, they aren't, Boy-ee. I heard about your talk today."

"Did you? I'm sorry. I don't want to worry you."

"Boy-ee, let me back you."

"I can't, Dad."

"Because of that old agreement?"

"Partly."

"Call it a loan, then. I can't stand by and see the paper licked by Pierce. Fifty thousand won't touch me. And it'll save you."

"Please, Dad, I can't do it."

"Is it because it's Certina money?"

Hal turned miserable eyes on his father. "Hadn't we better keep away from that?"

"I don't get you at all on that," cried the charlatan. "Why, it's business. It's legal. If I didn't sell 'em the stuff, somebody else would. Why shouldn't I take the money, when it's there?"

"There's no use in my trying to argue it with you, Dad. We're miles apart."

"That's just it," sighed the older man. "Oh, well! You couldn't help my paying the damages if Pierce wins," he suggested hopefully.

"Yes. I could even do that."

"What do you want me to do, Boy-ee?" cried his father, in desperation. "Give up a business worth half a million a year, net?"

"I'm not asking anything, sir. Only let me do the best I can, in the way that looks right to me. I've got to go back to the office now. Good-night, Dad."

The arch-quack looked after his son's retreating figure, and his big, animal-like eyes were very tender.

"I don't know," he said to himself uncertainly,—"I don't know but what he's worth it."

CHAPTER XXXVII

McGUIRE ELLIS WAKES UP

On implication of the Highest Authority we have it that the leopard cannot change his spots. The Great American Pumess is a feline of another stripe. Stress of experience and emotion has been known to modify sensibly her predatory characteristics. In the very beautiful specimen of the genus which, from time to time, we have had occasion to study in these pages, there had taken place, in a few short months, an alteration so considerable as to be almost revolutionary.

Many factors had contributed to the result. No woman of inherent fineness can live close to human suffering, as Esmé had lived in her slum work, without losing something of that centripetal self-concern which is the blemish of the present-day American girl. Constant association with such men as Hugh Merritt and Norman Hale, men who saw in her not a beautiful and worshipful maiden, but a useful agency in the work which made up their lives, gave her a new angle from which to consider herself. Then, too, her brief engagement to Will Douglas had sobered her. For Douglas, whatever his lack of independence and manliness in his professional relations, had endured the jilting with quiet dignity. But he had suffered sharply, for he had been genuinely in love with Esmé. She felt his pain the more in that there was the same tooth gnawing at her own heart, though she would not acknowledge it to herself. And this taught her humility and consideration. The Pumess was not become a Saint, by any means. She still walked, a lovely peril to every susceptible male heart. But she no longer thirsted with unquenchable ardor for conquests.

Meek though a reformed pumess may be, there are limits to meekness. When Miss Eleanor Stanley Maxwell Elliot woke up to find herself pilloried as an enemy to society, in the very paper which she had tried to save, she experienced mingled emotions shot through with fiery streaks of wrath. Presently these simmered down to a residue of angry amazement and curiosity. If you have been accustomed all your life to regard yourself as an empress of absolute dominance over slavish masculinity, and are suddenly subjected to a violent slap across the face from the hand of the most highly favored slave, some allowance is due you of outraged sensibilities. Chiefly, however Esmé wondered WHY. WHY, in large capitals, and with an intensely ascendant inflection.

Her first impulse had been to telephone Hal a withering message. More deliberate thought suggested the wisdom of making sure of her ground, first. The result was a shock. From her still infuriated guardian she had learned that, technically, she was the owner, with full moral responsibility for the "Pest-Egg." The information came like a dash of extremely cold water, which no pumess, reformed or otherwise, likes. Miss Elliot sat her down to a thoughtful consideration of the "Clarion." She found she was in good company. Several other bright and shining lights of the local firmament, social, financial, and commercial, shared the photographic notoriety. Slowly it was borne in upon her open mind that she had not been singled out for reprehension; that she was simply a part of the news, as Hal regarded news—no, as the "Clarion" regarded news. That Hal would deliberately have let this happen, she declined to believe. Unconsciously she clung to her belief in the natural inviolability of her privilege. It must have been a mistake. Hal would tell her so when he saw her. Yet if that were so, why had he sent word, the day after, that he couldn't keep his appointment? Would he come at all, now?

Doubt upon this point was ended when Dr. Elliot, admitted on the strength of his profession to the typhus ward, and still exhibiting mottlings of wrath on his square face, had repeated his somewhat censored account of his encounter with "that puppy." Esmé haughtily advised her dear Uncle Guardy that the "puppy" was her friend. Uncle Guardy acidulously counseled his beloved Esmé not to be every species of a mildly qualified idiot at one and the same time. Esmé elevated her nose in the air and marched out of the room to telephone Hal Surtaine forthwith. What she intended to telephone him (very distantly, of course) was that her uncle had no authority to speak for her, that she was quite capable of speaking for herself, and that she was ready to hear any explanation tending to mitigate his crime—not in those words precisely, but in a tone perfectly indicative of her meaning. Furthermore, that the matter on which she had wished to speak to him was a business matter, and that she would expect him to keep the broken appointment later. None of which was ever transmitted. Fate, playing the rôle of Miching Mallecho, prevented once again. Hal was out.

In the course of time, Esmé's quarantine (a little accelerated, though not at any risk of public safety) was lifted and she returned to the world. The battle of hygiene *vs.* infection was now at its height. Esmé threw herself into the work, heart and soul. For weeks she did not set eyes on Hal Surtaine, except as they might pass on the street. Twice she narrowly missed him at the hospital where she found time to make an occasional visit to Ellis. A quick and lively friendship had sprung up between the spoiled beauty and the old soldier of the print-columns, and from him, as soon as he was convalescent, she learned something of the deeper meanings of the "Clarion" fight and of the higher standards which had cost its owner so dear.

"I suppose," he said, "the hardest thing he ever had to do in his life was to print your picture."

"Did he *have* to print it?"

"Didn't he? It was news."

"And that's your god, isn't it, Mr. Mac?" said his visitor, smiling.

"It's only a small name for Truth. Good men have died for that."

"Or killed others for their ideal of it."

"Miss Esmé," said the invalid, "Hal Surtaine has had to face two tests. He had to show up his own father in his paper."

"Yes. I read it. But I've only begun to understand it since our talks."

"And he had to print that about you. Wayne told me he almost killed the story himself to save Hal. 'I couldn't bear to look at the boy's face when he told me to run it,' Wayne said. And he's no sentimentalist. Newspapermen generally ain't."

"*Aren't* you?" said Esmé, with a catch in her breath. "I should think you were, pretty much, at the 'Clarion' office."

From that day she knew that she must talk it out with Hal. Yet at every thought of that encounter, her maidenhood shrank, affrighted, with a sweet and tremulous fear. Inevitable as was the end, it might have been long postponed had it not been for a word that Ellis let drop the day when he left the hospital. Mrs. Festus Willard, out of friendship for Hal, had insisted that the convalescent should come to her house until his strength was quite returned, instead of returning to his small and stuffy hotel quarters, and Esmé had come in her car to transfer him. It was the day after the Talk-It-Over Breakfast at which Hal had announced the prospective fall of the "Clarion."

"I'll be glad to get back to the office," said Ellis to Esmé. "They certainly need me."

"You aren't fit yet," protested the girl.

"Fitter than the Boss. He's worrying himself sick."

"Isn't everything all right?"

"All wrong! It's this cussed Pierce libel case that's taking the heart out of him."

"Oh!" cried Esmé, on a note of utter dismay. "Why didn't you tell me, Mr. Mac?"

"Tell you? What do you know about it?"

"Lots! Everything." She fell into silent thoughtfulness. "I supposed that you had heard from Mr. Pierce, or his lawyer, at the office. I *must* see Hal—Mr. Surtaine—now. Does he still come to see you?"

"Everyday."

"Send word to him to be at the Willards' at two tomorrow. And—and, please, Mr. Mac, don't tell him why."

"Now, what kind of a little game is this?" began Ellis, teasingly. "Am I an amateur Cupid, or what's my cue?" He looked into the girl's face and saw tears in the great brown eyes. "Hello!" he said with a change of voice. "What's wrong, Esmé? I'm sorry."

"Oh, *I'm* wrong!" she cried. "I ought to have spoken long ago. No, no! I'm all right now!" She smiled gloriously through her tears. "Here we are. You'll be sure that he's there?"

"Fear not, but lean on Dollinger And he will fetch you through"—

quoted the other in oratorical assurance, and turned to Mrs. Willard's greeting.

At one-thirty on the following day, Mr. McGuire Ellis was where he shouldn't have been, asleep in a curtained alcove window-seat of the big Willard library. At one minute past two he was where he should have been still less; that is, in the same place and condition. Now Mr. Ellis is not only the readiest hair-trigger sleeper known to history, but he is also one of the most profound and persistent. Entrances and exits disturb him not, nor does the human voice penetrate to the region of his dreams. To everything short of earthquake, explosion, or physical contact, his slumber is immune. Therefore he took no note when Miss Esmé Elliot came in, nor when, a moment later, Mr. Harrington Surtaine arrived, unannounced. Nor, since he was thoroughly shut in by the draperies, was either of them aware of his presence.

Esmé rose slowly to her feet as Hal entered. She had planned a leading-up to her subject, but at sight of him she was startled out of any greeting, even.

"Oh, how thin you look, and tired!" she exclaimed.

"Strenuous days, these," he answered. "I didn't expect to see you here.

Where's Ellis?"

"Upstairs. Don't go. I want to speak to you. Sit down there."

At her direction Hal drew up a chair. She took the corner of the lounge near by and regarded him silently from under puckered brows.

"Is it about Ellis?" said Hal, alarmed at her hesitation.

"No. It is about Mr. Pierce. There won't be any libel suit."

"What!"

"No." She shook her head in reassurance of his evident incredulity. "You've nothing to worry about, there."

"How can you know?"

"From Kathie."

"Did her father tell her?"

"She told her father. There's a dreadful quarrel."

"I don't understand at all."

"Kathie absolutely refuses to testify for her father. She says that the accident was her own fault, and if there's a trial she will tell the truth."

Before she had finished, Hal was on his feet. Her heart smote her as she saw the gray worry pass from his face and his shoulders square as from the relief of a burden lifted, "Has it lain so heavy on your mind?" she asked pitifully.

"If you knew!" He walked half the length of the long room, then turned abruptly. "You did that," he said. "You persuaded her."

"No. I didn't, indeed."

The eager light faded in his face. "Of course not. Why should you after—Do you mind telling me how it happened?"

"It isn't my secret. But—but she has come to care very much for some one, and it is his influence."

"Wonderful!" He laughed boyishly. "I want to go out and run around and howl. Would you mind joining me in the college yell? Does Mac know?"

"Nobody knows but you."

"That's why Pierce kept postponing. And I, living under the shadow of this! How can I thank you!"

"Don't thank me," she said with an effort. "I—I've known it for weeks. I meant to tell you long ago, but I thought you'd have learned it before now—and—and it was made hard for me."

"Was that what you had to tell me about the paper, when you asked me to come to see you?"

She nodded.

"But how could I come?" he burst out. "I suppose there's no use—I must go and tell Mac about this."

"Wait," she said.

He stopped, gazing at her doubtfully.

"I'm tearing down the tenement at Number 9."

"Tearing it down?"

"As a confession that—that you were right. But I didn't know I owned it. Truly I didn't. You'll believe that, won't you?"

"Of course," he cried eagerly. "I did know it, but too late."

"If you'd known in time would you have—"

"Left that out of the paper?" he finished, all the life gone from his voice.

"No, Esmé. I couldn't have done that. But I could have said in the paper that you didn't know."

"I thought so," she said very quietly.

He misinterpreted this. "I can't lie to you, Esmé," he said with a sad sincerity. "I've lived with lies too long. I can't do it, not for any hope of happiness. Do I seem false and disloyal to you? Sometimes I do to myself. I can't help it. All a man can do is to follow his own light. Or a woman either, I suppose. And your light and mine are worlds apart."

Again, with a stab of memory, he saw that desperate smile on her lips. Then she spoke with the clear courage of her new-found womanliness.

"There is no light for me where you are not."

He took a swift step toward her. And at the call, sweetly and straightly, she came to meet his arms and lips.

"Poor boy!" she said, a few minutes later, pushing a lock of hair from his forehead. "I've let you carry that burden when a word from me would have lifted it."

"Has there ever been such a thing as unhappiness in the world, sweetheart?" he said. "I can't remember it. So I don't believe it."

"I'm afraid I've cost you more than I can ever repay you for," she said. "Hal, tell me I've been a little beast!—Oh, no! That's no way to tell it. Aren't you sorry, sir, that you ever saw this room?"

"Finest example of interior architecture I know of. Exact replica of the plumb center of Paradise."

"It's where all your troubles began. You first met me here in this very room."

"Oh, no! My troubles began from the minute I set eyes on you, that day at the station."

"Don't contradict me." She laid an admonitory finger on his lips, then, catching at his hand, gently drew him with her. "Right in that very window-seat there—" She whisked the hangings aside, and brushed McGuire Ellis's nose in so doing.

"Hoong!" snorted McGuire Ellis.

"Oh!" cried Esmé. "Were you there all the time? We—I—didn't know—Have you been asleep?"

"I have been just that," replied the dormant one, yawning.

"I hope we haven't disturbed—" began Esmé in the same breath with Hal's awkward "Sorry we waked you up, Mac."

"Don't be—" Ellis checked his familiar growl, looked with growing suspicion from Esmé's flushed loveliness to Hal's self conscious confusion, leaped to his feet, gathered the pair into a sudden, violent, impartial embrace, and roared out:—

"Go ahead! *Be* young! You can only be it once in a lifetime."

CHAPTER XXXVIII
THE CONVERT

Old Home Week passed in a burst of glory and profit. True to its troublous type, the "Clarion" had interfered with the profit, in two brief, lively, and effective campaigns. It had published a roster of hotels which, after agreeing not to raise rates for the week, had reverted to the old, tried and true principle of "all the traffic can bear," with comparative tables, thereby causing great distress of mind and pocket among the piratical. Backed by the Consumers' League, it had again taken up the cudgels for the store employees, demanding that they receive pay for overtime during the celebration and winning a partial victory. No little rancor was, of course, stirred up among the advertisers. The usual threats were made. But the business interests of Worthington had begun to learn that threatening the "Clarion" was a futile procedure, while advertisers were coming to a realization of the fact that they couldn't afford to stay out of so strong a medium, even at increased rates.

The raise in the advertising schedule had been partly Esmé Elliot's doing. As a condition of her engagement to Hal, she demanded a resumption of the old partnership. Entered into lightly, it soon became of serious moment, for the girl had a natural gift for affairs. When she learned that on the basis of circulation the "Clarion" would be justified in increasing its advertising card by forty per cent, but dared not do so because of the narrow margin upon which it was working, she insisted upon the measure, supporting her argument with a considerable sum of money of her own. Hal revolted at this, but she pleaded so sweetly that he finally consented to regard it as a reserve fund. It was never called for. The turn of the tide had come for the paper. It lost few old advertisers and put on new ones. It was a success.

No one was more delighted than Dr. Surtaine. Forgetting his own prophecies of disaster he exalted Hal to the skies as a chip of the old block, an inheritor of his own genius for business.

"Knew all along he had the stuff in him," he would declare buoyantly. "Look at the 'Clarion' now! Most independent, you-be-damned sheet in the country. And what about the chaps that were going to put it out of business? Eating out of its hand!"

Of Esmé the old quack was quite as proud as of Hal. To him she embodied and typified, in its extreme form, those things which all his money could not buy. That she disliked the Certina business and made no secret of the fact did not in the least interfere with a genuine liking between herself and its proprietor. Dr. Surtaine could not discuss Certina with Hal: there were too many wounds still open between them. But with Esmé he could, and often did. Her attitude struck him as nicely philosophic and impersonal, if a bit disdainful. And in these days he had to talk to some one, for he was swollen with a great and glorious purpose.

He announced it one resplendent fall day, having gone out to Greenvale with that particular object in view, at an hour when he was sure that Hal would be at the office.

"Esmé, I'm going to make you a wedding present of Certina," he said.

"Never take it, Doctor," she replied, smiling up at him in friendly recognition of what had come to be a subject of stock joke between them.

"I'm serious. I'm going to make you a wedding present of the Certina business. I guess there aren't many brides get a gift of half a million a year. Too bad I can't give it out to the newspapers, but it wouldn't do."

"What on earth do you mean?" cried the astonished girl. "I couldn't take it. Hal wouldn't let me."

"I'm going to give it up, for you. You think it ain't genteel and high-toned, don't you?"

"I think it isn't honest."

"Not discussing business principles, today," retorted the Doctor good-humoredly. "It's a question of taste now. You're ashamed of the proprietary medicine game, aren't you, my dear?"

Esmé laughed. Embarrassment with Dr. Surtaine was impossible. He was too childlike. "A little," she confessed.

"You'd be glad if I quit it."

"Of course I would. I suppose you can afford it."

As if responding to the touch of a concealed spring, the Surtaine chest protruded. "You find me something I can't afford, and I'll buy it!" he declared. "But this won't even cost me anything in the long run. Esmé, did I ever tell you my creed?"

"'Certina Cures,'" suggested the girl mischievously.

"That's for business. I mean for everyday life. My creed is to let Providence take care of folks in general while I look after me and mine."

"It's practical, at least, if not altruistic."

"Me, and mine," repeated the charlatan. "Do you get that 'and mine'? That means the employees of the Certina factory. Now, if I quit making Certina, what about them? Shall I turn them out on the street?"

"I hadn't thought of that," admitted the girl blankly.

"Business can be altruistic as well as practical, you see," he observed. "Well, I've worked out a scheme to take care of that. Been working on it for months. Certina is going to die painlessly. And I'm going to preach its funeral oration at the factory on Monday. Will you come, and make Hal come, too?"

In vain did Esmé employ her most winning arts of persuasion to get more from the wily charlatan. He enjoyed being teased, but he was obdurate. Accordingly she promised for herself and Hal.

But Hal was not as easily persuaded. He shrank from the thought of ever again setting foot in the Certina premises. Only Esmé's most artful pleading that he should not so sorely disappoint his father finally won him over.

At the Certina "shop," on the appointed day, the fiancés were ushered in with unaccustomed formality. They found gathered in the magnificent executive offices all the heads of departments of the vast concern, a quiet, expectant crowd. There were no outsiders other than Hal and Esmé. Dr. Surtaine, glossy, grave, a figure to fill the eye roundly, sat at his glass-topped table facing his audience. Above him hung Old Lame-Boy, eternally hobbling amidst his fervid implications.

Waving the newcomers to seats directly in front of him, the presiding genius lifted a benign hand for silence.

"My friends," he said, in his unctuous, rolling voice, "I have an important announcement to make. The Certina business is finished."

There was a silence of stunned surprise as the speaker paused to enjoy his effect.

"Certina," he pursued, "has been the great triumph of my career. I might almost say it has been my career. But it has not been my life, my friends. The whole is greater than the part: the creator is greater than the thing he creates. They say, 'Surtaine of Certina.' It should be, 'Certina of Surtaine.' There's more to come of Surtaine."

His voice dropped to the old, pleading, confidential tone of the itinerant; as if he were beguiling them now to accept the philosophy which he was to set forth.

"What is life, my dear friends? Life is a paper-chase. We rush from one thing to another, Little Daisy Happiness just one jump ahead of us and Old Man Death grabbing at our coat-tails. Well, before he catches hold of mine,"—the splendid bulk and vitality of the man gave refutation to the hint of pathos in the voice,—"I want to run my race out so that my children and my children's children can point to me and say, 'One crowded hour of glorious life is worth a cycle of Cathay.'"

With a superb gesture he indicated Hal and Esmé, who, he observed with gratification, seemed quite overcome with emotion.

"That is why, my friends, I am withdrawing certina, and turning to fresh fields; if I may say so, fields of more genteel endeavor. Certina has made millions. It could still make millions. I could sell out for millions today. But, in the words of the sweet singer, I come to bury it, not to praise it. Certina has done its grand work. The day of medicine is almost over. Interfering laws are being passed. The public is getting suspicious of drugs. Whether this is just or unjust is not the question which I am considering. I've always wanted my business to be high-class. You can't run a high-class business when the public is on to you.

"Don't think, any of you, that I'm going to retire and leave you in the lurch. No. I'm looking ahead, for you as well as for me. What's the newest thing in science? Foods! Specific foods, to build up the system. That's the big thing of the future here in America. We're a tired nation, a nerve-wracked nation, a brain-fagged nation. Suppose a man could say to the public, 'Get as tired as you like. Work to your limit. Play to your limit. Go the pace. When you're worn out, come to us and we'll repair the waste for a few dollars. We've got a food—no drugs, no medicines—that builds up brain and nerve as good as new. The greatest authorities in the world agree on it.' Is there any limit to the business that food could do?

"Well, I've got it! And I've got the backing for it. Mr. Belford Couch will tell you of our testimonials. Tell 'em the whole thing, Bel: we're all one family here."

"I've been huntin' in Europe," said Certina Charley, rising, in accents of pardonable pride: "and I've got the hottest bunch of signed stuff ever. You all know how hard it is to get any medical testimonials here. They're all afraid, except a few down-and-outers. Well, there's none of that in Europe. They'll stand for any kind of advertising, so long as it's published only in the United

States—provided they get their price. And it ain't such an awful price either. *I got the Emperor's own physician for one thousand five hundred dollars cash*. And a line of court doctors and swell university professors anywhere from one thousand dollars way down to one hundred. It's the biggest testimonial stunt ever pulled."

"And every mother's son of 'em," put in Dr. Surtaine, "staking a high-toned scientific reputation that the one sure, unfailing, reliable upbuilder for brain-workers, nervous folks, tired-out, or broken-down folks of any kind at all is"—here Dr. Surtaine paused, looked about his entranced audience, and delivered himself of his climax in a voice of thunder:

"CEREBREAD!"

The word passed from mouth to mouth, in accents of experimentation, admiration, and acceptance.

"Cere, from cerebellum, the brain, and bread the universal food. I doped it out myself, and as soon as I hit on it I shipped Belford Couch straight to Europe to get the backing. I wouldn't take a million for that name, today.

"See what you can do with a proposition of that sort! It hasn't got any drugs in it, so we won't have to label it under the law. It ain't medical; so the most particular newspaper and magazines won't kick on the advertising. Yet, with the copy I'm getting up on it, we can put it over to cure more troubles than Certina ever thought of curing. Only we won't use the word 'cure,' of course. All we have to do is to ram it into the public that all its troubles are nervous and brain troubles. 'Cerebread' restores the brain and rebuilds the nerves, and there you are, as good as new. Is that some plan? Or isn't it!"

There was a ripple of applausive comment.

"What's in it?" inquired Lauder, the factory superintendent.

"Millions in it, my boy," cried the other jubilantly. "We'll be manufacturing by New Year's."

"That's the point. *What'll* we be manufacturing?"

"By crikey! That reminds me. Haven't settled that yet. Might as well do it right now," said the presiding genius of the place with Olympian decision. "Dr. De Vito, what's the newest wrinkle in brain-food?"

"Brain-food?" hesitated the little physician. "Something new?"

"Yes, yes!" cried the charlatan impatiently. "What's the fad now? It used to be phosphorus."

"Ye-es. Phosphorus, maybe. Maybe some kind of hypophosphite, eh?"

"Sounds all right. Could you get up a preparation of it that looks tasty and tastes good?"

"Sure. Easy."

"Fine! I'll send you down the advertising copy, so you'll have that to go by. And now, gentlemen, we're the Cerebread factory from now on. Keep all your help; we'll need 'em. Go on with Certina till we're sold out; but no more advertising on it. And, all of you, from now on, think, dream, and *live* Cerebread. Meeting's adjourned."

The staff filed out, chattering excitedly. "He'll put it over."—"You can't beat the Chief."—"Isn't he a wonder!"—"Cerebread; it's a great name to advertise."—"No come-back to it, either. Nobody can kick on a *food*."—"It's a sure-enough classy proposition, with those swell European names to it!"—"Wish he'd let us in on the stock."

Success was in the air. It centered in and beamed from the happy eyes of the reformed enthusiast, as, crossing over the room with hands extended to Esmé and Hal, he cried in a burst of generous emotion:

"It was you two that converted me."

THE END